Haimya was a thing of beauty and terror alike as she made a thrust at full stretch, driving the point of her sword into the base of the attacker's skull. Even in the darkness, Pirvan saw life go out of the man's eyes—and also a fallen attacker roll over and grip Haimya's ankles.

Caught off balance, she staggered, and another man came at her with two daggers, getting inside her guard before Pirvan could even open his mouth for a warning. But a sailor stamped down hard on the clutching hands, and as they released their grip Haimya flung herself to one side, cushioning her fall on the man who'd thrown her off balance.

The sailor's sword ended the second man's threat to Haimya.

Then Pirvan's mouth went dry, as running feet thudded from the direction of the harbor. He turned, knowing that the wall at his back would buy him only time and hoping Haimya would fight close enough to him for a last word or two, if they could not hope for a touch—

D0790017

Saga

From the Creators of the
DRAGONLANCE® Saga
WARRIORS

Knights of the Crown
Roland Green

Maquesta Kar-Thon
Tina Daniell

Knights of the Sword
Roland Green

DragonLance ® Saga

WARRIORS
Volume Three

Knights of the Sword

Roland Green

DRAGONLANCE®
Warriors Series
Volume Three

KNIGHTS OF THE SWORD
©1995 TSR, Inc.
All Rights Reserved.

All characters in this book are fictitious. Any resemblance to actual persons, living or dead, is purely coincidental.

This book is protected under the copyright laws of the United States of America. Any reproduction or other unauthorized use of the material or artwork contained herein is prohibited without the express written permission of TSR, Inc.

All TSR characters, character names, and the distinctive likenesses thereof are trademarks owned by TSR, Inc.

Random House and its affiliate companies have worldwide distribution rights in the book trade for English language products of TSR, Inc.

Distributed to the book and hobby trade in the United Kingdom by TSR Ltd.

Distributed to the toy and hobby trade by regional distributors.

Cover art by Jeff Easley. Interior art by Valerie A. Valusek.

DRAGONLANCE is a registered trademark owned by TSR, Inc. The TSR logo is a trademark owned by TSR, Inc.

First Printing: December 1995
Printed in the United States of America.
Library of Congress Catalog Card Number: 94-68159

9 8 7 6 5 4 3 2 1

ISBN: 0-7869-0202-7

TSR, Inc.
201 Sheridan Springs Rd.
Lake Geneva, WI 53147
U.S.A.

TSR Ltd.
120 Church End, Cherry Hinton
Cambridge CB1 3LB
United Kingdom

Prologue

Unarmored, Sir Marod of Ellersford had never been a great burden for a horse. He was a head taller than the average, but also a span narrower. One who had trained him in youth was said to have jested:

"Think you to defeat all archers, by standing sideways? Think again, young Marod!"

That was forty years ago. Now Marod was no longer young, but a Knight of the Rose in the ranks of the Knights of Solamnia. Still he remained lean.

So his mount had easy work, carrying him up to the crest of a hill not far from Dargaard Keep. He did not look at the great mass of stone and the outbuildings that sprawled about it, but instead westward, toward the sunset.

Low but spike-crested hills rose there, where thousands of years of rain and wind had worn away soft outer rock from around harder cores. Some of the spikes rose against the crimson and gold blazing across part of the sky. Others were lost in spreading blue-grayness where storm clouds gathered.

A storm at this time of the spring could be great or small, doing much or little. Rather like the condition of the Knights of Solamnia—one reason that Sir Marod of Ellersford had been doing for some fifteen years the task that he hoped the True Gods would allow him to do for as long again.

That task was simple enough to put into words. It was to find for the knights resources of men, weapons, wealth, and skill not known to the priests who ruled in Istar the Mighty. It was also to keep those resources hidden from those priests—and insofar as Honor, Oath, and Measure allowed, from those knights who did not need to know of them.

The world did not fare so ill under the rule of Istar the Mighty that this was a matter of life or death. Even those lands that refused all but the most nominal allegiance to Istar did so politely (except the minotaurs, and they were no ruder to Istar than they were to anyone else, which Marod supposed was in some degree a gesture of honor). Istar ruled, peace prevailed, and men grew sleek in the arts of peace.

The Knights of Solamnia, given from youth to the arts of war, had little place in this snug world. Few came forward to fill their ranks; many left those ranks as soon as they lawfully could.

If the priests of Istar had not openly rejoiced in this, Marod might have been less uneasy. But it seemed to him that the priests rejoiced at the weakening of the knights as they would rejoice at the weakening of a would-be rival. Marod distrusted those who could not bear rivals.

An educated man, he knew well enough that even among the True Gods there were Good, Neutral, and Evil to keep the balance of the universe. Men, needing balance even more than the gods, needed to be careful about letting any among them gather too much power.

The knights would weigh in the balance against the priests merely by existing. Marod hoped earnestly that none of his and others' fears of harsher work ahead would prove true. Yet it was already known that the priests called against justice for races other than humankind, or at least for looking the other way when injustice was done.

There was also the chief among the priests openly calling himself the kingpriest, implying that he ruled both the worship of the gods and the daily affairs of the folk of Istar. And there were rumors, to which Sir Marod did not wish to give time, let alone credence—but which chilled him to the marrow when they did intrude on his thoughts.

What intruded on his thoughts now was the sound of a horse mounting the path at a trot, then blowing as its rider reined it in. Marod turned in his saddle to see Sir Lewin of Trenfar grinning at him.

Sir Lewin was a good load for a horse even when he wore only tunic and hose, cloak, sword, and dagger. Fortunately he had the means to support mounts of a size equal to bearing him. His own house was of the lower grades of Solamnian nobility, but it was related to half a dozen of the greater houses and at least one petty king. He had not needed to stint himself since he finished his training.

The grin had become habitual only since last year, when Lewin uncovered a plot among certain petty landowners farther east to turn robber baron. He had done this both at the risk of his life and by the sweat of his brow, and thus met any reasonable requirements for elevation to Knight of the Rose, the highest rank among the Knights of Solamnia.

One of those reasonable requirements, by the Measure, was the consent of all other Knights of the Rose. This included Sir Marod, and his consent had been readily forthcoming. Not without some doubt that the honor was being thrust upon his pupil a trifle too soon, but not enough to justify withholding consent.

The gods made all of us a mixture, from the days of Vinas Solamnus to now, and because a less savory part of the mixture is uppermost one day does not mean a man has gone over to evil.

Sir Lewin unpinned his cloak and offered it to the older knight. "It is heavier than yours."

"My years have not thinned my blood as much as you think, young knight," Marod said with a frosty smile. "And you have worked up a sweat, riding as you have. Take off your cloak and you risk taking a chill, for which there is but one cure."

Lewin's face twisted in mock horror. "No, not Guliana's tisane!" The White Robe healer was notorious for her belief that only through suffering could one win back to health.

"None other."

Lewin hastily wrapped his cloak back about his own shoulders. "I have read the letters you left for me. None seem to require action or even a reply, save to keep the writers content that we hear them."

Marod allowed himself no more expression than the marble of a temple staircase. Lewin frowned.

Marod knew that he was testing the younger man, and the younger man knew that he was being tested and would fail the test if he needed to ask which letter might require more than a formal reply. Both knights would be glad when this almost daily ritual was done.

"What of the rumors that Karthay intends to enlarge its fleet?" Lewin finally said.

Marod was not going to allow him that easy escape.

"What of them, indeed?"

"Our man in Karthay speaks of them as street tales. But he does not say which streets."

"Does that make a difference?" Marod knew the answer; he was playing Evil's advocate.

"More than a trifle. If it is a tale spreading along the harborfront streets—any sailor will talk of his dreams after the second cup. A larger fleet would be a dream for many sailors of Karthay, put ashore by Istar's traders."

"One sees. And if it is a tale spreading along the streets leading out from the Square of the Captains?"

Lewin frowned. The expression marred his good looks, of which he was prouder than a knight really ought to be, though not to the extent of violating any part of the Measure. Marod understood why the younger man usually grinned or at least smiled, even when there seemed little to smile about.

"One could read that in more than one way, like most auguries. Those who live on the streets beyond Temple Hill have wealth and rank. A larger fleet would need their consent. If they talk of it, that might prove its truth."

Lewin shrugged, then went on. "However, it is nowhere written in the Measure—or anywhere else I have looked—that wealthy men cannot dream of what will not be. So perhaps we should write those who have ears in Karthay, to listen to where the rumor runs, before we believe or deny."

"Very fine reasoning, Sir Lewin. We shall make a finished intriguer of you yet."

"Is that an honorable state for a Knight of the Rose?"

"A knight of any rank must serve his Honor, Oath, and brethren all at the same time. Nothing in the Oath of Knighthood says that this must be easy. Much in our history says otherwise."

The silence that followed Sir Marod's last words was unbroken, save by the breathing of the horses, until a distant rumble of thunder bid them leave the hilltop to meet the storm from drier vantage.

Chapter 1

He was twenty-two years old, six and a half feet tall, and strong in proportion. He bore the name Darin, because Waydol, the minotaur who had raised him, said that he ought to have a human name. However, he mostly referred to himself as "Heir to Waydol," or even "Heir to the Minotaur." That last title might not always be sufficient, if more than one minotaur came to inhabit this stretch of the northern coast of Istar.

Other minotaurs sailed along the coast, though fewer now since they faced death with scant hope of honor at the hands of Istar's fleet and coast garrisons. Beyond the sea lay all the lands of the minotaurs.

But when one spoke of "the Minotaur" in this land, one spoke of Waydol.

At this moment Darin spoke neither of Waydol nor of anything else. He wished to be as silent as one of the trees of the forest and as invisible as the breeze that crept through them. Even though the furtive breeze in the forest left him sweating and allowed the insects free play with his skin, he neither wiped away the sweat nor batted at the insects.

The call of a sunwing, three times repeated, made him turn his head. In the shadow between two immense pines was a darker shadow. Darin nodded.

The darker shadow stepped forward, turning into a man. He stepped to within arm's reach of Darin and, with two fingers and a thumb of each hand, tapped his message onto Darin's left forearm and hand.

Darin had learned the handtalk Waydol had given the band almost from the time he could use words. He could understand it as swiftly as common speech.

"The village is good prey," the man was saying. "Log wall with towers and ditch. Solid buildings. Fat cattle. Workers in field wear clothes—even women." If it was possible to convey disappointment in his touch, Darin felt it in the last bit of knowledge. Not that the man would do more than look; he had honor and also fear of Waydol's and Darin's wrath.

Yes, a village so furnished had wealth. It would not be easy prey, and it doubtless had a protector or lord who would seek vengeance for its raiding. It might even be directly under the rule of Istar.

Let would-be avengers thrash the forest as they pleased. Waydol's band knew paths to their stronghold that no one else did, and not only because they had made a good many themselves. In Darin's lifetime, the Minotaur had gathered a formidable band of the cunning and the crafty, as a legacy for his heir. He had also proved that a minotaur could lead humans, even against their own folk— something that both races doubted was possible.

What he expected his heir to do with the band over the next twenty years, Darin had realized some time ago that he did not really know. However, it was enough for now to keep the men from growing stale.

It would be a night raid if they waited much longer, and that Darin would not have. The only way to raid by night was to be ready to burn where one raided, to make light to find one's way about unknown streets or paths. That, or find a wizard with a flexible conscience and command of illuminating spells.

Darin had no scruples about the second, many about the first. There was not a magic-worker in the band, so the raiders would go in now, trusting to their own speed to confuse hostile aim as thoroughly as the gods' darkness might in a few hours.

The man tapped Darin's hand again. Darin nodded, squatted, and allowed the smaller man to leap onto his shoulders. The leaper caught a low-hanging branch and started pulling himself up, as silent as ever.

Darin remained kneeling, looking up as the man vanished in the branches with the speed of a squirrel. His name in the band was Stalker; after certain lessons, no one inquired too closely about his birth name. His birth blood was most probably sea barbarian; one seldom found that combination of agility and dark skin in other races. At last Darin heard from high above a faint *whttt!* That would be Stalker's shortbow, sending a signal arrow some two hundred paces through the forest to where the rest of the band waited in two wings. Each wing of twenty raiders was now to move to a position already scouted, one on each side of the village's fields.

The attack would come from two directions, forcing the villagers to divide their defenses. At the same time, the two wings would be able to help one another, and between them sweep up the people in the fields before they could reach the gate.

That was as far as Darin knew he could wisely plan. Waydol had taught him: "Never assume your enemy agrees with your notions of how to fight the battle."

Darin crouched and listened for any sounds of his men moving to the attack. He heard nothing that most listeners would not have called forest noises, and knew that the underchiefs could fitly punish the noisy. After a while he ceased to listen, and finished his arming.

A man of Darin's size could put fear in many opponents merely by drawing himself to his full height. However, he did not disdain a shirt of fine mail, knowing that a large man was also a large target. He also donned a good round helmet with a dwarven-work tailpiece and nasal added, a sword, and a dagger.

But Darin's principal weapons were his forearms and fists, guarded by elbow-length gauntlets of heavy but supple leather over still finer mail. Suppleness in leather that thick had to come from magic, or perhaps there was some other story behind those gauntlets that Waydol would not tell, not on the day he had given them to Darin or ever afterward.

Nonetheless, the gauntlets had allowed Darin to defeat a good many opponents while slaying few. He abhorred unnecessary killing even more than Waydol, and was not one to invent necessity where it was not found.

At last Darin had nothing to do but stretch and unknot his limbs for swift movement, as he took in deep breaths of forest-scented air. The forest smelled different than it did at home, no doubt through being farther from the sea, with less salt in the soil and leaf mold—

Chkkk!

Darin looked up. An arrow, twin to Stalker's, was quivering just below the second branch from the ground. A moment later Stalker slithered out of the tree, snatching the arrow from the trunk as he came.

The two men nodded. The two wings were in position. Now all they needed was Darin and Stalker in *their* position, from which to give the signal to attack.

The two men trod silently but swiftly, one behind the other, as they moved onward.

* * * * *

One sharp-eared villager must have heard something untoward from the forest, but courage or foolishness undid him. Or perhaps he wasn't sure of what he'd heard and wished not to make a fool of himself with a false warning.

The man fell before he could give any warning at all, as a slingball whipped out of the trees and into his skull. Darin waited a moment to see if any of the other workers had noticed the man's fall and took flight or came to his rescue.

If they came, they would find little to prove what had happened to him. The slingers of Darin's band carried balls of fire-hardened clay, fit to strike a man senseless and crumble into powder at the same moment.

If the villagers fled—

They did nothing. Perhaps none had seen their friend fall; perhaps they thought he had lain down from fatigue; perhaps they were too near the end of a long and wearying day to think of more than hot water and cold ale at home.

Darin licked dry lips. He himself had never drunk anything stronger than water when in health or herbal infusions when sick, but he understood weariness and thirst as well as these folk ever would! It seemed almost dishonorable to take them at such a disadvantage—unless one looked at the sentries atop the walls.

At that moment, one of those sentries seemed to notice the fallen man. He pointed with his spear, cupping the other hand to his mouth. Darin did not hear the words across the field, but he heard urgency in the man's tone.

Darin stepped into the open and slammed his fists against the trees to either side of him. The forest spewed men dressed in a motley of rust, green, and brown, all bearded and long-haired. Some of the men showed a trace or more of elven blood, and on the shoulders of a man nearly Darin's height rode a kender, belaboring his mount with a featherduster.

They raised no war cries; the only sound was of forty-some pairs of booted feet running hard. They had little breath to spare for shouting; it was also the custom in Waydol's band to be silent until first blood.

That would not be long; even now sentries were nocking arrows to bows. Darin raised his left hand, palm facing toward the ground. His archers unslung bows, opened quivers, and pulled out shafts, all without missing a step. Only when it came time to nock and shoot did they halt, for better aim. Darin's band had not nearly enough archers for an arrow-hail, which also led to unnecessary slaying even when one could use it.

So two sentries fell from the walls and one fell back out of sight, in return for one of Darin's men down with an arrow in his leg. Meanwhile, the onrushing line overtook the fleeing villagers. Before Darin drew ahead, he saw his men starting to bring down their captives, each in a different fashion.

Some men used clubs or fists. One man threw a woman over his shoulder and spanked her soundly; one could not tell whether she was screaming or laughing.

Stalker used his bolas, his own design, drawing on both Plains barbarian and kender styles. When he had used both, he drew from his belt a weighted belaying pin and stopped two more villagers in their tracks with that.

Now it was becoming vital to keep the villagers from closing their gate. A good dozen of their folk were still outside and free, but from the gate tower and from within the gate people were screaming "Close the gate *now!*"

Darin charged through the ranks of the fleeing villagers, slapping aside with his gauntlet one dagger thrust. He reached the gate just as it started to swing shut, gripped it with both hands, took a deep breath, and heaved.

The gate swung wide open again, and in the moment it stood so, two of Darin's archers shot down the men standing in the gateway. Darin leaped forward, snatched up the gate bar, which was twice as long as he was tall and as thick as his thigh, gripped it like a quarterstaff, and laid about him.

He struck only a few. Some fell in panic or simply lay down to save themselves, as others did by taking to their heels. In moments all those villagers who had been caught outside the gate were captives, and the gate stood open for the raiders to enter the village.

Darin would not give that order without giving the villagers a chance to yield. Even the briefest of fights at close quarters could strew more bodies in the village lanes than an honorable man could wish to see.

Darin cupped his hands. His voice was not quite in proportion to the rest of him—and a good thing too, Waydol said, or he would have deafened half his comrades by now—but it carried well.

"Ho, village of Dinsas! We have you at our mercy, and bid you yield at once. If you yield, little wealth and no blood will you forfeit. Fight on, and harsher fate awaits you."

Only after a long silence followed did the raider chief remember that these villagers might not understand his minotaur-accented Istarian speech. This was farther than he and his men had raided, so Dinsas should be within the area settled directly from Istar or cities that spoke its tongue. But every land had villages where the folk walked their own path, spoke their own tongue, and made rude replies to the polite requests of strangers whom they could not understand.

The silence grew longer still. Several of Darin's men picked up the gate bar; a battering ram was always a useful addition to the raiders' arsenal, but a heavy one to carry through the forest.

At last, a square-built man with a red beard appeared in the gateway, facing Darin. He wore a well-kept sword hastily slung over a cobbler's apron.

"My name is Hurvo, Speaker of Dinsas. Who are you?"

Darin looked down at the man. Hurvo looked more like an oversized dwarf than a short human, complete to the work-calloused hands. He did not appear to be short in courage, however.

"I am he who possesses your village," Darin replied, in measured tones. "I and my men wish to share that which lies within these walls."

"You possess the gate of Dinsas, no more," Hurvo replied, in an equally level voice. "What are you prepared to pay for the smallest portion of the rest?"

"As much as necessary, and if it grows to be too much,

we shall possess all of it when the paying is done. This will not be of much concern to you, for you will no longer need possessions beyond your graveclothes."

"Oh, you don't mean to eat us?" Hurvo said.

The kender mimed spewing all over the big man carrying him. The man hastily set him down.

"A kender!" someone said, in tones of loathing. Darin saw that several other villagers had come out from doorways and lanes to stand behind Hurvo.

"Imsaffor Whistletrot," the kender said, with an elaborate bow that turned into a handstand that in turn flowed into a somersault. The movement brought him close to Hurvo. Some of the villagers took a step backward.

Darin quietly hand-signaled to his archers. The first man to try taking Whistletrot as a hostage would get an arrow through his gizzard. He would also probably get Whistletrot's dagger in some less vital but surely painful spot if he survived the arrow.

Kender lived without fear, for which there were many explanations, some more fanciful than true. One explanation which Darin suspected might hold truth was that it was not easy to kill a kender if he seriously objected to the idea.

"Then you must be the Heir to the Minotaur and his band," Hurvo said, tugging at his beard as if trying to estimate the price of repairing a shoe. "Rather far afield, aren't you?"

"We have come as far as Dinsas, which is all that concerns any of us for the moment," Darin replied. He felt impatience creeping into his mind, but fought to keep it from his voice.

Never give a man the notion that he can fight you by delaying matters. That was another of Waydol's sayings that had proved true in many a skirmish, battle, and raid.

"I will hear your terms," Hurvo said. "Hearing them does not mean accepting them. Nor does offering you drink mean offering you our village. But we need not fight one another with dry throats."

The water was cold and clean, and, from the men's

sounds, the ale was good. Hurvo also sampled the first cup from each barrel before he allowed anyone else to drink.

* * * * *

"Speak now, Heir to the Minotaur, or is there another name you prefer?" Hurvo said, wiping foam from his beard.

"That one does most honor to he who raised me—" Darin began.

Several villagers hissed. One made a gesture of aversion and threw down his cup.

Hurvo sighed. "We have been through this argument before, Speko, and more often than you could count without taking off your boots. He may be heir to a red dragon, for all I care, but he is here, which makes it wise to listen to him."

Darin spoke quickly, before Speko or anyone else could complicate matters. "Our terms are simple. We shall remove from each house and shop one or two objects of value, as well as a certain amount of coin for the whole village. Also, we may eat and drink as we see fit tonight, and tomorrow when we break our fast before departing.

"If no harm comes to our people, none will come to yours. We shall even help heal your wounded. For every man harmed, though, a life will be forfeit. If battle is forced on us, the village will be burned, over your heads or not, as the gods allow."

Hurvo frowned. "Have you wizard or cleric with healing magic at their command?"

"Only the healing craft of those dwellers in the greenwood who must heal swiftly or die," Darin said. He felt a certain compulsion to honesty with this self-possessed village speaker, whose refusal to change countenance had begun to remind him of Waydol.

"Let it be so, if the village consents," Hurvo said. "I can decide myself if there is no time, but there will be a better chance of peace if I may hear the leading folk."

The sun was westering, but darkness made neither peace bloody nor battle kindly. Nor would eagerness escape Hurvo's sharp eyes.

Darin nodded. "Do not dally, or there will be a higher price. But you have until the sun touches the top of that tree over there." He pointed at what appeared to be a young vallenwood, at the southwestern corner of the fields.

Hurvo nodded and led his villagers back into the shadows. Darin quickly ordered wedges thrust into the gate, to keep it open, and three or four archers climbed into the gate towers.

The rest of the men set to guarding, tending the captives, and fitting the gate bar with handles to make a more useful battering ram. Even if Dinsas yielded, there was always someone who had lost a key, run away, or been killed, leaving no gentle way to reach the valuables behind a locked door.

* * * * *

Hurvo's argument with his village took nearly all the allowed time and most of Darin's remaining patience as well. The leader of the raiders was sitting on the battering ram, whetting the sword he had yet to draw in anger on this raid, when Hurvo reappeared.

"We consent to your terms," he said. Then he looked at Imsaffor Whistletrot. "Best keep that kender close by you."

"I am of this band, and go where I please," Whistletrot said. "If it doesn't please you—"

"Any harm to him is harm to one of us," Stalker said. He never raised his voice, even in battle, but Darin saw Hurvo take an exceptionally tight grip on his beard before nodding.

After that, the evening went well enough, if one can so speak of the looting of a village by a band of robbers, however moderate in their conduct. It helped that for the most part Darin's men chose to remain sober, although he noticed a good many water bottles in the piled loot. He'd wager that most of them would leave Dinsas tomorrow morning, tied to a man's belt and filled with ale or wine.

One man found a jug of mead and emptied it before he staggered out into the lanes again. Darin had him tossed down a disused well, then pulled up only when he was thoroughly frightened, half-drowned, and a little more sober. His chief hoped that the man would be fit to march in the morning. He had never left a living man behind on any raid, and few dead, but litters were always a burden.

Imsaffor Whistletrot was here, there, and everywhere, seldom in Darin's sight for longer than the chief needed to assure himself that the kender was still alive. Darin vowed to pass word to the kender's village, although, any word that implied system and order seemed odd applied to kender.

Regardless, it was not much more than a day's march from Dinsas, though hard to find if the kender did not wish visitors. Darin thought they ought to know that the poison of hatred for nonhumans had flowed all the way from Istar to Dinsas, and to be on the watch against their once-friendly neighbors.

Then he decided to leave the warning to Whistletrot, if in fact the local kender hadn't learned all they needed to know by their own methods. They would also have their own methods of dealing with hostile neighbors, and if it came to betting, Darin would not bet against the kender.

It was well after dark when Whistletrot reappeared for the last time. By now the village square was well lit with torches and bonfires, and the loot formed a glittering pile in the middle. The kender swung out hand over hand along a projecting rooftree to its carved head, then dropped lightly to the ground, turning a somersault in midair before landing.

Darin looked up from a plate that held meat pie, porridge, and brownfish pickled with onions. "There's a house that hasn't been visited, and it's locked," Whistletrot said.

Several men laughed. "You didn't get in, and you call

yourself a kender?" one said.

Whistletrot looked hurt. "I was told not to bring my lockpicks along on this raid. I—" He fished in the pocket of his coat. "Oh, my. I suppose I forgot to clear out my pockets before we left. Let me see."

Quite a few things turned up in the pockets, including the lockpicks. Another was a small, shiny metal ball.

"Ha, that's one of my bola balls," Stalker said. Short as he was for a sea barbarian, he still managed to loom over the kender.

"It is? Come to think of it, it does look like it came off a ship. Let me hold it up to the light and—"

Stalker tapped the underside of the kender's arm lightly with his belaying pin. The ball flew into the air. Stalker's hand plucked it from midair and pocketed it before it could fall more than a hand's breadth.

"You really ought to start putting your name on things you're going to leave lying around," Whistletrot began indignantly. "Otherwise there'll be so much confusion—"

Darin held up a hand for silence; Hurvo had appeared in the square.

"Yes, Speaker?"

"I heard you talking of a locked house. Did the kender—ah—do as usual with it?"

"No."

"As well for him. That is the house of Sirbones, our priest of Mishakal."

"Then why hasn't he come out to help us? We have enough work for three healers, I should think."

"Ah—we have been taking our hurt to him—eh—in private. He has been busy since it was still twilight."

Darin's first thought was of taking a villager's life—preferably Hurvo's—for this piece of deceit. Then he realized that he had not said anything about Sirbones in the agreement. It would be dishonorable to punish the village for not granting what had not been asked in the first place!

Also, none of the raiders were dead or even mortally hurt. There were two who needed healing to walk—one with an arrow wound and another because one of his captives had bitten him on the thigh—and several more who would march in greater comfort if they had healing.

Darin took a deep breath. "If he is done with your folk, then let him come forth and heal mine."

"I cannot command him. That was not part of the agreement."

"You have a fine memory," Darin said.

Hurvo smiled. "Not so fine for a villager, really. My great-uncle—now that was a memory. He could hold all the buying and selling of a village's three-day fair in his head, without writing a single figure on a wooden slab. Of course, he couldn't write in the first place, but—"

"That sounds like Uncle Trapspringer," Whistletrot put in. "He once had to judge a contest—"

Darin made a sound that plainly declared the unwisdom of continuing this contest of marvelous uncles.

Hurvo turned and led the others toward the healer-cleric's house, with Whistletrot riding on Darin's shoulder.

* * * * *

The house was a small one, only two rooms with a woodpile out back and a well-mortared chimney now trickling herb-scented smoke on the night wind. The door was ajar, and in the torchlight Darin saw that it bore what looked like blue scratchings.

A closer look suggested that it was intended to be a carving of a woman holding a staff. It was hard to tell if she was intended to be clothed or not.

Since Mishakal was supposed to be a rather chaste goddess, Darin decided in favor of her being clothed. He also decided that the carver had never seen a woman, clothed or not.

Then he knocked.

Two half-grown girls supporting an older man who limped but looked otherwise hale appeared in the doorway. "Bless you, Sirbones," one of them said. "I don't know what Father would have—oh!"

Darin stepped aside. The others scurried past, unable to take their eyes off his towering form. It was a while before he noticed a small man with a sleek and full head of silver hair standing in the doorway.

"Ah—you are Sirbones?"

"Oh. Yes. Hurvo warned me you were coming. He was not quite telling the truth about my being done with the villagers. However, I have worked on all the wounded as well as the regular sick. Kyloth was my last for the day, and for him it would take a greater healer than I to give him back his youthful pace. The one who healed his ankle the first time left some of the spell bound into the bone, which no doubt seemed a good idea at the time and might have been if the healing had been properly performed—"

Eventually Darin was able to get the priest's attention, though not before he'd begun to feel as if he were listening to an elderly gnome recite his entire name. In fact, Sirbones did look rather like an oversized gnome, much as Hurvo resembled a large dwarf—had there been mixing of blood with more than elves around here in days not only long past but wholly forgotten?

A fine jest, if some of those in Dinsas who loathe nonhumans have themselves the blood of elves or gnomes, kender or dwarves!

However, a chief with men in need of healing has no time for jests, or for listening to the babble of clerics. A chief who has sworn not to harm priests—and knows that threats against them are as useless as threats against kender—also must be exceedingly patient.

Darin was sure that spring had turned to summer before Sirbones finally ran silent. The priest looked up at the towering figure before him and said, in an entirely different tone of voice, "How many men have you who need healing, and what are their hurts?"

Darin wasted no time gaping, the more so in that the roster of his wounded was always the first thing he rooted in his memory after a battle. He could have recited it drunk or dying, and now spoke swiftly.

Almost before he was aware that the priest had vanished, Sirbones reappeared, carrying his staff and a small bag. The staff seemed to be plain, polished wood, with a blue glass tip—except that the glass glowed, was faceted like a jewel, and seemed to have some tiny figure dancing within its blueness.

"Lead me to your men."

"I must remain within the walls until we are done," Darin said. He pulled out a ring and handed it to the cleric. It was silver, with a dolphin engraved upon it. Waydol had worn it upon the little finger of his left hand, until he gave it to Darin, who had just turned ten.

"This is a sign that you come with my permission, and your healing is lawful." Darin tried to glower. "If it is not, and you live long enough in the face of my men's wrath—"

"Of course, of course. A traveling man am I, and I have fared in far lands and with men less courteous than yourself. I remember once—"

Darin pointed at the gate and muttered a frantic prayer to various gods that Sirbones was *not* going to go maundering again.

By the time the prayer was finished, the cleric was gone.

*   *   *   *   *

Darin did not see the priest of Mishakal again until the next morning. When he and the men inside the village gathered the loot and their breakfasts and marched out, Sirbones had already finished with the wounded raiders. None of them were quite as fit as they had been before wounds, but all could fight and march.

"I wonder if that healer is weak, or not giving us his best," Stalker said.

"Treachery is hard to believe in a priest of Mishakal," Darin said, then made a gesture of aversion for good measure. "As for being weak or fumbling—anyone can suffer that fate. It is something beyond even healers."

Stalker seemed about to reply, but then one of the

raiders came up with a jug of spring water, into which he had mixed cider and crumbled herbs. It was a refreshing drink that not only killed Darin's last thirst but made him aware of how long he had labored (it had hardly been worthy of the name "fighting") since dawn.

Darin drew off his gauntlets, wrapped them in his cloak to make a rough pillow, lay down, and was almost instantly asleep.

He awoke to see Sirbones standing almost over him, so close that Darin could have grabbed an ankle and snatched the little priest off his feet. Then he heard the sound of wailing and lamenting from the village.

He leaped to his feet and rested a hand on his sword hilt. Actually drawing it might lead him to the wrong conclusion.

"Who is weeping, and why?"

"Oh, it is the folk of Dinsas. They grieve for themselves, and for me."

"You?" Darin looked down at the priest. He seemed hale enough, but then with priests of Mishakal this could be an illusion.

Sirbones laughed. It was the laugh of a younger man than he had seemed to be last night. Darin also noticed for the first time that Sirbones seemed ready for traveling. He wore trousers and a loose coat, had a pack on his back and several pouches on a well-made belt, and had his healing staff slung across the pack and wore stout shoes instead of sandals on his feet. In one hand he carried a silver-headed walking stick.

"No. I am not sick or dead, and you are not talking to either a ghost or a carrier of plague. You are merely talking to one who wishes to continue his journey with you."

The way Sirbones said "journey" seemed to give the word ritual significance. Darin remembered that each priest of Mishakal had to go wandering for a few years, as part of his priesthood. He supposed that he should be honored, and he would certainly be grateful if the priest continued to do good work and did not talk men to death as fast as he healed them.

"Indeed. What have the villagers to say to this?"

"Nothing." Then Sirbones added hastily, "That is to say, they cannot go against my duties as a priest of Mishakal and the will of the goddess. They are not happy, however, and predict dire fates if I go with you into the Minotaur's lair."

"Waydol does not have a lair," Darin said. "He lives in a hut overlooking the seashore, like a civilized being. Nor will he hurt you, unless you talk to him at the same length as you have talked to me."

"Ah, that is a vice that comes when one has much of one's own company," Sirbones said. "But if one has no love for oneself, one is a poor healer, for one loves not others. Also, one's own company is what one finds most often on one's journey."

"How long ago did you begin your journey, if that is a lawful question?"

"Certainly," Sirbones said. "I left the Three Lakes Temple in Solamnia twenty-six years ago this summer."

"How long were you on the journey before you returned to the temple?"

"I have yet to return, young giant. I found that the farther I stayed from temples, the more the goddess favored me. I have been in Dinsas a full three years, which is the longest I have stayed in one place since I left the temple. It was time for me to move on."

Darin squatted. This brought his eyes almost to a level with Sirbones's. "I am not sure that I should not take back the—our prizes from last night. If I cannot ask you to return—"

Sirbones shook his head emphatically. "You cannot. Nor are you bound by any oath to return the villagers' wealth, which is but a fraction of what they possess. It would displease your men, and you will need their loyalty on the long journey home.

"Also, Waydol will need every man at his command, and soon."

Darin stood. "You have prophecy?"

"Only knowledge from your men, gained while healing

them—ukkkh!"

"Aaargghhh!"

The first sound came from Sirbones, when Darin snatched him up by the collar, to dangle him at arm's length. The second came from Darin, when fire seemed to shoot up his arm and make arm and hand alike go limp so that Sirbones dropped to the ground.

The priest picked himself up while Darin was still rubbing his arm. "I lack strength to do that every day, and you cannot afford to be hurt every day," Sirbones said firmly. "I have not stolen thoughts from your men's minds. I only listened to them and their friends talking. I added their knowledge to mine, and the sum was a need to help Waydol."

Darin sighed. "Well, if I cannot send you back or keep you from following me," Darin said, "I suppose the next best course is for you to march with us. You can keep up, I trust?"

"You may indeed trust me in that, and wisely," Sirbones said. He sounded maddeningly complacent.

Darin looked after the priest as he strode off toward the assembling line of men. He rubbed his arm and realized that the pain had vanished as swiftly as it had come. In fact, all the aches from yesterday's exertions had also vanished, not only from his arm but from the rest of his body. Even the mild case of the flux from a bout with bad water two days ago was gone.

Darin began gathering his own gear. He still was not sure that bringing Sirbones home would not be bringing an owlbear into the sheepfold. But it seemed hard to believe that the Minotaur and his heir could not between them deal with anything short of Mishakal herself!

Chapter 2

"All seems in order," Sir Niebar said. "I regret that it took so long to be sure."

Sir Pirvan of Tiradot frowned. "Do you imply a fault in our accounting?" He hoped his tone could convey a sense of injury rather than his taking refuge in the Measure's dictum that no knight will ever wittingly insult another.

Although if all knights had always lived up to every part of the Measure, the Solamnic chivalry would long since have either brought perfection to themselves and the world or gone mad trying to obey too many different rules at once.

The thieves of Istar had prided themselves on a complex and comprehensive set of customs to regulate the conduct of "night workers." They had, however, never committed the ultimate folly of the Knights of Solamnia, which was to write everything down in a multitude of stout volumes.

"It does not," Niebar replied. "Indeed, it reflects your

success and prudent management. Your manor is doing well."

"That is Haimya's doing more than mine," Pirvan said. "Fate had it that she leave off journeying for some years, when Gerik and Eskaia were young. In that time she discovered a gift, even a taste, for running a manor."

And if you even think too loudly that we should be able to spend more of our own money to support the knights' work, so that they have to spend less, I will knock you down and Haimya will geld you with a dull pruning hook.

Niebar rose to his full height, then bit back an oath. He had not been at Tiradot Manor long enough to remember which rooms were too low for his considerable height. He rubbed his scalp with one hand and thrust out the other to Pirvan.

The former thief turned Solamnic Knight took the proffered hand. He even managed a sincere smile, though the sincerity came more from the imminence of Niebar's departure than from a genuine regard for the man.

Well, somewhat. There is no pleasure in his company, but he is honest, brave, and courteous without making a show of any of these virtues. Worse men have taken the Knights' Oath.

The two knights walked down the spiral stair from the solar room atop the tower at the west end of the great hall. The outer door led to the courtyard of the fortified manor, where Pirvan's groom and stableboy had already led out Niebar's horse, and where Niebar's squire and serving boy had already mounted.

"Farewell, Pirvan," Niebar said. "I will not wish you a quiet year, because neither you nor your lady wife have much taste for that. But I will pray that what you wish for most will come to you, and soon."

Niebar had to be past forty, older than Pirvan, but he leaped into the saddle with the agility of a youth, without disturbing his horse, except for what might have been a sour look and a faint whicker. Then the gate swung open, three pairs of boot heels pressed into three sets of equine flanks, and the year's visitation party trotted off.

* * * * *

Pirvan waited until the last scrawl of yellow dust vanished from across the green horizon, then went in search of Haimya. Learning that she and the women were down by the millstream doing their best to wash winter out of the woolens, he went the other way, toward the ruined keep that was the oldest surviving human habitation on the Tiradot lands.

Built in the Age of Might, it had housed local lords of varying degrees of honor or rapacity until the Third Dragon War, in which it fell variously to both human and draconic foes. By the end of the war, it was uninhabitable.

When prosperity returned to the land, the then lords of Tiradot decided that the times of living in a fortress were past. They built a stout-walled, peak-roofed house with three floors and two wings, and all the appurtenances of a large farm as well, then surrounded the whole affair with a wall designed to keep out cattle thieves and cutpurses rather than armies.

Some generations later, another lord of Tiradot died without heirs, leaving the manor to the Knights of Solamnia. As the terms of the Swordsheath Scroll further generations afterward left the knights all property they had previously possessed, the Great Meld had made no difference in the status of Tiradot.

What eventually did make a difference was the need of the knights for the services of one Pirvan the Spell-Thief of Istar. When he prevented a renegade mage from unleashing Frostreaver axes on the world and helped bring down a black dragon revived untimely from dragonsleep, these feats were held to make him worthy of acceptance as a Knight of the Crown.

The price of his admission was to be as one of the eyes and ears set about the world, and particularly about Istar (in whose territory the manor lay), charged to him by Sir Marod. To do this properly he needed lands and other property suited to his station, and thus Tiradot Manor fell to his lot.

Pirvan was not sure to this day, some ten years later, who had fallen to whom. He had once heard a crown called "a splendid misery"; owning a manor often seemed much the same, on a more modest level.

At least one could say that the name "Pirvan of Tiradot" sounded better on the ear and in the heart than the name that he might otherwise have borne, one whispered behind his back but well known for all that:

"Pirvan the Wayward."

* * * * *

As always, when bleak thoughts paraded through his mind like a band of drunken ogres, Pirvan found relief in vigorous exercise. A swift side journey to the armory gave him climbing irons, leather trousers and sleeveless tunic, rope, tool belt and pouches, and spike-soled boots. All the metal hanging about him clinked and jingled like tinkers hard at work as he walked out of the gate, toward the old keep.

The walls still rose some ten times Pirvan's height on three sides, though they seemed even more cracked and crumbling than before. In places, the rubble core now dripped stones where before solid blocks had kept all tight and orderly.

Time to sell the rights to the villagers to quarry this old pile, Pirvan thought. *There's a good plenty of new houses and new rooms to old houses, not to mention stones for walks and walls, living up here. When I feel sour in mind or body, there will always be trees to climb.*

The keep was a quarter of an hour's walk, and the road to it was also the main road from the village that went with the manor. Pirvan passed a goatherd with her flock, a carter with a load of barrels (new, empty ones from the local coopers, judging from their polish, rattling staves and the speed the cart was making), several small boys doing nothing in particular, and an older lad carrying home two scythes freshly sharpened at the smith's.

One and all, they greeted Pirvan with courteous respect rather than servility. This was very much to his taste, and would have been more so if he'd been sure why they did it. Was it their natural custom, their knowledge of what an exceedingly odd sort of lord and knight he was, or the growing suspicion of the Knights of Solamnia spreading across Istar?

To be sure, even the last and worst reason hardly meant danger. Istar's claim to be the seat of all virtue in the world was more uttered than honored, and even many Istarians could not say the word "kingpriest" without smiling. It would be generations before the Knights of Solamnia had to contend with the hostility already shown toward nonhumans and human "barbarians"—unless the knights had to step forth as defenders of those folk.

Which, in truth, they ought to do. Indeed, ought to have done before now. But the knights had gained too much at the time of the Great Meld by fighting Istar's battles. Too much that they would be reluctant to lose over a minotaur thrown from a tavern without even being allowed to get drunk first, or a kender maid molested when *nothing* belonging to anyone else could be found on her person . . .

More dark thoughts, Pirvan realized. At this rate he would need to be going up and down the keep until noon to clear his head.

*   *   *   *   *

The keep walls were in even worse condition than Pirvan had remembered. His men-at-arms had the right to use them for climbing practice and other training, but there were only eight of them. A dozen knights climbing in full armor could hardly have left these gouges and cracks, and Pirvan wondered if the local boys were using the keep for wagers and dares.

Another reason for pulling the lot down, before one of those bold ones breaks his neck and his parents' hearts.

Pirvan had to find a new route to the top before he could climb, then just for the challenge found another new route for his second climb. That one proved longer and harder than it had seemed, and when Pirvan reached the top, he was drenched with sweat, bleeding on several knuckles and one cheek, and quite prepared to catch his breath, then turn homeward.

"Good day," said a cheerful voice from out of sight beyond the battlements. "May I offer you some water?"

Pirvan moved up another finger's breadth, slapped both hands down on a flat stone, and vaulted onto the roof of the keep. He drew his dagger as he landed, rolled, and came up with it held by the point, ready to throw.

But his wife, Haimya, had already drawn her own knife, as well as the buckler, hardly larger than a pot lid, with which she was so deft. They stood on guard against one another for a moment, then, as one, sheathed their knives and embraced.

"As well we didn't decide to practice," Haimya said, bending down. "We might have punctured the water bag, and Kiri-Jolith knows you look like a man who needs a drink."

Pirvan was too busy uncorking the bag to do more than nod. He spoke only after the water, laced with extract of tarberry and a hint of lemon, had washed the dust and sweat from his mouth and throat.

"Bless you, Haimya," he said. "It was a pleasure to see you. How did you come up?"

"By the stairs," she said, not quite meeting his eyes. No one could fault her courage or her skill with arms, but she had little head for heights and had never quite gotten over being ashamed of this.

"And how can it be a pleasure to see me when all you've looked at is the water bag?" she added, hands on her hips. The pose brought out the full splendor of her muscular figure, as tall as her husband's and, if anything, broader across the shoulder, without being any the less desirable.

She wore a loose tunic over men's breeches and low boots on her long-toed feet, and it did not hurt that the tunic was damp enough to cling closely in interesting places. The breeches, too—and Pirvan gently put a hand on each of his wife's hips, then kissed her on each cheek before his lips found hers.

They stood that way for some while, the pleasures of lovers, old married couples, and tried battle-comrades all mingling in the kisses and the embraces. It was impossible afterward to tell who first took a step backward, but both laughed.

"A good thing, too," Haimya said. "My knees were beginning to tremble from all this standing close." She brushed a hand across his cheek. "If they'd started shaking the keep—"

Pirvan made a rude gesture and trapped Haimya's hand with his. "Standing close" was the oldest of their pet phrases, going back to the time after their first quest when they had known that they must part for a while. Haimya had said that a time might come for them to "stand close," and so it had, which Pirvan considered the greatest good fortune ever to come his way.

At last he forced the pleasure of Haimya's touch from his mind. "Does anything call you down from here?"

"No duty that I can think of," she replied. "But if we stay up here much longer, surely something will happen. Besides, I promised the maids to help bring the laundry back from the stream."

"So be it."

Pirvan took another drink before he left, then Haimya drank, then he emptied the rest of the bag over her head and licked the drops off her cheek and neck, which had *both* sets of knees trembling before the last drop was gone.

* * * * *

Haimya drew a few stares on the way back to the house, as her tunic was damper and closer-clinging than before. However, none of the stares held anything that Pirvan could fault. It was well known in the land that the Lady of Tiradot was very fine to look at, but if you did more than look, she would not even waste time complaining of you to her lord, but settle the matter at once and in a way that might leave you inapt for any woman for years to come.

"I trust Sir Niebar the Nuisance found us trustworthy for another year," Haimya said as they passed the road-side shrine to Mishakal.

Pirvan nodded, stepping aside briefly to sprinkle the last few drops from the bag as a libation on the dusty stone.

"He does his best, and surely neither he nor his people ate the larders bare in four days."

"A wizard with a good scrying spell could have done the same work in a day or less, and eaten little or nothing."

"He would still have needed escorts," Pirvan said. "There is the odd bandit, and there is always the dignity of the order. Also, a wizard working truly potent magic can eat like a tree-feller in the winter woods."

Haimya's gesture was fierce, also eloquent of what she thought of upholding the dignity of the Knights of Solamnia out of her private purse or her children's inheritance.

"Besides," Pirvan continued, lowering his voice, "we are a trifle too close to Istar to play host to a wizard not from an Istarian temple without setting tongues wagging. Tongues whose wagging might reach the ears of those about the kingpriest."

"One day, the folk of Istar will have to choose between their worship of their own virtue and the worship of the True Gods," Haimya said with a grimace. "I suppose there's nothing we can do in the meantime, except pray that they make the right choice?"

"That, and serve the knights. They are not yet under Istar's yolk." *And one of Marod's purposes and mine is to see that they never are.*

They were almost to the gate now, and ran the last fifty paces. As they burst into the courtyard, laughing like children, they met their own children running toward them.

"Papa, Mama," Gerik and Eskaia shouted. "You have a visitor. He waits in the great hall."

Pirvan and Haimya stared at each other, a nearly audible prayer on both their faces that Sir Niebar had not returned.

"It is not that skinny knight," Eskaia added, reading her parents' mood as she did so often and easily. "This man is not skinny at all."

"Jemar the Fair?" Haimya asked, falling into the spirit of the game. Their old sea barbarian comrade-in-arms had put on a fair amount of weight since he had married Eskaia's namesake, a merchant princess of Istar, and taken to family life.

"No. He is not fat, either, but tall. Very tall," Gerik put in.

"How many eyes does he have?" Pirvan asked.

The children grinned. "We can't tell, because he has a patch over the left eye."

"Yes, and the other one we see looks red, as if he has been weeping or without sleep."

Pirvan and Haimya exchanged quick glances. Grimsoar One-Eye had been Pirvan's friend and sometime comrade during his thieving days, and was not much given to weeping. Nor did he often go without sleep, or sleep without snoring like an earthquake.

Except when he was in haste, and if he had come to Tiradot in haste, it would be well to learn why—also in haste.

"Gerik, go to the kitchen and have chilled wine and cakes brought to the small solar," Pirvan said. "Eskaia, you run down to the millstream and say that your mother has private business and asks the maids to forgive her for not helping them bring the washing up."

"Why do the maids need an apology from Mother?" Gerik said.

"Because she is breaking a promise she made to them," Pirvan said sharply. "Anytime you break a promise, you apologize to those to whom you made it. Your mother and I do it, the grand master of the knights does it, the king-priest does it." *If he still fears the True Gods, that is.*

"Therefore, *you* will also do it."

"Yes, Father," Gerik said. He sounded subdued, if not precisely repentant, and scurried off toward the kitchen with the air of not wishing to be under his parents' eyes any longer than necessary.

"He has been spending too much time with those three pestilential lordlings of Fren Gisor's," Haimya whispered. "We shall have to—"

"We can and will," Pirvan said, tucking her arm under his. "But after we hear Grimsoar out. If we are going to appear dressed like this even before an old friend, we owe him haste at least!"

Chapter 3

The green-walled chamber in Istar's Tower of High Sorcery lay so far below ground level that it could hardly be said to be in the tower at all. It would have surprised no one, wizard, cleric, or common citizen of Istar the Mighty, to know that it was shown on no plan of the tower.

It might have surprised some wizards to know that there were indeed plans of the five great Towers of High Sorcery, and that these plans were often seen by common folk. However, it would not have taken a long explanation to end their surprise or ease their concern.

Tarothin the Wizard remembered giving one of those explanations himself some years ago, to a bemused apprentice.

"In the first place, the rulers of those cities and lands where the towers lie do not much care for our being more mysterious than we need to be. So any little gesture of trust in the right place may be a potent force for goodwill.

Remember the Thirty-first Principle."

The apprentice had been bright and eager even while bemused. He recited the principle briskly, from memory.

"`A small spell at the right time has the power of a mighty one an hour late. A small spell in the right place has the power of a mighty one a thousand paces away.'"

"Exactly. Consider these plans of the towers a small spell for peaceful relations with those who wield power over our destiny without knowing much about us and often disliking the little they know.

"Also, there are times when one does not wish to use spells to unplug a drain or regild a ceiling in parts of the towers where nothing arcane or secret happens. Thus we bring in common workers, whose goodwill we earn by paying them for their labor, and who, when they see us as folk much like themselves, may lose a bit of their fear of us."

Tarothin had laughed harshly. Once his laugh had been full-bellied; one woman had even called it jolly. But there had been rather less to be jolly about these past ten years than before.

"Of course, anyone entering a Tower of High Sorcery with hostile intent will find the plans more menace than aid. An army using them would be lucky to find anything important, luckier still to find its way out again. And every tower is guarded by wizards whose skills are devoted to making sure that the invaders have no luck.

"So you can be sure that the existence of plans of the towers is no mystery, nor any great danger to us."

Mollified, the apprentice had returned to his studies.

* * * * *

I wonder what became of the lad, Tarothin mused, wiping his eyes discreetly as they watered from the smoke of the braziers. He had wits and a vocation, but seemed very firmly inclined to the White Robes. Too firmly for one his age.

It was unlikely that Tarothin would ever know. The full wizards of the White, Red, and Black Robes were not a multitude; the seats of a fair-sized games arena would hold most of them. But they were widely scattered, and it had become wiser with the years not to tell one another too much about their comings and goings, to say nothing of their secret refuges.

This meeting showed that problem as vividly as the freshly retouched gold inscriptions on the green marble wall behind the speaker's chair. The chamber held seventy wizards, and apart from those of Istar, Tarothin did not know the homes of more than one in five. He knew their faces and their skills, but he could not readily have said where they came from.

There were exceptions, of course, and one of them was standing beside a bas-relief carving supposed to represent Huma's minotaur companion Kaz. Rubina was a Black Robe who made no secret of being from Karthay, the great trading city near the mouth of the Bay of Istar and Istar's leading trading rival. She also made no secret of being as concerned for the fate of her city as she was for the fate of the towers and all their wizards, apprentices, and servants, which was not proper in a full wizard.

However, it was hard to work oneself up to a serious argument with Rubina. She was too gracious, too witty, and many times over too beautiful.

At the moment, Rubina's exquisite face was set in a mask of boredom, and her huge, heavy-lidded brown eyes were closed in a gesture not meant to be sensuous—at least Tarothin thought not. But then, the black robes weren't meant to be alluring, either—but it was hard to look at Rubina in them without thinking of what she might look like without them.

The speaker was now repeating himself for at least the fourth time (Tarothin had given up counting) on the iniquity of the title of "kingpriest" for the principal cleric of Istar. Tarothin thought that if there was any point to be made on this subject, it had already been made, and the speaker was continuing because he did not know how to stop and nobody had the wits or courage to tell him to be silent.

The matter of the title was of some moment, to be sure. It had always been one title of the principal cleric of Istar, since Istar had been a village and all its clerics could be gathered in a single tavern, which was probably where many of them spent most of their time. A century ago, it had become the sole title, but the old titles did not vanish from usage and the new one was seldom taken seriously except on the most formal ritual occasions. The merchants and artisans of Istar were a hardheaded lot, or at least had been. They liked the idea of being the seat of the world's virtue, but were not going to have themselves laughed at when there was work to be done.

Now, to be sure, people were actually fined or even imprisoned for failing to say "kingpriest." But one could put all the fines so far collected in a purse that a strong man could carry, and the sentences of imprisonment were less than those meted out to drunkards who fought with the watch.

To keep his muscles from freezing him like a statue, Tarothin took a step sideways and looked about the chamber. Within a staff's length he saw, wearing full robes, two kender, a full elf (Qualinesti, of course; the Silvanesti seldom lived outside their homeland, let alone entered any human order of priests, wizards, or warriors), two with the look of half-elves, and one who was short enough to be a dwarf, though he probably was not.

There lay what frightened Tarothin—the spreading notion that only humans, Istarian or otherwise, had virtue in the sight of the True Gods. This not only went against everything Tarothin had ever been taught, but it also went against everything he had seen or heard during a life now past its fortieth winter.

When the Istarians started enforcing *that* madness with fines and imprisonment—of humans or nonhumans, it did not matter—dire times indeed would be at hand. If the speaker had spoken so much as six words about that, Tarothin would have been content.

At last the speaker ran out of wind as thoroughly as he had long since run out of wits. Tarothin made polite noises as the man came down; he was, after all, a fellow Red Robe, and one needed harmony within one's own order even more than with the others.

A buzz of voices made Tarothin turn, to see Rubina mounting the speaker's stair and taking her seat. It could not be entirely his imagination that as she sat down she made her robes swirl a trifle more than nature allowed, revealing a well-shaped arm and truly exquisite ankles, as well as strong feet in sandals of leather with ebony clasps—and wine-colored toenails.

After this display, Rubina could have talked about the best formula for glue and still held at least the male portion of her audience. Instead, she bowed her head and said, solemnly:

"May the words of my mouth and the meditations of my heart be pleasing to all gods, and to this honorable company."

She then launched into a summary of a situation arising in the north that closely concerned her home city of Karthay.

"It will concern all here, and all magic-workers everywhere, before long. For how can we do our work in peace when there is no peace?"

That certainly won Rubina undivided attention. She continued, explaining that the outlaws and pirates of the north coast seemed to be growing in strength under the leadership—or so the tales ran—of a minotaur. They raided ever farther afield, and while moderate in their conduct, had everyone within several days' ride of the shore looking over his shoulder. They had not taken seriously to piracy on the open sea as yet, but that could well change.

Even before that happened, Istar would surely assemble a fleet and an army to scourge the outlaws. This might seem innocent, even useful, but fleet and army would sit squarely across the mouth of the Bay of Istar from Karthay. No Karthayan ship could move without Istar's permission, and it would be the easiest thing in the world to blockade Karthay over any slight dispute between the two cities.

"Istar has long been jealous of our prosperous merchants, and seeks to render them less prosperous. The scourge of the outlaws is real enough, but Istar will use it as a pretext for tyranny. And if we of Karthay resist, then the Knights of Solamnia will be bound to march, and the utter ruin of our city must follow."

From the looks and mutterings Tarothin noticed, not all of those present found the idea of Karthay's suppression as unpalatable as they ought to be. He also hoped Rubina would not notice any of this. Her temper was legendary; unleashing it now would render her cause stillborn.

Tarothin cleared his throat. "If I might take a moment to add my thoughts to the Lady Rubina's . . ." He waited a decent interval, then continued.

"Even if the Knights of Solamnia do not find cause to take part in this quarrel, Istar will have to increase its fleet and army. This means higher taxes, empty bellies, and people seeking to blame someone else for that fate. I will not judge either city, but I do call to your minds what has happened in other lands in other times.

"Istar has one great virtue—much of its empire it gained peacefully. What we can do to keep the city on that course in years to come, we should do."

The response to that bit of common sense was gratifying—a flurry of suggestions, some more practical than others. The arguments were long and loud enough to fill the chamber with echoes, adding to the headache Tarothin had already acquired from the brazier smoke. They ended with an agreement to appoint two people from each of the orders to sit in council on the suggestions, weigh their merits, and propose acting on the best.

Tarothin would have liked more, but he doubted that he was the only one here whose head was splitting and whose stomach was rumbling ominously. For the sake of secrecy, the whole conclave and its chamber had been bound with spells that required fasting, and Tarothin at least had eaten nothing since a dried apple tart just before he went to bed last night.

The conclave had been declared closed, and the wizards were drifting toward one of the four low doors that led out into the underworld of the tower, when Tarothin felt a hand on his arm. He turned to meet Rubina, with a face so lowering and thunderous that for a moment he actually forgot her beauty.

Then awareness of the lustrous black hair and the high cheekbones and full lips returned. So did knowledge that his gesture of support for her had interrupted her speech, perhaps even ended it before she had wished. If she resented that—well, he could plead good intentions, but with either woman or gods, that plea was apt to be rejected.

"My good lady, if anything important was left unsaid because of my eager tongue—"

The thunderclouds blew away, and the huge, dark eyes stared into Tarothin's with a warmth that, by a strange paradox, sent a chill creeping up his spine. Then Rubina laughed.

"Nothing I could have said was as important as having the conclave take the matter seriously. If it had not been for you, this might never have happened."

"I am sure someone else would have had the sense to do the same," Tarothin replied. "Our brothers and sisters sometimes *seem* witlings, but few of them actually are."

"Nonetheless, I am grateful. Indeed, my gratitude could extend to dinner in my chambers tonight."

Tarothin's mind told his body to cease baying like a hound on the scent, which it seemed about to do. The invitation might have many meanings, most of them innocent, and several outcomes, likewise.

Still, when one looked at Rubina and thought of her chamber, the picture that came to one's mind was a room largely filled by a gigantic bed, with every comfort ready at hand so that anyone in the bed need not leave it for quite a while. . . .

Tarothin lifted Rubina's hands and bowed until he could brush them lightly with his lips. He nearly chipped a tooth on one of her rings—three or four to each hand, he judged—but he was rewarded with a silvery laugh.

"I have nothing to do that could reasonably vie with the pleasure of accepting your invitation," Tarothin said, trying to assume the accent of a comic actor. This time Rubina's laugh made him suspect that the gods had not made him for acting.

"I rejoice," Rubina said, putting an arm briefly around Tarothin's waist and standing close so that honey breath tickled his ear and played over his cheek and neck. "But now I must leave you, to make my chamber ready for hospitality instead of merely work."

She seemed to vanish between one breath and the next, and it was a moment before Tarothin realized that while they talked she had maneuvered him close to one of the doors. She had simply stepped through it the moment her last breath flowed past him—though it was not entirely Tarothin's imagination that he could still smell her perfume in the air, and under the perfume the essential scent of woman.

What might come of this, Tarothin did not know; he was not even going to waste time guessing. However, there was one stop he would make on his way to Rubina's chambers.

Jemar the Fair was in port, with three ships, one of them *Sea Leopard*, whose Mate of the Deck was another old comrade of the quest into Crater Gulf, Grimsoar One-Eye. Grimsoar One-Eye was once comrade in night work with Sir Pirvan the Wayward.

What mortal men could know of matters along the north coast of Istar, Jemar and his men might know—or at least know who did. With Grimsoar helping, Tarothin might even be able to draw on Pirvan's wits—although as an oath-bound Solamnic Knight, the man could hardly offer more than advice without the permission of his superiors.

Tarothin told himself that he was *not* seeking all this to raise his standing in Rubina's eyes and advance himself toward a more agreeable conclusion to the dinner. He was seeking knowledge that might altogether prevent a needless war, or at least turn a large war into a small one. And those who said all wars were evil had never talked to those who lived because someone kept a war small.

For centuries, the world had accepted the reign of Istar because it had brought peace and a fair degree of justice. If this was about to change, by the folly of kingpriests or anyone else, it was not something to endure idly.

Chapter 4

It was only the remnants of a storm from far to the north, beating on the rocks at the foot of the cliff. But even those remnants turned into breakers two men high when they reached shoal water.

When the breakers reached the rocks, the spray leaped to the top of the cliff, silver as it leaped, leaving rainbows as it fell back. By long-nurtured and finely honed instincts, the homecoming raiders of Darin, Heir to the Minotaur, opened the distance between them and the cliff, as much as the narrow path would allow.

All except Imsaffor Whistletrot. He perched on a jutting rock, just above the highest reach of the spray, and stared down into the water.

"No shellfish for dinner tonight," he said with a grimace.

"I thought you hated oysters," one of the men said.

"Oh, I do. But most of you big folk love them, which is one reason I'm not sure the same gods created you and kender, and you'll be in a bad mood, which—"

Darin reached out one long arm, gripped Whistletrot by the collar, and drew him back to safer or even somewhat dry ground. This stretch of the coast seldom went long enough without rain for the ground to dry completely, which meant slippery footing for those unaccustomed to walking it.

Darin and his comrades did not complain of the weather. Their food came from root crops (which could well-nigh flourish in a swamp), from the trees and the animals of the forest, and from the sea. That this land was no friend to farmers was all the better for them, as they had no love for neighbors.

The big man looked up at the sky, alternately veiled and exposed by the dance of the clouds. "Best we make haste," he said. "I can endure a cold victory feast, but the cooks will mutiny if they must serve it, and Waydol will have something to say as well."

The pace quickened. Among the men, only Darin could have truly said that he loved Waydol. But every man here respected Waydol, valued his wisdom in war and council, and feared his tongue as much as, or more than, they did his fist.

Within minutes the path turned away from the sea and began to climb. No one who had not walked this path many times could have easily told where he was climbing to; the trees grew that quickly. Ferns and livid fungi that did not need sunlight also grew thickly where the trees left them space, and even a few ground-hugging vines flaunted dew-wet leaves among the decaying branches and needles.

Darin inhaled deeply. This forest was the true smell of home for him, for all that he had raided deep inland and far out to sea. He would ask nothing better of any god than to live out his life here, taking Waydol's place when the Minotaur at last lay on the pyre, and continuing Waydol's battle until the time came for him to pass the burden to his own heir.

Bird whistles sounded from ahead. Sirbones quickened his own pace, to draw level with Darin, curiosity plain on his face.

"Best not hurry," Darin said. "This path is treacherous."

"I think those bird whistles mean more than treacherous paths," the priest of Mishakal said. For all that he seemed old enough to be father to most of the raiders, he had kept up with them all the way from Dinsas without much effort.

"Oh?" Darin said. He was hardly surprised, though some of his men were a little uneasy at Sirbones's deftness in winkling out the band's secrets. None of them had been foolish enough to attack a man under Darin's protection, not to mention a priest of Mishakal, whom it would be impious and perhaps impossible to harm.

"Yes. Were I in your shoes—"

"I am barefoot, as you have doubtless noticed."

"So I have. But one need not say everything in the simplest fashion. Words, I have discovered, sometimes need to be caressed to bring them to a proper state."

Darin refused to contemplate how a priest would learn of caresses—though, to be sure, he had heard that celibacy among the followers of Mishakal was a common choice rather than a rigid law.

Pray that Sirbones has no eye for woman that will break the peace of the band.

"I am not worried about your words. I worry about your ears. Are they open to listen? Waydol says, truthfully, that our having only one mouth but two ears means that we should listen more than we talk."

Sirbones grinned and nodded in total silence.

"Very well. The paths and the land are a good defense against anyone less surefooted than a ranger or hunter. But if anyone should send a host of rangers or hunters against our stronghold, we have added to nature's defenses. Some intruders would be slain or crippled; we would have warning of the rest."

"You do not say that I should ask no more questions, but I hear it in your voice," Sirbones said.

"You hear truly," Darin said. "I also ask of you one further bit of wisdom: stay in single file with me and my men. Some of our gifts to strangers reach close to the edge of the path."

"Pits of poisoned spikes and the like?"

"You promised to ask no more questions."

"I made no such promise. I merely understood your command."

"Then why do you defy it?" Darin snapped. He was just weary enough and eager enough to be home and at rest to have small patience for the priest's jests.

"Your pardon, Heir to the Minotaur. I presume greatly on your hospitality."

Not so greatly, when you know as well as we that having a healer-priest among us will be a blessing worth enduring much worse than your tongue.

But Darin did not put his thoughts into words, not only from courtesy but also to save the breath he would need for the rest of the climb.

* * * * *

Pirvan and Haimya met Grimsoar One-Eye in the same solar where Pirvan had earlier that day dealt with Sir Niebar.

The great hall was the most honorable place for feasting an old friend, a guest who had traveled far, and a mate in the service of Jemar the Fair. It was also the most open to the curious and the indiscreet.

So when they were done with the wine and cakes (two platters, as Grimsoar was a light drinker but ate in proportion to his size), they gathered certain articles—maps, for one—from their hiding places and began to talk seriously.

"What brings you here, with the air of one who had rancid butter on his breakfast porridge?" Haimya said.

"I wish it was something as simple and harmless to others as my stomach," Grimsoar said. "But it concerns more. Karthay and Istar are on a course that may make them collide hard enough to sink the both of them."

Pirvan nodded. "We've heard that Istar's fleet is to sail north and scour the coast of outlaws and pirates. We've also heard that Karthay may have the notion of rebuilding its own fleet if Istar does this."

"I know naught of Karthay," Grimsoar said. "Or at least

no more than one can hear in the streets. Building new ships there is a matter for the higher councils, and even Jemar's got few ears there."

The hint that the Knights of Solamnia might have such ears was too plain to ignore. Pirvan sighed. Best clear the air among us at once, he thought.

"The Knights of Solamnia are sworn to aid Istar against its foes," Pirvan said. "If Karthay means to become one, then my oath demands that I end this discussion." Ignoring Haimya's looking not merely daggers but arrows and broadswords at him, for she was of Karthayan birth herself, Pirvan continued. "However, if our purpose here is to prevent Karthay and Istar from becoming enemies, then all that I know is at your service, as is all the strength of my arm."

"And mine," Haimya said, with a look at her husband so different from the previous one that he flushed, and for a moment his head spun from more than the heat of the ill-ventilated chamber.

Grimsoar's smile was a bit wry. "I didn't hear either of you promise anybody else's arms or anything else."

"We didn't hear you promise any aid at all from Jemar," Haimya said. "Or is it that you are placed as we are—you cannot make promises that you know your masters will keep?"

"I wouldn't call Jemar a master," Grimsoar said. "He doesn't have any mucking huge stack of books to tell him what to do and how to tell everyone else what to do. The sea doesn't allow that, so if you knights ever want to launch a fleet, you may need something a bit—"

"Grimsoar, old companion," Haimya said, in a voice as soft as silk and as chilly as the blade of a Frostreaver, "leave it be. Or tell us what you can honorably say, and we will ask for no more. But if we spend more time in rude jests, Gerik and Eskaia will be old enough to join us on this quest before we have decided to launch it."

The two men looked at each other, then burst out laughing. "Very well," Pirvan said. "I will sit silent and let Grimsoar talk. He has never needed encouragement to do that before, so I—"

"Good husband," Haimya said in a tone of gentle menace.

Grimsoar's rumbling voice broke the silence. "We began to smell trouble, those of us who had our noses to the wind, when they appointed Aurhinius to command in the north."

"Gildas Aurhinius?" Pirvan asked.

"The very same," Grimsoar said, then added, for Haimya's benefit, "and no friend to even retired thieves. The army sent him over to the watch about ten years ago, to put some discipline and order into them. I suppose they thought he was too rich to be bribed."

"Did he succeed?" Haimya asked.

Grimsoar nodded. "At the price of a few good men and women Pirvan and I knew, dead, rotting in dungeons, or slaving their lives out in quarries. Aurhinius loves fine armor, but he fights like a smith's masterpiece of a sword."

"Not one sent out lightly, in other words," Haimya said. The two men nodded.

"Aurhinius has gone north already himself," Grimsoar went on. "He took ten ships and about two thousand men, mostly to put some muscle in the garrisons up yonder. But there's recruiting going on, veterans being recalled, workers being hired on in the shipyards to speed refits and new construction—oh, Zeboim's own lot of trouble for honest sailors."

Pirvan managed not to laugh at Grimsoar's description of Jemar and his ilk as "honest sailors." Outright piracy was a smaller part of their work than before, but other ways of separating people from their gold still flourished among the sea barbarians.

Pirvan rose. "Old friend, my lady and I will have to think about this. But I promise you, we'll think toward the goal of doing something, or having it done if our own hands are bound."

Grimsoar's grunt made it plain that he would have preferred more, but knew he could not ask for it. Beyond that, friendship bound him to silence, at least as long as he was under his friends' roof.

* * * * *

The two paths converged before a vertical slit in a cliff face not much lower than the towering pines behind them. Darin saw Sirbones staring at the slit, wondering whether men could pass through it even if it led anywhere.

"Don't worry, friend priest," Whistletrot said. "The finest kender minds have worked on a solution to this problem."

"Aye," someone said, "and if we'd waited for a solution from them, we'd have been better off going to the gnomes."

Sirbones actually looked uneasy. "This isn't gnome-work, is it?"

Laughter echoed from the rocks and back into the trees. "No," Darin said. "Human, with a little help from a mino-taur, and quite trustworthy." He looked up at the top of the cliff and raised both hands over his head, palms outward.

A rumble started from deep in the rock, swelling until the ground underfoot seemed to be shaking. Sirbones was plainly uneasy, still more plainly trying to hide it.

Then the rumble faded. Darin walked over to a large boul-der to the left side of the slit in the rock and pushed hard. With a squeal like a flattened piglet, the rock slid to the left. Behind it lay a dark, dusty tunnel—or rather, a semicircular passage carved out of the living rock to one side of the slit.

At the far end, sunlight glinted on water.

"Be our guest, Sirbones," Darin said. "And be silent about all you see here and afterward. We will not harm you to keep you with us, but if any of our secrets depart with you, your priesthood will not guard you."

"I am guarded by Mishakal, whatever threats you make," Sirbones replied with dignity. "But *you* are guarded from my tongue's wagging by my own oaths and honor. It is the mark of a barbarian, Darin, to think that only he among all men has honor."

Before Darin could think of a reply to that, the priest unslung his staff, so that it would not catch on the rocks, and, holding it out ahead of him like a spear, vanished into the passageway.

* * * * *

Pirvan and Haimya made a point of doing their weapons practice with the men-at-arms or visiting fighters as often as possible. Too much practice with the same opponent could make a fighter used to that one opponent, no longer alert for the unpredictability of a new and unknown one.

This, they both agreed, was an excellent way to meet a swift death in battle.

Still, it lightened both their spirits to work against each other with wooden swords and padding. And today of all days, their moods needed lightening.

They had been at it now for a good part of the afternoon, and Pirvan's bruises were beginning to hurt, not to mention his eyes, where sweat ran into them. But Haimya was coming at him again, as light on her feet as a doe in the spring, and the bout was not over yet.

He risked closing, beat her sword aside, and thrust inside her shield with his dagger. She brought her blade around just in time for him to lock it with his, hilt jammed to hilt. Also nose practically touching nose, and her eyes—blue today, though he had seen them shine gray or green—staring into his.

Then she laughed, no dainty girlish trill, but a hearty guffaw. "A draw, this one?"

"Fair enough." He stepped back, not lowering his guard until Haimya shrugged her shield off her shoulder and dropped the sword on top of it. Then she sat down cross-legged and reached for the water jug.

"Are we going to help Grimsoar and all the rest?" she asked when she finished drinking.

"You mean, do we seek out the cause of this trouble between Istar and Karthay and seek to maintain peace between them?"

"You are talking to me, not writing a letter to Sir Marod."

"I had best practice for writing that letter, however."

"Not on me, I pray."

"Who else can I trust, for tolerance, discretion, and—"

She kissed him. He kissed her back, then broke away, smiling.

"—and interesting ways of interrupting me."

"I can make them more interesting still."

"The armory is a trifle open."

As if to underline Pirvan's remarks, Gerik and Eskaia came running in.

"Papa, Mama," Gerik cried. "Your friend Grimsoar says he will tell us stories about pirates if you let him stay for dinner."

"Grimsoar is staying for dinner, and even for the night," Pirvan said. "But you, lad and lass, still have to finish your lessons. The last time you showed me your tablet of sums, you had, between you, eleven wrong out of twenty."

"Oh, but—" Gerik began.

"Do *not* say that your clerks will do that sort of work," Haimya interrupted. "Remember that it takes time before you can pay a clerk's salary. Also, if he thinks you cannot find his mistakes, he will either work badly or cheat you, or both."

"Now run along. We will hold Grimsoar to his promise if you keep a promise to finish your lessons before we call you to dinner!"

The children scurried off, allowing Pirvan and Haimya to stand briefly with their arms about each other's waists before they started hanging up their equipment.

* * * * *

The ceremonial part of the welcoming-home feast was done. Now, at last, Darin could allow Waydol to lead him aside, into the Minotaur's stone hut, and speak where no one else could hear.

The first thing Waydol did was embrace his heir, for the fifth time since they had met at the end of the entryway. It was the fiercest embrace of all, and Darin knew that he had to give back, if not as good as he got, then the best he could do with merely human muscles.

This done, Waydol motioned his breathless heir to one of the stone stools on the rush-strewn floor. Waydol himself sat down cross-legged on the floor, and stared at Darin with that look that seemed to say the Minotaur could look into a man's soul and judge his honor and everything else in it.

Waydol did not have to look up very far to meet his heir's eyes. The shortest of adult minotaurs was Darin's size, and Waydol was taller than the common run of his folk. In his youth he had fought with a minotaur broadsword in each hand and, while that youth was past, he had not yet reached the age when even a minotaur begins to stoop.

"So, Heir Darin," Waydol rumbled. His Istarian vocabulary was excellent, but his accent remained strong, and no minotaur could ever sound less than guttural to a human ear. "Is there aught of this raid that I alone should know?"

"Nothing that comes to mind at once," Darin said.

"Do not ask to sleep and then speak," Waydol said, but the smile took the sting from his words.

"When did I last do that?"

"Oh, when you were sixteen or so."

"Ah, one of my first raids. I think I remember it, even though it was so long ago."

"It was, as you remember perfectly well, no more than six years ago. Or if you do not remember it, then I fear I must look elsewhere for an heir. *My* memory has not crumbled to rubble, at five times your years."

"Ah, but for a minotaur, your years are but those of a green youth."

"Indeed?" Waydol said, pretending to make a twisting pass with his horns at Darin's stomach. The young man rolled off the stool and came up holding it like a shield.

"Bring me the mirror and a polishing cloth," Waydol said, chuckling. A minotaur's chuckle sounded to most folk like millstones grinding together, but to Darin it was a sound of home.

Darin brought the bronze mirror and a sack of cloths impregnated with various scented resins, then held the mirror while Waydol carefully polished his horns. They were a fine pair, and the more precious to Waydol because he had narrowly escaped losing them.

This had been many years ago, when he suggested that one should learn the weak spots of the humans before one charged headlong at them. After all, honor did not require being foolish.

Some fairly powerful minotaurs thought this insulted their honor, and gave Waydol a choice: exile or dehorning—or death in the arena, of course, a battle Darin thought the other minotaurs should have been grateful never took place.

He chose exile. Shortly after that, he chose to make himself chief of a band of human outlaws, or at least those who survived their first encounter with him. And shortly after making himself chief, he adopted as his heir a stout-thewed child who had washed up on his shore, clinging to a timber from his family's lost ship.

That was nineteen years ago. The horns that Waydol had not lost in his homeland had continued to grow in exile, and were formidable weapons in their own right. Neither were the Minotaur's wits any less sharp.

Indeed, Darin thought that if the minotaurs had met in solemn conclave for months, they could hardly have picked one of their number better suited to learning the weak points of the humans. If those who remembered Waydol's insults were dead in the arena and those who lived had sharper wits, he still might carry out his task.

Which, to be sure, would mean a fearful burden on the honor and conscience of the Minotaur's heir. *When* it came about—and even without Waydol, Darin's life would have taught him that worrying about what may never happen deserves perhaps one minute out of the day, when one is using the privies or shaving or doing something else that makes small demands on one's wits.

"I think you should go out again soon, and with the greater part of the men," Waydol said.

"That will mean underchiefs," Darin replied.

"Kindro and Fertig Temperer are both seasoned enough to lead."

"And young enough to be spared if they fail?" Darin said.

"You may be such a cynic when you have a beard as long as my horns."

"If I have to ride with Fertig Temperer often, the beard will be white before it is long."

"He is no worse than most dwarves, and better than some."

"Then I pray I never meet the `some.'"

"Not one likely to be granted. The realm of Thorbardin is at our backs. We will need to withdraw into their lands if we are driven from the coasts."

Darin no longer marveled at a minotaur thinking of retreating in the face of superior force, rather than dying on the spot. What bemused him was where the superior force might come from.

By the time Waydol had finished explaining the significance of the coming of Gildas Aurhinius to the northern territories of Istar, not far from their own range, Darin understood more on the matter of superior force. He also wondered what he was supposed to do with, at most, two hundred men against ten times their number.

"If you find them gathered together, I expect little, apart from driving in their patrols, taking prisoners—the higher-ranking the better—and generally testing their fighting qualities. But you are not likely to find them all together.

"Aurhinius is, by all I have learned of him, a man with ambitions to rise high in the councils of Istar once he hangs up his helmet for the last time. Such a man will surely heed the cries of the northern towns for a hundred men here and fifty there to guard their walls, fields, and caravans.

"You and your men could eat any such handful for breakfast and save the odd survivor for a midmorning snack, lightly salted or sprinkled with vinegar. Do that once or twice, and Aurhinius will take the field against you. Then I leave it to your judgment—but do something to make the man *angry*.

"An angry opponent will charge straight ahead. He will not make the best use of his strength or weapons. He will not guard against surprise attacks.

"He will, in short, become the sort of man who can be beaten even with long odds in his favor."

Darin knew that well enough from personal combat—but this was the first time he'd be applying the principle in battle—indeed, on a full campaign against a civilized soldier at the head of a small army. He knew the uneasiness was lack of confidence in himself rather than lack of confidence in Waydol, and he also knew that the uneasiness would disappear once he had fought the first battle or two.

Meanwhile, he *was* Heir to the Minotaur. He slipped off the stool, took the mirror from Waydol's hands, and held it up in front of the Minotaur so that he could work more swiftly at polishing his horns.

* * * * *

"Good night, Papa."

"Good night, Mama."

The children's duet came from either side of the corridor. The years when they shared a single nursery and a single nursemaid were gone; now Gerik had a tutor as well as instruction from the men-at-arms, and the younger sister of Haimya's maid attended Eskaia.

Not that Haimya really needed a maid, but had she done everything for herself as she had during her years as a mercenary, tongues would have wagged in gaping mouths from streamside to hillcrest. Her one consolation for being waited on was that she had a chance to teach both her maid and her daughter the rudiments of fighting, and with bare hands as well as steel.

Pirvan heard the doors shut and slipped a hand around Haimya's waist. "I think we should be ready to say good night before long, too."

"You are not, I trust, in too much haste in that matter?"

"Not such haste as to displease a lady."

"I commend your honor."

"It's more good sense than honor, considering what displeased ladies can do."

Haimya drew closer. "Perhaps you should contemplate the possibilities of a pleased lady."

They did more than contemplate possibilities; they explored them thoroughly. They were lying close together when Haimya stirred and propped herself up on one elbow.

"Have we forgotten anything we need for going north?"

"We haven't packed the supplies yet."

"I was thinking of making sure that the knights do not accuse us of disobedience."

Pirvan drew Haimya down onto his chest and savored that pleasure for a moment before replying. "We do have to spend some time in Karthay. Sir Marod was quite firm in his letters about the duty of all who served him, to learn what Karthay intends with its fleet. If we spend even a few days there, that and what we learn from Jemar will satisfy Sir Marod and anyone else who may ask questions."

Haimya sighed and relaxed against her husband. Then he felt her shoulders quivering, and also warmth and dampness on his chest.

"Haimya?"

"Forgive me," she said, wiping her eyes with the back of her free hand. "It's foolish, but—this is the first time we're going off and leaving the children since they were old enough to understand danger."

Pirvan tightened his grip. "My lady and love, if you cry over that, you'll have me joining you, and the bed will be drenched. You think I do not slip into their bedchambers at night sometimes, to stand looking down at them and all of our hopes that they carry?"

"I thought that was my secret." She bit him gently on the shoulder, then started kissing him. The kisses made their way up his neck and cheek to his ear.

"My lady, in some ways you have no more secrets from me at all," Pirvan said as he tightened his embrace still further.

Chapter 5

Darin's raiders were four days' march from their stronghold before they reached the first town to the east. It had no garrison of picked Istarian troops, and indeed had not even heard of the soldiers' coming.

"Which is about the way Istar always treats us," one merchant said. "We wait a year to get the message with the permission to put new gates on the storehouse. Then the messenger comes, with two hundred mounted escorts who eat the storehouse empty so there's no need to put so much as a ribbon across the door, because what's left wouldn't feed a mouse!"

This was not the first time Darin had heard complaints from folk in the north, that the rule of distant Istar was capricious and as often harsh as helpful. That was certainly a weak point, at least of Istar, to bring back to Waydol.

Meanwhile, Darin felt no inclination to loot the town,

particularly as its walls were of well-laid stone and its people robust and determined, if not particularly skilled in arms. Instead of raiding, he paid some hundred and fifty Istarian towers for a dozen reasonably stout horses. This would give him a band of mounted scouts, to ride in the vanguard, on the flanks, or to the rear, wherever the need was greatest.

The raiders moved on, in two columns now, with the scouts carrying messages back and forth. Darin found Fertig Temperer no less harsh-tongued than ever, but under the harsh tongue was usually shrewd advice. The dwarves did not often come out of their mountains in great numbers to fight in human wars, but their own wars were the stuff of legends. A dwarf resolved on battle had everything a minotaur did except stature and strength, and frequently made up for those with keener wits.

The seventh day took them past two villages, whose farmers were all in the field when the raiders burst out of the woods. Panic sent the farmers fleeing, raising the alarm as they ran.

Instead of barring the gates, one village left them open. Out of those open gates thundered half a dozen horsemen, so well accoutred and sitting their saddles so well that for a moment Darin feared they had encountered Knights of Solamnia.

Instead of charging home, however, the mounted men circled wide around the fleeing villagers. They rode to Darin's flank, then charged that flank in as wide a line as six men could make, keeping beyond the reach of most of the archers in Darin's center.

The riders struck home with vigor and skill. They spitted two of Darin's men on lances, and a third fell with his skull slashed open. They wounded two more raiders, and one rider was dismounting to take prisoners when the archers finally came running to within range.

Unsettled, their shooting was wild, and narrowly missed adding to the toll of hurt and wounded friends. But two horses fell; the first dismounted man went down bristling with arrows, and Darin rode up to deal with the others unhorsed.

At least that was his intent. The two remaining mounted men turned their mounts hard about and flung themselves at him. The archers could not shoot, friend and foe being utterly mingled, and while Darin tried to learn the art of swordfighting from horseback the two dismounted men scrambled onto their dead comrade's horse.

Then all the survivors put in spurs and were out of sight in the woods before the archers realized that they had a clear target again. Darin dismounted, hoping that at least the fallen man was alive to talk, but two arrows in the face had pierced deep enough to silence him forever.

"This," Darin said, "was not well done. We were to annoy the enemy, learn his strength, and take prisoners. It would seem that Aurhinius has given his captains the same orders—and that this day, his scouts obeyed his better than we obeyed Waydol's."

The raiders made a cold camp that night, with extra guards posted in case the surviving Istarian riders returned with either darkness and surprise or greater numbers on their side. The night passed without either excitement or comfort, however, and at dawn the raiders moved out once more.

* * * * *

For the next few days, the land might as well have been uninhabited, for all that Darin and his company saw of the god-created races. There were farms and villages, and even one town to which they gave a wide berth, fearing it might house a garrison or scouts. But all of these were either deserted, or, as Darin thought more probable, wishing to seem that way.

They took to moving by night, reckoning that the local folk might have chosen darkness to do their business on roads free of raiders. But this only succeeded in getting the company thoroughly lost twice in as many nights, and three men wandered all the way into a bog, from which only one emerged alive.

Darin stood a little apart with his underchiefs as Imsaffor Whistletrot used his hoopak to sound a dirge for the lost men, while doing a kender dance that made the human chief think of a chicken on hot coals. As a musical instrument, the hoopak made a low-pitched roaring that reminded Darin of surf on the shore of a distant and haunted sea.

Which fit rather too well with his mood at the moment, he had to admit. The raiders had gone out with the intention of lowering Istarian spirits, or at least reducing their numbers. So far, the spirits and numbers most seriously lowered were the raiders'.

Waydol would be even less pleased with his heir than the heir was, at this moment, pleased with himself.

"What next?" Fertig Temperer asked, putting everyone's thoughts into two gruff words.

Darin used the excuse of the farewell to the dead men to not reply for a few moments. But that was all he had before Whistletrot stopped his dance, slung his hoopak, and scrambled up the nearest tall tree.

"I suppose he might see something without anyone seeing him," the dwarf said. "The gods look after fools, children, and drunks, and a kender counts for two out of those three."

"Here, now," Kindro began indignantly. The other underchief was genuinely fond of kender, whom he said were made to remind other races not to take the world too seriously. It was rumored that he was fonder of kender maidens than of their menfolk, and that for this reason the male kender were less fond of *him* than he liked to believe.

"Enough," Darin said. "We know where we stand, which is hip-deep in a midden pit. No need to talk over the fine points of the stink. The question is how to get out of it?"

Before anyone could speak further, a signal arrow thumped into the ground a sword's length from Darin's foot. Then Whistletrot thrust his head and torso precariously out from the branches of his tree, so far that he nearly fell out headfirst. He caught himself with ankles locked around a branch, and, hanging like that, frantically signaled the approach of a small party, men, on foot, not heavily armed, but otherwise unknown.

Darin and his underchiefs wasted no breath with orders. Every seasoned man who saw arrow or dangling kender passed on the warning to those out of sight, and the seasoned men everywhere rallied their greener comrades. In less time than it took Whistletrot to swing himself back onto the branch and start descending the tree, the raiders were prepared to receive their visitors.

The kender's observations were accurate, as usual. Darin wondered at times how a race commonly so maddeningly feckless could produce such a reliable scout as Whistletrot. But, then, the few humans who had spent time in Kendermore had come away with the notion that kender could be quite sane and sober when their homes and kin were at stake.

Perhaps Imsaffor Whistletrot had decided that Waydol's band was his home and kin. It made as much sense as any human notion about kender usually did.

Four men walked into the clearing, obviously aware that they were being watched, but showing no signs of fear. One of them carried a large earthenware pot, and another had a basket slung over his back. The rest carried packs, pouches, and daggers, and one unburdened man carried a boar spear nearly large enough for Waydol.

"Ah—where is the Minotaur?" the spear carrier asked, speaking in no particular direction, as if he expected the air, earth, or trees to answer.

"I am Heir to the Minotaur Waydol," Darin said, stepping forward. He did not bother to gather his scattered weapons, as there was no man in the band he could not have dealt with barehanded. That was, of course, assuming that the concealed archers did not put all the visitors on the ground at the first sign of treachery.

"Then we offer you these gifts," the same man said. He held the boar spear out butt-first and laid it on the ground at Darin's feet. The young chief saw that the shaft was cunningly wrought to provide firm handgrips, and that the head and crosspieces were good dwarf-work.

The other gifts included the pot, which exhaled a tantalizing scent of honey, and the basket, filled with cakes made of flour mixed with some scented herb that Darin knew but could not name. He ceremoniously raised the spear, licked a finger dipped in the honey, and broke a cake in half, handing the half he did not eat to the leader.

The man devoured it with more appetite than ceremony, brushed crumbs from his beard, and frowned. "Then you accept our gifts of peace?"

"That depends on what kind of peace you offer us," Darin said, and his underchiefs nodded. "If the price of peace with you is too great, you shall at least have these gifts back, to sustain you on your return journey, and we will not take you hostage or fall upon you on that journey."

The men looked at one another. "It seems the honor of Waydol and Darin is no legend," the leader said.

Another nodded. "Catch Aurhinius making that sort of bargain."

Darin was as careful to keep his voice steady as he would have been careful to be silent when crouching barehanded by a trout pool. "Aurhinius? The Istarian general?"

"The same," the leader said, then the other three men all seemed to find their voices at once. They had to lose their breath before Darin could make sense of their words.

"Aurhinius has a garrison in your town, or near it?"

They nodded.

"You wish us to drive it out?"

One man nodded, and the other three shook their heads.

"Best I make this short," the leader finally said. "We can't ask you to fight Aurhinius, or even the smaller band of soldiers he will leave behind when he moves on to the next town. His strength is too great for you to meet it, and even if you won, we would be dwelling amid ruins and ashes.

"No, what we want is for you to draw Aurhinius and

his men away from all the villages, so that we may hide what the soldiers might otherwise take. Aurhinius keeps firm discipline among his men in the matter of women, but only a god could keep a soldier away from mead or a gold necklace."

Darin nodded slowly as a smile spread across his face. If the villagers could deliver up Aurhinius to humiliation, the less bloody the better, the raiders would have their victory without any danger of having to wander the country for months, until their retreat was cut off or they returned to the stronghold to find it besieged.

Darin turned to his underchiefs.

"It could be a trap," Fertig said.

Kindro shrugged. "For that, we have the mounted scouts—as long as we keep them out of those folks' sight," he added pointedly.

Darin let the tone pass unremarked. Kindro had been a sell-sword for nearly as long as Darin had lived, before he came to Waydol. He was not jealous of the younger man's being heir to Waydol, but thought and sometimes said that he ought to make better use of the warcraft of his elders.

"That goes without saying," Darin said. "Let us learn where Aurhinius lies, then the best way to it, then pick another and send three or four of our best scouts. Whistletrot, too," he added, in a tone that left Fertig with his mouth open but unable to make a sound.

"So be it," the two underchiefs said in unison. Darin turned to the villagers.

"Now, it would be well if we arranged all this so that Aurhinius has no inkling of your part in it. If he suspects nothing, he will be less ready to burn houses or take hostages, let alone worse punishments."

"True enough," the leader said. "He's a warrior who follows Kiri-Jolith, not Hiddukel."

Hiddukel was the god of corruption, fraud, and theft.

Darin clapped the leader on the back, hard enough to make the man stagger.

"Your pardon," he said. The man choked out some sort

of reply.

It had been some while since Darin so forgot his strength, but he had reason if not justice on his side. To enter a contest of wits as well as strength, against a foe as honorable as he was formidable, and with little risk of death or suffering to the innocent—that was the greatest pleasure man or minotaur could contemplate.

Darin vowed to make offerings to Kiri-Jolith if he won the forthcoming contest. He also prayed, briefly, that Aurhinius's honor would lead him to do the same if the victory went to him.

*　*　*　*　*

The work of the scouts was less finding Aurhinius than keeping him from finding the raiders at a disadvantage. Had the riders not been out, the two companies of warriors might have met at a crossroads overshadowed by a half-grown vallenwood and set about with crumbling shrines so ancient that no one could tell which god they honored.

As it was, one scout rode back to halt Darin's advance. Two others trailed Aurhinius and his company, until they reached country too rough for safe riding. Dismounted, the Istarians' pace was such that a nimble kender, such as Imsaffor Whistletrot, could easily keep up with them—and report when and where they made camp.

"It's as well we're not trying to fight them to a finish," Darin said after listening to the kender's description. "Aurhinius has a good eye for ground."

He cleared his throat. "Or does anyone care to dispute my plan for this fight?"

A couple of men seemed reluctant to meet his eyes, but Darin held their attention until he saw them nod. What stories those men could have told was no affair of his. He and Waydol had long known that among their band were humans and perhaps other folk with a blood-debt to settle against Istar the Mighty. Someday the time might come to give them free rein. This was not it.

"Very well. The duty of the main body is to cover the retreat of those who attack the camp. This means dividing to cover both paths, though I hope to ride in by one and out by the other."

"And if all this moving around takes until after dark, or loses us surprise?" someone put in.

"After dark, a small band has an even better chance against a large one. If we lose surprise beforehand, however, we will seek another way of being fleas under Aurhinius's fancy armor."

"Never mind his armor," Whistletrot said. "Just give me that golden helmet he fancies."

"And how much else?" Fertig Temperer asked.

"Oh, Aurhinius seems to set the style for his men."

"More than any six kender could handle," Fertig interrupted. "Whistletrot, comrade of many brawls and a few real battles, take my advice. Get in and get out as fast as ever a kender moved."

"What do I win by that?" Whistletrot replied. Kender did not grumble, at least in the presence of other races, but he came close to it.

"Life," Fertig said briefly. "My friend, if we have to snatch you from a handling foray among the Istarians, I will throttle you."

"If I go foraying in the camp, I'm not likely to be alive to throttle," Whistletrot snapped.

"Very well," Fertig said. "If I must, I will gather up your pieces in a sack and take them home. I will have Sirbones enspell them back into a living kender.

"*Then* I will throttle you."

"Settle this after the fight, will you?" Darin said. "Right now, we have enough time for a bite and a trifle of sleep before we move. Best we have them, too, if we're going to be spending the night running for our lives."

Darin saw that his words put sober looks on most faces. This battle might be a jest, but it was against Istar the Mighty, favored with stout soldiers, whatever it might lack in virtue. One could never be sure in such a fight which way the jest would turn.

* * * * *

Getting out of the camp would be easier than getting in. The entrance was a level path barely two men wide, though firm and level for riding. Darin took care to have several men hidden on each side of the path where it reached open ground, so that alert Istarians could not readily block it against the riders.

One of the hidden men was Whistletrot. Fertig thought that was giving a drunkard the keys to the wine cellar; Kindro said that Fertig thought with his belly; Darin told them both to be silent, in somewhat less polite words.

The six mounted men all carried their choice of weapons for fighting on foot, as well as leather armor and brass helmets. They also carried, slung from their saddles, good, stout clubs, the only weapons any of them could use from horseback with more danger to the enemy than to their mounts or comrades.

This is not what the gods would choose to send against seasoned Istarian cavalry, Darin thought as he lowered himself cautiously into the saddle. The girths were tight enough that this time the saddle didn't slip, but he felt the horse sag and thought he heard it groan as well.

Or at least not unless they had been drinking late and were in the mood for rude jests, he thought further. Then Darin commended himself to the mercy of the gods, prodded his boot heels into his mount's ribs, and after an unnervingly long pause, felt the horse lumber into movement.

Aurhinius had no firm knowledge that enemies were close at hand, but he was a seasoned soldier who knew that he was in less-than-friendly country. Alert, vigilant, and well-armed sentries were posted, one on each side of the path.

They remained so until the moment when Darin led his riders into view. At the same moment the sentries' mouths opened to give the alarm, clay balls hurtled from the woods to smash into the backs of their necks. Both men went limp even as they fell, landing without a sound except for a faint clatter as one man's sword bounced into a clump of bushes.

One of the slingers, Imsaffor Whistletrot, leaped onto the back of Darin's horse and hung on behind him. Darin thought curses, but had no time to utter them.

"Why walk when one can ride?" Whistletrot whispered.

Darin's thoughts were louder. The horse must have heard them, because the overloaded beast blew hard, then picked up the pace from a slow trot to a fast one. It was trying for a canter when it reached open ground.

Across the open ground, not more than twenty paces away, a ruddy-faced, thick-set man stood while one attendant unbuckled silvered back-and-breast armor and another had already taken a golden helmet sprouting three scarlet plumes. The man wore a curly, dark beard and clothing of embroidered silk.

Chance had served up Aurhinius to Darin on a platter. No rummaging in tents, no need to wait for the man to mount up and charge—but there was still one flaw in the service.

Aurhinius stood on one side of a line of barrels and chests. Darin and his comrades sat their saddles on the other side. Unless their horses suddenly grew wings, there was no way over those barrels.

At least not for the humans. Kender were another matter. Darin felt small hands on his shoulders as Whistletrot vaulted onto them, then the kender jumped, turning a double somersault in midair. He flew over the barrels as lightly as a bird, landing next to the attendant with the helmet.

"Excuse me, but that's a fine piece," Darin heard the kender say as the human urged his horse forward, around the end of the barrels.

The attendant's reply was better not repeated, though the echoes were still repeating it as Whistletrot darted between Aurhinius and the other attendant.

Darin came around the end of the barrels and reached down. Without missing a step, Whistletrot tucked the golden helmet under his left arm and reached up his right for Darin's hand.

The kender flew into the air, and Darin dug in his heels again, keeping his horse moving at a ponderous trot. The attendants ran after him, just as the other mounted raiders came up in their leaders' tracks. Both men leaped aside without looking where they leaped, and while they landed unhurt, they also landed on their general.

Aurhinius's remarks to the world made those of the first attendant seem a model of politeness.

Good manners took a further hard blow as Darin led the riders on through the camp. Most of the men were dismounted, and as there were Istarians on both sides of the riders' path, even the archers with ready bows had to hold fast.

Darin's eyes were on a handful of men still attending their horses with feedbags or water buckets. But it was one mounted man who broke out of the shadows and rode straight at Darin who presented the first and greatest menace.

The man was riding loose-reined, guiding his horse with his knees, with a sword in one hand and a dagger in the other. Darin reached for his club and discovered that it had parted its thongs and fallen somewhere along the way.

This time the curses reached his lips.

Imsaffor Whistletrot wasted no time cursing. His slung hoopak was in any case a two-handed weapon, not at its best mounted, where kender seldom fought, anyway. His other weapons lacked reach.

So he tossed the helmet from left arm to right hand, catching it by the strap. Gripping Darin's belt with his left hand, he swung the helmet out and around as far and as hard as he could.

Both distance and speed were more than the oncoming rider expected. But then, the man was not the first to underestimate the strength and weaponscraft of a kender.

The helmet crashed into his sword as the blade swung down. The blade went wild. So did the rider's horse, for in going wild the blade nearly cut off the horse's left ear. A few moments of this wildness were all it took to unseat the rider. He parted company with his mount in midair, descended gracefully, and landed with a mighty splash in a puddle of well-ripened mud.

He was still struggling to his feet when the other riders trotted past him.

By now Aurhinius had left off calling down curses on the raiders and was rallying his men to pursue them. The rally was short-lived, however, as the archers on the entry path began shooting—not aiming to hit, so much as to distract.

They succeeded admirably. Instead of haring off in pursuit of Darin, Aurhinius's men went to cover, or snatched up their shields and formed a shield wall facing the archery.

This was the signal for Darin's archers on the other side of the clearing to begin shooting, hitting the Istarians in the back—or at least in the legs. Istarians cursed, howled, and danced wildly as they tried to keep up their shields, wield weapons, and pull arrows out of their legs all at once.

Not having three arms, they understandably failed.

Most of the men on foot had begun to pull themselves into better order by the time Darin's last rider disappeared down the outbound trail. Some had even mounted, and they spurred their horses after Darin.

At their head rode Aurhinius himself, without armor, with rents in his silk finery, as well as grass stains and mud smears all over it. He rode with sword in hand and on his face a look that would have curdled milk or turned the finest wine into vinegar.

He also rode without looking ahead of him. So it was another Istarian rider who saw the figures lurking in the trees and tried to give the alarm.

He might have succeeded, too, except that the extra weights Fertig had put on the net pulled it down before the riders could halt. They rode straight into the net, rising the height of a man above the path and securely bound to trees on each side.

Carefully sawed halfway through, so that when the mass of riders jerked hard on the net, both trees snapped off just below the net bindings and came down with a crash like a house falling. The net came down without killing any of the riders—though the horses were less fortunate—but blocking the path to mounted pursuit as if the earth had opened into a flaming pit.

Darin thought he recognized Aurhinius's voice among the curses again as he pushed his staggering, foaming mount to a final effort.

"Hope you're fit to survive on your own, my friend," he told the horse, patting the sodden, heaving neck. "We've no time for horse doctoring."

The horse at least was fit to stagger off out of sight as soon as Darin and Whistletrot dismounted. The other horses followed, none of them as close to dropping as Darin's, but then none had been carrying such a load.

"I wonder if the Istarians will trail them," someone said.

"For a while, perhaps," Darin replied. "But those Istarians have to be able to tell a loaded horse from one running free. They'll be seeking our trail soon enough—but not soon enough to find us, if we stop gabbing and turn homeward."

"No more raids while we've got the Istarians buzzing like we've kicked the hive?" asked one of the men who wanted Istarian blood.

"No. We're the bees, and we've stung Aurhinius enough for now. Fly around, and he'll bring smudge pots and wizards with poison spells. And there's the villagers to think about, for anyone who's forgotten our debt to them."

If anyone had, they dared not say it to Darin's face. Instead the men fell in behind him as he led the way into the forest, taking his usual care to find ground that would not show footprints or broken branches.

They were well inside the forest when Darin realized that a familiar face was missing. The whisper went along the line swiftly:

"Where is that confounded kender?"

Darin did not add, "Where is the golden helmet?" because *that* could start a panic.

He was about to quietly order the column to spread out and begin searching when a slight figure swung down from the trees on a vine. He bounced up as if the ground were a feather mattress and ran to greet Darin.

"I don't suppose I have the right to know where you've been?" the chief said.

"Oh, you certainly do, but it was nothing much. I tore the strap on the helmet when I swung it. Cheap work, that. Aurhinius ought to complain to the armorer and get a strap of good mail. I didn't think you'd want me to lose the helmet because of that.

"So I went up a tree and cut some vines for carrying the helmet." Whistletrot danced in a circle, showing Darin the golden helmet riding snug in a web of vines atop his pack. He danced in another circle while he unslung his hoopak.

Darin stopped him before he could start it roaring. Several other men swore to help him. One mentioned an old family recipe for kender stew.

"Really?" Whistletrot said. "Uncle Trapspringer said he had one, too, left over from a time when a lot of kender were besieged. I forget if it was ogres or minotaurs. No, wait, I think it was an island and there were sea trolls all around—"

"Later," Darin said, stopping Whistletrot with a firm hand on his collar.

"Or did they find a way to eat the sea trolls—?" Darin heard, as Whistletrot danced off out of reach.

He sighed. Victories came and went, as luck and the gods would have it. Kender never changed.

Chapter 6

Preparing for a quest or even a journey was a matter of no small complexity when one was a Knight of Solamnia.

Still, it was only in rare moments that Pirvan envied his younger self. To be sure, that younger Pirvan had few possessions he could not carry on his back, and no one to whom he needed to say more than "good-bye." And that only out of courtesy, and sometimes not at all, when he did not wish his departure known.

Also, when he reached his destination, if he was not seeking a new place for night work, he had little to do, and none of that in haste. To be sure, he needed a roof over his head and food in his stomach, but a host of cheap inns and lodging houses offered both, and in some of them fleas were rare and willing servant girls not unknown.

Now, of course, the effort required to go a-journeying sometimes seemed to Pirvan sufficient to take a large force of cavalry on campaign. Orders to the men-at-arms who remained behind, likewise the servants, likewise the stewards, bailiffs, village headmen, and all the others who could bring Tiradot Manor to ruin through malice or carelessness. Procuring horses (if any in the stables were unfit) and everything needed to turn a simple horse into a gentleman's mount, as well as food, drink, tents, money, and all else that might be needed if a day's journey ended short of a civilized tavern (the kind that had not been cheap when Pirvan's purse was lean, and were no cheaper now that it was fat).

Weapons—not so many hard decisions or so long a list, Kiri-Jolith be praised! Pirvan knew that he was still some distance from the full range of weapons skills that a true Knight of Solamnia had to master. At least Haimya's still being his master with the broadsword meant that he had a good teacher.

The armory gave up only sword and dagger for Pirvan, two swords and a shield for Haimya, and light armor—helm and back-and-breast. They also had various concealed weapons—concealed not only from the eyes of the passerby but from the armorer, who had to report such to the Knights of Solamnia.

Pirvan did not know what the penalty was for a Knight of Solamnia who carried a loaded cane or a swordstick. He did know that he much preferred to remain alive to find out.

Then all the days of preparation had fled, everything was packed or returned to the storerooms, and the horses themselves seemed to look impatient every time Pirvan passed through the courtyard. He did this several times on the last day, in his mind saying farewell to a place that had become home in a way he had never expected it would in the days when his new rank still sat on him like an ill-fitting helmet.

He and Haimya had gone journeying on the affairs of the knights many times, and a few times on their own affairs. More often than not, they had faced perils greater than Pirvan suspected this quest would offer.

Yet the farewell to the manor had become a ritual, and he suspected that his spirit would say it on his last departure, when they carried his mortal shell out to the burying ground beyond the stream.

There was also another farewell to be said, and there was no ritual to this, because it was to Gerik and Eskaia. No ritual, because with each farewell they knew more about what their parents faced than they had before.

What they faced, and what might take them from the world without so much as leaving a body.

There were times when the words of farewell nearly choked Pirvan. He wanted to say other words, words that would not choke him. Words such as:

"Ogres carry off Sir Gehbian and everything that is his. We are staying home." The affair of Sir Gehbian of Juhrwood had left Pirvan with headaches and Haimya with a limp for some months, and without exceedingly shrewd healing spells neither would have come home at all.

He dreamed of saying such words, but in the dreams the children did not leap about, shout for joy, and hug their parents. Instead they turned gloomy and sullen, muttering of "honor" and "you are not what you were" and other phrases that held no filial respect but rather a deal of painful truth.

"We bred them true," Haimya said one night, after Pirvan revealed the dreams to her. "True from the bone out, and no denying it."

"Who denies it?" Pirvan said, reluctant to be consoled. "But remember. Now we must say farewell when we march. In a while we will not be saying farewell, because they will ride with us. Then comes the worst part, when we must sit by the fire and watch *them* mount up and ride out."

"Both of them?"

"Any man who bids Eskaia sit by the fireside and embroider, she will stab with her longest, sharpest needle. And have you thought of how to reconcile Gerik to a life he would call less than honorable?"

"Hardly. It seems he has learned some good from those lordlings, as well as the rest."

"I suppose his mother had nothing to do with it?"

"Less than his father, I—"

Pirvan silenced her with a kiss, and that particular argument died aborning.

* * * * *

"Papa," Eskaia said. "May I ask you a question?"

"Is it one I must answer?"

"I think so, because it is one that both Gerik and I need answered."

"Why isn't Gerik here, to ask it himself?"

"He—I think he is afraid."

"Afraid?" Pirvan frowned, then said with mock seriousness, "It is unworthy of the blood of a knight—"

"It's the blood of a knight we're worrying about," Eskaia exclaimed. "Both of us. What will happen to us if you and Mama do not come back?"

Pirvan looked at the sky. No god appeared to offer guidance, advice, or even a rude gesture indicating that the problem was entirely his to solve.

For this last, Pirvan was grateful. He was in no mood to be told what he already knew.

He also knew that it was not a question of who would be the children's wards, who would pay for their education, how Eskaia would come by a dowry and Gerik his apprenticeship in the knights, and so on. They knew all this, and would be insulted if he repeated any of it.

"Eskaia, I am not sure what you want to know that we have not already told you."

The girl looked at her father with a pitying expression that Pirvan knew too well. It implied if he were not her father, she might call him too witless to be at large on the streets.

"Uhh—it's hard to say it right."

"Try. I'll listen to anything from you and your brother. So will Mama." Once, at least.

"Papa, if you and Mama die, who will train us so that we can avenge you?"

The words came out in a rush. Pirvan was conscious of standing mouth agape while his wits tried to assure themselves that his ears had not played them false.

He bought some time by hugging Eskaia, but his tongue ran away and he had to explain what he meant by "breeding true."

"Does this mean we will be able to fight as well as you?" she asked.

"Even as well as your mother, who is better than I am," Pirvan said. "Remember, when I was a thief, I went armed only to defend myself. I was no fighter."

"Yes, it was very honorable of you to try not to hurt anybody while you were stealing," Eskaia said calmly. "But if someone kills you and Mama, our honor means killing them."

"Indeed," Pirvan said. He could not escape the feeling that while his back was turned his daughter had changed into something he did not recognize. Love, yes. But recognize—that was another story, one he suspected that all fathers could tell.

He considered explaining how the children of Knights of Solamnia were bound to other notions of honor than blood vengeance—or at least ought to consider themselves so bound. From what Pirvan had heard in the way of complaints from his comrades, even those children who bred truest in the end sometimes made their fathers' hair stand on end.

Instead, he chose a more practical form of reassurance. "You will have all the training you can use, from all who have the care of you," Pirvan said firmly. "But worry about avenging us when we are dead and our killers are not. I hope you do not think that your mother and I will ever be easy prey?"

"Never!" Eskaia said. She stamped her foot. If she had been asked to spit on a temple floor, she could hardly have been more indignant.

"Then we are done with that, but not with the farewells.

If your brother could bring himself to come down—he need not wash—"

Eskaia was off like a stone flung from a siege engine.

* * * * *

Now all the farewells and even the scurrying about to retrieve vital items forgotten at the last moment were some days in the past. The journey from Tiradot to Istar lay over well-settled country, with good roads even in the hills and enough honest folk about at all times to discourage the other kind.

Not that Pirvan and his little company had much to fear from the common run of bandits and outlaws. They were too obviously armed and ready, promising no loot and many hard knocks, as well as an appointment with the executioner for any who survived the folly of the attack.

Indeed, at times those in Pirvan's company found themselves, in all but name, the guards of not-so-small caravans. Carters, pack trains, pilgrims, and the odd wayfarer who had no reason to be on the road but for the itch in his feet all seemed ready to stay within hailing distance of a Knight of Solamnia and his household.

It was during the long, ambling days on the road in such company that Pirvan learned a good deal more of the affairs of Istar, as the common man saw them. For the Knights of Solamnia, everything appeared in the light of a history stretching back the best part of a thousand years. For the common man, the world began when he was born and ended when he died, and the farthest he could think forward was his children and backward his parents.

At times, Pirvan wondered if that "common man's" view of the world was something Sir Marod had sought to find in him. No doubt Sir Marod had feared to be insulting by saying so aloud, but Pirvan found the idea no insult, indeed rather the reverse.

He would have taken up the matter with Sir Marod at some time, by choice over good brandy. Sir Marod would keep all the secrets he was required to keep and ten more besides, if he was allowed to do so. Pirvan had sworn some years ago to nibble away at Sir Marod's excess of secrets, like a mouse at a cheese.

The journey was agreeable in all save duration, which made Pirvan think yearningly of flying on dragonback, even precariously strapped to the exuberant young bronze Hipparan, except for one disagreeable incident. That came on the fifth night out, when lowering clouds that promised rain induced them to stop early, at a sprawling inn called the Chained Ogre.

The name itself rang harsh on Pirvan's ears, and he decided that making the innkeeper a trifle uneasy would only be fair pay for the man's dubious taste. The knight had not forgotten his old night work skills, including finding concealed routes into and about any building, being quiet and invisible, and picking locks.

The only difference was that now Pirvan put on the simple, patched garb that any manservant might wear, and he looked as if it had been dragged behind a wagon over several days' worth of road. Add a little work by Haimya on her husband's hair, and no one who had not seen him more often than the innkeeper and his servants would have been able to recognize him.

He had been about the inn for nearly an hour, and was beginning to expect to be disappointed in his suspicions. He promised to continue his search until the rain stopped, then retire. They would need to start early tomorrow, to make a decent day's progress over muddy roads.

Pirvan was now in the attic, which, from its mustiness, dustiness, and burden of useless articles, must be visited about once in the reign of each kingpriest. Then he heard a sneeze, and as he raised his lantern and drew his dagger, he saw something moving.

It was a small figure, and his first thought was some apprentice potboy or stablehand, eking out night after night amid the dust and debris of the attic after a day's exhausting labor. That was bad, but not something where Pirvan's duty or the law allowed him to interfere. Mutual recognition of each other's laws was part of the Swordsheath Scroll that bound Solamnia and Istar, and the laws of Istar said nothing against making apprentices sleep hard in filthy attics.

Then Pirvan looked more closely. The small figure was not a boy, but a kender—sex impossible to tell. Moreover, the kender had one eye half-closed in the middle of a purple bruise, and both its feet were chained to a log that must weigh as much as Grimsoar One-Eye.

Pirvan walked over to the kender so noiselessly that he was standing over the other before the kender noticed him. Then the kender gasped, went white, and covered his face with his hands.

Pirvan's first reaction was the impractical one of wishing to slaughter on the spot whoever had abused the kender this way. Kender had more than their share of annoying and even bad habits, but to make one this fearful—and thin as well—required brutality that no crime could justify.

Or at least no crime that the kender themselves would not punish readily. There was no part of Istar where one could not find within a day's ride enough kender to administer justice to one of their own. Why had the person responsible for this brutality not thought of that?

Pirvan decided it would be well to find out who that person was, and to assist his memory.

"I am Sir Pirvan of Tiradot, Knight of the Crown," he said. "I feel I am in the presence of injustice. Would you care to tell me your story?"

This took a while longer than Pirvan had expected, but not because the kender rambled and backtracked and generally made a hash of the story. It was because the first thing the kender did was to burst into tears. This made Pirvan resolve to find some way of killing the kender's persecutor slowly, but accomplished little else.

Finally the story came out. "So many things wound up on high shelves around here, the night I stayed, that it's no surprise that some of them fell into my pockets. I never thought anybody would put a brooch like that on a shelf, even if it was just pretty. When I heard that it was valuable, the first thing I thought of was returning it. That was what I was doing when they caught me."

Reading between the lines, Pirvan caught a tale of a kender staying in a human-owned inn where his kind were none too welcome, with fellow guests who openly hated nonhumans. Add a bout of handling that got a trifle out of bounds, even by kender standards (which was to say that the kender might have stripped the inn to the bare walls if he'd been able to carry that much), and the wrath of a good many humans descended even faster than a kender could run.

"I suppose you know that you have the right to appeal to the principal kender of the area, or at least inform them."

The kender looked away. "They know. I appealed."

"And—they left you like this?"

"There are not as many of our folk about as there used to be, not since the Brongon Hill fire."

Pirvan remembered that vaguely. It had wiped out a whole kender community—not killing many, but leaving the survivors destitute and forced to flee. Most went all the way back to Kendermore.

"That was a forest fire, though, wasn't it?" Pirvan added.

The wide kender eyes were suddenly as hard as granite. So was the voice, rasping through the dust.

"That is what they want humans to believe."

"They?"

"The ones who started the fire."

Pirvan filled a whole tablet with mental notes about pointed questions to ask in a variety of quarters. None of those would help the kender here in front of him, at least not tonight.

"Are there no kender left at all?"

"Few who think of fighting back. More than a few who think that if the humans go on this way, there's always the next hill and safety beyond it."

Pirvan noticed the kender's unusually forthright and direct manner of speech. But then a long-dead knight had said, "It concentrates your mind wonderfully to know you'll be beheaded in the morning," and no doubt starvation, exhaustion, and beatings could do the same to a kender.

"Uhh, there's more," the kender said. Kender could not really blush—fortunately, some said, or they would spend all their time blushing—but the kender suddenly could not meet Pirvan's eyes.

"How much more?"

"Ah—the real power among the kender are the Rambledin—I suppose you can call them a clan. I was courting Shemra Rambledin. You've never seen, or even imagined, anyone so lovely. She could sit on my lap for hours and—"

Pirvan coughed. The intimate details of the kender's courtship didn't matter so much as the fact that it had obviously gone awry. "So whatever happened, it turned the Rambledins against you. They wouldn't help you, or listen to your appeal, or pass the word on to Kendermore or anyplace else where they could help you without worrying about human opinions."

The kender seemed half-asleep, as if exhausted not only by the day's work, but also by telling his story. He still managed to nod.

"Well—and what is your name?"

The kender shook his head. Pirvan felt like shaking the kender.

"Not everybody may refuse to help you, even if you think you're dishonored. Those who want to help will need to know whom they're helping."

"Gesussum Trapspringer—and no, I'm not anybody's uncle. It's a real kender name, and I've heard all the jokes about it that you know and all the ones you don't besides."

Pirvan took a deep breath, then nearly coughed himself into a fit from the dust he inhaled. "What you need is some real solid food," he said when he could speak again. "I think it's time we improved the innkeeper's hospitality."

If it could have been done without danger to anyone, Pirvan would have cheerfully used his night work skills to burn the inn to the ground. The next best thing was using them to visit the kitchen, undetected, and return, also undetected, with a bulging sack.

"There's a meat pie and some apples for now, and hard bread and cheese for an extra meal a day until they run out. Better find some place to hide the bread and cheese—"

The kender was already snatching the meat pie out of Pirvan's hands and falling on it like a wolf on a lamb. The only sound in the attic for quite a while was the champing of the kender's jaws, followed by the crunching as the apples vanished nearly as fast as the pie.

The kender looked ready to weep when he was done, and Pirvan hoped this was not because he was going to be sick from eating too much too fast. Instead the kender brushed crumbs off his ragged clothing and managed a shaky grin.

"Do you know how long it's been since I've had a full stomach except in a dream?"

"No, but I do know about being that hungry. Honest thieves have to miss a meal every now and then."

"You were a thief? I thought you said you were a Knight of—"

"I was one, and now I am the other, and how I changed is too long a story to tell. I'm going to leave before anyone wonders where I am and starts asking in a way to make the innkeeper suspicious. I may not see you again, but I swear by Paladine and Kiri-Jolith that I *will* see justice for you set afoot."

The kender's grin was not so shaky now. "Just as long as it doesn't stumble on the way. That can happen, you know."

Pirvan had no reply to that, so he left in silence.

* * * * *

The rain continued all night and much of the next day. The day after that, it began to clear as they breasted the last hill before Istar.

The white towers of the mighty city leaped above the

walls, which themselves loomed like young hills marching across the flatland like a column of soldiers. The air smelled clean and fresh, if a trifle damp, like new laundry hanging in the courtyard.

Birds twittered in the bushes along the road, tarberry, verfruit, wild strawberry, and a dozen others. It was too early for even green fruit, but blossoms filled the eye with color and the nose with sweet scents. More birds hopped about in the fields, eyes fixed on the sodden earth for worms and ground-dwelling insects flooded by the rain.

Haimya drew level with her husband. "I hope the tower knows of our coming. It gripes my bowels to stay any longer in this place than necessary."

"If all else fails, we can claim a little of what House Encuintras still owes us, or so they said in their last letter."

House Encuintras had begun Pirvan's road to the Solamnic Knights, when he broke in to steal the Lady Eskaia's dowry jewels. Due to various circumstances, he'd found himself obliged to return them immediately, which ended in his being captured by Haimya and drawn into a quest that, to begin with, had no higher aim than ransoming Haimya's betrothed from the pirates of Crater Gulf.

"They will pay on their debt only as long as the old man lives."

"I have not heard that his health departs," Pirvan said. "Indeed, he may live to bury us all."

"If your tongue wags like this," Grimsoar put in, "that may well be a true prophecy."

Pirvan heard a harshness and a melancholy in the big sailor's voice that had not often been there before. "We will certainly not talk of the business of the knights. What else can bring harm?"

"I'm a sailor, not a soothsayer," Grimsoar replied. "But if tales of you and that kender have grown wings and flown to Istar ahead of us—"

Pirvan reined in and glared. "Now who is letting a tongue wag?"

"Our company is alone on the road, with no others in hearing," Haimya said, putting a hand on her husband's arm. "Let us hear Grimsoar out."

"It's a brief tale. I met a serving maid, for business that concerned us both, sometime before dawn. She spoke of how someone had been slipping up to the attic where they kept the kender. She hoped the man would soon be on the road, before the innkeeper found a way to make trouble for him."

Pirvan had no doubt as to the "business" between Grimsoar and the maid. What bemused him was the innkeeper's vigilance.

"Oh, by itself that's less sinister than you might think," Grimsoar replied. "Any innkeeper with a place that size and customers of the sort who often come there has enough spies to penetrate the inner circle of the kingpriest if he wants to. He may not wish to trade in his guests' secrets, but he doesn't dare let them keep too many."

Pirvan nodded. It would be well to learn if the innkeeper was, in fact, trading in his guest's secrets. Threatening to reveal that might allow settling the matter of the captive kender without a public scandal—always assuming, of course, that Grimsoar was wrong and that rumors were not already creating one!

They rode on, with more rain clouds beginning to build to the south. Pirvan did not care; the lowering sky well suited his mood.

* * * * *

They approached the city along what had been known for centuries as the Great White Road. The tale ran that originally it had been paved with chalk and crushed seashells, so that it blazed white in the sun. Now it had stone slabs like any other road, and after centuries of weather, earthquakes, hooves, and animal droppings it was the same color as any other high road.

It seemed to Pirvan that the villas and even palaces of the rich spread farther beyond the ancient walls of Istar each time he came to the city. In the last few years, he had noticed veritable villages growing up in the open spaces left among the more imposing homes, for those who served the rich.

Altogether, it made one wonder how Istar would defend itself from a foe advancing overland. Pirvan thought it would not be impossible if one fortified an outer ring of the villas and tore down an inner ring of them to leave five hundred paces of open ground beyond the walls. He also did not envy anyone who had to suggest this and listen to the screams of those whose emblems of wealth were to become fortresses or rubble.

Perhaps Istar did not intend to flaunt its wealth and power in the face of the gods. But even merchants, let alone priests, should remember that the gods saw everything, so they would see this piling of luxury on wealth on pride whether men wished them to or not.

The Great White Road divided inside the last of the villas, to lead to both the Water Gate and the Minotaur Gate. The first had its name from once being on a long-since-diverted stream, the second from being where a storming party of minotaurs had been fought to an honorable draw by picked Istarian warriors, including a few Knights of Solamnia.

When they rode up to the Minotaur Gate, they saw that it had been renamed. Now it was the Warrior's Gate, and at the crown of the archway a minotaur's skull carved in the finest Ergothian marble jutted out over the roadway. At least Pirvan hoped the skull was marble—he did not care to think what live minotaurs would say to the display of the skull of a dead one in such a public place.

Even less did he care to think what they would do; the next storming party would not be fighting for honor, but for blood, probably not caring much whose, either.

The gate was as well guarded as ever, though the guards seemed to serve three different masters. There were the men of the watch, the soldiers of the army, and the guards of the kingpriest, still in the white tunics that had raised so many protests from the White Robe wizards, and even some from the red and black.

At least the tunics were now cut so that it was harder to

mistake a temple guard for any sort of White Robe, even without the short swords hung on belts and the thrusting spears slung across their backs. The leader of the priests might call himself the kingpriest, and that louder each passing year, but the name of "king" did not yet carry with it the power—and Pirvan prayed, to any gods he thought would listen as well as those of Good, that matters would never come to that.

What came to Pirvan's party was a pair of men of the watch, both captains by the embroidery on their tunics and cloaks, and one fairly senior, judging from the gilded hilt of his sword. They approached Pirvan, made all the gestures of honor, then said:

"Sir Pirvan of Tiradot?"

"The same, and his party. To what do I owe the honor of this greeting?" Pirvan looked pointedly back at the line of travelers beginning to accumulate behind him.

"To matters contained in this letter." The junior captain handed a folded, sealed square of the best parchment to Pirvan. The knight looked at the seal. It was red, stamped with the open book of Gilean, chief god of Neutrality.

"He who sent this has dealt with all matters concerning your admission to the city as well," the captain went on. "You will find him, I am told, at the Inn of the Four Courts."

Pirvan's eyebrows rose. He suspected who they were going to meet, but at one of the largest hostelries in all of Istar—and also one far from both the Tower of High Sorcery *and* the waterfront?

Holding up other travelers on lawful business, however, solved no riddles. Pirvan took the parchment and thrust it inside his tunic, then made the formal salute to both captains.

"You stand in favor with the knights for your honor, service, and courtesy." At least until we find out what is going on here, he thought.

* * * * *

As Pirvan expected, it was Tarothin who met them in the sunny antechamber of a suite on the uppermost floor of the Inn of the Four Courts.

The courts were now, in fact, five, the owners having bought the whole street next door, closing it off and turning the houses into chambers that they rented to long-staying customers. Where the people in the houses had gone, Pirvan did not know, but this was *not* a cheap quarter of the city; he doubted that they were begging their bread in the streets.

"You are welcome, for all that you may think otherwise," the wizard said. His beard showed more gray than the last time Pirvan had seen him, but he still stepped as lightly, and his staff looked as ready as ever to swing into use as a weapon against foes too petty to require a spell.

They did not need Tarothin's pointing at his ear and then at the walls to be silent while they followed him to the innermost chamber of the four in the suite. It was also the smallest, and Pirvan noticed that the walls glittered slightly and the dinner of cold meat and pickles appeared to have been gnawed by rats. Wizard-sized rats, Pirvan suspected.

Tarothin shrugged at the question in Pirvan's eyes. "I warded this chamber against all listening, magical or otherwise. The spell should last as long as you need to stay here, unless Jemar takes more persuading than I expect, to take you aboard his ships—"

The travelers stood gape-jawed. Pirvan hastily signaled the men-at-arms and servants to repair to an outer room. When the door was closed behind them, with Grimsoar standing before it, Pirvan fixed Tarothin with a look as friendly as a couched lance.

"We are staying here? Not in the guesthouse of the tower?"

"No. I mean, yes—this is where you stay, until Jemar—"

"Tarothin. This doubtlessly excellent inn is far from the harbor. It is far from the tower. It is close to several temples, including one that houses the barracks for half the kingpriests' guards. We are here on business that the kingpriest and his minions may think dangerous to them. Does this suggest a logical course of action for you?"

Tarothin sighed. "Yes, and the same one I laid out for the hospitaler at the tower. He said that there was little danger to you, and more danger of giving offense to the priests by sheltering you. He has, however, sent silver to pay for all your wants here, up to five hundred towers— and you can *buy* most inns for not much more than—"

"What I want to know," Grimsoar One-eye put in, "is why you didn't come to me with some warning of all this, so that I could carry it to Pirvan."

Tarothin's face twisted in a the-gods-give-me-patience look. "Because before I knew any of what I have just told you, you had already departed. Nor would anyone tell me whither, so that I could send a messenger after you."

"A messenger who might have sent a copy of your letter to the kingpriest," Grimsoar snapped. "For the same reason, I did not wish anyone to know where I had gone."

Tarothin sighed. "And *I* did not wish it known all over Istar that Tarothin of the Red Robes sought Grimsoar One-Eye, mate aboard a ship of Jemar the Fair. That also might have reached ears better left unsullied by the news."

"By all means, let the priests keep their ears clean, to better listen to the voice of the gods," Haimya said. Her tone would have eaten holes in the floor. "All of which, however, does precious little toward bringing us to Jemar the Fair."

"It need not do so," Tarothin said, "because he already knows of your coming. He and no one else among his men. He has promised to see you this very night, if it is your wish."

"You may tell him that it is our wish indeed," Pirvan said. Then he stepped forward and embraced Tarothin. "Pardon, old friend, but it seemed that you had made a bad matter worse."

"Yes, and if you ever again give us such a fright, I will knock you down," Haimya said.

"And I will dance in my climbing boots on you," Pirvan added.

"And I will hang what is left from the maintop of *Sea*

Leopard until the gales have stripped your flesh from your bones and your spirit from both," Grimsoar concluded. "Meanwhile, I'm returning to *Sea Leopard* tond see about bringing a few trusted men here. I may even be able to speak to Jemar himself."

"Is Eskaia sailing with him?" Haimya put in. "I have yet to hear her named, but it would be a pleasure to see her again." Haimya had been Eskaia's bodyguard and confidante when the lady was heiress to House Encuintras, and, though far apart most of the time, they found they had more in common after ten years of marriage and motherhood.

"No, and it's pleasure that's the cause," Grimsoar said. "Or rather, the fruit of pleasure."

Haimya laughed. "Is this their fourth or fifth?"

"Only four," Grimsoar replied. "There is work to be done sometimes, after all."

Haimya slipped an arm through her husband's and briefly rested her chin on his shoulder. "You need not tell us about *that*."

"No," Pirvan said. "But if this wine is fit and safe—"

Tarothin muttered something rude.

"—then let us drink to Jemar and Eskaia. May their line be long and stout, and hold fast through all the storms of life."

They drank, but Pirvan and Haimya were looking at one another as they put their cups to their lips, with the same sobering thought.

Jemar and Eskaia live far from Istar when they are ashore, and have ships that can take them to sea if storms blow from the temples. We and our line are bound by duty to stand in the path of the storm and try to turn it aside from the innocent.

Yet Pirvan also saw in Haimya's eyes another thought that matched his own.

We would not love as we do, if either of us thought to do otherwise.

Chapter 7

They did not meet Jemar aboard his bannership *Windsword*, but in a chamber in the fortress-thick walls of a waterfront warehouse he owned through a discreet Istarian agent. *Windsword* was in the outer harbor, and Jemar would not have allowed a meeting that needed magical warding against unwanted listeners aboard the ship anyway.

"It's not that I don't trust you, friend Tarothin," the sea barbarian chief said. "The same for those who sailed with us to Crater Gulf. But there are plenty of new hands. They won't be easy, trusting a wizard, and I wouldn't be easy, trusting all of them to keep their mouths shut.

"Besides, I've grown a bit wary of spells taken to sea myself. There's more magic wandering about the water than before, and if a ship bound by one spell hits a storm bound by another—well, I can think of two ships like that who sailed into such storms and never sailed out again."

"I understand," Tarothin said. "It's the problem that

some wizards have with their staff, when they want to use it for both magic and fighting. I remember once a Black Robe who tried to knock a sword out of someone's hand with the end of his staff, and the sword had a spell bound into it that the staff released."

"Then what happened?" Pirvan said, trying not to let his impatience show.

Sea barbarian manners required some time spent discussing family, crops, successful voyages (or other kinds), and so on. Jemar was a friend, to whom Pirvan would not wittingly be rude, but he was also a friend to whom they had come in dire need and with the hot breath of enemies all but searing the backs of their necks.

"Released slowly, nothing might have happened," Tarothin said. "Released all at once—well, they never found either body, and the hole in the road was twenty paces wide and ten deep. A vallenwood a hundred paces away went over, too, but it might have been rotten—"

"As the gods send," Jemar said. A servant came in with salt fish, pickled vegetables, hard cakes with hot fruit sauce, and tarberry tea, wine, and brandy. When all had served themselves, Jemar seemed to consider the demands of manners met.

"Now, it seems to me that all the uproar Istar is making concerns this mysterious minotaur. So if we find a way to end his career, we will also end Istar's excuse for embattling the north shore.

"It won't be only Karthay that sighs as happily as a well-loved woman when that happens. A good few honest merchants with business in Solamnia and Thorbardin will be happy not to have Istarian captains looking over their shoulders.

"It's not so bad now, with Aurhinius commanding. He has the name of an honest man. But he also likes to lead from in front, which is another good thing about him but one likely to get him killed. An arrow or a rabbit hole, and he'd be in the family vault and in his place one of those sticky-handed merchant's boys who know how to make war pay for everyone except the men who actually shed their blood."

Jemar sighed and rinsed his throat with a hefty gulp of brandy. "Sorry to go on like that. Let me be silent and drink, while you speak. Lady Haimya, beauty should have first place, so if it will not offend Sir Pirvan—"

"So be it," Pirvan said, and nodded to his wife.

"I think we should begin in Karthay, and as swiftly as the winds and tides allow us to reach it . . ."

* * * * *

The meeting of Pirvan and his companions with Jemar the Fair was not the only meeting that night that altered the destiny of the races of Krynn.

In the northern town of Biyerones, Aurhinius met with his principal captains. Outside, the streets of the town were silent, except for the thump of boots on cobblestones as the soldiers of the guard patrolled on foot. He hoped the citizens heard the patrolling soldiers as protection rather than menace, but could not concern himself with their opinions now.

"We shall remain here, with the cavalry thrown out as a screen from the shore south to Krovari," Aurhinius said. "That will keep all the cavalry in the field, but there are not so many ways that a large band on foot can pass through such a screen. Small bands, the townsfolk and villagers can deal with themselves."

"One may doubt their loyalty," a high captain of horse said.

"One may, in private," Aurhinius said sharply. "Say nothing of this where others may hear, however. These northern folk are stubborn. Called traitors aloud, they may take a firmer stand against us. Also, everyone with a feud with a neighbor or an appetite for a neighbor's flocks and land will use the charge of treason as an excuse to assail that neighbor.

"Istar has not soldiers enough to bring peace to a land torn by such feuds. Nor would the city send them to us if she had them."

The high captain craved his general's pardon and was silent thereafter.

Aurhinius rose and strode to the map. "We defend, with both strength and skill, until the fleet comes north to secure our seaward flank. When we assail the Minotaur's lair by land and sea, he will have no way out. We will be able to maintain the siege with small forces supplied by sea, much longer than his stronghold can endure."

"And then?" It was another captain, one with a reputation for both valor and cruelty.

"Then we may have a real minotaur's skull for the Warrior's Gate, or we may have at least two prisoners who can teach us something of war. I think this—Waydol—has come to our shores at the behest of minotaurs of the highest rank. It never hurts, in war, to learn how much one's enemy knows about one, or by what methods they seek to spy one out."

* * * * *

Also in the north, but somewhat farther to the west, a minotaur and his human heir sat on a rock overlooking the sea. Only Lunitari shone clear of clouds, tinting a path across a sea hardly rougher than a millpond.

Waydol shifted in his seat. Over the years, his weight and tough hide had worn a virtual saddle in the rock. Then he drew a katar, a vial of oil, and a whetstone from a pouch at his belt and began sharpening the huge dagger.

As if it was not already sharp enough to shave with, Darin thought. But he knew that Waydol needed something to do with his hands when his thoughts ran in disturbing directions. Darin would throw no stones at Waydol for being uneasy, considering how ill he had slept since returning with Aurhinius's golden helmet. He had even thought of asking Sirbones for a healing spell to bring restful sleep!

"If Istar comes against us with all the force it can muster, it may go ill with us," Waydol said at last.

"Not without their paying a price, in more than red-faced generals," Darin said.

Waydol's laughter was a sharp, low-pitched boom rather than the long rumble. "I would have given a horn to see Aurhinius's face after his two attendants fell on him and drove him into the mud. But there is no pleasure without a price, and I think we are about to pay for ours."

Darin was silent, knowing that Waydol was less seeking advice and counsel than trying to define his thoughts by speaking aloud. It would not be the first time that Darin had played a sympathetic ear, for he had known since he was no more than eight that Waydol's lot was harsher than his heir's ever would be. Darin might die in battle tomorrow, but he would not have spent twenty-odd years before that battle alone on a foreign shore, with no sight of any other being of his own race.

Waydol was also silent for a while, so only the sigh of the wind and the distant murmur of waves disturbed the night. At last Waydol turned and looked at his heir. For the first time, Darin saw a pale clouding at the corner of Waydol's right eye, and vowed to speak to Sirbones about this, with or without Waydol's permission.

"I have taught you the minotaur way of war," Waydol said. "At least I have tried. How would you describe that way?"

For a moment, Darin thought he was more likely to be able to sprout wings and fly than to answer that question. Then before shame could silence him for even longer, his lips found words.

"To always be fit and armed. To use all the strength needed in a fight, which is not the same as all one's strength. To never begin a fight which is dishonorable, and to never yield to a foe who has done so, or who asks your honor as the price of your life."

This time, Waydol's laughter raised echoes from the cliffs all around the hidden bay. He clapped an arm across Darin's shoulders, and for a moment Darin was sure his spine was jarred from neck to waist and several of his ribs cracked. It was a while before he could breathe easily again.

Meanwhile, Waydol sat on the rock, while looking rather as if he wanted to dance, caper, fling his arms about, and sing to the moon like a satyr. As Darin drew his first deep breath in a while, Waydol gave a gusty sigh.

"Well, Darin. I asked many years ago if I could raise you with the soul of a minotaur and the soul of a human in the same body. I forget what I vowed if this prayer was granted, and I know I have not kept those vows.

"Yet somehow, some gods—yours, or mine, or some who care not what shape of body a soul inhabits—granted my wish. This night, I do not think there is a more content being on Krynn than I."

Waydol stood up and rested a massive hand on Darin's forehead, then rumpled his hair. "Go down and sleep well, Heir. I think it is best that I keep a vigil tonight, before we talk of whether Aurhinius is an honorable foe or not."

Darin saw there was no disputing or cajoling Waydol, so he went down to his hut and wrapped himself in stone-warmed furs. He expected another restless night, but it was as if Waydol's touch had been the sleeping spell from Sirbones. Darin slept without dreams until the sun was well above the horizon.

* * * * *

In Istar, the Conclave of Wizards met once more beneath the Tower of High Sorcery, without accomplishing much. Tarothin was absent, which everyone expected and no one remarked on.

Rubina was also absent, which no one had expected, and on which more than a few people did remark, even at length.

Also in Istar, the kingpriest met with a certain priest who served Zeboim the Sea Queen. At least the man was said to be a priest, and not a renegade mage.

The man spoke wisely and well, but not even the king-priest, let alone those who ushered the man to and from the kingpriest's chambers, could look unmoved on the visitor's mask.

It was made in the shape of a gigantic turtle's head, the beak studded with barbed fangs. To be sure, the Sea Queen took the form of a giant turtle when she moved through the waters, but when she did, she brought evil and destruction.

Also, whatever shone in the eyeholes of the mask, it was not wholly the priest's own eyes.

* * * * *

Clouds had swept across most of the sky, effacing Lunitari and most of the stars, when Pirvan and his companions came out of Jemar's warehouse. Tarothin remained behind, promising to join them in the morning after visiting certain friends from the towers.

The harborfront streets were narrow and ill-lit at the best of times, and not improved by the darkness the clouds had spread across Istar. Pirvan took his bearings from the masthead lights of ships tied along the wharves, then turned on to a street that proclaimed itself Glad Girls' Lane. This close to the harbor, Pirvan suspected that he knew when and why the girls were glad.

They were three streets up from the water, and only two streets from the better-lighted avenues, when Pirvan held up a hand to halt the band. Then he cocked his head, seeking to pick human sounds from the rising wind.

"I think we're being followed," he whispered. "Grow eyes in the backs of your heads, and be ready to run at my command. But *don't* be separated."

Their men-at-arms and Haimya nodded. After a moment, so did Grimsoar One-Eye and his two sailors from *Sea Leopard.* The hesitation made Pirvan uneasy. Treachery in Grimsoar was unthinkable—or was it? Every man had his price, and with the stakes as high as they were someone might have been able to put forward—

The darkness came alive, but it was the darkness *ahead* of them.

That and silence gave the attackers surprise at the

outset, and they did not waste it. One man-at-arms died with his throat gaping, and the second gurgled with steel between his ribs. But he did not die before his own blade flew clear and thrust up under his killer's chin, to drive onward into the brain.

This left the two sailors, one with a purse from Jemar, as well as Grimsoar, Pirvan, and Haimya, fighting against at least thrice their numbers. Grimsoar cut down the odds somewhat by chopping down one attacker with a sideways cut that nearly severed the man at the waist. Then he slowed a second man by kicking him in the knee and opening his cheek with a dagger.

Pirvan thrust low to find his dagger point grating on armor under the ragged workingman's clothes, then brought his knee up into his opponent's groin. That doubled him over, bringing his head down far enough that Pirvan could slam the hilt of his sword across the back of the man's neck. The knight leaped back as the man fell, twisting in midair so that he landed with his back against a solid wall.

One sailor was slowed by the weight of the purse, but his reach was long enough and his arm strong enough that he kept himself safe for a while without changing position. Then an attacker worked around behind him and raised a short sword to thrust the sailor through, but Haimya saw the man even before Pirvan, and she was closer.

She was a thing of beauty and terror alike as she made a thrust at full stretch, driving the point of her sword into the base of the attacker's skull. Even in the darkness, Pirvan saw life go out of the man's eyes—and also a fallen attacker roll over and grip Haimya's ankles.

Caught off balance, she staggered, and another man came at her with two daggers, getting inside her guard before Pirvan could even open his mouth for a warning. But the sailor stamped down hard on the clutching hands, and as they released their grip Haimya flung herself to one side, cushioning her fall on the man who'd thrown her off balance.

The sailor's sword ended the second man's threat to Haimya.

Then Pirvan's mouth went dry, as running feet thudded from the direction of the harbor. He turned, knowing that the wall at his back would buy him only time and hoping Haimya would fight close enough to him for a last word or two, if they could not hope for a touch—

A man only slightly smaller than Grimsoar One-Eye loomed in the alley, a sword in hand and a steel cap on his head. His sailor's beard was plaited with two yellow ribbons. Behind him a dozen more men, all in sailor's garb, all well armed, crowded forward.

Grimsoar embraced the newcomers' leader. "Well, Kurulus, if you ever want a place with Jemar—"

Pirvan stared. Kurulus had been Mate of the Tops aboard *Golden Cup*, the ship that had carried the companions of the quest to Crater Gulf most of the way to their destination. His reward from House Encuintras for a stout fighting arm and sound seamanship had been his own command.

"I've my own ship, Grimsoar, and you know that Jemar lets no one start save as a mate. Now let's see if we've trapped the right set of rats."

"Would somebody please explain—?" Haimya began.

Grimsoar put a finger to her lips, and nearly had it bitten off for his pains. "Later," he rumbled, and Pirvan nodded. He did not know what the sailors might be about, but it was seldom that a knight was not allowed to defend himself from those who sought his life. A mystery, yes, but not likely a matter for a Judgment of Honor.

Half the newcomers were standing guard. The other half were helping Grimsoar and Kurulus turn over the bodies and examine them. Pirvan counted ten dead, including a couple of men whose wounds did not at first look that deadly.

A sharp hiss that turned into a whistle made all heads turn. Grimsoar was holding up a body with one hand. With the other, he'd torn open the man's tunic. Mail showed under, and also a dark spot in the man's exposed armpit.

"Pirvan, Haimya, you need to see this," Grimsoar said.

The knight and his lady knelt by the body. By lantern light, the dark spot in the dead man's armpit turned out to be a tattoo of a crown, a stylized one gruesomely different from the emblem of the Solamnic Knights of the Crown. A circle surrounded it; a closer look showed it to be a representation of one of the woven cords that senior clerics wore around their foreheads on ceremonial occasions.

Senior clerics and, so it was said, the kingpriest.

Pirvan stared at the crown-in-a-circlet tattoo, and knew that one of the uglier rumors about the kingpriests of Istar had just revealed itself as the truth.

"Did you set a trap for footpads, or was catching the Servants of Silence part of your plan?" Pirvan whispered to Grimsoar.

"I swear we were only after the Vlyby brothers and their runners," Grimsoar said. He seemed to be talking as much to himself and Kurulus as to Pirvan. "I should have realized that you and Haimya might draw different fish."

Grimsoar could deal with his guilt and shame later. Right now it was most unlikely that the kingpriest would look benignly on tonight's events: ten of the men sworn, tattooed, and trained to silence his opponents dead, against only two of their prey, and those the least important. The existence of the Servants of Silence was now known to a Knight of Solamnia and other witnesses, too many to eliminate before they talked. The knight and his companions warned of their mortal danger.

In a similar situation, Pirvan knew his curses would shatter glass and crack roof tiles.

"Very well," he said. "We have to return to Jemar and go aboard one of his ships at once, if he will still hide us."

"He gave oath," Grimsoar snapped. "Do not insult him by doubting."

"He did not give oath to be our friend after we have smitten the kingpriest with the open hand," Haimya pointed out. "We offer no insult by giving him a chance to pick which battles he shall fight."

"Well, I say we fight this thing through," Kurulus said.

He turned to his men. "We are all sworn to House Encuintras, and they still owe a debt to these people. I suggest we pay it by going to—where were you staying, Sir Pirvan?"

"Inn of the Four Courts."

"Right, lads. If Sir Pirvan will give us some proof of our right, and a bit of silver to grease palms, we'll be off to the inn and back with your baggage and servants before the live temple rats stop running."

Pirvan forced sensible words out of his mouth, as reluctant as they were to come. "Ah—we were thinking of leaving everything—"

"Leave everything," Grimsoar said, "and we leave things the kingpriest's minions might want to get their hands on. Not to mention that Jemar's likely to be happier taking us aboard if he also doesn't need to equip us from the skin out."

"Are you sure anyone owes us enough to quarrel with the kingpriest—?" Haimya began.

"Oh, hush, Lady," Kurulus said unceremoniously. "We're sworn to House Encuintras, and that means more than their debts being ours. It also means that who attacks us attacks them, and satyrs will turn celibate before any tower or temple picks a quarrel with House Encuintras."

Pirvan handed over one of the room keys and a double handful of silver towers from the sailor's purse. Kurulus divided his men, four to stay with Pirvan and his companions and eight to go to the inn. Then he led the eight off up the street at a pace that would have done honor to minotaurs.

"Pleasant to have friends," Haimya said. Her brittle tone said that she was trying to keep up with the night's events, but rather wished they would slow their pace a trifle.

"More than pleasant when one has enemies like the kingpriest," Pirvan said, drawing her close. "I would call it the difference between life and death."

* * * * *

The clouds kept their promise of more rain. As Pirvan led his companions back to the harbor, the sky opened and unleashed a downpour that turned the gutters into streams and the streets into shallow rivers.

At least it also offered some protection. While the rain was at its height, a herd of centaurs could have trotted four abreast through any street in Istar without being noticed. By the time it began to slack off, they were in one of *Windsword*'s boats, beating toward the outer harbor with the lateen sail up, to take advantage of the dying storm's wind.

They made good time at the price of nearly being seasick on the way. Haimya had to rush to a shadowed section of the railing, where darkness veiled the sights and the wind the sound. When she returned, she was pale but striding proudly.

"I do hope it doesn't take as long as it did the last time for me to get my sea legs," she said. Then she gripped Pirvan's arm so hard that the knight winced, and when he saw where she was pointing with her free hand, he muttered unknightly language.

Tarothin was standing at the break of the forecastle, not quite with his arm around his companion but so close that she clearly would not have protested the gesture. The companion was a woman, nearly as tall as Haimya, with black hair flying in the breeze as well as gleaming in the lantern light.

She also wore black robes.

"Of course, that might be just her traveling clothes—" Pirvan heard himself saying.

"It seems the boat ride made me sick and you witless," Haimya said, so sharply that her words reached Tarothin and his companion. Both turned as Haimya advanced on them with the look of being ready to heave the woman overboard and the wizard after her if he protested.

Perforce, the knight followed his lady and caught up with her as the two women stared at one another. Pirvan was reminded of two wolves deciding whether or not this was the time to fight for pack rank.

The silence was broken twice over, by Tarothin's clearing his throat and by footsteps from behind, which turned out to belong to Jemar the Fair. The Black Robe turned her gaze on Pirvan, and he suddenly felt like a satyr faced with a woman ready to amuse herself with him.

Except that "amuse" would be the wrong word, if this woman had serious notions of bringing him to her by magic. Or by any other means, his reason added, noting the vast, dark eyes, and the gleaming, dark hair that framed everything.

I suppose once a year or so she meets a man too old or too young for her to try her wiles on. Otherwise she sees us all as prey, and that has given her bad habits.

Pirvan thanked all the gods of Krynn in a single comprehensive prayer of gratitude that Haimya was with him on this quest. Then he smiled.

"My lady. I am Sir Pirvan of Tiradot, and you may have heard of me as Pirvan the Wayward." Then he thought, *Which was not what I intended to say, and may give the lady ideas—not that she needs any help in such matters.*

To Pirvan's surprise, the woman's smile was as grave as that of a white-robed cleric. "I am Rubina, Black Robe of Karthay. I found that what I serve and what your friend Tarothin serves are much the same. So, with the permission of Jemar the Fair, I am taking passage to Karthay aboard this ship, and as much farther as I can be useful."

From Tarothin's way of standing and looking at her, one of her uses was too plain to require comment. Pirvan and Haimya exchanged glances. This gave Jemar time to find his voice.

"I trust you will not presume to object to whom I may carry aboard my own ship?" It was not a question.

"Do I look like that big a fool?" Pirvan asked.

"No. A wise man as well as a knight, and the two are not always the same," Rubina said.

Haimya giggled, which she did seldom, and which seemed to put Rubina out of countenance. The woman turned and, with regal grace, put an arm around Tarothin.

"Come, my friend. I think the wind is rising, and neither of us thrives on chills and coughs."

When the deck was empty except for sailors carefully devoting themselves to their work, Haimya burst out laughing.

"What amuses you so, my lady?" Jemar asked.

"I was jealous at first. Then I saw that she had taken Tarothin for hers and was not seeking elsewhere. But she can hardly open her mouth to a man without saying something inviting. She must waste rather a lot of time better spent on other matters."

Pirvan looked everywhere but at his wife, and was rewarded by her fingers slipping inside his tunic and tickling him in the short ribs. When he got his breath back, he turned to Jemar.

"Old friend, I trust your judgment, but is taking this Black Robe wise or necessary?"

"Tarothin thinks so, and I know from my own eyes and ears in Karthay that she has much influence in the towers there. Have your knights told you nothing about her?"

"Not even her name."

"The knights will be well advised to talk more with the magic workers and less with one another in the coming years," Jemar said.

"And we will be well advised to seek a warm cabin, out of this chilly wind," Haimya said. This time Pirvan caught her hand before it reached inside his tunic, then lifted it to his lips and kissed the sword-calloused palm.

Chapter 8

Their cabin was small and sparsely furnished, and Pirvan realized that if their baggage ever did catch up with them, most of it would have to go into the hold. However, of most concern right now was that they were out of the wind and the rain, together, and alone.

They were just drifting off to sleep in a bunk barely large enough for one and distinctly cramped for two, when a fearful din from above jerked them both back to full wakefulness. To Pirvan it sounded as if the Servants of Silence might have followed them and were now trying to carry *Windsword* by boarding.

He leaped out of bed, snatched for his clothes and sword with one hand, and with the other tried to gather up decent garb and adequate weapons for Haimya. He ended by thrusting both of his legs into one leg of his breeches and falling on his face hard enough to cut his lip when he tried to leap for the ladder.

When he rose, all he could see of Haimya was bare shoulders, one bare arm holding a sword, and a face rapidly turning bright red from holding in laughter. About that time, Pirvan also recognized Kurulus's voice, cheerfully reporting the arrival of everybody's baggage and a few new hands.

Pirvan was curious about that last item, but not so curious that this time he failed to dress properly and appear on deck like a knight, complete to weapons and low boots. He nearly tripped again, over a line on which several sailors were hauling, but leaped over it as a chest he recognized as his and Haimya's spare armor swung into view.

The clatter and clang of loading made conversation impossible; Pirvan went to the side to be out of the way. It was then that he saw Grimsoar One-Eye's *Sea Leopard* close to port, and equally close to starboard a ship he didn't know but which flew the Encuintras banner at two mastheads and the aftercastle. That, he supposed, was Kurulus's ship.

And here came Kurulus himself, grinning rather like a kender who's just made off with a whole crock of piping-hot biscuits and somebody's wedding cake from a baker.

"All well?" Pirvan asked.

Kurulus laughed aloud. "Oh, we'll be telling our grand-children about this night. We got to the inn in fine style, hiring a few porters on the way with that purse of Jemar's.

"It took more than the key to prove we had the right to enter your room. Also, a few of the servants seemed ready to slip out and tell someone—I'll name no names—about us.

"So we had to climb the stairs as if the water were rising at our heels. We entered the chambers, picked up every-thing we could carry—"

"Not being too careful whether it belonged to us or the inn?" Pirvan interrupted.

"Sailors in a hurry don't much care to read badges, if they can read at all. Anyway, we got clear, and with a little help from a carter we persuaded to go out of his way—"

"Did you steal his cart, or just force him to drive it down to the harbor?"

"Ask no questions and you'll hear no sea stories," Kurulus said, so piously that Pirvan burst out laughing.

"And then?"

"Well, the four of my lads who'd taken you down to Jemar's boat then launched ours, and warned my own *Thunderlaugh*. We put our launch over the side, then hoisted anchor and drifted down to join you. I reckoned that three sea barbarian ships and the Encuintras flag is enough protection from anything the kingpriest is likely to send after us.

"If he whistles up the whole Istarian fleet, we're fish food, but I'd wager all the wine aboard that he'll do no such thing. There's plenty in Istar who think virtue means honoring the gods instead of just a man who thinks he's one."

Drums began thudding, calling the hands to make sail, and Pirvan stepped aside as men swarmed toward the ratlines to go aloft and toward the sheets to work from the deck. Kurulus gave Pirvan a bone-crushing handshake, then swung over the side into his launch.

Lunitari was shining again, though veiled by clouds, and Pirvan saw, one by one, the sails shaken out and swelling with the wind. Then the drums and pipes beat for the capstan hands to raise anchor, and Pirvan himself ran forward to push on the bars, smoothed by many years of sailors' hands.

It was not knight's work, but at this moment Pirvan would have mucked out pigsties to speed his departure from Istar.

* * * * *

They had a slow but easy voyage to Karthay, with many fluky or contrary winds, but no storms. By the second day Haimya had her sea legs, and although she still looked pale, she could sway with the motion of the ship and lock one arm around the standing rigging as if she'd been at sea half her life.

They passed so far offshore of the Flower Rocks that Pirvan had to climb to the maintop to get a glimpse of them, dark and low above the sun-dappled water. There he, Haimya, and Tarothin had helped save *Golden Cup*, at the price of narrowly escaping drowning and a sea naga.

Now the sea sparkled and danced so that it was hard to believe it could hold anything dangerous. Rainbows of spray rose as the four ships sliced through the little waves, sails flapped and filled alternately with drum cracks, and gradually the coast of the Bay of Istar fell behind them.

Three days brought them into sight of the mountains beyond Karthay, without bringing any sign of pursuit. Pirvan wondered aloud at this, and his curiosity was hardly idle. He had much to do in Karthay, whether they went seeking the Minotaur's outlaws or not. He could do it faster if he did not have to slip through the shadows of the city, to avoid its own rulers or the Servants of Silence.

Jemar tried to put him at ease. "To my mind, the danger of pursuit ended at the waterfront. The Istarian fleet's mostly commanded by the merchant families. They'll not take kindly to chasing a ship of House Encuintras.

"Nor will they be too happy over the Servants of Silence. Custom has been for the temple guards to stay in the temple precincts. Sending sworn killers roaming about the streets could bring down the kingpriest, or at least leave him with no power except to decide when he should go to the privy!"

Pirvan could only hope that Jemar was right. The sea barbarian chief believed in little except his own strength and shrewdness, for all that he professed to honor Habbakuk, Lord of Mariners. He did not know how corrupting it could be to tell a man that he is virtuous above all others.

At least the Knights of Solamnia required that one practice the virtues—and made their practice so demanding that one had no time to sit and think how wonderful one was. Without that discipline in their followers, the kingpriests were threatening to sow corruption in the name of virtue.

* * * * *

On the fourth day, they found themselves off an anchorage on the western shore of the bay. On the charts it bore the name "Istariku." In a dialect so ancient that only a handful of scholars and clerics knew more than a few words of it, this meant "Eye of Istar."

What that eye had been meant to watch in the days when the anchorage gained its name, no one knew. Today it plainly was meant to watch Karthay and the mouth of the bay, neither more than a day's good sailing from the anchorage.

There were also ruins on the hills that suggested Istariku might once have been a considerable town, but of more interest to the travelers was a small village of tents on the shore. Also on the shore, drawn up on the beach, were a dozen light galleys, and anchored in deeper water were several heavier ships, some clearly merchant vessels, but others flying the banners of the Istarian fleet.

Kurulus volunteered to take his *Thunderlaugh* in to see if he could find buyers for some of his cargo. Even more important, he would seek out captains who might grow loose-tongued after enough wine.

"Everybody expects the worst of sea barbarians when it comes to a drinking bout," he said. "They'll have suspicion close to their hearts and their hands close to their steel. But House Encuintras will be my shield and my staff."

Jemar could not but agree. He also could not help cautioning Kurulus not to presume too much on his house flag. "From what I have heard, old Josclyn Encuintras is not what he was, and may not be here to help us much longer."

Kurulus lowered his voice so that only Jemar, Pirvan, and Haimya could hear him.

"That's what he wants the world to think. I'd wager the

price of one of those galleys that he'll see out another ten years. He might even welcome a good brawl with the kingpriest while he's young enough to enjoy it. He'll enjoy even more finding out who in his house will kiss the kingpriest's arse, and turning them into fish food."

As Josclyn Encuintras would not see seventy again (Eskaia was the last child of his third wife and the only survivor out of four they had borne him), Kurulus's tribute made Pirvan briefly jealous. At barely half the old man's age, he thought as often of the pleasures of hearth and home as the honor of smiting foes.

But then, he had Haimya, which Josclyn Encuintras did not.

* * * * *

Kurulus took *Thunderlaugh* into Istariku at midmorning, while Jemar's three ships began their beat offshore to Karthay. Kurulus might have departed sooner, save for an argument begun by Rubina, who thought that she might well learn much that was useful if allowed to accompany Kurulus.

Tarothin not only looked displeased but said more than he should have, in Pirvan's opinion. Rubina looked displeased in return, but said nothing.

Jemar played peacemaker. "My lady, I doubt not that your power to make men babble exceeds that of the finest wine. Nor do I question your right to use whatever powers you see fit to loosen their tongues." This last was said with a sharp look at Tarothin.

"But merely by going aboard *Thunderlaugh* you will reveal more than you learn. Our enemies will learn, sooner rather than later, that a Black Robe accompanies us, a Black Robe of Karthay. Consider that this might arouse suspicion enough to make some captain willing to defy the might of House Encuintras to make trouble for us."

Rubina nodded slowly. "True enough. I am one of those weapons best brought out only at dire need. Also, the more help I can give Sir Pirvan in making the best use of his time in Karthay, the better for us all."

Pirvan *hoped* she was referring to their plans to recruit mercenaries, with or without the help of the rulers of Karthay and the eyes and ears of the Solamnic Knights in the city.

The Black Robe then rose slightly on tiptoe and brushed her lips against Tarothin's ear. "Also, I would be depriving myself of your company. It would take a greater prize than anything I could learn from the Istarians to make that worthwhile."

Her tone almost oozed sincerity, and Pirvan understood clearly the impulse that he had read on the faces of a good many of his fellow voyagers:

Throw this wench overboard and her black bedgowns after her. Nothing she can do for us is worth listening to her in the meanwhile.

But a knight was sworn to both honor and prudence, and disposing of Rubina at this point in the quest would show neither. Also, they were going to need all the help they could obtain to muster enough men to carry out their plans.

So Rubina stood with Tarothin on the aftercastle of *Windsword* and waved farewell to Kurulus as he turned *Thunderlaugh* in toward the anchorage, from which boats were already putting out to greet him.

* * * * *

The Boatsteerer was a fair-sized inn of moderate comfort and with a discreet landlord, in the West Port quarter of Karthay. Even if the landlord had not had a reputation for discretion, according to the knights' watcher in the city, he had prudence enough to develop that gift when dealing with Jemar the Fair.

The sea barbarian had never had the name of a bloody-handed killer for pleasure. He did have the name of one with a long memory for indiscretion or betrayal, and a short way of dealing with the indiscreet or treacherous when he caught up with them.

From a back room in the Boatsteerer, Pirvan and Jemar set out to recruit a band of warriors sufficiently numerous and redoubtable for their purposes. Haimya offered what help she could, but she was years past her sell-sword days, and more than a few of her old comrades were retired or dead, as were all but a few distant kin.

Grimsoar went about the streets, picking up the odd sailor or craftsman through his knowledge of both the seafarers and those who practiced night work, not to mention a few old friends from his days as a wrestler. He was also the one charged with procuring weapons, as the lords of Karthay might well grow uneasy if they saw the same men both recruiting soldiers *and* assembling armory.

Pirvan was not, to his dying day, sure whether Rubina helped or hindered. It took him equally long to forget one evening at the Boatsteerer, when Rubina chose to join him and Jemar in discussing the hire of fifty men through one Birak Epron.

Epron was a sell-sword of some reputation, so short and wiry that one might suspect kender blood in him, save for the fact that at first he was about as talkative as one of the inn's tables. He sat on his bench opposite the three questers, sipped from a single large cup of ale, answered questions with single words or grunts, and asked only two questions during the whole earlier part of the evening.

One was "What is the bounty on Waydol's head?"

"That depends on how many other heads we bring in besides Waydol's," Pirvan said. "There are ten towers a man for everyone in the expedition that brings down Waydol, and much honor besides. If we bring down the rest of his band as well—why should generals with golden helmets to protect empty heads garner it all?"

"Because Aurhinius's head is not empty," Epron said, which was the longest speech he'd made thus far.

Pirvan decided that he would not again try to persuade a seasoned sell-sword that the quest would be easy.

The second question came later, and was "Have you

healers with you?"

Rubina answered that, before either of the men could speak. "Of course we do. Any wizard of my stature can command healing spells, perhaps not of the highest order, but sufficient to keep alive many who would otherwise be dead.

"I am no follower of Mishakal, but if you will offer a pain to my healing, I think I will prove satisfactory."

A cunning look came to Birak Epron's face, and he found his tongue. "If you must lay hands on what most needs healing, this room is no place for it. It's against my nature to remove my breeches save behind a closed door."

"Then by all means let us repair to a room with a door that can be closed," Rubina said. She rested a hand on Epron's shoulder, and Pirvan would have sworn that he actually floated several fingers clear of the bench before his boots touched the floor.

Rubina had her head on his shoulder, and he had his arm around her waist, by the time they reached the foot of the stairs to the sleeping chambers. It did not help that it was at that same moment that Tarothin entered the room.

He looked at Rubina disappearing up the stairs with another man, and his face turned the same color as his robes. He looked about to burst into furious oaths—or cast a spell to make the inn burst into flames.

Before he could do either, Jemar rose, hand on the hilt of his sword. "Tarothin, leave be! You are too old not to know a lightskirt, even if her skirts be black. You are too young to let one make a fool of you. And by Habbakuk and Kiri-Jolith, you are too wise to know that a lightskirt will not change her ways for your charms, such as they may be!"

For a moment, Pirvan thought he was going to need to step between the sailor and the wizard, lest they come to blows. Certainly that fear was on the face of everyone within earshot, which probably included everyone in the Boatsteerer and in the street outside!

Tarothin at last took a deep breath, forced his hands down to his sides, and licked his lips.

"Pirvan, make my apologies to your lady, and to others whom you think deserve it. I find that I cannot continue on this quest. Rubina commands all the magic you will need, even if she cannot command herself any better than Jemar."

The sea barbarian took on the look of a bull walrus about to attack. "I command both myself and my ships. And I say that if you think otherwise, then you can spare yourself ever setting foot aboard any vessel of mine!"

"That will be a pleasure I did not anticipate," Tarothin nearly snarled, and he strode out so furiously that he collided with a serving boy and brought down both boy and a tray of dishes with a resounding crash.

"This does not seem to have been the best-spent evening since we met," Jemar said, somewhat later. It had taken some while for the men to pay the landlord for the damages and for Haimya to use her old field-nursing skills to patch up the boy. He would hurt more on the morrow than if Rubina had healed him, but no one was prepared to seek out the Black Robe and interrupt her "healing" of Birak Epron.

Pirvan shortly thereafter declared himself exhausted and strode off for the chamber he shared with Haimya. He was not in the least sleepy, but the need for sleep would serve well enough as an excuse to avoid others until his own temper healed.

He would not have believed Tarothin capable of such folly as that jealous rage. He did not believe Rubina would prove any kind of an adequate replacement for Tarothin, for Karthayan or kender, for she was a Black Robe and therefore a servant of Takhisis. The Dark Queen stood for all that Paladine, patron of the Knights of Solamnia, opposed.

He even wondered if it was lawful, let alone prudent, for *him* to continue on the quest.

The one consolation he found before he blew out the candle was that he had actually grown sleepy while washing himself and pulling on his nightshirt.

* * * * *

There was someone in the room with Pirvan, and he had his dagger out from under the pillow the moment after he realized this. Then he lay perfectly still—until, by the smell and sound of breathing, by the sound of clothes being removed and boots being slipped off, he recognized Haimya.

He needed no further recognition, but he had it anyway as she slipped into the bed and threw her arms around him from behind. Her warm breath was soft and soothing on the back of his neck. He slipped the dagger back under the pillow and lay still.

"Kurulus has returned," Haimya said at length. "He says it would be well to make haste, to set our plans afoot. More ships—twenty at least, and soldiers in proportion—are gathering in Istar, to join those already here."

Pirvan frowned. The plan was simple enough: Jemar would carry Pirvan and some two hundred mercenary soldiers across the bay and land them secretly. They would then march overland, toward the region where Waydol the Minotaur held sway.

Meanwhile, Jemar would sail out of the Bay of Istar, carrying another hundred hired swords, and proceed westward, to meet his remaining ships and men. He would bring them to the coast where Waydol's stronghold was believed to lie, at the same time as the marching column reached its landward side. Then, having no need to collect Waydol's head or anyone else's in order to accomplish their plan, the companions would offer Waydol and even his band safe passage beyond the reach of Istar's fleets and armies.

If Istar was going to send further strength for sea and land into the north, however, it was now a race. It was not only a race of the companions to reach Waydol's stronghold before Aurhinius did. It was also a race of the companions against Istar's preventing Jemar from sailing or the sell-swords from marching.

Also, there was the danger that the Istarians, in their

arrogance, might do this by blockading Karthay or landing soldiers in territory that the Karthayans considered they ruled directly, rather than Istar. Either could make the breach between Istar and Karthay open. Preventing that open breach was the whole purpose of Pirvan and Haimya assembling their companions and resources and leaving hearth and home at the behest of the Knights of Solamnia!

Even Haimya's warmth against him did not ease Pirvan.

She felt that tautness and unease in him and drew him harder against herself. "What troubles you, my lord and love?"

He told her of his thoughts and added his disgust with Tarothin. "I do not know if a man is ever too old to make a fool of himself over a woman. But Tarothin is far too old to throw a tantrum like that, and to endanger sworn companions by it."

He felt Haimya shaking then, and started to roll over, wanting to hug her and kiss away the tears that would be falling in the next moment.

What happened in the next moment, instead, was her teeth nearly meeting in the lobe of his left ear. The pillow fortunately stifled his yell, and by the time the pain had faded he realized that Haimya was not weeping but quite the reverse.

"My lady," he whispered. "You can have a pillow to stifle your laughter. But if you do not tell me the jest afterward, I shall stifle you."

Slowly, Haimya sobered. "I wish we could have told you before," she began, "but we knew—"

"We?"

"Jemar, Tarothin, and myself. I believe Grimsoar guessed, but he can hold his tongue and countenance."

"You are adding to the mystery, rather than dispelling it," Pirvan said, wearily. "Please go on."

"Simply enough, the quarrel was feigned. Tarothin remains behind, his loyalty to Istar and the kingpriest apparently restored. With a trifle of luck and a few bribes, for which Jemar has provided the silver, Tarothin will be able to sail with the Istarian fleet. This gives us eyes, ears, and magic among our enemies—or at least those who may become so."

Pirvan shifted position. The warmth of Haimya beside him was so comfortable that he would have gone back to sleep if his mind had not still been whirling like a carnival dancer.

"Did you not trust me?"

"Your honor, yes. Your face, no."

"My face?"

"It would have been a scroll on which enemies might read what they ought not to. I suppose you were too honest as a thief to be a good actor, and of course you have been a Knight of Solamnia for ten good years—"

It was a while longer before Haimya finally persuaded Pirvan of the truth of the matter. When at last she did, his first reply was to laugh softly into her hair.

Then he took her in his arms.

"Well, I may not be the actor Tarothin is, but I have one blessing for the rest of this quest that he lacks."

"And that is?"

"He must remain celibate for the remainder of this journey. I, on the other hand—"

Haimya ended the conversation with her lips.

Chapter 9

The little expedition had to retrace its course somewhat to be sure of landing Pirvan and his men securely. Directly across from Karthay would be too close to Istariku and its swelling garrison and fleet. Going north to near the mouth of the bay would mean a long march across territory already garrisoned, where it was not rank tropical forest.

Sailing south meant a long march, but one free of large towns, hostile garrisons, or the more formidable sort of natural obstacles. It was also well-watered country, with plenty of game; there was no hope of the marchers carrying enough food for the whole journey.

What they could not hunt or pick, they intended to buy, and the gold and silver gathered by Jemar and the knights together would go a long way toward opening store-houses. Pirvan hoped that the money would go even farther toward closing mouths.

At least they knew more than before about how the folk

of the north looked askance at the rule of Istar. With some, this was ancestral memories of being ruled by Karthay, or more recent experiences of being put off their land by the "barbarians" suppressed, with the aid of the Knights of Solamnia, at the time of the Great Meld.

With most, however, it was the simple fact that the farther from Istar, the less benign the mighty city's rule. Pirvan was not a great student of history, but he had read enough in the libraries of the knights' keeps, as well as in his own, to have learned somewhat of the lessons of the past.

One of those lessons was that any empire needed to be exceedingly careful that its outlying provinces were well governed. Farthest from the center of power, they were the easiest prey for corrupt governors and captains—and also found it easier to shift their allegiance to other rulers, a fertile source of every kind of war.

Not that there was anywhere the folk in this land could shift their allegiance, even if they wished. The dwarves of Thorbardin would laugh at the idea of human subjects, and Solamnia could hardly rend the Swordsheath Scroll. But a land perpetually steaming with discontent like an untended pot of soup was not a land at peace.

All of this weighed heavily on Pirvan's mind as he watched the last of the overland column climb out of the boats and wade ashore. The sky was sullen from both cloud and the early hour, but the breeze had vanished. The water was black and so calm that it almost seemed oily.

Farther offshore, mist and rain were already swallowing even *Sea Leopard*, the nearest of the four ships. Several boats that had already unloaded were laboriously crawling back to the sea barbarian vessel. Pirvan wanted to believe that he could see Grimsoar standing in the prow, but knew that had to be mostly his imagination.

A very real splashing close by made him turn. Rubina was wading ashore from the boat, holding her skirts well above her knees to keep them dry. She had not been entirely successful in this, and she was being entirely too successful in attracting a great deal of notice.

Birak Epron cleared his throat. "My lady Rubina. I

think you should have changed into more practical garb before entering the boat. I am sure that once your baggage is landed, the Lady Haimya will be glad to keep watch while you clothe yourself anew."

Rubina stepped out of the water and let her skirts fall. Pirvan saw faces fall as well, as those shapely limbs vanished from sight.

Now the Black Robe stepped up to the mercenary captain and gave him one of her dazzling smiles. "I would far rather have your company in that endeavor—" she began.

Epron cut her off. "Lady. Never think me ungrateful. But I have duties to my men. For that matter, so do you. One we both have is to keep discipline among them."

Rubina frowned. It was the frown of an exceedingly shrewd woman pretending to be a silly one. "My dear friend, you seem to wish to make my first war very harsh for me. Not only have I lost Tarothin, now it seems that I am to lose—"

"Lady Rubina," Haimya said, in a tone that excluded all possibility of argument. "Let us go aside, and I will tell you, while you change your clothes, just how harsh war is."

She then took a firm grip of Rubina's arm. For a moment it seemed that the Black Robe would resist, physically or even magically, and Pirvan met Epron's eyes in total agreement.

Unaware of her narrow escape, Rubina allowed herself to be marched off to a discreet clump of dragonstooth bush, which here on this coast grew to the size of young trees. When the women had disappeared, Pirvan turned to the mercenary captain.

"I thank you."

"I guard my men from all dangers, and they me, Sir Pirvan. I keep that bargain even against all the Towers of High Sorcery. Has anything ever made you think that sellswords have no honor?"

"Nothing whatever, and much to the contrary. But I have also learned not to overlook the power of—of—"

"A woman like Rubina making a man think with other parts of his body than his head?"

"That's one way to say it, I suppose."

The last boat's keel grated on the gravel of the beach as it pushed off. Pirvan contemplated the mountain of equipment and supplies left behind, and the men already moving it to hiding places.

It was as well that Birak Epron was the senior mercenary captain and therefore next only to Pirvan in command ashore. His men were not only the best of the lot, but they were also doing a fair job of hammering their own skills and discipline into their motley comrades.

As for Rubina, Pirvan vowed to do his best to leave her to Haimya and Epron. If between them they could not make her more useful than useless to the expedition, then he would have to step in himself.

* * * * *

"I ask your pardon for this hospitality, but we lost our fields last year," the man kneeling before Darin said. He placed a wooden tray of dried fruit and nuts surrounding a piece of salt meat harder and darker than the tray in front of the Heir to the Minotaur, then rose and stepped back.

By the flickering torchlight, Darin saw that his men were as alert as they needed to be in a strange camp. He could give his attention to the leader without worrying about surprises from the other band's men.

Men—and others. Somewhere in this land, over the last few generations, ogres had made free with human women more than a few times. Of the thirty men Darin had counted (without seeming to do so; doing that openly could bring on a fight at once), at least ten showed signs of ogre blood.

Among them was the leader, who had just placed the gift of food before Darin. He was as tall as Darin, and would have been nearly as broad and strong had hard labor and scant food not fought against ogre blood. Nor was he even truly ugly, let alone misshapen. Brow ridges, the shape of his skull, the jawline, and the matted hair that grew everywhere except where old scars seamed the leader's skin were all he showed of the ogre look.

But they had been enough to make him an outlaw. Not a successful one, though, from the state of his men, their weapons, and their camp—not one, in short, who could afford to refuse an alliance if one were offered him.

Darin wished for the tenth time in as many days that he was holding the stronghold and Waydol was moving about the country, offering alliances to outlaw bands, lone robbers, and the merely discontented or wild-spirited all across the land. However, this could not be. No horse could carry Waydol, and the work needed to be done quickly.

Nor, in truth, were all the outlaws of this land well disposed toward minotaurs merely because they were ill disposed toward Istar, or whoever happened to claim lawful authority over the land. The Heir to the Minotaur did not arouse suspicion or anger, as the Minotaur himself might have done.

Darin motioned his men forward on each side of him. When they formed a half-circle, opened toward the half-ogre and his fire, Darin began to eat.

He felt no hunger to lend savor to the coarse food, but as he ate he saw his men looking across the fire to see when their food would be ready. He frowned. It did not seem likely that the half-ogre had a meal for another twelve men in his storehouses. He himself was eating entirely as a gesture of peace, but he was eating when his men were not, much against his custom, honor, and sense.

"Brother of the greenwood, may I ask of you two things?" he said to the half-ogre.

"All may be asked here, but as to what may be granted . . ."

"I understand. First, is Pedoon the name by which you are known, or the one by which you wish to be known?"

The leader ran a thumb across his brow ridges. "I've answered to Pedoon and nothing else for years. I don't think I'd know you were talking to me if you used any other."

"Very well, Pedoon. Then is there aught to eat in your camp for my men? If there is not, are we at liberty to hunt on your land, so that we need not choose between tightening our belts and eating them?"

The laugher from Pedoon's men was harsh barks. Looking at them, Darin could well believe that they found little humor in jests about hunger.

"Will you be content with bread and salt and hunting rights thereafter?" Pedoon said.

Darin nodded. Whether bread and salt bound Pedoon against all treachery as they would have many humans, he did not know. Much depended on where Pedoon had been raised, whether among ogres or among humans, but there was a question to be asked when the chiefs were alone.

The bread was barely half-baked, of flour made from some plant surely never intended for that purpose, and the salt was the coarsest of rock salt. But with the eyes of both chiefs on them, Darin's men dared not refuse, particularly when they saw Darin himself eating the bread and salt.

They had just finished their ritual, and some were reaching for their water bottles, when a man three paces to Darin's left rose to his knees. Then his mouth opened, and he began to claw at his throat. Mucus ran from his eyes and his nose, and it seemed that he wished to spew.

A small figure at the right of the line leaped up and ran into the darkness, where the horses and their guards stood. Pedoon shouted, and half a dozen of his men leaped up and followed Darin's runner.

"Hold!" Darin shouted. One man was well out ahead of the rest, and as Darin turned, he raised a spear.

Darin was not wearing his gauntlets, but the strength of his arms was the same, gauntlets or not. He gripped the shaft of the spear as it thrust at him, jerked it from the man's hands, and slammed the butt end up under the man's jaw. He crashed backward into the midst of his comrades—and all the men on both sides rose to their feet as if pulled by a single cord.

In the next moment everyone had a weapon in hand.

In the moment after that, a bloody slaughter would have begun, except that out of the darkness, the small figure returned. Now he was carrying a staff, from whose head an unearthly blue light shone, faintly but visible to all even in the glare of the campfire.

"Hold!" Pedoon shouted, and Darin echoed him. Sir-bones hurried over to the choking man, who had now fallen on his side in convulsions. He laid the staff on the man's throat, then on his belly, then on his chest, and finally stepped back, singing in a voice that sounded like a giant earteaser in full cry.

It seemed that the man emptied his stomach of everything he'd eaten since he left the stronghold. Sirbones and two of his comrades helped drag him to clean grass and wipe him clean with leaves and water. Then they laid two cloaks over him, and Sirbones stepped up to Darin.

"Most of the poison is out of him, and my healing will fight off what may remain."

"What kind of poison was it?"

"In that kind of bread, you could hide a dozen at once without tasting any of them," Sirbones said. "Ask the poisoner. Or I can—"

"No!" That was Pedoon, now standing beside the man who had tried to spear Darin. "He has violated the laws of the gods and of this band, and was a fool and a traitor as well. But you shall not enter his mind."

"Will he be the better if you thrust hot coals into his body until he loses his voice from screaming and dies without speaking?" Sirbones snapped.

Darin stepped between the priest and the half-ogre chief. "Will you answer Sirbones? There will be no war between us over this, but you will not be called our friends without some fit answer."

Pedoon shrugged massive shoulders. Even his shoulder blades sprouted hair, though much of it was gray. "Ansik always walked a little apart. I don't know where he obtained the poison. I trust that any of his comrades who do will see that nobody else is as stupid."

Pedoon's hooded gaze swept the ranks of his men like a fire spell. "As for why he did what he did—there is a price on your head, Heir to the Minotaur. All men know it. Some are less honorable about how they try to collect it than others.

"Does that content you?"

Darin looked at Sirbones. The little priest shrugged. His face said that the answer might not content him, but they had small chance of getting a better one.

Darin nodded.

"Then may I have Ansik's spear?"

Darin handed Pedoon the captured spear, butt first, while keeping a hand on his own sword hilt. But he had no need to fear. Pedoon stood over Ansik, who had barely recovered his senses, and drove the spear down into the fallen traitor's chest with all his strength.

Ansik hardly even twitched before life left him.

Silence enveloped the camp, as complete as if every man there had followed Ansik into death. Pedoon broke it, with a long, harsh, wailing cry.

The rest of the band took it up; plainly it was a lament for the dead, neither ogre nor human but partaking of the ways of both. Darin signaled to his men to listen in silence, until the lament was ended.

When the night birds and insects stunned into silence found their voices, Pedoon stepped close to Darin.

"Will you walk apart with me, Heir to the Minotaur?"

"Gladly."

Darin was not happy with the dark trail where Pedoon chose to lead him, but followed in silence. If death by Pedoon's treachery was his fate, he could not turn it aside by seeming a coward or refusing to give ear to the chief.

"It would be as well, I think, if our bands did not unite," Pedoon said. "Hunger and hard beds are easier than worrying every day about treachery, from one side or the other. Tempers grow short that way, steel flies, blood flows, and in the end we all have less than we did."

"I was thinking the same," Darin said, and those words would have passed the test of a high-level truth spell. "I had not thought your—you—"

"You hadn't expected such good sense in an ogre?" Pedoon said, laughing. In the dark woods, an ogrish laugh was an uncanny sound. "Shame on you, who follow a minotaur."

Darin could think of no reply. Pedoon laughed more softly.

"I owe you, though, for not treating Ansik's foolish treachery as cause for blood. And I can pay this debt, at least. There was a man who spared me and my band over by the bay, some ten years ago, whom I've never seen again. I'll probably die with that debt weighing on my spirit. But you I can pay."

Pedoon explained how he and several other chiefs of small bands had agreed to warn each other of hostile visitors to the land. He would swear, and ask the others to swear, that anyone who came against Waydol and his heir would also be cause for warning.

"Not fighting, unless they are few or we can band together faster than we ever have before. But warning— on this you can trust us."

Darin gripped Pedoon's knob-knuckled hand. "And you can trust my huntsmen to share whatever they bring down before we leave your land."

They walked back to the camp with silence about them save for the night sounds of the forest.

* * * * *

"Any room at this table?" came the voice from behind Tarothin.

The Red Robe remembered to look owlishly about him before focusing slowly on the bland-looking man standing behind his chair.

"Suppose so," he said. The slur in his words was just a hint. He was supposed to have emptied only three cups of good wine, which would barely fuddle a hardheaded drinker. No one would take him on if they thought he'd turned sot over his broken heart.

The man sat down without further invitation and signaled the serving maid for another jug of wine and a plate of sausages. Tarothin had to let his cup be refilled when the order arrived, but it was no hardship not to drink the wine.

He was able to pretend to drink, and to let the drink

work on him, until the man leaned over and whispered, "Do you want back at those people who left you?"

"What people?" Tarothin said.

The man started to say something loud and out of character, then took a deep breath. "You know which ones. The tale's all over Karthay by now."

If it was, somebody had been giving it boots, wings, or even a ride on a dragon. However, if this fellow had heard it and was from where Tarothin hoped he was, the tale had traveled far enough.

"Oh, Rubina and her friends?"

"That's the name I've heard for the woman. What about the others?"

"If you've heard the tale, you know who they are. Damned Istarians. Triple-damned knights."

Tarothin spent the next five minutes expressing what he'd like to do to Rubina, certain Istarians, and any Solamnic Knight who fell into his power. Occasionally he raised his voice enough to draw dubious looks from nearby tables.

Some of the details were Tarothin's imagination. Some of them came from one of the most unpleasant experiences of his life, the trial of a renegade mage who'd used healing spells to torture his victim. Most of that, Tarothin sincerely wished, *was* his imagination.

His visitor kept a straight face until Tarothin was done, then ordered more wine. The wizard hoped the man would get to the point, if any, before he had to drink enough wine to really fuddle his wits.

The True Gods were with Tarothin. Halfway through the next cup, the man leaned over and said, "Look, you. I don't know what would come of you going back to Istar. But we have a band of good Karthayans who are tired of this fight against Istar. The gods have plainly shown their favor to the city, and we're not folk to fight against the gods.

"So we're chartering a ship, a big one, to carry plenty of stout Karthayans ready to take up arms for Istar. We'll need wizards aplenty, but the tales say you're worth three of the common kind. Can we trust you?"

The wine had fuddled the man more than it had Tarothin, and it took him quite a while to get this out. By then, however, he was past noticing that Tarothin had stopped drinking.

That was no bad thing for Tarothin. He didn't dare use even the smallest self-healing spell to sober himself up, or further befuddle the other man. The other might say he was a Karthayan loyal to Istar's rule, but if he was a Karthayan, then Tarothin was a kender!

"Is there a place I can come, to go aboard?" Tarothin asked.

"Eg—Egalobos's place. It's on—on Shieldmakers' Wharf."

"Egalobos's place on Shieldmaker's Wharf." Tarothin made a great show of looking in his purse, ready to pay for the next round.

"Friends—friendssh left you—w'out g-gold?" the man got out.

Tarothin nodded, but the man was nodding, too; then he fell forward onto the table, knocking over the wine cup. Tarothin felt he deserved to lie there with his beard in the wine, but instead called a serving boy.

He was careful to stagger as he left the room. The man probably hadn't come alone. No conspirators worth spying on would send as their only agent a man who passed out after three cups of such villainous wine! It would embarrass Tarothin to even pretend to be associated with them.

But sots and witlings had brought down thrones before. When war and peace were in the balance, one Red Robe's embarrassment weighed very lightly.

* * * * *

The letter Pirvan wrote from Karthay had eased Sir Marod's mind.

The letter just received from Istar did the opposite.

Sir Marod looked at the letter as if wishing hard enough would change the words on the parchment into something innocent, such as a love poem or a laundry list.

Wishing had no effect. Putting the letter in the candle would have some effect, but not a good one. Regardless, much of the letter was already carved on Sir Marod's mind.

The kingpriest was sending certain powerful and ruthless servants of Zeboim the Sea Queen aboard the fleet about to depart from Istar. They went by his command, with his blessing, aided by the resources of the great temples, and specifically freed from most of the normal bounds to their use of magic.

That was the worst part. Black, red, and white wizards and the priests of Good, Neutral, and Evil gods kept the balance on Krynn as it was kept among the stars by honoring certain rules. Not as complex or binding as the Measure of the Knights, but serving well enough.

Sending priests of Zeboim to sea with orders to do whatever they needed to gain victory could be pulling the keystone out of the delicate arch of the balance on Krynn. Then chaos would be unleashed and all beings alike buried under the ruins.

Sir Marod decided that he was developing a taste for dramatic figures of speech that could as well be left to poets and pageant-makers. The priests of Zeboim would not go unopposed, by either magical or human powers.

But their presence would increase the peril into which Pirvan and his friends were sailing or marching before they could learn of it and be on their guard. And this was quite apart from their having magical aid only from Rubina, since Tarothin had left the company in a jealous rage.

Sir Marod had ordered men and women to their deaths before—not too many to count, but enough to sometimes deny him easy sleep at night. But he had always done his best to be sure that those who went forth knew what they faced, *before* they departed.

This time, it gnawed at him that he had sent knights forth with broken lances and blunted swords, against foes who might rise from the ground or fall from the sky without warning.

Chapter 10

"hulloooo!" came from the rear of the column. "Sir Pirvan! Is this the last hill?"

Pirvan cupped his hands and shouted back, "Yes. The next one's a mountain!"

Good-natured curses and weary laughter echoed from the rocks as the column approached the peak of the trail. Pirvan forced strength into his legs, knowing that he was taking it from some other part of his body that would probably need it before he had a chance to rest.

He was in the lead when they reached the crest, and nearly went limp with relief when he saw that the downward slope was easy, and the trail broad, without sharp drops. When one loses two men in a single day from their straying too close to a drop edged with mud or slippery rocks, a war leader comes to value slopes so gentle that a baby could roll down them without being hurt.

He also comes to value able junior leaders. Haimya was

one he would have valued even without love, likewise Birak Epron, and, more than somewhat to his surprise, Rubina. The Black Robe now wore male attire, though no soldier ever campaigned in such a hat, and this definitely altered her charms so that they were less distracting to the men.

It also did not hurt that when they stopped for the night, she would go along the column, laying on hands and staff for blisters, pulled muscles, thorn stabs, and the like. Like any Black Robe, her healing powers were modest, but so far the overland column had taken no serious injuries. Everyone was either dead or marching on.

Pirvan found the flattest and driest rock by the side of the trail and sat down. Then he drew from a pouch on his belt a tightly folded, leather-backed map of this land.

This area had never been part of Solamnia, so the knights had not been mapping it as they had some lands, ever since maps were first invented. Instead, they had trusted the Swordsheath Scroll and the Great Meld to induce Istar to provide maps out of courtesy.

In this, as in much else, the knights received less than their due. The most Pirvan could tell from this map was that their march had taken them almost out of the hills, and beyond lay more level country. This level country stretched from here to the seacoast, and somewhere on that coast was Waydol's stronghold.

So they were now entering lands where the Minotaur's band might be roving. The inhabitants might be friendly or hostile, largely depending on what they thought of Waydol. Their thoughts on Istar's rule might also make a difference, and Pirvan took a crumb of comfort in most of the men with him being Karthayan.

Pirvan squinted against the westering sun and looked downhill. The trees grew tall enough to hide much, even on this slope, so it took him a while to spy the trails of chimney smoke from well beyond the last visible bend.

"Village ahead," he said to Haimya and Epron. "It's downhill, so we can surely reach it with time to spare before dark. But can we trust it to be friendly?"

Epron nodded. "The oldest question I know, for the captain of a marching column. How far to push the men? For if the village is friendly to Waydol, we might be safe only if we go farther than might be well for the men."

Pirvan had not and would not defer to Epron's opinion so much so that the men questioned who led the column. But he could not deny that he had never before led two hundred men in battle, and Epron had led that many more times than he had fingers (of which he lacked two, thanks to a sword wound to his left hand).

"Very well. We'll march as close to level ground as we can, make camp, post guards, then scout out the village. Once we're out of the forest, we should think of striking out across country, well away from settlements."

"We're supposed to learn how the people are disposed toward Istar, Waydol, Karthay, and, for all I know, the Irda and the ice barbarians," Haimya said. "Of course, if that was so important, they might have sent two men marching and the rest could have gone by sea."

"There's truth in that," Epron said. "I do not call your friend Jemar—"

"Let us not discuss Jemar while the men are passing by," Haimya put in. "Moreover, let us remember that he is on the sea with Istar's fleet, which cannot touch us the moment the water is too shallow for their keels."

Pirvan wanted to point out that Jemar was, in turn, safe from Aurhinius, the moment the water reached the depth of a horse's belly. But he knew that weary bickering could too easily turn into sharp quarrels.

* * * * *

In the end, there was no need to pass the village too closely. A narrower trail forked off from the main one well before the village, and scouts sent down it reported that it reached open country well clear of other villages.

The trail led, however, through what was almost another village of charcoal burners, who had their furnaces set up in a score of different clearings along the next day's march. By now, Pirvan looked like anything but a knight, and indeed the column could be recognized as soldiers only by their being armed and keeping in some sort of order.

"Hunh," one of the burners said, wiping her (at least Pirvan thought it was a woman) hands on a leather apron as black as tar and cracked like ice in the spring thaw. "You fellows will never do Waydol's business for him, even if you don't fall down afore you gets to his gate."

Pirvan shrugged. "Who says we're going to do anything at his gate besides knock? What we do then—it's up to him and how he replies."

"You're not one to call him enemy, then?"

"Not unless he misnames us that first, and even then we'll try not to fight him harder than needed to force a parley."

The charcoal burner—definitely a woman, for all that she was not much shorter than Grimsoar One-Eye—seized Pirvan in a dusty, malodorous embrace. "Gods be with you, then. But be wary. There's plenty of folk out for the bounty on Waydol, and you may be fighting your way through them before you're done marching."

So it went much of the day, with Pirvan and Haimya feigning every sort of opinion about Waydol, to draw out the charcoal burners and their kin. By the end of the day, it was plain that, at least among the charcoal burners, Waydol was considered no great enemy, sometimes a friend, and very surely one who made Istar the Mighty angry, so could not possibly be all bad, even if he was a minotaur!

It was harder to tell what the village on the main road thought, for the charcoal burners and the villagers were not the best of friends. The woods-dwellers suspected the villagers of kissing Istar's hand (or other parts) simply because they were the sort of folk who would do that sort of thing. But as to details, they could give none, and after a while Pirvan gave up asking.

"It's not marvelous that we don't get along with nonhumans when two human settlements so close can't make peace," Epron said as the last soldier filed past the last clearing.

"It may not be a surprise, but something doesn't have to be an ambush to be deadly," Haimya said. She looked long and hard at Epron, and Pirvan remembered that Epron not only had solely humans in his band but also had not urged recruiting any other races. Not that there were that many such in Karthay, but one could wonder.

Except that in this matter, wondering led nowhere but to sleepless nights that Pirvan could not afford, if he was to keep putting one foot in front of another until they knocked on Waydol's door.

* * * * *

Haimya thought for some time afterward that perhaps she had spoken an ill-luck word, in mentioning ambushes. For they encountered one not two hours past the forest of the charcoal burners. Blessed with greater strength or skill, the attack might have cost the marching column heavily.

As it was, the villagers who laid the ambush on the trail could not make up their minds which side of the trail they ought to take. So they were still darting back and forth across the road and sometimes standing to argue in the middle of it, when Pirvan's scouts came within sight of them.

The scouts saw without being seen, slipping into the woods at once and creeping forward until they could count the enemy's strength and positions. Then their messengers scurried back to Pirvan, who promptly halted the column while he listened to the reports.

Birak Epron thought that on the left at least the woods were thin enough that a small party might slip secretly behind the villagers and turn the tables on them. He even volunteered to lead it himself, but Pirvan thought he had more of an eye on a feat to impress Rubina than on sound tactics.

The Black Robe had been faithful to Epron, as far as Pirvan knew, but he also knew that Epron would always doubt, always be seeking some new way of making himself stand taller in the lady's eyes. His remarks about not letting her turn him from his duty were much more than wind, but something less than the whole truth. Fortunately, his men seemed tolerant—as yet.

"Send your best sergeant, with ten or a dozen picked men," Pirvan told the mercenary. "None among us doubt your courage. None among us could do your work, if you were to be slain in a skirmish against foes not worthy of your steel."

Epron looked dubious. "Good sergeants do not grow on tarberry bushes either," he said. "Nor have I kept faith with my men all these years by sending others to do what I would not."

"All these years, you have not been so badly needed." Weariness brought to Pirvan's mind the notion that perhaps Birak Epron wanted a war between Istar and Karthay, which would surely fatten the purses of sellswords from every land.

And leave a trail of burned towns, weeping widows and orphans, young men dead or crippled in their prime, and much else not beloved of the gods.

He kept the insult off his lips. "Epron, choose. I do not think the folk ahead are finished warriors, but they are not asleep or drunk, that we can wait forever to strike."

Epron shrugged. "Have it as you will, Sir Knight."

Epron's sergeant and ten men swiftly vanished. Other men vanished into the woods on the other side of the road. Their task was to cover the retreat of the main body, if by some ill chance the ambush forced one.

The rest of the column was to simply march down the trail, like a worm dangled in a fishpond, to bait the ambushers into striking. Pirvan prayed briefly to Kiri-Jolith that the fish would not be unexpectedly large and hungry, then took his place at the head of the column.

Pirvan's guesses as to the strength and skills of the enemy were not far off the mark. They were hardly more than fifty, and of all places to strike, they chose one where broad, deep ditches ran along both sides of the trail.

So when the first arrows flew from the trees, a soldier or two dropped. Most, even the less well trained, dove into the ditches on one side or the other. Both ditches held water, one up to a man's knees, so the diving soldiers were neither dry, clean, nor comfortable in their refuge. Nor did all the archers keep their bowstrings dry.

But enough did so that they were able to beat down the enemy's archery, picking off bowmen almost as fast as they showed themselves. A few minutes of this, and the enemy grew desperate enough to charge, even against more than thrice their number.

As they charged, so did Epron's sergeant and his band. The enemy to the left of the road found themselves caught between two fires, driven onto wet ground where they could barely fight and not even hope to fleet, and they were subdued in moments. They could have been cut down to the last man where they stood, but Pirvan had given strict orders against needless killing. For the most part, he was obeyed. On the right, where Pirvan himself led, the fighting was more than a trifle sharper. Here were the village's stouter hearts and more skilled sword arms, and Pirvan actually had to draw his sword to beat back one of two men who'd picked Haimya as an opponent.

The knight finally ended the affair by a feigned retreat, which drew the attackers out of the forest, across the ditch, and onto the trail. As they reached it, the rear guard came storming up at a run, drawing a band of steel around the villagers. They began to wave their bows, reversed and unstrung, and soon there was nothing left to do but bind the prisoners.

No, not altogether. It was in Pirvan's mind to learn why the villagers had committed this particular folly. In spite of his orders against needless killing, of the fifty attackers some six were dead past healing, and Rubina found herself with burdensome work to do with many of the rest.

Pirvan sat on a stump before the oldest of the hale men and contemplated them. Then he motioned to the ground.

"Sit."

"You have us in your power, Captain," the man grumbled. "No need to be gracious."

"On the contrary," Pirvan said. "Great need, unless you are evil as well as foolish. Sit or stand as you wish, but tell me why you attacked us."

It seemed that the village had heard, no doubt from a spy among the charcoal burners, that the mercenaries were marching to join Waydol. This meant they might ravage the country on the way. Also, if they were allowed to pass without resistance, the vengeance of Istar, in the form of one of Aurhinius's captains and his riders, would sooner or later descend on the village.

"Then we'd lose as much as we lost today in blood, and more in treasure, women, and children, besides our honor. At least our blood today bought freedom from all that."

Pirvan sighed. His own men had too little to spare of anything, save Rubina's healing spells, to make up any of the village's losses.

But there was parchment and an inkhorn in one of Pirvan's pouches, and he could do something for the village with them. He drew them out, wrote swiftly, then called Haimya for wax. Into a blob of green sealing wax he pressed his ring with the sign of the crown on it, then folded the parchment and gave it to the villager.

"Take this to a keep of the Knights of Solamnia, as proof that a knight wishes you to be heard. They will listen, and I think you will have some justice, perhaps even more than you expect."

The man looked dubiously at Pirvan. "It's known about the country that the knights are not what they used to be."

"The knights never were what the legends say, most of them. The gods know, I'm not. Do you know that I was once a thief in Istar, before the knights found more honest work for me?"

The villager now looked completely bemused. Pirvan stood and lifted the man to his feet. "So don't kneel before me. Just lay that letter before the knights, and *then* judge how much we're worth. You may find yourself surprised."

"I'm already surprised, Sir—ah—?"

"Sir Pirvan."

"Like I said, I don't know what to make of all this. But maybe folk like you make the knights worth asking."

By now, most of the wounded villagers had been healed enough to walk or to be carried on improvised litters of branches and cloaks. Pirvan stood by Haimya and watched the villagers move out of sight, then turned to Birak Epron.

"Rally the men, put the crippled and dead on litters, and let us be out of here. I want to be well out of the forest before nightfall."

* * * * *

Being out of the forest before nightfall proved impossible. Strips and patches of woodlands wandered all over what, from the ridge, had seemed open country. Pirvan would have sworn that some of the trees were following them about.

They finally made camp in an easily defended field with woodlands on one side and a clear stream on the other. The light tents went up, the wounded were laid in them under Rubina's charge, and a party went off to bury the two dead.

Pirvan leaned back against a stout maple and took off his boots. He had neither removed nor dried them since the battle, and raw red strips around his calves told him that he had been less than wise. He was pulling off his socks and luxuriating in the feeling of grass against bare feet when a shadow moved in the darkness.

He was reaching for his sword when the shadow moved again and turned into a silhouette outlined by the campfires.

"Good evening, my lady Rubina."

"Good evening, Sir Pirvan. I sense a need in you for healing."

"Nothing that fresh air won't cure without you needing to exert yourself."

"Perhaps, perhaps not. At least let me look at it, lest it

grow so serious that I must weary myself further in healing it."

"True. You have done honorably and well, and it would be ill-done to ask of you more than you can give."

"I am known for my generosity, but thank you anyway," Rubina said. Pirvan caught the double meaning, but knew that the best way to keep Rubina from going on in such a manner was to be silent.

It was hard for him to remain silent for long, however, once Rubina's long, supple fingers began playing around his chafed calves. Little sighs of contentment escaped him, though at least she did not insist that he remove his breeches.

Unfortunately, it did not seem to matter much to Rubina's subtle love spells what a man was wearing. By the time Pirvan felt a burning desire to pull Rubina down into his lap and kiss her, he knew he had to get away.

He lurched to his feet, conscious that anyone looking at him could tell that desire was in him, and Rubina stood also. She pressed against him so that it was plain that she wore little under her soldier's clothes, then raised a hand to brush his cheek and lips.

Then she laughed—for once not a mocking laugh, but one in which real tenderness glowed—and kissed Pirvan on the chin. "I—well, you know what I wanted, and I know your thoughts. But because I know your thoughts, I also know that—I do not need that power over you, Sir Pirvan. Nor would I gain it by coming between you and your lady.

"You have something very rare, the two of you. I think it has a power to protect you both. If ever I could work a spell for you, it would be to bring out that power."

Rubina kissed Pirvan again and strode off, with a hip-swaying motion that spoke plainly of her own desire and a firm intent to satisfy it. Pirvan stood against the tree for a moment, rubbing the places where the Black Robe had kissed him. Not to cleanse himself of some impurity, but simply to help himself believe what had happened.

Eventually Pirvan decided that the traditional remedy

of cold water might serve. He walked upstream from the camp, beyond the sentry line, and in a secluded clump of bushes by a quiet pool stripped off his clothes and plunged into the water.

It was invigorating, soothing, cleansing, and much else, all at once. Pirvan was luxuriating in the water's embrace as he never could have done in Rubina's, when a splash too large for any fish sounded close by him.

He turned as a human head broke the water, a head with straight, fair hair hanging down all about it and eyes without color in the darkness, but with a familiar shape.

"Well met, my lady."

"It seems a bath was in both our thoughts," Haimya said.

"Indeed," Pirvan replied. Although that was no longer his only thought; even cold water had its limits when he shared it with Haimya.

She took him by the hand and led him toward shore. As the water reached their waists, he put his arms around her from behind and kissed the back of her neck, wet hair and all. She turned to face him—and very little was said thereafter, for so long that what finally awoke them was the sound of searching parties from the camp.

They slept again soon after reaching their own tent, and Pirvan's last thought before slipping down into oblivion was: *All warriors should have mates like Haimya. But then, if they did, they would never want to leave them to go to war.*

Is that a way of making peace everywhere, one that even the gods have overlooked?

Chapter 11

Tarothin was not the world's happiest sailor, even aboard a large ship such as *Golden Cup*. He was even less happy now, clinging desperately to any handhold that offered itself, as the boat thrashed its way out of the west port of Karthay. The wind was blowing half a gale, the rain slashed his face like tiny knives, spray soaked everything the rain left dry, and *Pride of the Mountains*, the "Karthayan loyalists'" chartered ship, might have been on Nuitari for all Tarothin could see of it.

He had the modest consolation that he was standing up to the rough ride better than a good many of his boat-mates. The new recruits looked like the cheaper sort of sell-sword, the scrapings of every tavern in Karthay.

They also looked as if they would gladly sink to the bottom of the harbor if that would end their misery. How miserable they were, Tarothin's nose told him plainly.

Then something cut off the wind, the sails flapped,

someone shouted "Out oars!" and those few aboard fit to handle or even recognize an oar lurched to their task. Tarothin decided that it was not beneath his dignity to handle an oar himself, and he had worked up a good sweat by the time the boat slid alongside *Pride of the Mountains*.

He was sweating harder by the time he finished helping unload the boat. Both cargo and passengers had to be swung up on deck in nets, and Tarothin's sweat stung the fresh blisters on his hands.

Eventually the last barrel and sack was stowed below, leaving the decks to the crew and the groaning, prostrate forms of the recruits. Somebody with what looked like a mate's sash summoned Tarothin over to the break of the aftercastle.

"Can you do anything by way of healing for those poor clowns?" the man asked, pointing at the deckload of sea-sick victims.

Tarothin frowned. He didn't want to use major healing spells this soon or on minor ailments such as seasickness. He needed to conserve his strength, the more so in that he knew *Pride of the Mountains* was very ill-provisioned and he would be doing all of his magic on scant rations. Also, the less these people knew about his real powers, the better his chances of surprising them when it came time to use them.

"Well, these lads can heal themselves, for the most part, if I can bring them to where they'll keep down water and broth. If someone will show me the galley, I can mix up a kettle of any of two or three potions that will settle stomachs. All the magic I'd need is a little spell any hedge-wizard could do in his sleep."

The mate looked dubious. Tarothin shrugged. "I can enspell them all back to health, but do you want that much magic hanging over the ship when we're about to put to sea?"

"Who told you we're about to put to sea?" The mate still looked dubious about whether he should call for help and have Tarothin clapped in irons.

Tarothin feigned total indifference to this fate and the mate's goodwill. "Nobody told me, but I've eyes in my head, and this isn't the first time I've been to sea. Also, ugly as this wind may be, it's fair for heading offshore. Wait for the spells to blow away, and they could be blowing away on a dead foul wind."

"Aye," the mate said with a sour look. "And our Istarian masters will not be thanking us for that."

Tarothin memorized the directions to the galley and left the mate trying to get a few of the seasick newcomers to help their worse-off mates. He also wondered if the mate's remarks indicated some discontent on the part of the crew, or merely a sailor's age-old reluctance to be at the beck and call of landlubbers.

At least he could do himself no harm with anyone aboard *Pride*, if his first work aboard was bringing twoscore seasick recruits back to a semblance of health!

*   *   *   *   *

Some days' sailing to the northwest, Jemar the Fair peered out of a port in the aftercastle of *Windsword* and also contemplated a scene on deck. If he had been able to compare his emotions with those of *Pride*'s mate, they might well have found themselves kindred spirits.

Not that *Windsword*'s waist was littered with green-faced recruits too seasick to care whether they lived or died. It held, apart from the usual hands at work preparing to get under way, three women sensibly clad in hooded cloaks over tunics, trousers, and low boots, and surrounded by a modest ring of bags, trunks, and crates.

One of the women, even clad loosely, was plainly with child. And there was what soured Jemar's mood. The woman he loved as much as life itself and almost as much as the sea was proposing to embark with him while halfway to bearing their fourth child.

At least no harm ever came of a civil greeting, even to a blood enemy, let alone to one's own wife. Jemar took a deep breath and stepped out on deck.

A moment later he could hardly breathe at all, because Eskaia was hugging him so hard. She had surprising strength for a woman who barely came up to his shoulder, and warmth flowed through him from her embrace, even as he felt her roundness amidships.

"To what do I owe this greeting?" Jemar said with raised eyebrows.

"To your giving permission for me to come aboard and sail with you," Eskaia said, her smile dazzling white in her olive-hued face.

"Indeed," Jemar said, trying to avoid even a tone, let alone words, that would bring on a public quarrel. "And to whom do I owe the honor of your fellow passengers?"

Eskaia stepped back and punched her husband lightly in the ribs. "If you have forgotten Amalya, my first maid, then I wonder that you propose to command the fleet. It is as well that I am here to take your place, if your wits—"

Jemar could not hold in his laughter. It was not quite a joking matter; had Eskaia been born to a family like her husband's, she might indeed be striding the deck of her own ship (although, one hoped, not so far along with child) and aspire to fly her own banner someday. She had taken to the life of a sea barbarian's lady as if she had been born to it, instead of heiress to one of the great merchant houses of Istar.

Jemar stopped laughing when he realized that Eskaia was still speaking. "—is Delia, a Red Robe with special command of healing spells and midwifery. To be sure, I do not expect us to be at sea long enough for the babe to be born, but Delia also has it in her to prevent mishaps."

Miscarriages *is what you will not say*, Jemar thought.

They had been lucky with their brood: three healthy babes in succession, and remaining healthy through all the years since the midwives held them up for the proud parents to contemplate. But sailing on this voyage seemed to Jemar to be tempting fate.

By now, all hands on deck had dropped their work in favor of scrambling to pick up Lady Eskaia's baggage. They would have picked up her as well had they not been leaving that honor to their captain.

Perhaps it will be for the best. Habbakuk knows they love her, and if they see her as a good-luck charm . . .

Everyone on the deck of *Windsword* cheered as Jemar the Fair lifted his wife and carried her into the aftercastle.

* * * * *

Tarothin found *Pride of the Mountain*'s galley as ill-stocked as he had expected. However, there were herbs and spices enough for one of the potions, not the best but likely to be good enough with a little help from magic and a great deal more from the gods.

The Red Robe wizard worked swiftly, following the principle that if it didn't taste bad, nobody would believe it was any good. The smell of the potion as it boiled nearly drove the cooks and their mates out of their own galley, and the boys who carried the pots on deck did so with their kerchiefs wrapped over their noses and mouths.

But it worked. By the time *Pride of the Mountains* was ready to sail, the still-pale recruits were on their feet—and promptly set to work by the boatswains's mates, at the capstan, hauling on the sheets, or lashing loose gear in place.

Once offshore, of course, the weather and the ship together did their best to put the recruits back on the sick list. But that best was not good enough; all were still on their feet and working, or else off watch and sleeping off honest fatigue, when *Pride* met the Istarian fleet.

The weather was still nothing for a pleasure cruise, and Tarothin would have sworn that he saw fog, rain, spray, and clouds in the air all at once. He clung to the railing and tried to count the Istarian fleet, and made a guess of some fifteen ships, of a size to hold some thousand or more soldiers beyond their own crew.

Some of them were making heavy weather of it; the galleys were all under sail and had their oar ports lashed firmly shut. Even the heavier sailing ships were rolling with a lazy motion that could have made Tarothin queasy if he'd looked at them too long.

He did no such thing. Instead, he went below and locked himself in his cabin, his services having earned him quarters to himself. Then he lay down and bound himself with a light spell that would put him into a trance and a stronger one that would make him acutely aware of any magic or magic-workers in the fleet.

It would not allow him to interfere with any spells; that was another and more serious matter, not to mention far more perilous. Neither would he be as able as he wished to defend himself from magical attack, let alone physical, while he lay in the trance.

But the combination of spells did have one great virtue. He was like a fly on the wall of a room, undetectable by those going about their business below, who would remain unaware of his scrutiny.

When he awoke, the fleet of Istar would have fewer magical secrets from him.

* * * * *

Lady Eskaia lowered herself into her husband's second-most-formal cabin chair, the vallenwood one, with inlays of polished, wine-hued coral and hornwhale ivory. Her husband noted that she moved with both caution and grace.

Indeed, she would not lose that grace until the last months of her pregnancy, when no woman could avoid taking on the shape of a melon with legs or moving like one. Otherwise she might have been an elf, perhaps one with the wild blood of the Kagonesti behind her dark coloring, with an instinctive grace of movement ashore or afloat, walking or dancing, clothed or—

Jemar did not force that thought from his mind. He did force his tongue to draw inspiration from it, to shape words that he hoped might send his wife back ashore.

"You are too beautiful to be real, even when I see you sitting here before me."

"Even when I am bearing?"

"Even so."

She blew him a kiss. "I will never cease to marvel at how a rough sea warrior became so honey-tongued."

"I had inspiration, my lady."

"Then if you were so inspired, my lord, why do you seem so ill at ease over my presence here? Am I bad luck?"

"No." That was mostly the truth; those who believed women aboard ship were bad luck were a diminishing handful, and Jemar did not care to have any of them serving him.

"You have been my good luck for as long as I have known you," he went on. "I owe—"

"Something to my dowry and to the connection I brought to you, with House Encuintras and its allies, I would say."

"You *would* say that, when here I am speaking words of gentle passion—"

"Better than words of not-so-gentle passion to see me back in the boat and headed ashore."

Jemar leaped from his chair. He wanted to go down on his knees, put his head in Eskaia's lap, and beg her to consider what folly she was about to commit. Instead he stood, hands clenched into fists and pressed against his side.

Eskaia's gaze seemed to pierce him like an arrow. Was she suspecting he might be about to raise a hand to her? He had done this twice; he was quite sure that his life would be forfeit if he did it a third time. It had made him guard his tongue, temper, and wine-bibbing, none of which in moderation, he supposed, would do him any harm.

Indeed, moderation would give him more years to spend with Eskaia, who was some seventeen years his junior and would probably be a silver-haired beauty when he was a mumbling wreck of a sailor or a corpse long since reduced to bones by the fish of some distant sea. He wanted those years. He wanted them so badly, he could taste them on his lips—

Eskaia rose and embraced him, so that he tasted his dreams on her lips instead. "I do not think lightly of the dangers that might come on this voyage, Beloved. But remember that I survived a winter storm while carrying Milandor, and he is now up to my shoulder and hearty as a minotaur."

"A storm is not a battle. If the ship stays afloat, all aboard are apt to live out the storm. A battle is another matter. A battle that might pit us against the fleet of Istar, with the odds on their side—"

"You need not draw me a detailed chart of the perils of this course," Eskaia said. "But consider how many perils I may avert.

"First, I may well know some of the Istarian captains, or at least those under them. If we come to negotiating rather than fighting, that will be useful.

"Second, Istar's fleet might well be prepared to send Josclyn Encuintras's son by marriage down among the Dargonesti and the sharks. They will be less willing to sink Josclyn's daughter. My father is not too old to be a bad enemy."

"You ask me to sail into battle with all knowing that I am ready to shield myself behind my wife? My wife who is with child?" Jemar's fingers twitched, and his voice climbed to the pitch of wind shrieking in the rigging.

Eskaia did not move. Instead she smiled. "Choose. Be thought a coward by little minds for so shielding yourself. Or be thought a fool, by me and likely others, for refusing to avail yourself of every weapon that the gods can possibly allow you."

Jemar's shoulders sagged. Eskaia would not slash him with her tongue like a storm slashing sails to ribbons if she thought his pride had made him a fool. But something would depart from between them, something that made life sweeter than he had ever dreamed it could be.

"If I know you as I ought to, there is another reason," he said. His smile was forced, but she answered it with one of her own. "You want to see our old friends again, our friends of the quest to Crater Gulf."

"You are not as witless as you sometimes pretend to be, Jemar," Eskaia said, raising herself to kiss him. "I would be very happy indeed to see them."

"Just as long as we are not too busy dodging galleys' rams and showers of arrows to give anyone even a simple `Good day,' " Jemar put in. He gently embraced his wife.

"Now, send in that magic-working midwife or that midwifely wizard or whatever she is, and let her satisfy me as to her skills. For if she is not what she says she is, you still may find yourself going ashore."

"That is only just," Eskaia said as demurely as a girl of nineteen instead of a matron of past thirty.

Jemar wanted to grind his teeth at the futility of his bluster. But had he not forsworn that habit some years ago, being wed to Eskaia would have reduced his teeth to stubs and his diet to gruel and ale.

* * * * *

Tarothin would have seemed asleep to eyes ignorant of magic. Indeed, it would have taken magic of the fourth order or more to penetrate the disguise of sleep—and such penetration would turn the trance to true sleep and leave much less for a curious wizard, friendly or not, to learn.

This was as well, for Tarothin was listening to the minds of magic-workers so close by that they had to be aboard ships of the fleet. He could not tell which ships; he had a vague notion that they were in a chamber so damp and dark that it must be well below the waterline of a large ship.

That was all he saw of the physical surroundings of the others. He had the impression that they were clerics rather than wizards, but could not have sworn to it had he possessed a waking tongue to swear.

Far more vivid was the next image—a stormy sea, with ships plowing across it, reefed sails taut-bellied, green water pouring over waists and sometimes forecastles. Ahead of the ships flew a misty shape that sometimes solidified enough to be recognizable as the Blue Phoenix, a common form of Habbakuk.

Suddenly the sea in the path of the ships erupted into a mountain of water, crowned with foam. Darkness swelled within that mountain of water, which held its shape in defiance of the power of the wind and its own weight.

The darkness surged free of the water—the monstrous turtle shape of Zeboim, who brought Evil to the waters as Habbakuk brought Good. She leaped completely clear of the mighty wave, and her beak closed on a wing of the Blue Phoenix.

Now wind blew outward from the mountain of water. Ships already heeling over as they fought to clear the wave heeled farther. Some went right over and lay keel up before foundering; others lay on their beam ends as men clung to the last few handholds until their strength vanished, and so did they, into the boiling sea.

Thunder and fire burst from the battling gods. The wind stripped the sails from every ship still afloat, dismasted several, and threw another on its side. It went down almost at once, as if a giant hand—or beak?—had snatched it down into the depths.

The fire held all colors and none, and most of the colors were not ones to which a wise man would care to give a name, for that would mean studying them too closely for too long. It also held heat, and steam exploded from the top of the wave as enough water to fill a small lake flashed into white vapor.

Tarothin saw the wall of vapor expanding toward him, knew that his flesh was about to be seared from his bones, struggled to either awake or cast a protective spell, or both if he could contrive it—

—and awoke bathed in sweat, with the bedding of his bunk almost as sodden as if his cabin had been flooded. He looked up at the port; it was sealed beyond allowing even a trickle. He looked at the deck; it was dry, with not even a dark spot on the cheap woolen rug that his last few towers had bought for cabin gear.

What had become of Habbakuk in this joust of the gods,

Tarothin did not know. He suspected it would not be prudent to dwell too long on this—vision, dream, nightmare? He had known the magic-hearing spell for only a few years, and it was not common among the Black Robes, rare among the Reds, and virtually outlawed among the Whites.

But priests of Zeboim so openly plotting to seek their mistress's victory over Habbakuk might be confident because they commanded some unusual spells. Tarothin might find before the voyage was over that his mind was as open to them as theirs to his.

Then victory would be a matter of who struck first.

Tarothin drank half his jug of water, then stripped and washed the sweat from his body with a cloth dipped in the other half. He felt cleansed not only in body but somewhat in mind when he was done.

He also felt clearheaded enough to know where his duty lay. Neutrality suggested that he should not strike first if the danger was only to him. But his neutrality also suggested even more strongly that he should have no such scruples if his friends were in danger.

Chapter 12

To the northeast, the canyon slashed deep into the side of the mountain. The mountain's upper slopes lay hidden in sullen, dark clouds, and more clouds were piling up to the east and north. A sharp-eyed observer could make out lightning flashes within the clouds.

"That looks like no natural storm," Birak Epron said. He had looked about him carefully to see that no one but Haimya and Pirvan were within hearing. Now he looked down at the river, winding along the bottom of the valley below. Pirvan looked at Rubina, but Epron shook his head. That did not mean the Black Robe was innocent, only that the mercenary captain would not willingly hear an accusation against her.

Not that there was a great deal one could expect from such an accusation, besides a furious quarrel and certainly not the truth. But Pirvan was beginning to wish that circumstances had dictated he travel either with Rubina or with the column of sell-swords. He could deal with either alone; both together made him feel out of his depth.

However, the plain fact was that the day was drawing to a close. Beyond the river, in places shallow enough to wade, were several concealed campsites. On this side it was all bare rock and grass, without even a visible spring for fresh water. A ridge also overlooked the south bank of the river, studded with perches for archers to play on anyone below.

Crossing the river this late in the day was not much to Pirvan's taste. All the alternatives were even less so.

"I will take Rubina up with the leaders," Pirvan said. "You keep well back, in the middle of the column."

"Very well. As fond of her as I am, I could wish she had not quarreled with Tarothin. Two wizards are better than one, and Tarothin was apt to speak his mind. Rubina unveils her body but keeps her mind invisible to mortal eye."

Pirvan refrained from congratulating the mercenary captain on his belated achievement of wisdom.

* * * * *

The river was one of those ill-natured streams too shallow to float a boat, too wide to jump across, and too deep to wade easily. It was also full of dead animals, so neither drinking from it nor swimming across it was an agreeable thought.

The column cast up and down along the near bank, seeking a ford. In time they found a sandbar that cut most of the way across the river, and made a path shallow enough to cross if not quite dryshod, then without ruining clothes and weapons.

"Let us not forget the food," Haimya added. "If we ruin the trail biscuit and then run into a land hunted bare, we may be leaner than elves before we reach Waydol."

Two of the tallest soldiers crossed the river with stout ropes, tying them to trees on the far bank. Further tall, strong soldiers entered the water, stationing themselves at intervals along the ropes in case anyone lost his grip. Pirvan did not expect much of this; the current appeared sluggish, except for an occasional eddy.

Pirvan and Haimya led the way across. Rubina followed. In spite of her height, she somehow contrived to be soaked from head to foot, so that when she emerged from the water her black garments clung to her like a second skin. She stood in the open like that, wringing the water out of her hair, until several men stumbled into potholes because they could not keep their eyes off her.

Pirvan was about to drag her forcibly out of sight when he heard a distant rumbling sound, like thunder but nearer the earth. He ran to the bank and looked upstream and down. Downstream showed nothing as far as the last visible bend.

Upstream, a faint haze seemed to rise from the river. Pirvan strained his eyes and saw the base of a prominent tree upstream seem to vanish. Then the lower branches also vanished. The same thing happened to other trees, and Pirvan cupped his hands and shouted, "Flood! The river's rising! Everybody out of the water to high ground!"

Not everyone could obey this prudent command. The river was a hundred paces wide at the crossing point, and even those men who remained calm did not all survive. Pirvan saw Haimya run down to the water's edge, stripping off her armor and clothing as she went, clearly intending to use her swimming prowess to save whomever she could.

The knight wanted to shout, or run and grapple her away from the water. Instead he pointed to two soldiers already crossed over.

"Take the Lady Rubina to high ground, or climb a tree if you find nothing better."

Then Pirvan himself ran down to the bank, where the water was rising toward him almost as swiftly as he descended toward it. There could be no stopping Haimya; his choices were letting her risk her life or shaming her before all in a way that she would not forgive.

The knight hoped that his wisdom would console him

somewhat if it was his fate today to see his lady drown before his eyes.

One of the soldiers who'd carried the ropes had already leaped in and been swept away with his comrades. The second was firmer on his legs, and also giving ground before the rising water. As men thrashed to within reach, Pirvan's long arms snaked out and caught them by the handiest part of their bodies or piece of clothing. Then he drew them in like a fisherman with an oversized catch, and thrust them up the bank to Haimya. She supported them as far as dry ground, and there Pirvan and others made sure that they spewed the water out of them and were not caught by any further rising of the river.

Had the ropes gone entirely, the death toll might have been the stuff of nightmares. But they held for a vital few minutes, allowing a good many men to stay on their feet until they could lighten themselves enough to swim. Then those who could swim went thrashing off downstream, slanting toward the banks, many of these finding safety. All along the bank downstream Pirvan saw soldiers shaking themselves like wet dogs—and in the stream, the bobbing corpses of those whose luck had run out.

On the far side of the river, the gentler slope of the bank made for a swifter spread of the water. Those who reached dry land soon found it turning into knee-deep, then waist-deep, then swimming-deep water. Again, this happened slowly enough that a good many men lightened themselves and swam to safety.

Pirvan hoped for a while that the river would go down as swiftly as it had risen. The hope was vain. As twilight crept across the land, he and Birak Epron stared at each other across five hundred paces of water, much of it two or three men deep, carrying a freight of drowned animals, drifting tree trunks, and patches of weed. A few more human bodies also floated by, foresters or farmers to judge from their garb, and at least one who seemed to have ogre blood in him.

"Now what should we do?" Pirvan asked, half musing and less than half aloud.

Rubina, busy combing her hair, shrugged. "Ask Birak Epron or your lady before you ask me."

"My lady is setting the guards, and Birak Epron is five hundred paces away. I cannot shout or shoot a message arrow that far. Do you propose to give me wings or conjure me up a boat?"

"Your pardon, Sir Pirvan."

"I will pardon you when you swear to me, by whatever a Black Robe will swear by, that you had nothing to do with the flood."

Stark amazement spread across Rubina's face. In one less accomplished in feigning what she was not, Pirvan might have believed Rubina's face alone. Instead, he listened while she swore by Takhisis, Gilean, *and* Paladine that she was as innocent as a babe unborn of aught to do with raising the flood.

As neither falling trees nor gaping crevices in the earth nor thunderbolts from the sky punished Rubina for using Good and Neutral gods in her oath, Pirvan was prepared to accept it. Not with much more pleasure in her company than before, but at least with less stark fear.

"In truth, I could not have conjured up that flood. I did not even detect it before your senses did," the Black Robe added. "In the sphere of water I have very little power. I would not be prepared to swear that the flood was wholly natural, but on the other hand, we were downstream of a land where it has been raining heavily."

"Just hold your tongue about the unnaturalness of the flood, if you please," Pirvan said more sharply than he intended. But his tone bounced off Rubina like a pebble off a battle helm, and she replied with a dazzling smile that made him feel ready to leap to his feet and grapple stout opponents.

The sensation did not last, but the need to grapple remained, and with problems as stout as any foe with a body. Pirvan began pacing up and down the riverbank, ignoring the mud that sucked at his boots and the low-hanging branches that slapped his face.

On his side of the river, he had twenty men, a third of

them armed and equipped. On the other side, Birak Epron had the rest of the survivors, and it was hard to tell how many of them had weapons or gear. Perhaps half, certainly not more.

The river would, of course, go down before long. But even when it shrank back to its previous size, it would not bring the dead back to life, or farm and reequip those who now had nothing but the sodden garments they stood in.

Go forward or go back? Someone had to go forward and learn more about Waydol. Or if that was impossible, at least reach the coast and warn Jemar the Fair. If he cruised off the north coast long enough, the Istarian fleet would arrive and might fight him merely for lack of anyone else to fight, or because he was a sea barbarian in the wrong place at the wrong time.

Pirvan knew that he and Haimya—with Rubina, if she could be trusted—could make the northward trek on their own and do as much as a larger band. However, there was that larger band to think about, and to take care of, seeing how many of them would be next to defenseless in the face of serious attack or even common footpads.

Divide the band, taking some forward and sending the rest back? Seemingly prudent—until one realized that the armed men would also have to be divided. Divided, there might not be enough of them to defend their unarmed comrades in either party. Also, the country behind was alert and more likely to spawn attacks.

Take all the men onward? A dangerous course, but perhaps the least dangerous one. If all else failed, Pirvan could march them up to one of Aurhinius's garrisons. His rank as a Knight of the Crown would be surety enough for the men's correct treatment. They would be humiliated, although not as greatly as he, but they would live, instead of dying miserably in the wilderness.

If luck held and they were able to reach the coast, a small party of picked, armed men could scout Waydol's stronghold. The rest could find their own perch on the rocks, living on fish, seabirds, and game until Jemar appeared offshore.

Furthermore, they need not remain ill-equipped. Spears had been cut from branches long before armorers took them in hand, snares could bring down men as well as game, and clubs had their uses in close-quarters fighting. One of the more important classes knights in training took was called "The Dangerous Man," which showed you how to turn anything into a weapon and keep to the last your hopes of an honorable death, if not victory.

Then the bubble of Pirvan's hope burst. These mercenaries were not Knights of Solamnia or even those admitted to training for knighthood. Half of them were the wastrels or brawlers of their hometowns, and the rest were accustomed to treating employers who left them ill-armed with disdain if not outright mutiny.

What would he do if they refused to go on? What would he do if Birak Epron refused to punish the would-be deserters? That would be foolish; Epron had to know, better than the others, that making one's way alone back through a hostile countryside could end only one way. But Epron could not stand alone against fifty men thinking only of a way out of this wilderness.

Pirvan sat down and began throwing pebbles and bits of bark into the turbid river rushing past his feet. The sense of having failed those for whom he was responsible ate at him from within like a worm at an apple.

The Measure discussed this, of course; there seemed little that it did not. It said that such a state of low spirits was dishonorable for a knight and should be ended as swiftly as possible. It did not say how.

It also said that important decisions should not be made while in this lowness of spirits. It did not say what was to be done if the decisions were urgent and the lowness of spirits not likely to depart before you needed to make them!

It seemed to Pirvan that another two or three seasoned mercenary captains would have done as well as any sort of knight. However, he had his orders, his men had him—and both, to be sure, had Haimya. She had spent time enough as a mercenary so that she could at least advise him how much these men would be prepared to endure. Pirvan suspected that Birak Epron's men would follow their captain to the uttermost ends of Krynn; he was less sure of the others.

Now to find Haimya. Pirvan rose—and as he did, two of the armed sentries backed into view. They had their swords drawn, but were not wielding them, and seemed immensely careful to make no sudden moves. One of them was so careful that he tripped over a tree root and sprawled backward. His mate helped him to his feet, but did not take his eyes off whatever it was that was following them, invisible to Pirvan but with its own source of light.

Then a little procession stepped into Pirvan's sight. In the lead was a man carrying a torch and another—man, though showing ogre blood—carrying a white flag.

Behind these two càme four more armed men. Two of them had drawn swords. The other two were carrying a blanketed form on a litter of branches and blankets.

Bringing up the rear was a tall half-ogre, with a cloak and helmet that suggested he was the leader. He also held a spear out in front of him, with the point bobbing only a handbreadth from the throat of the person on the litter.

Then the litter bearers set their burden down. The tall half-ogre lifted the blankets away from the person's throat with the point of his spear.

A knife seemed to drive between Pirvan's ribs, then twist in his heart.

The person on the litter was Haimya.

Chapter 13

Tarothin had nearly the complete run of Pride of the Mountains after his potion put the new recruits back on their feet. The captain was grateful, the Karthayan leaders were grateful, and the men themselves were grateful.

The only one not grateful was the man who'd offered Tarothin the place aboard *Pride* to begin with. But then, expecting gratitude from an agent of the kingpriest was like expecting charity from a moneylender.

As the fleet beat its way out of the Bay of Istar and westward toward the meeting with Aurhinius, Tarothin found himself doing other work besides healing. The first money he'd ever earned was for dealing with unruly drunkards in a local tavern, and from that he had progressed to learning the quarterstaff. Except for one year of his training as a wizard, when the work had been too physically demanding and his teachers too strict, he had kept up that skill ever since.

So he was able to serve as an extra instructor at drill for the new recruits, at least when the deck wasn't at an impossible angle. Walking among the new recruits by day and among the sailors in the evening, he was able to listen a great deal without saying much or drinking anything at all. He thought that it would have been cheaper to buy honest vinegar, rather than pay the price charged for what the vintner had passed off as wine.

One thing he heard about was a good many nightmares similar to his vision of Zeboim and Habbakuk. Nobody was sure what they meant, but rumors of priests of Zeboim being aboard the fleet were rife enough to make some of the mates frown.

Tarothin tried to reassure anyone who seemed seriously alarmed that the priests of Zeboim were as devoted to the balance as anyone. Furthermore, the kingpriest would hardly be so lawless or foolish as to favor one kind of priest to the point of endangering the balance, even if the priests themselves might be less than honest.

The replies to *that* notion were eloquent, even blasphemous. They made it clear that even Karthayans who favored the rule of Istar did not thereby also favor the rule of the kingpriest.

Long days led to Tarothin sometimes taking a nap in the afternoon, though he no longer needed to prepare himself for long nights with Rubina. It was during one of those afternoon naps that his own nightmare came to him.

A circle of priests wearing the fanged-turtle masks of Zeboim's devotees was conjuring storm clouds over a mountain. The clouds poured down rain, streams swelled rivers, rivers rose, and men downstream from the mountain were swept away without warning. He thought some of the men were soldiers, but he awoke too soon and with too muzzy a head to be sure.

He was not too muzzyheaded to know that he should keep this dream to himself.

* * * * *

Pirvan's first decision was to leave his own steel sheathed. He then ordered all the armed men to do the same, including the two sentries who had led the whole procession. Finally, he threw Rubina a look eloquent of what would happen to her if any foolish spellcasting by her put Haimya in further danger.

All of this would no doubt persuade both friend and foe that he was weak where danger to Haimya was concerned. But there was small point in veiling a self-evident truth.

Instead, he stepped forward, hands in plain view.

"To what do we owe the dubious honor of a visit under such circumstances?"

"I should think that we are owed the explanation, as you committed the first offense," the half-ogre said.

Several of Pirvan's men turned red and were plainly fighting not to draw their weapons. Pirvan crossed his arms on his chest. This also allowed him to have both of his daggers in their chest sheaths within easy drawing distance. He thought he could put down the half-ogre before the enemy chief's spear pierced Haimya, but did not intend to put the matter to the test unless matters grew desperate.

They did otherwise. The half-ogre stepped away from Haimya, raised his spear, and thrust it point-down into the ground. He still had a sword large enough for a minotaur at his waist, and several knives slung variously about his person, but he was now standing out of striking range of Haimya.

"I am unaware of any offense we have committed," Pirvan said in warmer tones. "However, ignorance, while no excuse, is certainly as common as snow in the winter or rain in the summer. If we have been ignorant, we will accept teaching."

"You came into our territory without warning or asking permission," the half-ogre said. "We don't allow this to rival bands. We could hardly allow it to soldiers."

"We are soldiers on lawful business," Pirvan said. "That business need not be dangerous to you, but we are prepared to fight if need be."

"I'm sure your comrades beyond the river will avenge

you well enough," the chief said. "But I would rather not speak of fighting and revenge at all. Unless my memory is fading, I think I owe you a life-debt."

Pirvan ran as much of his life as he could through his mind, trying to remember where he might have encountered the half-ogre and saved his life. The face and voice rang faint, distant bells in his memory, but the winds of time distorted them—

"Did you lead the band that came down on us the night we took—something—from Karthayan possession? On the western shore of the bay, on a steeply sloping path?"

Half-ogre faces are not made for smiling, but the chief made a fine show of yellow teeth. Then he laughed.

"Yes. I am Pedoon, and that night you could have killed me and all mine. You did not. Was it for such that they made you a Knight of Solamnia?"

"How did you—oh. I suppose word has flown ahead of us, that I am called Sir Pirvan. Well, in truth I am Sir Pirvan of Tiradot, Knight of the Crown. I lead these men on business that I swear is not dangerous to you."

Pirvan's voice hardened. "The woman on the litter, whose life you threatened to begin this parley, is my beloved wife, Haimya. I know not what customs you have in the matter of parleys, but I assure you that you were in more danger than you realized by so beginning this one."

"Not against a Knight of Solamnia. Also, as you said, word flew ahead, and it was known how you were, each to the other.

"Now," Pedoon went on. "I believe it would be as well if we went to my camp, you and some guards. I pledge my honor and that of all my men, likewise the blood of any oathbreaker, that no harm will come to you or yours."

Pirvan was not sure that he had much to gain from speaking with Pedoon. But if the outlaw chief considered that he owed Pirvan a life-debt, that made long odds against treachery, with either ogre or human. Therefore, Pirvan also had very little to lose.

"I shall accept, under two conditions."

"What are they?" Suspicion returned to Pedoon's voice.

"That I signal my men on the far bank, so they will not cross in the morning to avenge the blood which you have not shed. Also, that our healer Lady Rubina examine my wife and give assurance that she is not gravely hurt."

And if she is, you owe me a debt payable only in blood.

"Fair enough."

This set off quite a flurry of movement as two of the soldiers lit torches and went to the riverbank to signal to the far side. Pirvan told them to pass the word that he was negotiating with a powerful local leader, who seemed honorable. But if they heard nothing of him by noon tomorrow, Birak Epron was in command and should act as he saw fit.

By the time the torches winked in reply from the far bank, Rubina had been kneeling for some time by Haimya, running her hands over the unconscious woman's face, listening to her pulse and breathing, opening and closing her eyes, and looking into her mouth with all the intentness of a horse buyer who suspects the seller of sharp practice.

At last she rose. "It is a powerful distillation of phyloroot. Did you make her drink it, or force a cloth over her mouth and nose?"

"The second, and I have the scratches to prove how she resisted," Pedoon said.

"You are lucky to have only scratches," Pirvan said. "Very well. What does this potion do?"

"Very little beyond inducing heavy sleep," Rubina said. "Or at least that is what the books say. I see no sign of any other injury, but I would suggest that Haimya be allowed to sleep until nature purges the drug from her system. I could wake her with a moderate spell, but she would be too fuddled for serious business, almost too fuddled to walk. Think of a drunkard after the tenth cup."

Pirvan did, and the thought was not agreeable. He would have to negotiate with Pedoon without Haimya's counsel, and Rubina was a poor substitute. But complaining about what couldn't be helped was a vice thrashed out of him by his father before he had ever heard of the Knights of Solamnia, except as distant, godlike warriors far beyond the ken of town boys like himself.

"We have until noon tomorrow to dispose of all matters between us," Pirvan said. "Otherwise, I do not know what a seasoned captain like Birak Epron will devise, but I doubt it will please you."

Pedoon jerked his head, pulled the spear from the ground, rested it on his shoulder, and nodded to the rest of his men. Pirvan, Rubina, and three of their armed men fell in behind, and the whole procession was out of sight of the riverbank within fifty paces.

* * * * *

Waydol was practicing with the cesti when Darin walked up the path to the Minotaur's hut.

The spiked, armored gloves were sufficiently vicious-looking when sized for human hands. Fitting the hands of a large minotaur, they became monstrosities.

Waydol's exercise target was a log, wrapped in leather and suspended from a tree by heavy leather thongs. The leather was already showing scars, and as Darin watched, another strip dangled and splinters flew.

But then, the power in Waydol had always been some-thing Darin accepted as part of nature. He had seen the Minotaur break a mutineer's spine by slapping him across the back of the head with less than full strength, lift anvils that two strong men could barely move, carry on his shoulders a boat large enough for five men, and otherwise show strength far beyond what one expected of any mortal being.

Waydol feinted with his left hand, drove home with his right a punch that snapped two of the thongs, then noticed his heir. He turned, unstrapped the cesti, tossed them on the bench, and signaled for Darin to bring him water.

"You are bleeding," Waydol said when he had drunk. He was sweating heavily, and Darin knew that most humans found a minotaur's odor as foul as a gully dwarf's midden. Again, to him it seemed natural.

Darin rubbed his fingers along the left side of his neck. "Oh, so I am. I believe one of the brawlers caught me with a wild slash. He will not be slashing anybody, with that knife or anything else, until Sirbones heals his arm. It was a comrade who broke it, to keep the peace."

"Good," Waydol said. "But it should not have happened at all."

Darin frowned. The Minotaur laughed shortly. "No, it is not that I doubt you. Had I done so, I would have come down myself and put matters in order. You have done well what you should not have had to do at all."

Darin had to admit Waydol's point. Their ingathering of outlaws and robbers in the north country was proceeding well enough, if one spoke only of numbers. Bands large and small were coming in, along with many single men, some of whom had plainly left their villages for the good of the other villagers.

Some of these men had already deserted, a few were undoubtedly spies, and far too many had been long accustomed to living without order, law, or discipline. There had already been brawls and stabbings over wine, women, and quarters—not as many as Darin had feared, but even one was too many. No one was dead yet, but that was luck and Sirbones's healing, and the luck could not last.

Waydol's band seemed at the moment in no small danger of choking on its own success, like a snake attempting to swallow too large a pig.

Darin licked dry lips. He was about to presume greatly, but the time to discuss desperate measures was before they become necessary.

"We could send north for help," he said. "To your homeland," he added, in case Waydol had not caught his meaning the first time.

The Minotaur stared, looking for a moment as if he had been poleaxed and was about to drop at his heir's feet. Then he laughed softly and embraced Darin, so gently that the embrace would not have annoyed a housecat, let alone a stalwart warrior.

"In this moment, I feel almost like a god. I have put the soul of a minotaur into the body of a human. Do you really believe that the time has come to bring my folk south, to help us against yours?"

"If there is no other way but seeing our band and all its new recruits fall apart like a biscuit in hot soup from brawls and disobedience . . ." Darin found that he could not finish. He shook his head, but that failed to jar his thoughts or tongue into motion again.

Finally, he blurted out, "Whatever we must do for those whom we have sworn to lead well must be done. If it must be done by other minotaurs, so be it."

Waydol sat down on the bench. It gave a faint creak, then a sharp crack, then snapped in two. The Minotaur picked himself up and contemplated the wreckage.

"A good thing that no one who believes in omens is in sight." He lifted half of the bench in each hand and tossed both pieces on the pile of firewood behind the hut.

"I honor you, Heir, but I also ask you to think on this. Few minotaurs would come here at the behest of one said to have lost honor. None would come, save in the hope of bringing this band under their authority in place of mine. Then the brawls and wrangling we have seen would be like childish quarrels compared to what we would see.

"Also, none would come at all, unless I returned north with the message myself. That would leave you with the whole burden of keeping our band from turning into a pack of wild dogs."

"I could accept that, as needs be."

"I will trust you with it if the time comes, but I think my fate and the band's now begin to drift apart. I must sooner or later return north, with what I have learned of human strengths and weaknesses. More of the first than of the second, I would say, and I do not expect to live long after speaking that truth.

"Those who follow us, however, must be given a safe path out of this land, and out of reach of Istar if there is such a place. We must labor together until that is done. Then you will need to remain behind and lead, while I take one of the boats and sail north."

"Alone?"

"One could crew a large ship with those who have sailed alone from this land to the minotaurs' coast or the other way. In the good sailing season, with a well-made boat, it is hardly a perilous enterprise."

"Are we then to begin to consider our line of retreat now?" Darin said. "You spoke of the dwarven nations."

"Yes, but that was before I spoke with Fertig Temperer. He said that the dwarves might not let us in, though if they did, they would not give us up readily. His fear was that Istar might make the dwarves' taking us in a pretext for a war against Thorbardin."

"Such a war would not sit lightly on my conscience," Darin said.

"Nor mine," Waydol added, emptying the water jug. "Hand me the brush and comb, please." He began grooming himself, though even Darin's hardened nose suggested that the Minotaur really needed a complete bath.

"Besides, here in the stronghold we at least command ground from which we cannot easily be driven. Even Istar might let us go rather than pay the blood-price of a fight to the finish. And there are other folk, less set in their ways than the dwarves."

Darin was not sure whom Waydol meant by that, other than its not being the kender or the gully dwarves, but the Minotaur was right. Here in the stronghold, brawls or no, they could buy time at a price they could afford.

* * * * *

Haimya was awake, but only able to smile and press Pirvan's hand, by the time they reached Pedoon's camp.

The camp had the air of having been hastily enlarged to accommodate many newcomers within the last few days. It still held no more than fifty armed men, that Pirvan could see. Allowing for half as many more on guard, that meant fewer than a hundred, even counting those women and children old enough to throw stones and wield spears.

No match for Pirvan's soldiers, had they not encountered the flood and left much of their weapons and gear at the bottom of the river, along with twenty of their comrades. As it was, the ragtag force posed a real peril to Pirvan's march, if Pedoon wished to offer one.

It seemed that he did not.

"We both want to go to the same place," the half-ogre said. He handed Pirvan a piece of what appeared to be bread and a lump of what was most likely salt. Pirvan's tasting did not resolve all doubt, but faces around him eased nonetheless.

"And what is that place?" he asked after drinking to cleanse his mouth.

"Waydol's stronghold," Pedoon said.

"If this were so, what is your reason for—?"

"Sir Pirvan, do you think me a fool? I know that you are trying to bring Waydol to heel. This bothers me not at all. I was thinking only of how we might work together for this."

"Your pardon," Pirvan said, though he felt not in the least apologetic. It seemed prudent, however, to listen rather than talk.

Listening was rewarded. Pedoon had gathered under what might be called his banner more than a hundred forest-dwellers, most of them human or with ogre blood. He wished to march them north to Waydol's stronghold, but feared rival bands and also the cavalry patrols of Aurhinius.

"But if you marched with us, Sir Pirvan, we'd be too strong for rivals to attack. As for the Istarians, if they see that I've given oath to a Knight of Solamnia, a sworn ally of Istar, they might leave us be."

Pirvan's rank as a Knight of the Crown had not been granted to him to serve as a shield to outlaws. But if letting it so serve removed these folk from this land, and carried both them and his soldiers peacefully to the north, that seemed honorable enough.

Yet there was something in the way Pedoon spoke of Waydol that set Pirvan's teeth on edge. He rose and brushed soot and mud off his breeches.

"I would like to think about this alone for a short while. Will I be in danger if I remain within your circle of sentries?"

Pedoon pulled from a pouch at his belt a cloth that might have been white about the time Pirvan was cutting his first tooth.

"Wear this around your head and it will be a sign of peace between us."

The rag was not only filthy, but it also stank. Pirvan did not know what he might attract on his walk. The stink might keep away insects, and if the rag itself kept away arrows and spears from quick-tempered sentries . . .

"I thank you, Pedoon."

* * * * *

From *Windsword*'s deck, gray walls of water seemed to shut out the horizon as gray clouds shut out the sky. Last night the ship had been sailing along a coast where barren headlands, terraced hills, and stretches of woodland alternated. Now it might have been in a world that held nothing but wind and water.

With no duties to keep him on deck, Jemar the Fair went below to his cabin. Eskaia was in bed, with Delia sitting on the carpeted deck, apparently listening to one end of her staff as if it were an ear trumpet, while the other rested on Eskaia's belly.

Wondering if he'd stumbled on some women's mystery, Jemar turned to withdraw.

"No, stay," Eskaia called. "She is nearly done."

"Done with what?" Jemar nearly snapped. Bad weather this close to shore always made him uneasy. They had plenty of sea room unless the wind changed, but that could happen, and the coast hereabouts made the worst sort of lee shore.

"I am listening to the babe," Delia said. "Not with the ears of my body, but with a spell bound into my staff."

"Oh?" Jemar said. "And what is the babe telling you?"

"Nothing much, other than it is well," the woman said. "It is not yet time for me to tell lad from lass, or hear a heartbeat."

"This is not our first," Jemar said. "Pray do not treat me as a witling in the matter of babes."

"Fathers are seldom much better than that," Delia said,

but Eskaia squeezed her hand hard so that she turned the sharp words aside with a smile.

"I'm a sailor," Jemar said. "As fathers, we're apt to be around for the laying of the keel, but the building and the launching are mostly mysteries. Are you done?"

"Yes," Delia said, and she gathered herself to make a retreat with more dignity than haste.

"I thought a sour-tempered midwife was bad for the babe," Jemar said when the cabin door was closed.

"Oh, she has merely had more trouble than she cares to remember, with fathers who want nothing new done for their babes," Eskaia replied. "But the babe feels well, say I who have borne three, and I feel better yet. May I go on deck?"

"No."

"Not in this common storm?"

"It is a short, steep, inshore sea, and the ship's motion is sharp."

"I remember walking the deck when the wind was slicing off the tops of waves and hurling them at the ship. To be sure, I saw men looking at me as if I were mad—"

"You did, and one of them was me. My heart was in my mouth every moment you were `taking the air.' Also, you were not as far along as you are now."

"Very well. I shall be most docile and withdrawn, on one condition."

Jemar sighed. Eskaia was not the daughter of a master bargainer for nothing, as he had learned to his cost—and as rivals and enemies had also learned, to a much greater cost. There were times when he thought that Eskaia would have made a much better adviser than wife, but those times had grown rare as the years passed.

"What is that?"

"You shall be honey-sweet to Delia. And if she smites any of the crew who look at her unlawfully, let it pass. Otherwise you shall have a sour midwife, which may not harm the babe but will surely put me out of temper."

Jemar did not sigh again. Instead, he grinned, though somewhat ruefully. Living with Eskaia had taught him

much, including when there was nothing to do but gracefully accept defeat.

* * * * *

The forest shrouded Pirvan in utter darkness outside,
and there was more darkness within. This journey seemed
to be taking him very far afield from what it had been
intended to do, as well as from a knight's honorable
course.

His honor he would leave to Paladine and his fellow
knights to judge, after he had done his best. But he could
not leave to future judgments the very essence of his purpose in this land, which was to end the Minotaur's threat
before Istar did so by means that unleashed war. As far as
he could see, he and his men had covered a great deal of
country with their bootprints without taking more than a
few steps toward that goal.

Now he heard the footsteps he had been waiting for, in
the darkness behind him. In a moment he knew from the
heavy tread that it was not Haimya, in her right senses
and come to give him counsel.

It was instead Pedoon, the other he had been hoping to
see. The half-ogre shortened his stride and fell in beside
the knight.

"Have you orders concerning Waydol about which you
can speak to me?" Pedoon asked.

Pirvan shrugged. "There are secret details, but they do
not change what I have told you."

After a moment's silence, Pedoon nodded. "But—is
there law or custom that says you cannot accept the
bounty?"

Pirvan suspected this conversation was going in a direction where, by the strict interpretation of the Measure, he
could not honorably continue it. However, he was the only
Solamnic Knight within many days' march to judge honor
or dishonor. Also, his own honor, as well as that of the
knights, rested heavily on bringing his men to safety.

"There's little point in dividing something one has not

earned. Even scholars know that."

"I'm no scholar, Sir Knight. Just an old outlaw you once saw fit to spare. Am I now unworthy of being even heard?"

Pedoon sounded ready to weep, and the weariness in his voice seemed genuine. Pirvan punched the hairy shoulder lightly.

"Your pardon, again. I think my wits washed down the river with my biscuit bag."

"No matter. But I think this. If we bring our united band into Waydol's camp, we may be the largest there. I've heard there's discontent with Waydol. Who better than us to rally it? For if Waydol is overthrown by men led by a Knight of Solamnia, we'll all have earned the bounty and pardons to boot, and no one will say aught against us."

Pirvan's first thought was regret that he had spared Pedoon ten years ago. His second was that this might be unjust; what did he know of living as an outlaw in a world far harsher than the streets of Istar or its empire's towns?

His third thought was that he must find a way of turning Pedoon aside from this course without a quarrel. That took a while to accomplish; the knight sensed Pedoon's impatience before he was done.

"I think we price the calf before the cow is brought to bull," Pirvan said slowly. "First, we have to bring our men safely to Waydol's camp, past outlaw bands, Istarian patrols, flooded rivers, and, for all I know, earthquakes, forest fires, and plagues of stingflies!

"Second, the discontent must be real instead of rumored. Waydol has held his band together since I was a youth. That is not the feat of a common chief. Going against him might be mere folly.

"Third, even if there is discontent, we may still find it best to stand beside him. If he wishes to negotiate from strength, *and* I add myself to that strength, it may be the better for us all. Had you the choice between the bounty and losing your men to Istar's justice or starvation, which would you choose?"

"My men, of course," Pedoon said, and Pirvan could

hear no untruth in the half-ogre's voice. "We have been in the woods a long time, Sir Knight. Too long, I think. How to end it . . ."

Pirvan put a hand on Pedoon's shoulder. "Two bands, like two heads, are better than one in that, I should think. Let us return to camp and set it afoot."

Which does not mean I shall not speak to Haimya about keeping a sharp eye on Pedoon as we draw closer to Waydol's camp. Treachery is a snake with many heads; cut off one, and others may still bite.

* * * * *

The messenger who brought the letter to Aurhinius arrived in camp on a lathered horse. He ran from his mount to the general's tent, and all but flung himself through the door and onto his knees before Aurhinius.

Aurhinius thanked the messenger and ordered him and his horse given proper care. He made no great haste to open the letter, however.

It was his experience that the haste with which a message was sent depended less on its importance than on the rank of the commander to whom it was being sent. A message destined for one of Aurhinius's rank always flew as if on the wind, even if it was only an invitation to some self-important archivist's party celebrating his new theory of the origins of the kender.

However, after a half cup of wine, Aurhinius found curiosity prickling under his tunic. So he opened the letter—and let out a long, hissing breath.

"Bad news, my lord?" his secretary inquired.

"Not trivial news, certainly, but whether good or bad remains to be seen." Aurhinius put the letter down and smoothed it out. "It seems that Jemar the Fair's ships have been sighted off this coast. At least eight of them, perhaps more. The report is two days old. There have been no sightings since the storm blew up."

"Jemar," the secretary said, musingly. "Is he the one who married—?"

"Into House Encuintras? The very same. Which means he is not commonly called enemy to Istar. Yet he is also a sea barbarian, and such as he are seldom enemies to outlaws like Waydol. Unless there is a quarrel over dividing the loot," Aurhinius added.

The secretary laughed dutifully. "Shall I file the letter, or do you wish me to take down a reply at once?"

"File it, but I will answer it as my first task in the morning," Aurhinius said. He rose and blew out the candle on his camp table.

In spite of the comfort of his cot, a gift from his dead wife, Aurhinius could not rest easily at first. The storm that was hiding Jemar's ships from observers ashore would also be blowing in the face of Istar's fleet at sea. Whether Jemar meant good or ill to Istar, he was more likely to be able to accomplish it unopposed.

Unless the opposition came from other than natural means. The rumors running about Istarian lands had long since reached the camp; Aurhinius was too skeptical of both rumors and magic to believe the half of them.

But what would happen if the campaign was to be decided by a duel of magic on the high seas? Such duels on land left havoc in their wake; Aurhinius could not recall hearing of any such at sea.

Yet Zeboim was daughter to the Dark Queen herself, by Sargonnas, the Lord of Vengeance. Call them clerics, wizards, or mages, anyone wielding untrammeled spells in Zeboim's name was to be feared, even if they said they were on your side.

So were those who had sent them forth.

Aurhinius hoped rather than prayed that Jemar had some magical assistance as well. Otherwise the oceans would see not a duel but a massacre, if Jemar made the slightest hostile move.

At least that gave Aurhinius the text of his message—Jemar the Fair is not to be attacked or interfered with unless he makes some hostile move—and with that in his mind he at last found sleep.

Chapter 14

The storm in the north affected more than one of those who fought what chroniclers later recorded as Waydol's War.

Although the storm did not rise to full-gale strength, it forced both Jemar's ships and the Istarian fleet out to sea. "The waves have some mercy, but the rocks have none," was in the thoughts of men aboard both fleets.

This kept Tarothin busy aboard *Pride of the Mountains*, as seasickness once again spread through the ship. He faced it this time with a nearly empty galley, and not even much water that wasn't green and ripe-smelling from too long in the cask.

He did his best, however, with hot water and a few spices in a mixture that smelled and tasted even worse than his first effort. The vileness of the brew was so overwhelming that many of the seasick forced themselves to recover to avoid drinking it, and it did the rest no harm.

The sea also had its way with Amalya, Eskaia's personal maid. She collapsed, groaning and green-faced, and Delia found herself maid, midwife, and healer all at once. This kept her busy and out of Jemar's way. Also, watching Delia work on rope burns, sprained ankles, and the occasional broken wrist or cut scalp made Eskaia aware of the power of the sea and more willing to keep to her cabin.

Aurhinius had decided that nothing would assure the proper use of the fleet, for peace or war, save his personal command of it. So he rode north as hastily as the messenger had ridden south, to a wretched fishing village found on no map and with a name he could neither spell nor pronounce.

Instead of a ship to take him out to the fleet, however, he found a gale keeping everyone in port or else driving them far offshore. He remained weather-bound in a fisherman's hut for some days, fearing the consequences of delay, knowing that he was useless, and suspecting that his temper was a trial to those about him.

Inland, Pirvan's soldiers and Pedoon's outlaws marched north, along muddy trails and across fields that sometimes imitated swamps. They faced no more killing floods, but swollen streams and washed-out bridges delayed them as much as the mud. The weather also ruined clothing and footwear, and made the long marches on empty bellies so harsh that even the soldiers began to desert and some of Pedoon's men simply collapsed and were left behind, to catch up as best they could.

Pirvan and Birak Epron kept their men together, at least. Also, at every night's stop, there was the *chkkk* of knives carving wood. Straight branches or saplings became spears, lances, or pikes, depending on their length and the fancy of the woodcarver. A few even became rude bows, with strings of deer sinew.

A lucky stop at an isolated smith's forge produced a treasure trove of metal scraps that could be turned into spear points, and a few axe heads as well. By the time Pirvan had paid out nearly the last of the knights' silver, his men were fit to fight at least treachery from Pedoon's band, if nothing worse.

The weather also blinded curious or hostile eyes, besides keeping their owners mostly indoors or under shelter in the first place. None could take advantage of the weak armament of Pirvan's men, because few could see it at all. There were days when mist, rain, and wind made the world so murky that Pirvan's men could have marched in breechclouts and carried only willow wands, and still been as safe from attack as babes in the nursery.

What the servants of Zeboim had to do with all this weather, no one knew, nor did any of them speak afterward.

* * * * *

They reached Waydol's stronghold and camp the first day the sky showed any blue.

Pirvan had known that they were approaching the coast from the seabirds flying overhead, white wings flashing against both blue and gray. He'd also known that they were approaching Waydol's stronghold, or at least entering a land torn by war, by what they'd passed for the last two days.

Trails beaten wide and deep by the booted feet of many men. Traces of their passage, including discarded clothing, scraps of food, midden pits, the pitiful remnants of efforts to make campfires, and twice unburned bodies.

Pirvan stopped the columns for those, at the insistence of his men, who formed hasty grave-digging parties and even let Rubina utter a few words of honor over the graves. Pedoon's motley band might leave their sick to die, but Pirvan's either carried them onward or gave them decent burial.

Besides the trails, there were abandoned farms, and on one of these they found a half-starved horse. This served as a mount for Pirvan, though he had offered it first to Rubina.

"I cannot ride," she had said. "Besides, I began this fool's journey on my own feet, and I will finish it that way or you may put me into the ground, too!"

Pirvan promised Rubina a decent burial, mentally noted not to bury her too close to anybody's well, and mounted the horse.

With only one horse and him no war charger, there was small point in Pirvan's chasing the mounted patrols that came out of the murk, watched from far ahead, then vanished again as if they were spirits. Pirvan doubted that, and they did not look Istarian; perhaps Waydol had mounted scouts.

At last, toward noon, one of the patrols did not stop beyond bowshot, but rode straight up to Pirvan. Their leader, a dwarf who seemed to perch on his horse rather than ride it, gave Pirvan a half-polite wave of greeting.

"You be?"

"Pirvan the Wayward and Pedoon, with men seeking the goodwill of Waydol the Minotaur and his heir."

"Hunh. They neither of them give goodwill without getting good service. You've come to give that?"

"We've come to give our best," Pedoon spoke up. The dwarf returned a sour look, then shrugged.

"All right. Line up, if you aren't already, and follow me."

Obeying this command took a while for Pedoon's men, who had their share of stragglers to round up. Pirvan's men were at least all together and all on their feet, even if their order would have given a knight instructor apoplexy.

Looking back over the double column of men, Pirvan felt his spirits lifting. Shared hardship and sound leading, in which Pirvan thought he could claim a modest share, had turned a collection of sell-swords into a stout and hardy band of warriors, who kept discipline and order and guarded one another, at least against Pedoon's gang. They would make Waydol think well of their leaders. Properly armed, they would also be very hard to kill.

Having neglected to equip himself with spurs, Pirvan had no way of urging the horse forward but heels and voice. Neither of them had much effect, in any case; the horse was wind-broken as well as half starved.

* * * * *

Waydol's stronghold was not what Pirvan had expected. It was a log-walled camp large enough to hold a thousand men, with earthworks around the gate, a ditch around much of the wall that didn't border on a stream, huts, tents, latrines, cook sheds, and much else. Piles of firewood, wagons, and even stables stood in another circle, this one unditched and only half walled as yet.

Waydol's ambitions seemed to be growing, and so was his strength. And the discipline involved in getting this much work out of bands of outlaws, even if they had nothing else to do, was considerable.

Pirvan of Tiradot had suffered a most miserable journey, but at the end of it he was at least facing a not unworthy opponent.

The dwarf, whose name was Fertig Temperer, reined in and pointed off into the woods. "Over yonder's the real heart of Waydol's strength. But don't be even thinking about getting into it, until you've proven yourself trustworthy."

How they were to do that was a serious question, but one that could wait. Food was one that could not.

"What about rations?" Pirvan said. "If my men have to tighten their belts any more, we might as well eat them while there's something of them left."

"We've fish and porridge," the dwarf said, turning to address all the men at once. "Now, we want you to divide up into fifties, which is what the huts will hold. You'll most likely have to build your own, but—"

"We've come a long way to be told that we have more work to do," someone shouted from Pedoon's ranks. Heads turned in Pirvan's columns, too, but Haimya and Birak Epron glared along the ranks, as if daring anyone to open his mouth.

"As you please," the dwarf said. "Any road runs two ways. If you start back now, you might be out of Istar's reach before dawn tomorrow."

A seabird gave a high, shrill cry above Pirvan—drowning out the whistle of an arrow that suddenly sprouted from Pedoon's left eye.

"There, in the woodpile!" Haimya shouted, drawing her sword and pointing. Fifty sets of eyes turned in that direction, to see a tall man leap down from a woodpile, holding a bow in one hand.

"Hold!" Pirvan shouted, echoed by Birak Epron. Their men held.

But Pedoon would never give another order again, or hear one. As Pirvan watched, his remaining eye glazed and set, staring blindly at the sky. His sharp-nailed fingers twitched briefly, clawing up mud, a final shudder ran through him, and he lay still.

"Get the bastard!" someone screamed from the outlaw ranks. This time it was fifty voices that took up the cry— and then Pedoon's band was charging at the one man toward the gate of camp.

Pirvan shouted orders to his men and curses to his horse. "Left column to the gate! Keep Pedoon's people out while we parley. Right column, form square."

Again Birak Epron echoed Pirvan's orders, though not his remarks to the horse. The beast lurched in motion, staggered a few steps, then dropped dead. Pirvan was barely able to roll clear without getting his leg caught under his falling mount.

By the time Haimya had lifted Pirvan to his feet, Pedoon's men were well on their way to the gate. The soldiers were a bit behind but catching up fast, thanks to their better condition. Meanwhile, what looked like a small army was gathering in the gateway, prepared to defend the camp against what undoubtedly seemed a serious piece of treachery.

The treachery had been on the other side, but no one would hear the newcomers' case if they sparked an all-out battle in the camp. Pirvan's run to the camp gate was something out of a nightmare. He'd been fast on his feet as a youth and was not much slower as a man, but now he wore boots, one leg had taken some harm in the fall, and the mud tried to suck him knee-deep at every step. Without Haimya at his side, he might have fallen three times instead of only once, and perhaps not risen again until it was too late.

It was almost too late anyway. By the time Pirvan reached the gate, the race was over and the battle begun. Several bodies already lay in the mud, and Pedoon's men had formed a circle around the archer. He was a large man with both sword and dagger in hand, his bow now slung, and he was defending himself viciously and well.

Pedoon's men did not dare close; most of the bodies were theirs. But the circle kept the men in the camp gateway from coming out, and also kept Pirvan's soldiers from coming at the archer. Everybody was too close-packed to allow use of the archer's own weapon against him. Altogether, it looked as if the matter would go on until lost temper or drawn steel unleashed general slaughter.

"Surrender!" somebody yelled from inside the camp. Pirvan did not know whom the voice was addressing.

The murderer took the cry as addressed to him. "I saved Waydol from Pedoon's treachery! He would have sold Waydol to the Istarians. Him and the Knight of Solamnia!"

Pirvan wanted, not to sink into the earth, but to grow claws like a dragon so he could rip out the archer's throat before it spewed any more venom. Somebody had spied on him and Pedoon the night of their walk in the woods, and brought word to Waydol's camp. How many had he told? How many more waited to defend their chief, by stretching Pirvan in the mud beside Pedoon?

Useless questions. Now there was only honor—and anyone who thought it useless was a fool beyond all hope.

Pirvan stepped forward.

"I am Sir Pirvan of Tiradot, Knight of the Crown. I take this man into my keeping, until he can be fairly tried for the death of Pedoon Half-Ogre." He hoped that they would find some other name for Pedoon, but better folk than he had been buried under shorter names.

The archer whirled. One of Pedoon's men took advantage of his distraction to try closing. The archer slashed with his dagger, opening the bold outlaw's throat into a bloody fountain. The man stumbled, then fell atop the body of a comrade.

Pirvan stared at the archer. His wide, dark eyes seemed to see everything and nothing, and the knight suspected he was looking at madness. Also looking at his own death, if he underestimated this foe.

Haimya stepped up beside her husband. "We had best go in against him—"

Pirvan jerked his head. "That's hardly better than Pedoon's men mobbing him. The Measure—"

"—may kill you."

"Then take good care of Gerik and Eskaia," Pirvan snapped. Haimya looked as if he'd slapped her. He spent no time on apologies, but pushed his way through the circle of Pedoon's men and spoke to the archer so that all could hear.

"Now, yield to me and accept my custody as lawful, or I must take you by force."

The man's reply was a ragged madman's scream. Pirvan had already drawn his sword, or he would have died the next moment, cut down in the mud. As it was, he felt the wind of the archer's sword on his cheek, flung himself frantically to one side while parrying a dagger thrust. He avoided falling only by a miracle, then drew his own dagger and settled down to serious work.

How serious it was, Pirvan realized only afterward, when those who watched told him about the fight. It seemed an endless blur of largely defensive work, as the archer launched one wild attack after another. The man was larger and stronger than Pirvan, and driven by rage as well. Fortunately he was not as fast, and was even less polished a swordsman than Pirvan.

The knight had all he could do to stay alive for the first few minutes of the battle. His one hope was that everyone else would let him and the archer fight it out, and that included Rubina's not intervening on his side with any spells. That *would* be the end of his days with the knights, if he was saved by a Black Robe's magic!

After a time that seemed hours, Pirvan realized that some of Pedoon's men had been dragged out of the circle and replaced by his own soldiers. That at least would help keep the fight fair. But there were more of Pedoon's men still holding the gateway, and the risk of a bigger fight if the men inside tried to come out.

At that point Pirvan nearly lost fight and life together by stumbling over a corpse. He rolled fiercely aside from the archer's downward cut, and, as he rolled, slashed at the man's leg, wildly but with effect.

"First blood!" tore from a dozen throats.

Pirvan stood up. Blood was running down the archer's left leg. He did not seem to be limping, however, but the Measure was strict in the matter of first blood.

"Do you yield?"

The reply was a stream of obscenities that would have knocked birds dead from the sky if the din of the fight had not already frightened them away. Also another furious attack.

But this one was not as fast as the others. Perhaps it was the leg wound. Perhaps it was all the strength poured into the earlier attacks, strength now gone forever. Perhaps the man's feet weighed more heavily—Pirvan discovered that, sometime since the beginning of the fight, he had kicked off his boots and was now fighting barefoot.

It felt good, familiar, like his old night work—and it made him a great deal lighter on his feet.

The archer was now fighting with one leg of his breeches soaked with blood and both feet burdened with mud. He also showed half a dozen minor wounds that Pirvan could not remember inflicting, but which had to be slowing him even further.

Pirvan knew that he had to end this fight before passions rose higher or the archer's still considerable strength got a lucky stroke through the knight's guard. He played the archer around in a circle until he had firm footing under him, then closed using speed he had saved until now.

Inside the man's guard now, Pirvan locked dagger to dagger, immobilizing both weapons for a moment until the other's greater strength would break the lock. He dropped the sword—and ignored the screams and howls all around him. Pirvan drew a dagger from its chest sheath, quickly, as the archer tried to get his sword around.

Then Pirvan thrust up—and felt the knife go through the windpipe, past the mouth, up into the brain—as the man fell away and backward.

Pirvan bent to retrieve his fallen sword—and a howl went up from inside the gate.

"Kill the knight! Kill the other traitor!"

Instantly Pedoon's men turned from Pirvan's possible enemies to his staunchest defenders. They had seen him avenge their fallen chief; they would fall beside him rather than let him down. They began striking wildly, though with not much vigor or skill, at the men in the gateway.

The men there struck back, more of Pedoon's fighters went down, and the men in the gateway pressed forward. In that moment they would be out in the open and the great battle begun.

Pirvan had no breath left for curses. But he still saw clearly, and what he saw was that not all the men inside the camp were pushing forward. Some were drawing back, and dragging or trying to drag others with them.

The men inside the camp seemed of two minds about Pirvan and his men.

"Back from the gate!" he shouted. "Everyone back from the gate, out of bowshot, and form a square! Now, you triple-cursed fools!" He called the men quite a few other things as well, most of which he knew about only afterward, told by those who heard him in awe and admiration.

At least Pedoon's men obeyed, breaking all at once in a desperate rush to get clear of the gateway. Apparently they felt their obligation to the knight avenger had been fulfilled, because Pirvan suddenly found himself standing as Pedoon's men streamed past.

The next moment he was alone, facing a dozen men from the camp. The moment after that, Haimya was beside him, her face frozen in a battle mask that Pirvan feared was aimed as much at him as the enemy.

But Haimya's blade was as quick as ever, and took down two opponents. Then out of nowhere whirled a bola, wrapping itself around her blade and pulling it out of line. She gave ground as her guard went down, and a lean, dark man leaped out of the crowd, wielding a short club.

Haimya drew her dagger as Pirvan closed to protect her, but something smashed him across the ankles and he staggered, knowing that his own guard was down and that the dark man could kill either him or Haimya or probably both—

But the dark man and his partner—a kender, of all things!—were stepping back. They seemed to be herding the rest of the men from the camp backward as well, so that suddenly Pirvan and Haimya were alone.

Alone, fifty paces from their nearest men—now all formed in a ragged but thick square, Pirvan noted with approval. Alone, with Haimya swordless and Pirvan barely able to walk, the fire in his legs adding to exhaustion until he knew he had about three more steps in him before he could be cut down like ripe wheat.

Yet not alone, either. Pirvan wanted to ask Haimya's forgiveness for his sharp tongue, but knew that if it did not come in words, it would come in a few moments, when they went down together.

The few moments came and went, but no enemy advanced.

Pirvan turned to Haimya. "Forgive me, my love." At least that was what he tried to say, or rather, croak.

Haimya turned toward him, blinked, and started to speak.

The words never came. From the right a howling war cry tore at Pirvan's ears. He wanted to drop his sword again and clap his hands over them.

In another moment, from the left came the reply to the war cry. It was as wordless as the first, but it came from no human throat. Only one race on Krynn had that thundering bellow.

The Minotaur had come—and Pirvan would wager that his heir was not far away.

* * * * *

The first to arrive was a man leading one of the mounted patrols, on what seemed to be a raw-boned pony. It was only when the man dismounted that Pirvan realized he'd been riding a full-sized horse. It was the size of the man that had deceived Pirvan.

There was nothing awkward about the man's movements, however, as he approached Pirvan and Haimya. "I am Darin, Heir to the Minotaur. It would be well if you explained how your coming to our camp brought such disorder."

"Lord Darin—" Haimya began.

"Heir," the man said firmly.

"Oh, be easy for the moment, Darin," rumbled a voice from the left. Pirvan and Haimya could not have kept from turning to look if they'd been transformed into statues.

A form still more gigantic than the rider was walking steadily across the field toward them. He could not have been much less than eight feet tall and, like all minotaurs, was broad in proportion.

His progress was as much a march as a walk. He seemed to refuse to allow the mud the dignity of thinking itself able to impede his progress, as feet rose and fell as steadily as the rotation of a millwheel. He wore short breeches, a sleeveless tunic, and a shatang, the heavy minotaur throwing spear, slung across his back.

His hide showed patches of gray amid the red and the black, but his horns shone like the finest crystal. They were also the longest horns Pirvan had ever seen on a minotaur.

It took long enough for Waydol to cross the field for Pirvan to tear his gaze away and look elsewhere. All of his own men were also gaping, but they were holding their weapons and maintaining their square well.

The gateway of the camp was solid with men, and more

had climbed atop the wall. Apparently for many of Waydol's recruits, this was the first time they had laid eyes on their chief.

None of the men in the camp seemed to have a weapon raised, which was good. Less good was a number of bodies that were not Pedoon's men or the archer. There would be a blood-price to pay, which was not Pirvan's notion of the best way to begin negotiations with Waydol.

At last the Minotaur was close enough for a formal greeting. Though he had reproved his heir in public, there was nothing friendly about his demeanor as he approached Pirvan and Haimya.

Neither knelt. With minotaurs even more than with men, that yielded superiority before it was even asked.

They did not even bow their heads. Instead they stood, hands held out and fingers spread to show that they intended peace. As Waydol halted, Pirvan spoke.

"We greet you, Waydol."

"Your first greeting was less than friendly," Waydol said. Most minotaurs sounded as if they were angry or at least had a headache, even when they were speaking politely. Waydol did not sound angry. His voice sounded more like an avalanche—which is not angry with what it crushes, but does not admit to being stopped, either.

"We came, if not in friendship, then without any ill wish toward you," Pirvan said. "Yet your greeting also did not speak of friendship. My comrade in leading our band, Pedoon Half-Ogre, whom I once spared in battle, was shot down like a mad dog by one sworn to you."

"There is a blood-debt, indeed, on both sides," Waydol said. Pirvan began to hope. Admitting that placed a considerable burden on an honorable minotaur, and it was never wise, safe, or even sane, to assume that a minotaur did not regard himself as honorable—even if he had chosen to dwell for twenty years as an outlaw chief among humans.

"So shall we let the gods judge?" Waydol said. He seemed to be asking the question of Pirvan and Haimya, of his heir, even of the sky above and the mud underfoot.

"Let the gods judge," the heir said, but with a questioning note in his voice. He did not sound disobedient as much as bemused.

"Then the trial shall be in two days' time," Waydol said. "I shall take my heir Darin as my companion. Who will be yours, Sir Pirvan?"

Before Pirvan could realize that what he had heard was really what had been said, Haimya said, "I will, the gods be my witnesses." Then she whispered to Pirvan, "The only alternative is Birak Epron, and I'm better in close combat than he is."

Haimya might be as accomplished a warrior as Huma Dragonsbane, but she had still most likely signed her own death warrant. "Trial," as the minotaurs used the term under these circumstances, meant personal combat, Pirvan and Haimya against Waydol and Darin.

Regardless of what weapons and armor were allowed, the odds were definitely in favor of the Minotaur and his heir. But participating in such a trial was lawful, and indeed if one had sworn to let the gods judge, the Measure commanded it.

"Regardless of the outcome, the blood-debt shall be considered settled," Waydol went on. "Beyond that, the loser shall give oath of peace to the winner."

It was on the tip of Pirvan's tongue to say that his Oath as a knight forbade him to offer such, but he bit his tongue into submission. What Waydol had just said implied that the combat would not be to the death.

It might carry a whole cargo of other meanings as well, but Pirvan would think about those later. For the moment, he would accept that he had entered a game where he did not know all the rules and where his life might be forfeit, but where the prize could be so great that it was worth the danger.

Even when the danger was to himself and Haimya both.

Chapter 15

"This goes beyond folly," Rubina said. "It is madness."

Birak Epron said nothing, but rose and stepped out of the room, low and smoke-blackened, in the abandoned farmhouse that would shelter Pirvan and his companions until after the trial of combat two days hence. He looked as if he wished to slam the door, which had miraculously survived, behind him, but instead closed it gently. In another moment his footsteps on the gravel faded into the misty twilight.

"What does he think of this, I wonder?" Rubina asked, speaking more to the stone walls and moldy straw of the floor than to Pirvan or Haimya.

"He thinks that we have sworn to do it, therefore we must do it or be forsworn, and nothing he or you can say is worth the breath taken in uttering it," Haimya said briskly. Pirvan sensed that the lightness in her voice was still largely feigned, but that she wished to avoid any more quarrels with anyone.

"Also, I think he wishes to be sure that only trustworthy men are within hearing," Pirvan added. "This whole quarrel has arisen from a lying tale borne by some double-tongued fool, and believed by one with more ambition than sense. The gods alone will stand between us and ruin if it happens again."

"Is that not already how matters stand?" Rubina asked.

Pirvan's mouth was dry from fatigue, fighting, and an uneasy mind. He tipped the water jug up over his wooden cup and drank. The men outside were not sleeping cold or hungry, thanks to firewood and salted fish sent out from Waydol's camp, but they had nothing more than water to drink. At least it was clean; none on either side in the recent fighting had sunk so low as to poison wells.

"No," Pirvan said, when he had rinsed his mouth. "You heard Waydol speak of what the winner may ask of the loser. Does that sound like he means the combat to be to the death?"

"Perhaps. But that great lout Darin looked doubtful. Deny that if you can."

"Doubt or surprise?" Haimya put in. "I think Waydol is setting afoot a plan secret even from his heir. I hope this does not mean a breach between them."

"I should think you would be praying and sacrificing for a breach between them," Rubina said. "What scant chances of victory or life you have would be greater, if so."

"I doubt it," Pirvan said. "Nor would it come without a price. A breach between Waydol and the heir would divide the camp into still more factions. Sooner or later they would come to blows, unleashing chaos."

"I do not speak as a Black Robe in this," Rubina said, "but only as your friend. Would not chaos in this case serve our cause, both of escaping and of reducing Waydol's power?"

"Not in any honorable way," Pirvan said, and he went on in spite of Rubina's grimace, as though the word "honor" were a foul smell. "Besides, what of our men?

Even if we escaped, they would be caught in the chaos, and in the end fighting one another, most likely. I will cut my own throat before I wittingly send men sworn to me to such a fate."

"If Waydol and Darin don't spare you the trouble," Rubina said.

Pirvan could not help but admire the lady's persistence, which was as evident as her beauty. However, he had doubts about the uses to which she put both.

Light knocking made the door sway on its one remaining hinge. "It is I," Epron's voice came.

He entered without waiting for a reply, stamping mud off his boots. Rubina gave him a reproachful look over his desertion.

"Is there anything you can say to our friends to save them?" To do her justice, the pleading note in her voice seemed real.

"I have spoken with the chief of the wagons who brought the food," Epron said, in the manner of one making a formal report to a captain. "He says they have no wine or ale to spare for now. This is as well, as our men have been empty-bellied too long to endure either.

"Tomorrow an armorer will come to repair those weapons needing it. He says that it is likely, though not certain, that, regardless of the outcome of the trial, all who join Waydol's service will receive arms from his stocks."

That said a good deal about Waydol's storehouses— and more than hinted at his being able to buy, not merely steal, weapons, from sympathetic towns and villages in the land about his stronghold. It also made Pirvan more certain than ever that Waydol was minotaur to the core; even if he had set up his own standard of honor, he would thereafter hold to it until death.

"Keep the men at work, and allow no wandering to the camp," Pirvan said. "Also, I will speak to them tomorrow, praising them for their discipline and courage today."

"I doubt many of them will be disposed to wander all the way to the coast out of mere curiosity as to whether they will be killed on sight or not," Epron said, with the first smile Pirvan had seen on his face in days. "But you have the right ideas. Soon I will not be able to teach you anything about leading formed bodies of soldiers."

"Yes, and what good will all this learning do him in the trial?" Rubina snapped. She seemed on the edge of tears. "I propose no serious magic, but even the lightest touch to their joints—"

"Is forbidden!" from Haimya.

"Will cost me my honor!" shouted Pirvan.

Into the echoing silence, Birak Epron inserted himself, speaking as calmly as a farmer discussing how many hogs he should slaughter before the onset of winter.

"My lady. I am sure these good people have told you that they cannot do otherwise than fight Waydol and his heir. They speak the truth.

"Now I will say more that they cannot. By what we have shared, by the honor in which I hold you, by—by whatever more we may say lies between us—I will not see you dishonor yourself as you propose. By all gods who judge honor and enforce oaths, I will kill you with my own hands unless you bind yourself to stand aside from the trial."

If Birak Epron had turned into a minotaur, the silence could not have been more complete. It lasted until Pirvan laughed.

"What amuses you so?" Epron said in a stony voice. He moved to sit beside Rubina, who did not resist his putting his arm across her shoulder.

"I was thinking that if you turned into a minotaur, you would probably crack one of the roof beams and bring this whole house down on our—"

He broke off, because Rubina had begun to cry. It needed no command from Birak Epron's hard eyes for Pirvan and Haimya to rise and walk together out into the night.

* * * * *

Gildas Aurhinius climbed the swaying ladder from the

fishing boat to the deck of his bannership, *Winged Lady*, with as much dignity as anyone could. He was fit and agile under the layers of fine clothing and good living, and he had never been seasick in his life.

The other captains accompanying him to sea were less fortunate. None of them fell into the sea, but two had to be hauled up in a net. Another, who had survived thus far, promptly knelt in the scuppers and spewed.

"There is a wizard aboard the Karthayan *Pride of the Mountains* who makes potions that work against seasickness," the captain said. "Shall we signal him to come over?"

"Where is the Karthayan?"

The captain pointed. On the remotest horizon, silhouetted against the sunset, Aurhinius made out a three-masted ship with the yellow foresail that Karthayans commonly sported.

"My thanks, but I think we can leave the wizard in peace."

It was an answer Aurhinius gave reluctantly, but with the knowledge that it was the right one. Bringing the wizard aboard might allow a private conversation, in which Aurhinius could inquire about priests of Zeboim and other such matters.

It might also drown the wizard on the way, or make him as seasick as those he came to heal, or put him in such a temper that he would be slow to answer questions put to him by a god. Also, he might be in league with the servants of Zeboim.

Aurhinius disliked situations in which he could not carry the fight to the enemy, pushing him off balance and forcing him to respond to Aurhinius's moves. However, he had the patience to endure waiting if he must, and had won several battles and at least one campaign thus.

Neither did one have much choice, patience or no, if one did not know how many enemies one faced or where half of them were!

* * * * *

Darin swept the crumbs of hard bread from his lap. The mice in the walls promptly scurried out and began feeding. Waydol smiled and emptied his plate for his furry little tenants.

"Is there anything we have not settled to your satisfaction?" the Minotaur asked.

Darin wished he could say, "No," but this was not the time to begin telling Waydol even the smallest lies.

"Yes. What if we win?"

"If they yield—"

"No. I mean, if they die."

"I think we can manage to avoid killing them without too great a risk of losing the fight. Certainly if one is crippled, the other will most likely yield to save him or her."

Darin thought of asking whether he and Waydol would follow the same rule, as he wished. But that would be treading too close to the border of a dishonor that no minotaur would ever accept.

"But if the worst happens—?"

"If the worst happens, then we will have killed a Knight of Solamnia. I will take the oath of peace from that sellsword captain, Birak Epron, to settle the matter of the men. They will then be no danger to us, even if they do not join our ranks.

"Meanwhile, the Knights of Solamnia will be taking the field to avenge one of their own. They will end the war far more swiftly than those Istarians, who seem to be trying to fight the cheapest rather than the best war. Also, the knights are disciplined and well supplied, will not loot the country or mistreat the villagers, and will take prisoners and treat them with honor.

"To them, you may yield the band with some confidence that the men will at least be spared. If there is danger of the knights wanting your head, you may join me in the boat north—though I would trust the knights more than my own folk, given a choice."

"I see." At least Darin thought he did. The idea of arranging a fight so that defeat could be turned into victory, or the reverse, and with equal ease, would have been difficult to understand coming from a human captain. From a minotaur, even from Waydol, one had to force oneself at first to believe that neither the minotaur nor oneself had gone mad.

"There is something else that you did not see," Waydol continued. His voice was harsher now. "No more than you saw the planning of treachery against Pedoon."

"I cannot be everywhere, and spying on the men—can I have honor, and still trust men with none, even if I need them?"

"A dilemma, to be sure," Waydol said, with infuriating blandness.

"Not one easily solved, when I have so much to do," Darin snapped.

"I know that there is five times the work for a leader than there was before, and that you do nine parts in ten of it," Waydol said reassuringly. "But that means you must spend some of your time training new underchiefs. Kindro and Fertig Temperer will not be enough if you are to lead the men after I am gone."

"I will seek them after the fight. But what is the other thing that I did not see?" Darin was as close to anger with Waydol as he had been in many years, and knew that weariness was only part of it.

"Forgive me. I think you did not see it, because you were not in the right place. I could see more clearly how Pirvan and Haimya fought. It was as if one mind were controlling four arms and four legs.

"You and I have fought as partners in a few practice bouts, but never in real strife. I would wager that the knight and his lady have fought together for their lives more times than we have practiced. So our victory will be honorably earned, and by other than their deaths."

"The way you put it, they might even win!" Darin exclaimed.

"Yes," was Waydol's only reply.

* * * * *

Sir Marod's pen left a small blot on the parchment as he finished the letter. But the sand dried it along with the rest of the ink, and he was shortly able to read back over the letter with satisfaction.

> Dargaard Keep
> Fourth Holmswelt

Sir Niebar:

You are hereby directed and commanded to take three trusted knights and study the matter of a kender named Gesussum Trapspringer, unlawfully held captive at the Inn of the Chained Ogre, just west of the town of Bisel.

If you determine that you may need more men, you may draw on the men-at-arms at Tiradot Manor. You are not to communicate with the local kender community until you have freed Trapspringer and discussed the circumstances of his captivity with the innkeeper of the Chained Ogre.

I appreciate that this is the sort of work we commonly leave to Sir Pirvan. However, he has other tasks in hand, which he cannot leave. However, I command this action on the basis of letters from him, so you may know the information is reliable.

> By the Oath and the Measure,
> Marod of Ellersford
> Knight of the Rose

The old knight folded and sealed the letter, then summoned a messenger to take it, as well as a servant to remove the remains of his dinner. He was eating alone in his chambers more often than he ought to of late, and less than even his aging body needed.

Yet there was so cursed much to be done, so little time to do it, and now nothing heard from Pirvan in so long that one had to prepare for the possibility of his death.

Jemar the Fair was reported well and offshore, but he had scant power to affect anything happening on land.

Marod decided to keep a vigil on his arms tonight. He would have ill rest in any case. A vigil once a month was a requirement for Knights of the Rose, and perhaps it would even ease his mind as it was supposed to, according to the Measure.

* * * * *

In every direction but one, the darkness about the farm was so complete that Pirvan and Haimya might have been plunged into a thick sack of black velvet.

In the direction of their soldiers' camp, the watch fires still burned, though the cook fires were fading embers. By the light of those watch fires Pirvan could make out sentries, the least armed with spear and helmet, making their rounds. Others, he knew, waited in the shadows, to surprise anyone who slipped past the visible watchers.

His men were fit and ready for whatever might come of the trial. If his speech to them tomorrow was fated to be a farewell—

He swallowed. That meant a farewell to Haimya, too, and he would have to use all the discipline of mind he had learned to keep that thought from unmanning him before the soldiers. They would understand; he had heard their praises of the knight's lady and comrade when they thought he was not listening.

But it would still seem ill-omened, and he needed to raise more hearts than his own tomorrow.

An arm stealing around his waist made him jump, but he recognized the touch before he drew steel.

"You came so quietly I did not hear you."

"Forgive me."

"No, you forgive me. Please, Haimya. What I said when you seemed commanded by your fear—"

"You speak truly about my fear getting the best of my tongue. That shames me as much as you think your reply shamed you."

"I note that you were yourself again before the fighting started."

"Yes, and when the trial is over I am going to sit down with that bola-tosser and that kender and learn how they work together. I had not thought a kender had the discipline for that."

"Waydol seems to bring out from many folk what even they did not know they had in them."

"Yes. It would be well if we all lived past the trial. I want to learn more about Waydol. Either he is the shrewdest minotaur ever calved, or his folk can be even more formidable enemies than we have thought."

"Both could be true. But we can think on how to fight for a bloodless victory tomorrow. Tonight is ours." Her arm tightened, and her head rested on his shoulder.

"Ours?"

"The house has three habitable rooms, my love. Birak Epron and Rubina are at last asleep, the gods be praised, in the one at the far end of the house. In the nearest one I have laid blankets and furs. I traded a dagger for them, to one of Waydol's sergeants.

"We can sleep soft, for this one night."

Pirvan turned and let Haimya lead him into the house, and when at last they slept, the blankets and furs were soft indeed.

Chapter 16

Pirvan finished smearing the oil on Haimya's back and started working farther down her body. Briefly, he let his hands linger.

She laughed, turned, and kissed him, then spat. "Kah! That fish oil tastes worse than it smells."

"No doubt we should have asked for fresh oil, or perhaps bear grease."

Pirvan finished smearing his lady from head to toe, then turned while she returned the favor. As she picked up her fighting garb, two strips of leather, she frowned.

"Is this oil really going to do anything, save make our friends and foes alike fight to stand upwind of us?"

"Believe me, every thief I knew had done it three or four times in their night work. Mostly they did it to slip through small spaces, but it made them hard for any thief-taker to grasp as well."

Pirvan donned his own fighting garb, a strip of leather

over a padded loinguard, and walked to the corner where their quarterstaves stood. He picked them both up, twirled one in each hand, and grinned at Haimya. She might have seemed more desirable and more deadly at other times, but Pirvan could not remember them.

Haimya took one of the staffs, dropped into fighting position, then whirled and jumped at the same moment. But her smile as she turned back toward him was a bit uncertain.

"What if they do wear armor?"

"We'll have a bigger edge in speed than we would otherwise. But I doubt that they'll shame themselves that way. I made sure that everyone knew that you and I would be fighting without armor."

The trial would certainly be not only without armor, but also with no overabundance of rules. They would fight in a square a hundred paces on a side, and anyone who stepped outside the line of stakes marking it would be out of the fight. Neither side would use edged weapons, spears, or bows. Anything found within the square could be used as a weapon, but nothing could be given to the fighters after the fight began.

Once it began, it would go on until one side or the other declared that they'd yielded, or became clearly unable to continue the fight. Death, if it came, was intended to come only by mischance—but both sides would have guards posted against anyone tempted to follow in the footsteps of Pedoon's murderer.

"My lady?" Pirvan said, with a bow in the direction of the door.

She brushed his cheek with her lips and stepped through the door. As Pirvan followed her, the horses sent by Waydol whickered softly.

"Come along," Fertig Temperer, leader of the escort, growled. "Some trader slipped into the cove last night with a load of wine. Give those loons an extra hour, and there'll be no keeping the peace."

Pirvan swung into the saddle. A breeze blew, chill on his bare skin. The oil would make him hard to grip, but gave little protection. At least the sky was a uniform gray, so that there should be no time wasted maneuvering to get the sun in the other man's eyes.

"Forward!" Pirvan called, and his men's newly acquired drummer started pounding out a slow march beat. As the column fell in behind the mounted escort, Pirvan admired their order and how they'd managed to clean their weapons and even try to clean their clothes.

The drumbeat went on, a small but determined voice calling out against the vastness of the gray sky and the scarred land.

* * * * *

The breeze had dropped by the time Pirvan and Haimya led their men up to the fighting square. It had been laid out the day before, at a safe distance from both camps to avoid disorder. Pirvan studied Waydol's men, saw no signs of any drunkards, and looked for his opponents.

What he found was a large brown tent, erected at one end of the square. It had the look of an improvised affair, probably an old sail, but it meant that Waydol and Darin could step straight from hiding into the square. No chance for their opponents to study them in advance, while Pirvan and Haimya were fully exposed in more than one sense of the term.

Your pardon, knights, for not thinking of that myself.

"Ah," came a familiar woman's voice. "I thought you would be fair to the eye, Sir Pirvan. Now I am certain."

Pirvan took a firm grip on his staff and turned to Rubina with a thin smile. "I thank you, my lady. But I also warn you. If you distract me so that I perish in this fight, I will come back to haunt you, if Haimya does not have your blood."

Rubina put her hands on her hips and laughed. "Your pardon, Sir Knight. I gave oath to let this fight be fair, and I would not break it."

"Good," Pirvan said shortly and, turning his back, began exercising to loosen his muscles.

Haimya did the same; then they each picked up their staffs and worked with those, though they did not work against each other. The less known about how he and Haimya made a fighting pair, the better—though if Waydol was half as shrewd as Pirvan thought, he might well have guessed something.

Which is as the gods will have it. We can do no better than our best.

What was no doubt intended to be music broke the waiting silence. Waydol's band had five drummers and even someone who thought he could play a trumpet. Pirvan thought that if anyone ever broke the sleep of the knights at a keep with such wretched braying, he would be swimming in the moat before the echoes died.

Pirvan's one drummer started to reply, then cheers drowned out all the musicians as the tent opened and Waydol and Darin stepped out. Pirvan swept his staff onto his shoulder, took Haimya's hand, and began walking toward the line of stakes, as their own men began cheering.

The cheering fought its own battle, as Pirvan studied his opponents. One gamble he'd won: neither of them wore armor. Darin had even forsworn his armored fighting gauntlets, which could turn those massive arms of his into deadly war clubs. Indeed, neither he nor Waydol wore anything at all except heavy loinguards.

Pirvan listened intently for any undercurrent of discontent with him and Haimya having weapons against opponents with none. He heard nothing, and breathed brief prayers of thanks.

Darin looked like a champion out of some tale of the days of Vinas Solamnus. Big he was, but there was nothing uncouth in his proportions or clumsy in his movements. As for Waydol, Pirvan had never seen any living creature so embody raw physical strength. He wished he could have seen Waydol in his youth.

The Minotaur might be showing his age, but his heir was in his prime fighting years. Both had a huge advantage in reach and striking power over any unarmed opponent.

Without their staffs, Pirvan's and Haimya's efforts might prove more entertaining than useful.

Haimya now stepped away from Pirvan and began marking circles in the ground with her left foot. Pirvan could not see what need she had of rituals or testing the ground, as it was as level as a tabletop and neither hard nor soft in any pattern he could make out. But if it eased her, then so be it.

One herald from each side stepped forward and, with drums rolling again, read out the rules of this trial by combat. Mercifully, the trumpeter stayed silent until the reading was done, then he brayed forth all alone, like an ass being whipped.

"Waydol!" Pirvan shouted. "When you give me oath after this fight, I will demand one thing at least."

The Minotaur tossed his horns. "What is that?"

"You find a new trumpeter, or teach the one you have how to play!"

Laughter joined cheering, and from both sides. Then the drums rolled again. The two heralds raised their staffs of office (they looked to have been carved from whale ribs), and held them aloft while the drums rolled.

Then the drums ceased, the heralds scampered for the sides of the square, and the four fighters advanced to battle.

* * * * *

The first few minutes passed in feints and maneuvers, as each side tried to learn about the other without revealing anything about themselves. This put a burden on Pirvan and Haimya, to not show their team-fighting too soon or weary themselves using their greater speed to stay clear.

There was only a single touch in this part of the fight, when Waydol launched a full-strength, straight punch at Pirvan's staff. The blow was only glancing, but it jarred Pirvan's arms all the way up to his shoulders. He rolled with the punch, turning a somersault that opened the distance, then rose, spat out dirt, and looked at Waydol with new respect.

The Minotaur laughed. It was not a cruel laugh of pleasure at another's pain. It was instead the laugh of one caught up in the joy of combat.

I want to live through this fight, Pirvan thought. *It will be one to remember. Even talk about with Waydol and Darin, if we all live to grow old in comradeship.*

Future camaraderie did not seem to be much in Darin's mind, however. He was faster than Pirvan had expected, not agile but able to gain speed swiftly with those long legs. Several times he ran at Haimya, and only her darting left or right faster than he could change direction saved her from a close and perhaps final grapple.

Twice she thrust at Darin's knees with her staff, and once she got home hard enough to make him stop for a moment and test the knee. But it could still bear his weight at any pace he needed to use; Haimya could not even claim first blood.

Pirvan also had to move faster, in order to try a few strikes at Waydol. He would have been willing to strike from behind at first, but saw no way of doing any damage there. So he played at Waydol's elbows and hands, and struck three times without doing more than make the Minotaur stop to suck a knuckle.

But the knuckle was bleeding; that tough minotaur hide could be broken. Also, it was first blood.

Pirvan went through the first blood ritual, as he had with the archer. Waydol's reply was another boisterous laugh; Darin, less polite, spat on the ground near Haimya's feet.

The fight began anew.

* * * * *

Before much longer, both sides were pouring with sweat and breathing heavily. Pirvan did not mind the sweat; over the fish oil it would make him and Haimya still harder to grasp firmly. But they would need to hold back some breath for the inevitable climax of the fight, which would come, barring a miracle, when Waydol and Darin thought their opponents were slowed enough.

Then would come a rush to close, a grapple of strength and size against speed and quarterstaves, and only the gods knowing how it would end.

All four fighters also showed more than sweat and heaving chests. Darin favored one arm, where Pirvan and Haimya had each caught him with a clean, hard strike. Pirvan had grazes and bruises from too-close escapes from both of his opponents.

Haimya had an ugly swelling on one hip, where Waydol had caught her with an unexpected kick. Had the hoof struck with its intended force, it would have shattered her bones like a dropped pot. But she rode with the blow, Pirvan knocked Waydol farther off balance with a blow to the stomach, and Haimya nearly put him down altogether with a thrust at his throat.

But Darin came in behind Haimya, and she had to dart aside again, without even a chance to strike at his weak arm. Waydol seemed slower on his feet after that, but his arms could still fling those massive fists about in a way to make any sane opponent wary.

Wariness, however, could take one only so far. Sooner rather than later, Pirvan and Haimya would also have to risk closing, to strike a vital spot that would slow one or both opponents.

If that minotaur *has* any vital spots, Pirvan added to himself. Any minotaur's vitals were as well protected by his bulk as a human's would have been by armor, and Waydol had more bulk than the common run of minotaurs, nor much of it fat, either!

Knight's and lady's eyes met, and they looked at Darin. Then they ran in, swinging wide to each side of Waydol to close on the heir. The Minotaur was less vulnerable, and had so far fought a coolheaded battle that would keep him that way. Pirvan and Haimya needed to heat Waydol's temper, and taking down his heir seemed to be the best way.

They closed and struck, and for a moment it seemed

they had succeeded. Shouts and cheers roared all around them. But Darin's arms and legs flew out at impossible angles and with unbelievable speed.

Pirvan felt his staff brushed aside like a twig, and a hammerblow to his cheek. He rolled with the punch as much as he could, went down, and rolled without getting up while holding his staff over him as protection.

He lurched to his feet and nearly went down again, but stayed upright with the aid of his staff. Haimya was between Waydol and Darin, a position that spelled doom, and Pirvan could not force his feet into movement!

Instead, he saw Haimya wait until the last moment, as both the Minotaur and his heir lunged at her. They had not agreed on who should pursue and who should block, and both tried to pursue. They pursued straight toward each other, and when Haimya darted out from between them, it was too late for them to stop.

Six and a half feet of human and eight feet of minotaur collided with a slaughterhouse noise. The impact knocked Waydol backward off his feet, and staggered Darin. He still had the wits to lunge at the escaping Haimya, but he lunged with his weak arm. He missed a firm grip on her slippery shoulder, caught her upper strip of leather, tore it free, then went to his knees.

Cheers and shouts rose higher, from both sides. Pirvan wasn't sure if the men were cheering the bold fighting, or the fact that Haimya now wore nothing above the waist.

This mattered little, compared to the fact that his own fighting strength was coming back. He'd felt for a moment that his brains were rolling about inside his skull and all his teeth would fall out of his jaws if he sneezed. But all he could swear to was a bloody lip and a monstrous ache in one cheek.

Haimya, meanwhile, could not have been less concerned at her sudden disrobing. She saw both opponents on the ground and closed, trying to finish at least one.

Instead Waydol rolled, coming up to grip Haimya's down-thrusting quarterstaff with both hands. Haimya let go, threw herself backward into a somersault, and came up at a safe distance, as Waydol snapped the quarterstaff like a twig and threw the pieces away.

This left Darin still sitting, with his back to Pirvan. Pirvan couldn't close fast enough, however, and Waydol shouted a warning. Darin leaped up and turned, giving Pirvan only an opening to thrust at the hand holding the leather strip. The blow went home, the leather fell, then both Waydol and Darin were backing away, for the first time in the fight.

Pirvan's men were outnumbered four to one by Waydol's, but they made up for it with their lusty cheering.

Pirvan darted in, picked up Haimya's fallen garment on the end of his staff, and held it out to her as she came up.

She was filthy, glazed with sweat and oil, and bleeding where Darin's nails had torn her shoulder. She looked like every vision of a warrior goddess ever given to mortal men, all combined in a single splendid body.

"Thank you for considering my modesty," she said, tucking the upper strip inside the lower one. "But I think I see other uses for this now. Can we lead the fight back to where we began?"

"Eh?"

"Where I was making circles in the dirt with my foot and you thought it was some ritual?"

"Oh." Light penetrated the darkness of Pirvan's aching skull. He nodded cautiously. "We'll have to pretend to be worse hurt than we are, to draw them after us."

"Another grapple with either of those monsters, and I at least won't be pretending," she said, rubbing her rib and shoulder.

"Onward," Pirvan said. It came out more of a grunt than an exhortation, and Haimya actually managed to laugh.

* * * * *

The cheering and shouting slowly faded into an awestruck silence as Pirvan and Haimya gave ground before the advance of Waydol and Darin. It was a slow retreat, matched to a slow advance, and both knight and lady were trying to judge the state of their opponents every step of the way.

Were the Minotaur and his heir hurt? Or were they merely being cautious, perhaps themselves feigning injury? On the right answer might hang life and death—but there was no assurance of any answer at all.

At last Haimya signaled that they were at the right spot. Pirvan nodded, and moved off to the left to draw Waydol. He still had two good arms and a longer reach than Darin, who was now definitely favoring one arm.

Darin lunged. Haimya went down, rolling and coming up with the upper strap in her hand—and something wrapped in it.

She ran, and Darin whirled to run after her. She ran like a deer, Waydol turned to join in the chase, and Pirvan dashed in to strike him at the base of the spine. Haimya had to have only one opponent for a few seconds.

Waydol whirled, arms flying, and Pirvan once again ducked and rolled clear. As he came up, Haimya whipped the leather strap in three quick circles around her head, then let go of one end.

A stone the size of a child's fist flew out of the improvised sling. It flew as straight as a mason's maul coming down on a wedge, at Darin. It struck like that mason's maul, squarely on his forehead.

The big man stopped in midstride, swayed, but did not quite fall over. Instead he reached out in front of him, as if groping in a fog for something to guide his footsteps. Then he sank to his knees, looked at Haimya, and at last fell over on his left side.

Waydol's men seemed too appalled to cheer, and Pirvan's seemed too grateful.

The Minotaur was not so tongue-tied. He glared at Darin and spoke a few words in his own tongue. Pirvan did not know the minotaur language, but suspected that blood-feuds had begun over softer words.

Indeed, it seemed that they had finally made Waydol

lose his temper.

For the next few moments, Pirvan and Haimya had a busy time keeping Waydol from tearing them limb from limb. If he had not been trying half the time to catch both of them, one in each hand, he might have succeeded with one of them.

As it was, Waydol was pouring with sweat and breathing like a blacksmith's bellows when his burst of speed was done. Pirvan and Haimya looked at each other. Both bore new hurts, where Waydol's fists and nails had connected. Pirvan could barely talk; Haimya was favoring one leg and new scratches had bathed the upper half of her body in mingled blood and sweat.

Victory would come soon or not at all.

They closed with Waydol, coming at him from opposite sides to divide his attention. He lowered his head, ready at last to strike with his horns—and Pirvan forced from his mind a picture of Haimya spitted on one of those horns like a roasted pigeon.

But lowering his head was Waydol's fatal mistake. Pirvan and Haimya ran at him—and Pirvan tossed his quarterstaff to Haimya, while she tossed the leather thong to him.

Pirvan had never run so fast in his life as he did over the dozen paces it took to get behind Waydol. He leaped up on the Minotaur's back, kicked him hard at the base of the spine, and looped the leather thong around the base of his great neck.

Waydol reared up, so that Pirvan was dangling by the thong. But the tough leather tightened under his weight, against the Minotaur's windpipe. Waydol reached back, to grip Pirvan and tear him apart—and left himself wide open to Haimya and her staff.

She thrust furiously at his throat, his belly, his groin, both knees. Then she started all over again. Somewhere in the middle of the flurry of blows, Waydol sank to his knees, and a moment later Pirvan stepped out from behind the Minotaur and gripped Haimya's arm.

"Hold, my lady and love. He's done fighting."

Waydol nodded painfully. He tried to speak, but the blows to the throat had taken his voice for the moment. Instead he lifted both hands and placed them in Pirvan's. Pirvan took the Minotaur's bloody hands in his own battered ones, and from far off came the thought that he and Waydol were, in some sense, blood brothers now.

Then the world dissolved in a tumult of shouting, in which each man seemed to have a brass throat and be trying to make more noise than all the rest together. All it did for Pirvan was to make his head ache worse.

Haimya was standing before him, and he held out the leather strip to her. Instead she leaned against him. He thought this was a touching gesture but the wrong time and place, until she went to her knees. He had just time to squat down and catch her before she fainted—and then when he wanted to get up, he found that his legs had finally mutinied.

Pirvan didn't faint. He remembered what seemed like a small army of people running onto the field, with Birak Epron and Rubina in the lead. From somewhere else came Fertig Temperer, a kender, and a small man with silver hair and muddy blue robes.

He remembered being told that the man had a name, though not what it was, and that he was a priest of Mishakal. He remembered Rubina hugging both him and Haimya, and dropping her staff, which was nearly trampled before Birak Epron drew his sword and drove the crowd back to a safe distance.

Then Sir Pirvan of Tiradot did not precisely faint. But he took Haimya's hand, and for a long time after that he did not remember what he did or what happened around him in any great detail.

Chapter 17

The logs in Waydol's snug hut crackled pleasantly and gave off a soothing smell of pine.

Those were just two of many pleasant sounds and smells—and sights and tastes—that Pirvan had savored in the days since the trial. He always savored them more after he'd put his life in the balance, and for a time he wondered if he would ever savor anything again.

He sipped from a cup of Sirbones's mulled wine. It had no effect against great hurts, the priest of Mishakal had said, but it did not slow their healing by proper spells. As to the minor hurts not worth serious magic, it at least makes one forget them for a while.

This time Pirvan drank deeply. He wanted to forget many things besides minor hurts, then sleep beside Haimya, to wake and savor her warmth and the soft sound of her breathing. . . .

A time would come for all of this, but that time was not yet.

Waydol emptied his goblet, which was larger than Darin's, and Darin's was as large as Haimya's and Pirvan's put together. He set the goblet down, wiped his mouth with a clean cloth, and, with a delicacy of movement that showed his hands still pained him, he coughed.

"I fear I cannot dismiss the trumpeter," Waydol said. His voice was hoarse, like a man's with congestion, but otherwise undiminished. Sirbones was a healer of high skill, and while all of the fighters would have aches and pains reminding them of the trial for some days, none would suffer lasting hurt.

"It would shame him," the Minotaur added. "He came to my band fleeing from apprenticeship to a harsh master. Playing the trumpet was his only pleasure."

"It is only pain to all who listen," Pirvan said. "Let us strike a bargain over the trumpeter. If he goes into the world, I will find him a teacher who can tell him if he has any musical art. If he does, well and good. If not, then we can seek some other work for him."

"You are firm in your honor," Darin said. He spoke softly, so that he did not need to move his head. Of the four fighters, he had come closest to death; without a skull thicker than most, he might have gone before Sirbones could heal him.

"I am a Knight of Solamnia," Pirvan said. "I know that only begins the explanation, but I do not have time to tell you every thought that I have had about honor. Leave it that I will no more abandon your men than I would have abandoned mine, and let us go on to the best way of saving them."

When he accepted Waydol's oath of peace, Pirvan demanded only that Waydol agree to allow any of his band who so wished to go free. Jemar the Fair's ships would bear them to Solamnia, where, if they chose peaceful lives, it was unlikely that Istar would seek them out.

Waydol was not bound by anything save his loyalty to his men. Pirvan suspected that the Minotaur intended to seek his homeland again, with his precious burden of knowledge about human ways.

No doubt the minions of the kingpriest would say that Pirvan ought to halt Waydol, even slay him if necessary. No doubt, also, Pirvan would not lift a finger to stop Waydol, and would offer bare steel to anyone else who attempted it.

The knight's major regret in letting Waydol sail north was not what he might tell his folk. It was losing the chance to know the Minotaur better. Waydol could teach the knights a thing or two about honor and oaths; Pirvan wanted to learn them.

"What of those who do not wish to flee to Solamnia but wish to give up the outlaw life?" Darin added. "Can you do anything for them?"

"The knights would doubtless honor any pledges I made for them, if they took the field," Pirvan said. "But I think Aurhinius means to settle matters before that happens. So I would urge that all who wish to flee by land do so before we find ourselves besieged. If they quietly vanish from your band and reappear elsewhere as honest men, I doubt that anyone will trouble them.

"The one thing to be avoided like dishonor is anyone trying to be chief of an outlaw band in your place. Then the Istarians will harry this land until it lies ruined, and their fleet and army will loom over Karthay until that city loses patience."

Those words were out of Pirvan's mouth before he realized that, to a minotaur, Karthay and Istar spending each other's strength in a witless war could be a welcome prospect. Yet he did not fear Waydol thinking along those lines.

Waydol believes in the superiority of the minotaurs, as do all his folk. But he believes that they must show their superiority by winning honorably.

"I will have words with any ambitious little men," Waydol said. "Darin, are you fit to take *Gullwing* to sea and seek out Jemar the Fair?"

"I feel well, Waydol."

"Has Sirbones said you *are* well?"

"Not yet."

"Then you remain ashore until he speaks," Waydol said. There could be no more arguing with him than with a battle-axe.

"Jemar may well find us without Darin's voyage," Pirvan suggested. "Also, there are signals that he will recognize. If you can build beacon fires on the headland above the cove, they will be visible far out to sea."

"To the Istarians, as well as to Jemar," Darin put in.

"I think the place of our stronghold is no longer much of a secret," Waydol said. "Now we must help our friends win the race to it, against our enemies."

*   *   *   *   *

Aurhinius awoke to the sounds of a great deal of shouting and running about overhead. This seemed to be his normal manner of waking aboard *Winged Lady*, or indeed any other ship. Fortunately he was a sound sleeper; his good digestion gave him more than a certain roundness of belly.

The running ceased, but the shouting continued. Aurhinius began to make out words. It seemed there was an unidentified ship in sight.

He decided to dress and go on deck, to see how the captain dealt with this. It was the first such sighting since he had come aboard; all the others had been plainly merchant ships of one nation or another. All except one, a low-built sailing vessel that had darted off into a fogbank at a speed that suggested its crew did not wish to be identified.

Aurhinius made less of a business of dressing than usual. Fond as he was of fine attire, he was fonder still of his own dignity—and dressing aboard a warship as though one were at audience with the kingpriest was a sure way to be laughed at.

In long woolen tunic and linen hose, Aurhinius came on deck, about the time the lookout called from the masthead.

"Deck, there! It's a light galley, under sail. No flag that I can see, but she's coming toward us."

Aurhinius looked at the captain, who shrugged. "None of our scouts are missing. Could be a messenger ship, though if she's coming from the west, she's likely to be from Solamnia. Can't be carrying too many men, though, so I won't hope for knights joining us."

"Much as I think," Aurhinius said.

The next hail from the top surprised everyone. "She's resting on her oars and raising a truce flag. No banners yet, but there's something painted on her foresail."

"Nothing hostile, that's for certain," the captain said. "Otherwise she'd be running." He raised his speaking trumpet and shouted aft.

"Port your helm. I want to run down and speak to this galley. And send the men to quarters."

"Signal the same to the rest of the fleet," Aurhinius said.

"Begging your pardon, my lord," the captain said, "but there's no call for that. If *Winged Lady* can't handle a light galley by herself, then you can take your banner elsewhere with my blessings."

"I can't think of that," Aurhinius said, smiling. "Your figurehead is too enticing."

The captain returned the smile. The bannership's figurehead was a life-sized carving of a splendidly proportioned woman, wearing nothing but a pair of spreading wings, with every feather exquisitely carved and gilded. There were many different opinions as to which goddess or heroine the figurehead represented. The one that Aurhinius favored was that it was a likeness of the woodcarver's mistress.

Before the men had taken their stations for battle, the lookout hailed again.

"Deck, ho! The galley's turned toward us and shaken out her foresail. I can just about make out—Habbakuk guard us!"

"What do you see?" the captain shouted. "Answer, or Habbakuk won't save you from me!"

"It's a minotaur's head on the sail, Captain. A great,

huge red minotaur's head."

"Any minotaurs aboard?"

"Can't—no, wait. I can see the people on deck. All human, looks to me."

Aurhinius snapped his fingers, and one of his servants stepped forward. "My everyday armor and sword, if you please."

"Yes, my lord."

He turned to the captain. "We have been seeking Waydol. It appears now that he has also been seeking us."

* * * * *

Since he set sail three days before, Darin had wondered what his fate would be, if he met the Istarians before he met Jemar. He had not expected to encounter the whole fleet, and with the wind blowing so that *Gullwing* could not possibly flee.

However, since he recognized Aurhinius's banner as well, he decided that honor did not require a fight to the death. He ordered the truce flag raised, and considered what he would say to Aurhinius if that flag was to be honored.

He had not expected the Istarian bannership to come down on *Gullwing* itself, looming over the galley like a draft horse over a pony. Neither did he expect the hail from amidships.

"Ahoy, Waydol's galley! If there is one aboard with the power to speak for the Minotaur, Gildas Aurhinius would be pleased to host him aboard *Winged Lady*."

"Mark my words," the galley's Mate of the Deck muttered. "It'll be hoisted, and by the neck, not hosted."

"Then we'll learn that the Istarians have no honor, without losing any of our own," Darin said.

"But we'll lose—" the mate began.

"We lose time already, and soon I will lose my patience," Darin said. His voice did not rumble like Waydol's, but he managed to be as emphatic.

"Aye-aye, Heir," the mate said.

Darin went across to *Winged Lady* in a boat sent from the bannership, a further unexpected courtesy. It arrived so quickly that he barely had time to change the shirt he had worn since sailing day and give his boots a quick rub with a coarse cloth.

Then he swung down into the boat, conscious of a great many of his men directing their eyes upward as if in prayer. He himself wondered if he should ask the gods at least to keep him from saying anything stupid.

He had little chance to say anything at all for a while, as he was courteously rushed aboard and then below, rather as if he were to be hidden from eyes elsewhere in the fleet. If this was so, whose eyes?

That concern left him swiftly as he was ushered into Aurhinius's cabin. Confronted with a man whom he had gone to some trouble to embarrass, and who now had the power of life and death over him, he knew he needed to do more than to avoid anything stupid. He really needed the eloquence of a scholar-priest.

"I trust my helmet is receiving proper care," Aurhinius said. He made no move to rise.

Darin kept face and voice bland. "I entrusted it to Waydol himself. He honors trophies from worthy foes."

"Then perhaps I may return the courtesy, in time," Aurhinius said. "If you had left it with that kender—"

"Imsaffor Whistletrot is a trusted and loyal comrade of many battles," Darin said.

"I do not doubt that. But kender are not the best folk for taking care of others' valuables."

Now Aurhinius rose. He still did not offer to shake hands or step out from behind his desk, let alone suggest that Darin sit.

"I believe that we both seek Jemar the Fair. It that not so?"

Lying seemed futile or worse. "Yes."

Aurhinius clasped his hands behind his back. "Now, Heir to the Minotaur. We can either sink your ship and take your men aboard to continue the quest for Jemar as our guests, or we can sail in company. The choice is yours.

"What will earn you your ship and your men's freedom is an answer. For what purpose do you seek Jemar?"

"None that can injure Istar or offend the gods."

"You seem to believe that you know all about Istar's intrigues and also the will of the gods. That makes you wise beyond your years. Also beyond belief."

Aurhinius slapped both hands down on the desk. Inkwells and pens jumped. "Do not take me for a fool! I have no reason to trust you and every right and power to take your head and those of your men."

"You have those," Darin said, then swallowed. "But you also have the wisdom, and I believe the sense of honor, not to do so."

Before Aurhinius could reply, Darin continued. "Lord Aurhinius, let us therefore deal honorably with one another. Let each of us say why he seeks Jemar, under oath to tell the truth. If we do this, and you mean Jemar no harm, I will sail with you.

"Otherwise, you will have to pay for *Gullwing* and every man aboard her in blood. Do not be sure that your blood will not be part of the price, either."

Darin had not expected the threat to move Aurhinius to either fear or violence. Even less had he expected what came next, which was laughter.

"If you are what comes of a minotaur's teaching, then perhaps we should hire minotaurs to teach more of Istar's young men. You have an old head on young shoulders, which is far too rare these days and promises to become rarer."

Aurhinius pushed a stool out from behind the desk. "Sit down, Darin, and tell me if Jemar means to aid Waydol in any way that can harm Istar."

"He does not. Waydol is oathbound to Sir Pirvan of Tiradot, Knight of the Crown, by right of Sir Pirvan's victory in a combat trial."

"A human beating a minotaur?"

Darin flushed. "Two humans, beating a minotaur and—another human."

Aurhinius was too polite to ask the obvious question.

"So Waydol means to withdraw from Istarian land—at least what he holds now—and trouble our peace no further? And he will do this aboard Jemar's ships?"

"The gods willing, yes. You may also have something to say about that."

Aurhinius had a good deal to say about what he and Istar's sailors and soldiers could and could not do. But in the end, Darin felt that the Istarian could be trusted to make no hostile move against Jemar, as long as the sea barbarian removed Waydol and the outlaws and did nothing else.

But how to warn against treachery, if Aurhinius was not perhaps complete master in his own house? Darin realized that, indeed, his sailing with the Istarian fleet would give him the earliest warning of any treachery. He would then have to gamble on finding darkness or bad weather to slip away, as well as the soundness of his ship and crew, and even then hope for the favor of the gods.

But he was being given as a free gift what he now realized he should have eagerly sought. Perhaps the gods were already with him.

The handshake between the Istarian general and the Minotaur's Heir was that of two men who each felt that they had come out ahead in honest bargaining.

* * * * *

Sir Niebar contemplated the four men-at-arms standing in front of him, and the locked door behind them.

"I am asking you to accompany me and two other knights in a matter of grave concern to the Knights of Solamnia and the peace of the realms. If any of you feels that you cannot promise to obey me as you would Sir Pirvan, you may leave now. You will lose nothing thereby."

All four men stared back. No doubt they found him far more mysterious than he found them. None of them, however, so much as looked toward the door.

"Very well. This matter is one not only of concern to the

knights, but it is also close to Sir Pirvan's heart. It concerns the unlawful captivity of a kender."

He told briefly of Pirvan's discoveries at the Inn of the Chained Ogre, then continued. "Since Sir Pirvan embarked on the remainder of his journey, we have learned more about the inn. It may be a center of certain— rites—conducted without the knowledge or blessing of the kingpriest."

The training of the Servants of Silence was only partly a rite, and Sir Niebar and Sir Marod both gravely doubted it went on without some blessing of the kingpriest. But to ask these men to follow him into open warfare against the kingpriest would be asking too much. Moreover, if they could claim ignorance of the true purpose of the raid, any vengeance would be more likely to fall on Sir Niebar alone.

Beyond the loss of honor, through lying to these good men.

"So—the kender's a witness?" one of the men said.

"Of that, and other things."

"Against humans, or kender, or who?"

Niebar reined in tongue and temper. "Does it matter?"

"Well, Sir Niebar, to my way of thinking, it's overdue for us to be taking a hand on the side of the other folk. I'm no great lover of any of the odd breeds, but I think—I won't say the kingpriest, but maybe some close to him— are trying to gull us. Let folk get into bad habits toward kender, and next thing you know, they'll be doing it to each other."

"Aye," said a second man. "I'd do this, too, for anyone but a gully dwarf."

Who are not likely to need our help, Niebar considered. What the gully dwarves lacked in wisdom, they made up for in centuries of experience in hiding, so that would-be persecutors often gave up even trying to *find* them.

Kender, on the other hand, were about as hard to overlook as the Towers of High Sorcery.

* * * * *

Darkness clamped down on the sea like a vast lid on a bowl. Tarothin stood in the waist of *Pride of the Mountains*, judging the distance to the ship with the minotaur head on its foresail.

All he could see of it now was its stern lantern. Darkness had long since swallowed the minotaur head and everything else aboard, including the young giant, as tall as a minotaur himself, who strode the deck.

The Minotaur had sent his heir to sea, probably in search of Jemar rather than what he had found. The heir had even survived this unexpected meeting, thanks to the favor of the gods, the honor of Aurhinius, and very probably the ignorance of the priests of Zeboim.

Tarothin had used the spell-hearing trance sparingly since the first time, and not at all in the past few days. The priests of Zeboim seemed quiet for the moment, and the wizard would have given ten years of his life to know why.

Did they think that victory was already won, without further need to exert themselves? Or were they saving their strength, to fight desperate battles they saw ahead?

Which, of course, depended on how they defined "victory"—and Tarothin would not even venture a guess at that. The priesthood of Zeboim was more secretive than most, and priests of Zeboim set afloat with all restraints removed by the command of the kingpriest himself were likely to defy ordinary human or even wizardly understanding.

However, if Tarothin could not understand them, he could at least carry a warning. The Red Robe ran through his mind the estimate he had already reached, about the distance to Waydol's ship. He was not an accomplished swimmer, having come to that skill late in life, but he was not what he had been aboard *Golden Cup* on the voyage to Crater Gulf, a man who would have sunk like a stone if he'd gone overboard.

Also, the water was warmer than farther south, the wind light, and the darkness fit to hide him. If he could just get overboard without a splash that would have the alarm up and boats scurrying about in search of him—

Boats. Like many ships of the fleet, *Pride of the Mountains* was towing a couple of seagoing barges, fitted to sail or row and able to carry heavy loads of soldiers or stores. The towlines trailed from the waist. If he could just climb down one of them, without being seen, then slip quietly overboard from the barge . . .

This was one of those decisions, Tarothin realized, that had to be turned into action before thinking about it drained the courage to even try. He had his staff with him, and a waterproof pouch of herbs for certain spells never left his person, even when he bathed.

He was as ready to go now as he ever would be. He refused to think about losing his way, about encountering hungry fish, about being in the water so long that it chilled him to weakness.

Instead he waited until no one was looking toward the port side. Then he climbed over the railing, wrapped arms and legs around the towline, and began a clumsy slide down it toward the barge.

Chapter 18

"Halt! Who goes there?" a sentry called.

Pirvan had been about to dismount, but stopped with one leg still over the saddle. Then he swung back onto his horse. It was still no proper charger, but at least it wasn't the ravens' fodder he'd ridden the first day at Waydol's camp.

Waydol had ordered the patrols increased, mixing cavalry and infantry now that they had nearly forty horses. Pirvan, as a Knight of Solamnia, was assumed to be the best leader of mounted troops, as well as expected to be the most skilled in the difficult art of patrolling.

Along with Birak Epron and Haimya, Pirvan had a good laugh over that.

Less amusing was the danger that he might have to fight Istarian soldiers or their allies. Honor bound him to lead and defend Waydol's men until Jemar arrived to carry them to safety. However, if his honor ended by forcing him to kill Istarian soldiers, the rulers of the city might have something to say to the Knights of Solamnia about one Sir Pirvan of Tiradot.

So far, however, there had been no such awkward encounters. Pirvan had provided biscuit and salt fish for starving bands of fleeing farmers, sighted Istarian cavalry patrols at great distances, and given would-be recruits for Waydol directions to the camp. He had yet to draw, let alone bloody, a weapon since he began riding the patrol rounds.

Tonight's patrol was five mounted men, including Pirvan, and ten more on foot. Half of the foot soldiers were Birak Epron's veterans, who were teaching the other half, from Waydol's recruits.

From the edge in his voice, the sentry sounded like one of the new men.

Pirvan urged his horse forward, while signaling the others to spread out to each side of him. He doubted that they faced an ambush or serious opposition, but it was always well to have a few men clear of any trap, to ride or run and bring warning.

It was a night of patchy clouds, but otherwise clear, and Solinari was waxing as Lunitari waned. There was enough light to tell friend from foe, with a little luck, which was the best a warrior could hope for, in night fighting.

"Halt!" came again. "Who goes—ahhh!"

The sentry's scream was that of a man caught in the jaws of a monster. Pirvan shuddered in spite of himself, and of the certainty that only human foes roamed tonight. Now he dug in his heels, and the horse moved up to a canter, the fastest he dared take it in darkness on uncertain ground.

Pirvan and his riders overran the sentry post almost before they knew it was at hand. The knight had a brief glimpse of a body lying gape-throated on the ground, with two figures in dark clothing standing over him. Then a third and fourth enemy loomed out of the darkness, both mounted, both also dark-clad. Pirvan realized that all four of the attackers were far too neatly dressed to be outlaws, but were not Istarians unless the dark clothing was a disguise.

That was his last untroubled thought for some time. In

the next moment both mounted figures charged Pirvan, swords in hand. Pirvan was between them, and he and they swept past one another so fast that all he had to do was duck his head for their swords to clang together over his head, showering sparks but no blood.

Not so harmless was their charge into the middle of the infantry. The new recruits scattered, screaming. The veterans ran too, but silently and in a formed body, spears thrusting out like the quills of a porcupine. Pirvan drew his own sword, wheeled his horse, and rode back to help his men.

By the time he reached them, or where he thought they had been, the moonlight had faded, to leave Pirvan in that dreaded situation of not knowing where either friend or foe might be. So when a man on foot ran at him, thrusting with a spear, he did not cut the man's head from his shoulders. Instead he slashed at the man's arm, controlling his horse with his knees while he gripped the spear shaft with the other hand.

The man howled and let go of the spear as the sword tore his flesh. Pirvan lifted it, tested its balance, and realized that he had just acquired a serviceable lance.

This realization came not a moment too soon. The man was running at him again, a short sword in his good hand. Pirvan shifted his grip on the lance, wheeled his horse, and thrust downward.

The lancehead took the man in the throat, ripping it open, then tearing free. The dying man toppled to the ground; Pirvan's horse nearly unseated him trying not to step on the writhing body.

"Behind you!"

Pirvan crouched low, wheeled his horse, and couched his lance in a single flow of motion. The enemy rider was too surprised to see a lance coming at him to do anything before the lance took him in the chest. He flew backward off his horse with a thump and a clang of armor, screamed once, screamed a second time as the man behind him rode over him, then lay still.

"We've taken the other two, Sir Pirvan!" a voice called from the darkness.

"Which two?"

"The ones who killed the sentry."

"Keep them alive if they're not dead. Or I'll ram this lance up somebody's arse!"

Both men turned out to be alive, which made two prisoners and three dead among the attackers, against three dead and one wounded among Pirvan's men. It was not an exchange to be proud of, even if for the first time in his life he had fought in an actual battle like a knight of tradition, wielding a lance from horseback.

The best thing he could hope to salvage from tonight's wreckage was learning who had sent these men into the jaws of his patrol. Somebody very bold, very careless of the lives of his men, or very eager to learn Waydol's secrets—and none of these made for pleasant thoughts.

Darkness again lay within Pirvan, as well as around him, as the patrol turned about and marched for camp.

* * * * *

Aurhinius was perusing the last of a pile of letters, most of them concerned with one matter.

Several towns on the north coast were sending their levies west against Waydol. Their total strength might be as much as three thousand men. Add this to the two thousand Istarian regular troops already ashore, and if they concerted their attacks, they might overwhelm Waydol by sheer weight of numbers.

It would be a bloody victory even if a certain one, but blood would not daunt the commander ashore. Next in seniority to Aurhinius, High Captain Beliosaran had been the inevitable choice, in spite of his reputation for cruelty as well as courage.

However, it would take time for Beliosaran to gather all his men, more time for the town levies to assemble and march. Some of the towns might insist that Beliosaran detach some of his men, to take the place of their absent levies.

This, of course, risked making the whole bounty-hunt even more futile than it would be otherwise. Aurhinius wondered idly if even Beliosaran would dare attack Waydol with the number of men likely to survive hunger, fluxes, fevers, shoddy boots, swamps, snakes, ambushes, and simple loss of enthusiasm for war.

His secretary entered, as was his right, without knocking.

"Signal from *Pride of the Mountains*," the man said.

He uttered the name with more than a touch of disdain, which was nearly universal toward the Karthayan ship in the fleet. It had proved neither well found nor well manned. The only reason Aurhinius had not prayed for a storm to dismast it was that it would then need an escort home, else the Karthayans who thought they were winning favor with the kingpriest would howl like starving wolves—probably for Aurhinius's head.

"Anything important?"

"Possibly. They think their wizard, that Red Robe Tarothin, fell overboard."

Aurhinius did not groan or utter other unmanly sounds. He did briefly wish *Pride of the Mountains* afflicted with shipworms and its crew with blue scab and the choking fever.

"Tarothin?" Aurhinius said. "Is he the same—?"

"Yes. The one who went to Crater Gulf, with Sir Pirvan, before the knights took him in. They say he was going with Pirvan to Waydol, but quarreled over a woman. A Black Robe, they say."

"First wizard I've heard of with that much sap in him," Aurhinius said. "Well, put some boats over and have a search made. It's all but a flat calm, so there's no danger to the boats and perhaps even some chance of finding Tarothin, if he's not already drowned. It would be best if we could tell Sir Pirvan that we *tried* to find one of his old comrades."

"Aye-aye, my lord."

Alone, Aurhinius looked at the messages again, and then at the map on the bulkhead. Perhaps there was something he could do about matters on land, besides leaving them to fate, town levies, or Beliosaran.

The fleet carried close to a thousand seasoned soldiers,

though many of them the worse for seasickness. They could be landed closer to Waydol's stronghold than any Istarian or town soldiers now stood. Marched inland, they could enforce a truce between Waydol and his enemies, until Jemar the Fair removed the Minotaur's men *or* it became plain that the Minotaur and the sea barbarian were plotting treachery.

Then there would be ample strength both ashore and afloat to deal with open enemies as they deserved.

* * * * *

Pirvan and Waydol walked side by side up the path to the Minotaur's hut. It was narrow for two when one was a minotaur, but Pirvan had come to know it well in the last few days.

They said nothing for much of the way. Indeed, it sometimes seemed to Pirvan that he and Waydol said the most when they were silent. It was as if they had been friends for years—and it was a grief to Pirvan that the future could not hold such a friendship.

Waydol was adamant about returning to his homeland, resigned to whatever fate might await him there as long as he could first tell his people what he had learned about the humans. He was equally adamant about seeing his people and Darin provided for before he set sail.

Far off in darkness and fog, a pinkish glow pulsed and flickered.

"They have lit the beacons," Waydol said. "It may help guide any friends who are joining us by sea. I doubt that it will help Jemar much. Any ship of good size close enough to see the beacons will be too close to the rocks. If she takes the ground now and the surf gets up before morning, we will be rescuing her people instead of they us."

"Jemar's a cautious man—for a sea barbarian, that is," Pirvan added, as he heard Waydol trying not to laugh.

Another twenty steps brought them to the top of the path. The hut was a dim bulk in the fog, with a lantern burning golden above the door. Haimya wanted to learn the secret of Waydol's lamp oil, which gave that particularly pleasing color as well as an agreeable scent.

"We have questioned the prisoners," Waydol said, unbarring the door.

Pirvan was silent. His honor was involved in their not being tortured. He also could not stand alone against Waydol's whole band if they thought such necessary.

"They talked freely enough," Waydol added. "They're levies from Biyerones, trying for the glory of the first kill against us among the townsfolk. I suppose they can claim it if they wish, but also the first dead."

Not the last, though. Aloud, Pirvan said, "Are the towns all going bounty-hunting?"

"I doubt it is the bounty that lures them," Waydol said. "They are most likely doing it to purge doubts of their loyalty. High Captain Beliosaran commands ashore now, and he has a reputation for being harsh with enemies, and for seeing them everywhere."

Just the sort of man needed to change an honorable campaign into butchery, if given time, thought Pirvan. "Let us pray that the winds bring Jemar faster than Beliosaran or the town levies."

"In my way, I shall do so," Waydol said. He turned and now his voice was softer, as close to a whisper as nature allowed in a minotaur.

"There is something else I have wished to ask of you. No oath binds you, but if you had a son of an age to be looking upon women . . ."

Pirvan would have given much to be able to relieve the Minotaur's evident embarrassment. Unfortunately he had not the remotest notion of what was on Waydol's mind.

"Darin will remain behind when I sail," Waydol continued. "His life is not bound to me forever. But in time, our band will also cease. Then he will be a man alone among men, needing to make his way in the world by what is in him."

"I can give oath to guard him as if he were my own blood kin," Pirvan said.

"You will do that without any oath, I know," Waydol

said. One immense hand rested on Pirvan's shoulder—lightly, but after a sleepless night and a brisk fight, it made the knight's knees sag.

"What I ask is that you—that you keep him from Lady Rubina. He—she does not seem the kind of woman that a young man should find first."

This is asking me to light a fire in a barn full of hay and keep the barn from burning down. But Waydol had the right to ask anything of him, even the impossible.

"Lady Rubina hardly listens to me, though somewhat more to Birak Epron."

"He is not oath-bound to me."

"He is to me, and therefore to you. Also, he is a man of sense." Pirvan grinned. "One of vigor, too, or so I have heard. He may well entertain the lady so that she has no time to cast eyes elsewhere."

And gully dwarves are really dragons in disguise.

"Do not give me false hopes, Sir Pirvan."

"Very well. Then I will give you a real one. My good lady calls your heir so splendid a young man that he will not be long in finding a woman worthy of him. What Lady Rubina may do will neither make nor mar him."

"May it be so," Waydol said. "Sir Pirvan, I must bid you good night. Can you find your way back alone?"

"He will not be alone," came Haimya's voice from the darkness.

"No," Waydol said. "With you, Lady Haimya, he cannot be alone. May Darin be so fortunate."

And as we end the night's work with a prayer for a miracle . . .

The door thumped shut, and Haimya put an arm around her husband.

* * * * *

Tarothin managed at first to keep from his mind any thought of the vast depth of the water under him, and what it might hold.

Then he could not forget that the bottom was as far

below him as the foot of a hill from the top. All of the distance was dark water, with the-gods-knew-what swimming about in it in search of food.

Natural creatures only, of course. He would have sensed it if the priests of Zeboim had been calling up anything else to their aid or the aid of their patroness.

Tarothin swallowed water, nearly choked, and for a moment floundered desperately. He calmed both breath and limbs, then resumed a steady stroke. It upheld both his body and his courage that he'd found the water warmer than he'd expected, and his swimming surer.

Yet even the warmest water will leech away a man's strength if he is in it long enough. Slowly Tarothin felt his limbs grow heavier, his breath come harder, his thoughts come slower until they hardly came at all.

He was swimming almost by instinct when he struck something hard and slimy. He looked up, and redness glared down at him. *Stared* at him, for it was a single enormous red eye, and the hard, slimy surface he'd touched was the shell of a gigantic turtle—

Tarothin screamed—which was the best thing he could have done. The sound did not carry far in the fog, but it roused everyone aboard *Gullwing*.

The wizard had just time to realize that he'd touched the weed-grown rudder of a ship, and that the "eye" was its stern lantern, when a line splashed into the water beside him. He gripped it, determined to hold on with not only hands but also teeth and toes if need be.

He went on gripping it as the sailors hauled him in like a dead fish, over the railing, to land with a thump and a splash on a well-scrubbed deck. He made it to his knees before all the water he'd swallowed came back up, and stayed on his knees until his stomach was empty.

By then he had a circle of sailors around him. None of them were minotaurs, and none of them were the young giant who had to be the Minotaur's Heir. Neither were their faces particularly friendly.

I suppose a half-naked, half-drowned wizard is not something that a respectable ship hauls aboard every night, he thought.

That thought reminded him of his staff, and stark terror at the thought of having lost it heaved him to his feet. He rose so suddenly that he found his staff by its cracking him across the back of the head. He unslung it, held it in both hands, using it partly as a crutch, and would have kissed it if he hadn't been surrounded by those staring sailors.

Then the ring parted, and from what seemed to be near the masthead a strong man's voice spoke.

"What has Habbakuk brought us now?"

* * * * *

Darin had invoked Habbakuk more to please his sailors than out of his own beliefs. But after he'd heard Tarothin out, and been satisfied that the Red Robe told the truth, he thought that the Fisher God had indeed done him and all his friends a favor.

"We must leave the fleet," he told the Mate of the Deck. "There is danger, and we must warn Waydol and Sir Pirvan."

"Eh, what about our oaths?" the mate asked.

"We cannot be bound by them now," Darin said. "Not to Aurhinius. Our oaths to Waydol and Sir Pirvan come before those, though I doubt that Aurhinius personally has a hand in this."

The mate looked bewildered. Darin groped for words that would sound true without revealing truths too horrifying to be spread abroad.

"The fleet sailed from Istar divided within its ranks. A faction opposed to Aurhinius plots mutiny, with the aid of certain mages. If they prevail, or even if they attempt to seize power, Aurhinius's pledge to protect us will be worthless. If they prevail, the fleet may make war without mercy, against both us and Jemar."

The mate whistled. "Well, then we'd best be about taking our leave. I'll have one of the boats put over the side, with a mast and sail, and hang a lantern at the masthead. That's close enough to the same height as our stern light, so anybody looking at it will think it's us, until it's too late."

Darin wished he could do more than thank the mate for a cool seaman's head in this crisis. He wished even more that he could be certain of being alive in a few days, to give that reward.

"Oh, and we'll pad the oars a trifle, and douse the sails to make our shape smaller," the mate went on. "And if any of the lads makes a noise, I'll have his guts for a hat-band!"

No one made a noise, the sails came down and the oars slid out in silence, and the lantern-bearing boat drifted off until it was lost in the fog. Then, at a soft whisper from the mate, the oarsmen began backing water, and *Gullwing* slipped astern out of the fleet and off into the night.

Chapter 19

Aurhinius slept through the dawn uproar of turning out the morning watch, cleaning the decks, and setting to rights anything that had gone awry during the night. What eventually awoke him was his secretary, shaking him. He stared up into the young man's face.

"What now?"

"The Minotaur's ship—gone."

"Sunk?" Aurhinius allowed himself a pleasant moment's fantasy in which *Pride of the Mountains* had rammed and sunk *Gullwing*. Then he could offer the Karthayans to Waydol as the price of peace—

"No. Stolen away, in the night. That heir was treacherous, after all."

"Either that or a bad navigator. Did he possibly follow the transports when they parted company, thinking they were the main fleet?" The landing party was on its way south; Aurhinius had spent all the time that he could spare, praying for their safe arrival.

The secretary shook his head dolefully. "It was no mischance, my lord. We found a boat they'd set adrift with a lantern tied aloft in her midst, to deceive us."

Aurhinius put his feet out of bed. The deck seemed colder than last night. So did the air. In these waters, such a drop in the temperature often meant a storm. Several other things seemed more useful at the moment.

"I presume the fleet is pursuing?"

"Yes. The foremost scout reports she has *Gullwing* in sight, but may not be able to close with her before nightfall even if the wind stays fair and the weather clear."

"I am ecstatic," Aurhinius said. Another matter left dangling suddenly struck him. "Has anything been seen of Tarothin?"

"Nothing, my lord."

"Where was *Pride of the Mountains* when *Gullwing* disappeared?"

"Ah—in the next column, or so I have heard."

"Within—shall we say—swimming distance?"

"For a strong, bold swimmer, perhaps, but wizards are—"

"More apt to use their heads than anyone in this fleet seems to be doing at the moment."

Aurhinius retained the powers of speech after this last remark, but declined to waste words that would accomplish nothing. He pointed at the door. The secretary could not have departed, or the servants entered, more swiftly, if Aurhinius had sworn the sails from the masts and the masts from the deck.

* * * * *

Darin wanted to climb to *Gullwing*'s masthead and study his pursuers himself. Instead, he kept his feet on the deck and his faith in the lookouts. They were carefully chosen for keen eyes and cool heads, and the least of them was more agile aloft than he was.

Find good men under you, and you will not need to be every-

where at once and do everything yourself. It was as if Way-dol's voice had spoken to him on the sea wind.

"Deck, there!" the lookout called. "I can see some more ships behind the lead one."

No need to ask if they were Istarians. Darin looked aft. At first sighting, the Istarian pursuer had been visible only from the top. Now he could make out its sails from the deck. The other Istarians were still too far off for anyone but the lookouts.

"Think we ought to lighten the ship?" the Mate of the Deck said.

"How?" Darin asked. "I don't like dropping ballast when it may be coming on to blow, and that's slow work anyway."

"I was thinking of the food and water. We're either not going to be out here long, or we'll be out here forever and needing no food or water."

"You are in fine spirits this morning," Darin said in gentle reproof.

"I can count fingers held up in front of my face," the mate replied. "Leastways, until after the fourth cup."

Darin considered. *Gullwing* had been loaded with stores for a long voyage with a full crew. They'd reckoned that if the ship returned early, it would be to carry off Waydol's men, with no time for loading new stores.

Now it seemed that the first task was to make sure that *Gullwing* returned at all.

"Start with the water casks," Darin said. "Broach them and pump the water overboard. Then lay out sails to catch any rain the storm may bring. And have Tarothin come to me. I trust he is well?"

"Oh, well he is, Heir. Willing, that's another matter. But he'll see reason."

* * * * *

Jemar and Eskaia stood side by side atop the midships deckhouse of *Windsword*. It was not as high as Jemar wished to go, but it was as high as he dared allow Eskaia.

Also, climbing aloft and making the lookouts uneasy would speed no sightings of friend or foe.

What made Jemar more uneasy was the sudden drop in the temperature overnight, together with the rising wind. The fog was long gone, but he felt in his bones that a storm was coming.

A natural storm, for now. But it's no secret that weather magic is easier when you can play with power already set afoot instead of doing everything with your own spells.

Tarothin commanded some weather spells; Jemar hoped the Red Robe was looking for a chance to use them.

"Deck!" called the lookout. "Signal from *Thunderlaugh*. She's sighted beacons ashore. Says they're your private signal."

Eskaia's sigh of relief nearly matched the force of the wind, and she gripped her husband's hand. Jemar would have danced if he'd no dignity to think of.

"Well and good," Jemar said. A messenger ran forward, to the sailors at the signal halyards. Soon flags were soaring up to the yardarms and breaking into blazes of color against the sullen sky.

Thunderlaugh signaled back, with the course and distance to the beacons. Jemar sent thanks and promise of reward to Kurulus, shouted the same to the lookout, and then unbent enough to hug Eskaia.

"Almost done?" she said, returning the embrace.

"Call it a good, long step forward," Jemar said, freeing one hand reluctantly to make a gesture of aversion. The sea gave men victory only reluctantly, and it could strike back in many a natural way before the men ashore were safe.

Jemar made another gesture of aversion, this one with both hands. He had just performed it when the lookout called down again, this time in a voice cracking with excitement.

"Sail, ho! It's a galley with a minotaur's head on her foresail. *Gullwing* for sure, and she's coming on fast, like someone was chasing her."

Jemar frowned. The galley would be out of signaling range for some while yet, and even then its crew might have no way to read sea barbarian signals. Should he deploy his ships for battle now, or wait until he knew more?

One thing he knew: His ships were already beating hard to windward. Maneuvering them into battle formation would slow them still further.

Something else he also knew: The time to take care was when danger was only a possibility. True enough on land, and ten times truer at sea.

Jemar looked at his ships, then began inking three signals on a smooth-shaven wooden message board.

"I see what you want the ships to do," Eskaia said, looking at the board. "But why?"

"This way, we'll leave the heavier ships in open water, to meet *Gullwing* and her pursuers. They'll stay between the enemy, if there is one, and the lighter ships will go in to Waydol."

"Will it come to a fight?"

"You sound almost eager."

Eskaia flushed. "I beg your pardon. The fight aboard *Golden Cup* was quite enough for me. Besides, I am quite unfit to wrestle minotaurs now."

Jemar embraced her again. If it was the Istarians pursuing *Gullwing*, he wasn't sure they wouldn't be better off facing minotaurs!

* * * * *

Tarothin lay in his bunk, not because he was sick, reluctant, or entranced. He merely needed all his concentration to understand the message he was receiving.

He also needed more than concentration to believe it in the first place.

The first ticklings of the message were not in his mind, but in other parts of his body. Parts associated with certain ancient rites that he had performed with Rubina, more than once and with great joy. At least on his side, and he was gentleman enough to hope that she had taken as much as she gave.

This was the first time he had ever begun magic in such

a fashion, as he was not skilled in the kind of spells normally associated with that particular rite. *Although a man could become accustomed to this kind of magic,* he mused.

It was about this point in the message that he began to put a name to the person sending it.

"Rubina?"

The reply came not in words, but in an image. It was an image that did nothing for Tarothin's ability to concentrate.

Then words came:

I wanted to be sure you would recognize me.

Rubina, I am quite sure that there are many other men who would also recognize that image of you.

I do not kiss and brag. Besides, you are the only wizard.

So? That does not explain why you are seeking me out. This is a potent spell you seem to be using for idle chatter.

Rubina's image returned. Now she stamped her foot, her eyes turned red, and her hair transformed itself into green snakes with purple eyes and fangs that Tarothin did not care to observe too closely.

Was that Takhisis or temper, Lady?

I should leave you to the Dark Queen and her daughter's servants, if you go on like this!

Nothing could have restored Tarothin's concentration more quickly than the hint about Zeboim.

Rubina apparently plucked Tarothin's surprise and fear from his mind, turned it over in her own mind to look at it from all sides, and then replied.

The servants of Zeboim are at work. Or will be soon, to shape the storm. Can we—work together, that they may not succeed as they wish?

Many possible answers poured through Tarothin's thoughts, regardless of his knowledge that Rubina might be aware of every one of them.

He decided that what she *had* to know could be said briefly and plainly:

You are a Black Robe, servant of Zeboim's mother, yet you propose to fight the Sea Queen. How can I trust your word?

The first image danced along the fringes of Tarothin's mind. He replied brusquely.

That is not enough to bind me to you in treachery against our friends.

The reply came with surprising speed and clarity.

You speak truly. They are our friends. Also, there is Karthay, my city. Finally, it is not clear that those against us serve Zeboim, true daughter to Takhisis, or only those aspects of Zeboim that the kingpriest allows them to see.

That was wandering off into scholars' territory, besides imputing an alarming amount of power to the kingpriest. However, the thought of a magical storm sending Jemar's ships to the bottom and marooning Pirvan and Waydol's band at the mercy of the Istarians was still more terrifying.

What do you propose?

You have weather spells at your command that you can work on the water. Mine avail only on land, unless I join them to those of another wizard who is already on the water.

Tarothin was again briefly skeptical. Indeed, it would have been within reason to say that he was appalled. Such links were neither impossible, unknown, nor even particularly dangerous—except for such as Rubina proposed, which would link a Black and a Red Robe, who had never linked before, at least magically, over a considerable distance, using exceedingly potent spells, against equally potent and unrestrained enemies.

At that moment, the only virtue to Rubina's proposal seemed to be that, linked to her, he could at least neutralize any attempted treachery before it had fatal effects—at least to his friends. His own fate—

Will you put our friends in danger, while you fret like a child with a toothache about what I have no intention whatever of doing?

Her tone reminded him of more than one of their bedtime quarrels.

Yes, I am in the same mood. But I remember how those quarrels often ended.

Tarothin sighed, both with his body and with his mind. He thought longingly of oaths of celibacy. Then he replied to Rubina.

Shall we begin now?

Yes, if it is not already too late.

* * * * *

Darin repeated his request for Tarothin to come on deck, growing less polite in his choice of words each time. Then he began to make the request an order.

In due course, it was discovered that the Red Robe had locked his cabin door. He was the only man aboard besides Darin with a cabin to himself.

"Break it down," Darin said.

Those who heard the order, from the Mate of the Deck on down, looked dubious. They did, however, obey—or at least attempt to obey.

Minutes later, they streamed up on deck, babbling and shouting so that Darin had to roar for silence before he could hear what had happened.

The cabin door had resisted all efforts to open it. It was as if it had turned to stone. When they brought up logs of firewood from the galley and began trying to smash their way through, the logs flew out of men's hands.

Then they tried to remove the hinges, and the hinges glowed red-hot, without setting the door or anything else afire.

Finally, they tried to pry out the latch—and it turned into the head of a serpent, with fangs dripping venom that painfully burned several men who did not back away in time.

Darin looked at the swollen red marks on several of his crewmen, and noted that Tarothin owed these men a healing and an apology when the wizard had dealt with other, more urgent matters. It also seemed to Darin that perhaps he owed the wizard an apology, for not remembering the folly of disturbing a magic-worker when he is casting potent spells.

The only question left unanswered was this: If Tarothin was casting potent spells, what were they doing? The closest of the pursuers was now hull-up from the deck. The sharp-eyed on deck could make out the topsails of other Istarians to the east.

Darin decided to take a turn at the pumps, which were emptying the water from the casks out of the bilges. Exercise might settle his mind; it would at least keep him from standing around, plainly wondering what Tarothin might be about.

He had just set foot on the ladder to the hold when the lookout shrieked.

"Sail, ho, dead ahead! A whole squadron! We're trapped!"

Darin saw panic born on the faces of the men on deck and bellowed, "Nonsense! That's either a merchant fleet or Jemar!"

That halted the panic for the moment, though the Mate of the Deck whispered in Darin's ear, "What if it's minotaurs coming to help Waydol?"

"Then they'll have to fight the Istarians for the privilege," Darin replied. "Every ship and man the Istarians send to fight somebody else is one less to fight us."

The Mate of the Deck looked like a man who would believe in the virtue of one minotaur at a time, but he nodded.

Then the lookout screamed again, no words in his cry. He needed no words, and in fact need not have spoken at all. No one aboard *Gullwing* or any other ship in sight needed lookouts to see the storms rise.

* * * * *

No two men saw the storms in quite the same form. Indeed, few men agreed on how many storms there were. The lowest guess was two, the highest ran into the scores.

By and large, what men saw was a gray-green wall rising from the sea, as hard-edged as if it were made of stone, as translucent as if it were made of glass, swirling within those hard edges as if it were mist. It grew just ahead of the closest Istarian pursuer, and the water at the base of the wall turned into foam as a fierce wind blew from it.

Then a wave rose opposite the wall, as tall as the mast of a ship. Incredibly enough, it remained that tall for longer than any natural wave could—until it broke on the wind and the wall. Where there had been foam before, now there was a caldron of white, leaping so high that the wall sometimes disappeared.

Wind and water fought each other. Gusts and waves spread out in all directions from the battlefield, like ripples on a pond.

But these were not ripples. *Gullwing* heeled under the combined force of wind and wave, until water slapped at its leeward railing. The aftersail blew off its yard like a kerchief snatched from a child's head. Most of it flew away on the blast, flapping like a dragon's wings; a few forlorn rags remained standing out from the yard.

Darin did not need to order the foreyard down; men were already cutting its ropes with axes and knives. The broken rope ends lashed about, knocking men into the scuppers, and the yard itself came down with a crash that drowned out the storm.

But *Gullwing* now rode under bare poles, and men were already dashing below to close the oarports. Lightened both below and aloft, the ship had at least more than a prayer of staying afloat. If the wave storm and the wind-wall storm balanced each other long enough, it might even make enough headway to learn if the newcomers were Jemar or someone else, friend or foe.

* * * * *

Pirvan and Haimya had risen early and ridden out with a small escort, to scout possible landing places outside the cove, for friend or enemy. The cove's entrance was narrow, for all that this made for a sheltered, deep anchorage inside and easy defense.

Enemies would need to land somewhere else; friends might wish to. Hence the scouting.

Pirvan did much of the actual climbing, though Haimya scrambled up and down many of the steeper slopes along with him. She was less agile, and certainly kept her eyes fixed firmly on the sky, but in a few more years she would be able to climb wherever she needed to.

Sirbones had offered a spell to remove the fear of

heights from her mind; Haimya had refused it so fiercely that it took a while to soothe the priest of Mishakal back into an equable temper.

It was Haimya, with her eyes on the sky, who first saw the motion in the clouds. "Pirvan!" she called. "We'd best ride for home. That storm's breaking!"

Pirvan looked up. It seemed that an immense whirlpool had opened in the sky, with the clouds swirling into concentric circles. If they were moving, it was too slowly for the eye to catch; it was as if the whole sky had been conjured into this shape in a moment.

A storm was indeed breaking, but Pirvan's instincts told him that it was no natural storm.

"Hulloooo!" one of the horse-holders up the slope shouted. "Someone says there's a waterspout out to sea, the biggest he's ever seen! Can't see it from down there, but up on the cliffs you can see everything. They say there's ships out to sea, two or three squadrons of them right to each side of the waterspout, too."

To Pirvan, that settled the question of the storm's causes. He could only wait and pray, to see its consequences.

A wave higher than usual broke over the rocks only a man's height below Pirvan. A second wave followed it, at an impossibly short interval. This one was solid green water.

It rose like the river's flood, and if Pirvan had not leaped for the next higher rock, it would have risen as high as his knees, perhaps pulling him off in the backwash. But Pirvan leaped, then leaped again, then Haimya was pulling him up past the last bad ground, squeezing his hand, and kissing his cheek where he'd grazed it bloody on one leap.

"Send messengers!" he shouted to the horse-holders. "Everybody is to stay a good height above the water."

"How good?"

"If you're washed away, you know it's not good enough."

The horse-holders laughed as if Pirvan had made a fine jest. He did not feel in the least amused; magic unleashed did

not always stop where the magic-workers intended it to—
and in this battle, one side might not intend to stop at all.

* * * * *

Windsword took several large waves as gracefully as it
usually did. Jemar had just begun to let pride in his
favorite ship overcome his doubts about the unleashed
magic when two waves struck together.

They were the vanguard of two chains of waves, which
chose to collide exactly at *Windsword.* Jemar had heard of
such wave chains and how they could produce monster
waves by their collision. He had never seen one. Still less
had he expected to ever be in the middle of the collision.

Windsword did not heel. There was too much water
pouring onto the ship's deck from both sides. It merely
sank lower, then lower still, until the entire main deck was
awash. The railings dipped under, boats and deck gear
began breaking loose, stays flew free, and the foremast
swayed and crashed over the side.

Jemar was too busy clinging to anything that offered a
handhold and thanking the gods that Eskaia was below,
to think about his ship for a moment. Then he knew that
he'd have to get men forward to cut away the foremast,
take in sail on the other masts, do what he could for the
injured—

The waves rolled on away toward the horizon, the
water drained from *Windsword*'s deck, and like a pig rising from its wallow, it lifted.

As it did so, the last ropes holding the broken foremast
snapped. Instead of remaining to batter at *Windsword*'s
bow, the foremast went sailing off on a voyage of its own.

Jemar fought a ludicrous urge to wave farewell to it.

Instead he looked down. The decks looked as if they had
been ravaged by drunken minotaurs with axes, with wreckage everywhere and more than a few men sprawled flat. But
most of them were moving, some cursing lustily, and the
two who did not move had shipmates helping them.

His own ship was afloat, for now, and its crew needed

no help from him in rigging it for foul weather, magical or otherwise. Jemar turned his own eyes outward, to look first for *Gullwing*, then the rest of his ships.

He had to count twice before he could begin to believe that every ship—his ten and *Gullwing*—was afloat. Some of them looked as if they'd met gale-force gusts or deck-swamping waves, too, but so far he had no lost ships to mourn.

Also, he had lost none of the strength he would need to remove Waydol and his band from that stronghold behind the beacons.

Just to be sure that his wishes were not deceiving his eyes, Jemar started a third count. He was halfway through it when a sailor popped up the ladder.

"Captain! You're needed below! Your lady's hurt!"

* * * * *

Waydol was trying to meditate when Birak Epron ran in so suddenly that the Minotaur had snatched a katar from a side table before he recognized his visitor.

"If you wish to tell me of the magic storm at sea, that is stale news," Waydol said, mustering as much patience as he could.

"This is more. We have sighted the main body of the town levies. Two thousand at least, with half that many soldiers of Istar with them."

"How close?"

"Their vanguard is already past the place of your trial."

"Honor lingers there. May they hear its voice," Waydol said, in a voice that made Epron flinch. "Is there other word from the sea?"

"Istarian ships in two squadrons. One close to shore, likely carrying a landing party for when the sea goes down. The other is on the far side of the storm from Jemar's squadron."

"That is certain? Jemar has come?"

"He has come as far as he can while the wizards conjure up this ravening sea!" Epron snapped.

Meditation at this time would not only be dishonorable,

it was becoming impossible as well. Waydol rose and began opening his weapons chests.

At least *he* would not have to wait on wizards to finish their games before he found enemies within striking distance.

* * * * *

No storms troubled the land where Sir Niebar and his six companions rode swiftly toward the Inn of the Chained Ogre. Yet they rode in shadow, for they were taking byroads and trails through the forest wherever it lay thick enough to hide them from unfriendly eyes.

For the moment, Sir Niebar assumed all eyes were unfriendly. They might not be able to do harm out of that lack of friendship, for the seven riders were none of them recognizable as Knights of Solamnia or men-at-arms in the service of any respectable house. They looked more like tavern brawlers in search of a tavern to empty with their fists; the rest of their weapons were carefully hidden inside tunics, under cloaks, and in saddlebags.

The only eyes that might not be unfriendly were those of the nonhumans who inhabited these woods. Niebar was certain of kender and suspected gnomes; gully dwarves were everywhere, but made poor spies when a man wanted accurate news quickly. Centaurs also lived hereabouts, at least one small herd, but they so seldom cared much about what humans did (as long as it wasn't trapping, shooting, or poisoning them) that they were no more a menace than the gully dwarves.

The kender had eyes to see, wits to understand, and tongues to tell. There could have been no warning to the local kender that did not risk warning the innkeeper and his friends. So Niebar could only pray to Paladine, Kiri-Jolith, and Majere that the kender would realize he and his men were coming to end their kinsman's torments, not add to them.

* * * * *

Jemar tried to compose his face before he entered his cabin. Coming to Eskaia with a look of stark terror ruling every feature would not help matters.

From the look Delia gave him as he came in, Jemar had not been entirely successful. Then he abandoned self-restraint, rushed to the bed, and knelt beside it.

Eskaia smiled. It reminded Jemar of the smile he had once seen on the face of a criminal being impaled, but it made Eskaia seem real once more.

How long would she remain that way?

"What happened?" he asked. Now he thought he had command of his voice, if not his face. Eskaia actually raised both hands in salute—then dropped them again as pain twisted her face.

Delia favored the captain with a grim smile. "She fell. Hard. Forward."

"Of course it was forward," Eskaia murmured. "You've always said I was well padded—ah—astern . . ." She bit her lip, and Jemar noticed that blood had dried on both lip and chin.

"Can't you at least put her out of the pain?" Jemar asked. He wanted to snarl, scream, roar, or otherwise sound like bull thanoi in the mating season. He kept his voice low, for Eskaia's sake.

"Not without making things worse," Delia said. "I don't know if I should tell you this—"

"Jemar knows that I had some potential to be a cleric," Eskaia said wearily. "Delia, talk quickly, or let me tell my lord the story."

Delia swallowed, and Jemar had to do her the justice to admit that she then told the story quickly and even well.

Eskaia had fallen during the great wave-collision. She had so shaken her womb that she was in grave danger of miscarrying. Also, she might be bleeding from within.

There were spells Delia knew to heal each condition separately, but both had to be healed together if they were not to lose babe or mother. The only spell that could do that had to be performed on dry land. Attempted out at sea, and in the presence of so much magic already unleashed, the spell would surely fail, probably killing both babe and mother together.

"We must put in to land at once," Delia concluded. "In hours, it will be too late. I have heard there is a safe harbor we can reach in that time. Steer for it, Captain, in the name of all good gods!"

"Delia, Jemar can't take his bannership off and leave the rest of the fleet to—oh—to face the—the enemy," Eskaia got out, between gasps.

"He can if he wants you to see another sunrise," Delia snapped.

"I could go to another—" Eskaia began.

Delia squeezed her eyes shut and her hands into fists. Jemar wanted to shake her, then saw that she was weeping. Over that, he had no right to quarrel with anyone.

"If she stays aboard *Windsword*," Delia said, hoarsely, "what I can do, and the help she gives me—this may keep her alive long enough. Putting her in a boat—you may as well fling her over the side!"

She glared at Jemar, as if daring him to raise hand or voice to her.

"It won't help me to have you quarreling," Eskaia said, with a ghost of her old fierceness in argument. "Jemar, do what you judge best. I will have no quarrel with anything you do."

"Well, I cannot turn into a dragon and fly you to shore," Jemar said. He bowed his head briefly, in remembrance of a bronze dragon who had died a hero at Crater Gulf, for all that he had been waked from dragonsleep for no other purpose than to balance a black dragon waked by a renegade mage.

"But we can steer for Waydol's cove, I think. Delia, is speed all we seek, or will easing the motion of the ship help?"

"It will help if you can do it," Delia said. "I am no sailor, but I think those wind-conjuring wizards out there will make it less easy than it could be."

For once, Jemar found himself agreeing with the mid-wife-healer.

Chapter 20

Darin no longer had to fight an urge to climb to *Gullwing's* tops. The ship had no mast left standing.

Even from the deck, the view was less clear than it had been. The magic storms were filling the air with clouds, rain, mist, spray, and everything else to block the eye. Also, the ship was a trifle lower in the water.

The Minotaur's Heir wondered if Tarothin's cabin was still watertight. If *Gullwing* sank much lower, the crew was going to have to rescue the wizard whether he wished it or not, unless he could conjure up a fish's gills and go on working magic underwater.

The magic storms were still visible, however. Both now reared as high as hills above all the mist and spray. The green mist wall was fighting back with lightning bolts; great clouds of steam erupted as the onrushing waves quenched them.

At least no actual magic seemed to be spilling out of the storm area to endanger the ships at sea, either Jemar's or

Istar's. Even wind and waves seemed less of a menace. Darin had six oars out on each side, and *Gullwing* was slowly opening the distance.

Meanwhile, a keen-sighted crewman said that he had seen Istarian ships sailing close to shore. Darin himself had seen Jemar's ships heading about, straight for the mouth of the cove.

He hoped that they were doing this to carry out their task, and not because they were in distress. No one ever sailed to safety aboard a ship grounded to avoid sinking or holed on rocks.

At least there were other sailors besides Darin who could pilot Jemar's ships through the passage. Darin could give his full attention to keeping his own ship afloat—and with it, the wizard on whose efforts all still might stand or fall.

* * * * *

Waydol's armor was an old-fashioned leather shirt sewn with iron rings, a helmet large enough to cook dinner for a dozen men, and bronze greaves. His weapons included a clabbard, the saw-edged minotaur broadsword, two katars on his belt, plus a third strapped to his left wrist, and an arena-fighter's rack of four shatangs on his back.

Pirvan suspected that before the day was over there would be men dropping dead from the sheer sight of Waydol fitted for war. He would hardly need to touch them with any of his steel.

He himself was profoundly grateful that this time he was fighting at Waydol's side, and not against the Minotaur.

"Any word of Darin?" he asked.

Waydol shook his head. Pirvan noticed that he'd put sharp steel tips on his horns, to keep them from splitting if they struck armor. It reminded him of the efforts some Knights of Solamnia devoted to protecting their mustaches, a problem that had never concerned Pirvan. His chin was well arrayed when he chose, but his upper lip had failed to produce anything that didn't look like an undernourished caterpillar.

Birak Epron came up and greeted both Pirvan and Waydol. Behind him his men were drawn up, reinforced to more than three hundred by some of Waydol's men and deserters from the levies. There was even a rumor of an Istarian cavalry sergeant.

The sea breeze had now risen to a brisk wind, and the company banner rippled and snapped. The breeze was also blowing every form of murk in from the sea, though not letting it pool into vast, impenetrable banks. Jemar's ships ought to be able to make their way into the cove safely, and ashore the fighting men would not have to fight half-blind.

"I've sent out boats to pilot Jemar's ships into the cove," Waydol said. "They should also bring word of Darin, if Jemar has sighted him."

No one cared to put any of the other possibilities into words. Pirvan had wondered if there was anything in the Measure against praying for the survival of outlaws, then decided that he did not care. He would leave nothing undone to turn aside from his friend and comrade Waydol the fate of losing heir, band, and stronghold all in one day.

A mounted messenger came up, trotting as he'd been told to. Pirvan had knocked one galloper out of the saddle with his own fists, and after that, orders about sparing the horses were taken more seriously. Everyone probably feared that Waydol would punch the next galloper.

"Lord Waydol! The Istarians are coming ashore about an hour's march to the east. Those who saw reckon not less than a thousand."

The Minotaur nodded. "Then those who face us will be two-thirds levies, if the battle begins now."

"It might. Beliosaran has a reputation even beyond Istar. He is quite capable of throwing the levies at us, to use us up and spare his own Istarians until the reinforcements arrive."

"That is the tactics of a butcher, not a captain in war."

"Do I seem ready to argue?"

Waydol grunted amicably. "No. Just be ready to fight,

though. You may dislike fighting the innocent, but half the men will lose heart if you and your lady aren't in the front."

As if Waydol's words had summoned her, Haimya rode up, leading Pirvan's horse. Thanks to more captures, the knight had now awarded himself a proper cavalry captain's war-horse, not trained for knightly fighting, but fit for everything else.

"Have we searched the outer camp for women and children?" Pirvan asked. "Deserters can work out their own fate now, but I won't leave refugees behind."

"I would rather have held the outer camp with a rear guard," Waydol said.

Pirvan looked at Birak. They'd argued this point before, and both knew that it was sentiment overruling sound judgment. The Minotaur could not readily bear to give up easily even a trifle of what had been his for so long.

"They'd just surround it with a handful of men, then move on to the stronghold," Pirvan said. "Then the men in the outer camp would be cut off. We've agreed long since that everyone who's sworn to you should have a chance to make it back through the gap and aboard ship."

Waydol nodded. He seemed too downcast to speak. Then they all heard trumpets—some as discordant as Waydol's, others the silver-throated tones of Istarian battle signals.

Drums followed.

And Waydol threw back his head and gave a bellow of challenge and defiance that made all the martial music of the attackers seem like children with toy instruments.

* * * * *

Jemar forced himself not to stand looking over the shoulder of the leadsman as *Windsword* crept through the gap in the cliffs and into Waydol's cove. The leadsman had enough work to do, and that work meant life or death for everyone aboard the ship, without his captain dripping sweat on him!

Life or death for more than *Windsword*, too. If she got out of the channel and struck, it would likely as not block the way for the ships behind. Some might even join her aground. All were following as closely as a file of sheep passing through a gap in a fence, with the pilot boat Waydol had sent out ahead of them all.

At least the channel was wide enough for every ship to use its oars or sweeps. Some of them could only make bare steerageway without wind, but all could navigate in—and Habbakuk grant that they could make it out again.

The last rocks slid past, the channel began to open out into the cove, and Jemar looked up at the cliffs. They surrounded the cove on three sides; the fourth was a more gentle slope, covered with huts, gardens storehouses, and everything else needed for a band of outlaws the size of a fair village. Atop the slope were stables, forges, and a few stone huts that looked older than the rest of the place, or perhaps were just built minotaur-style, which hadn't changed much since elves had ruled Ansalon.

Jemar looked around the cove, measuring it with a seaman's eye. If there was enough deep water and the holding ground was good, it had room for twice the ships he'd brought. There also seemed to be a fair number of boats drawn up on the shore, and the ships would be putting theirs over the side even before they anchored.

Another step forward, not to be taken again. They could still fall, though, and from a fatal height.

The anchoring gang could do its work with even less watching by its captain than the leadsman. Now he could remain on deck until the last of his ships was safely through the passage.

Jemar wanted to howl like a maimed wolf. Instead he called for a messenger.

"Go below and see how Lady Eskaia fares."

"Aye, Captain. We—we're all praying for her."

"Well begun is half-done, lad. Now, run!"

* * * * *

The levies came straight out of the mist, and Pirvan and Waydol met them head-on.

At least they did for all of five minutes, long enough to force the levies to deploy from what might be called a column of march into what was no doubt intended to be a battle line.

It took them nearly half an hour and language that made even Haimya blush to make that battle line fit to advance.

By then Pirvan and Waydol had their three hundred men well in hand, and ready to give ground at whatever pace might prove necessary.

Most of the levies carried pikes, spears, or swords. Few had much armor, and the archers were still few and badly scattered.

"Probably no one captain commanding all of them," Birak Epron said. "Certainly no Istarian, or they'd be better arrayed."

"Then where are the Istarians?" Waydol asked.

"Probably off to the seaward flank," Epron said. "Ready to join up with their comrades, then work around our flank and run right up our arse while the levies hold us in front."

Then the thud of fast-moving horses on damp ground reached their ears—from the right, or landward flank.

Epron spat. "Remind me never to take up prophecy when I'm too old for soldiering."

Pirvan nodded, and Epron bawled, "Form square to receive cavalry!"

The men managed the feat of not only forming the square, but also moving off at an angle while they were forming, opening the distance between them and the levies. They had just finished when the flank patrols rode into sight, hotly pursued by several score horsemen.

None of them looked like the dreaded Istarian cavalry. This time Pirvan gave the order directly.

"Square—kneel, archers—shoot!"

Unlike their opponents, Waydol's picked rear guard was well supplied with archers. Indeed, the captains had eagerly sought men who were proficient with more than one weapon, and as a result a good many of the spearholders had bows slung across their backs.

The spears wavered and dropped, the square wriggled and writhed as the archers opened clear lines of sight, then suddenly an arrow-hail soared overhead. It was only a momentary blur against the clouds, and the wind sent some of the arrows badly astray.

Enough flew straight, however, considering the size of the target. The horsemen all looked like wealthy merchants for whom playing at knight was a hobby. Like their brethren on foot, they lacked the discipline to deploy quickly into their battle formation.

So they rode into range, a target a hundred paces wide and nearly that deep, just as the arrows came down.

Horses and men screamed. Men toppled to the ground, to writhe until other horses trampled them into stillness. A few horses fell; more went mad with pain, hurling otherwise sound riders to the ground.

The cavalry attack dissolved before the archers could shoot for the third time.

But the sight of their townsfolk dying under the arrows touched the courage of the infantry levies. Some of them darted out in front, screaming and shouting. Then a whole mob several hundred strong thrust out from the line and charged in a ragged mass toward the square.

At the same time, another score of horsemen rode out to join the survivors of the first attack. They slowed to pick their way over the bodies, but came on steadily toward Waydol's square.

Waydol stepped to the side of the square facing the horsemen, drawing two shatangs from his rack as he went. The men in front of him crouched low. He raised his right arm, swung it back, then snapped it forward so that it was a blur.

The shatang flew even faster. One moment it was in Waydol's hand. The next moment it was buried halfway to its butt in the chest of a horse. The horse, dead in midstride, crashed down on top of its rider.

Before the horsemen could even notice their comrade's fall, the second shatang was in the air. This time Waydol took a man.

He took the man in the chest, and the man flew backward off his horse. He was in midair long enough for Pirvan to see that the shatang had pierced completely through breastplate and body, to stick out a good arm's length behind the man's back.

The second cavalry attack was more prudent than the first. They fled, for the most part without having to be killed. A few archers sent farewell arrows after them, before turning their attention to the onrushing infantry levies.

Pirvan knew this was a crucial moment for Waydol's men. If one town's infantry hurt them seriously, others would be encouraged to swarm in. If they stood off the first assault, it might dishearten the rest.

Then Pirvan could lead the square back to the stronghold and the sea, with no fear of anything except Istarians, magic, storms, treason, and falling off his horse. He could do something about the last danger by walking, but as for the rest—

Then the infantry was on the square.

Waydol seemed about to draw his clabbard, then to realize that he couldn't wield it without lopping heads and limbs of friends. Instead he drew the third shatang for thrusting, while the other hand sprouted a katar.

For all his preparations and might, Waydol was not at the place where the square gave way. That honor fell to Pirvan and Haimya.

It began when one shrewd levy swordsman ducked under a spear thrust and stabbed the spearman. This opened a gap, and the swordsman had comrades with equal courage, skill, or luck. Suddenly three spearmen were down, four levies were pushing back the second rank, and some archer from the far side of the square loosed a wild shot and hit a friend in the second rank.

Pirvan vowed to kick the wild shooter in a vital spot at his first free moment, which he suspected would not come quickly. What came instead was what seemed half the population of a village, shouldering its way into the square.

They met Pirvan and Haimya, Pirvan with sword and dagger and Haimya with broadsword and shield. An attacker tried pulling her shield aside with a billhook; Pirvan stabbed him. His comrade swung an axe down at Pirvan's unprotected head; Haimya sidestepped and caught the axe on her shield, then cut the axeman's legs out from under him.

Meanwhile, Pirvan had shifted to Haimya's temporarily unprotected side, wielding sword and dagger in a blur of motion. It was intended less to kill than to alarm. It succeeded. Several advancing levies became retreating levies.

Not all, however. A man ran at Pirvan with a spear, to be lifted off his feet on the point of Waydol's shatang. The man was still screaming as Waydol shook the heavy spear, flinging the man into the middle of his comrades.

Trying to avoid the flying body, some of those comrades moved the wrong way. Some came within reach of Waydol. One of these screamed as a hoof crushed his foot, another died gurgling as the katar sliced his throat.

On the other flank, Pirvan and Haimya faced four men, all with swords and apparently either brave enough or witless enough to stand and fight. It did them little good.

Haimya hooked one sword aside with her shield and slashed the next man to the right with her sword. Pirvan ducked under Haimya's shield and stabbed the man with the immobilized sword. This put him behind the two other men, with Haimya in front. The two men between them drew about three more breaths before they were both stretched on the ground.

Pirvan whirled to see to his back, but discovered that it was safe. Seeing their point slaughtered, the rest of the attacking column was retreating. In fact, they were running as if they expected Pirvan, Haimya, and Waydol to sprout wings and fly after them.

Pirvan wished he could. It would do no one any harm, least of all the levies, if they kept running until they were back in their local taverns, telling lies about their prowess over the wine.

As it was, the whole line of the levies drew back out of bowshot. From the way their ranks heaved like boiling porridge, Pirvan suspected that they would be slow to attack again.

"I think we have outstayed our welcome here," he said. "Send the messengers to bring in the mounted patrols, and let us be off."

Waydol nodded. "I did not have half the fighting I had anticipated, you know. However, there was a reward. I saw you and your lady fighting as a team, when I could appreciate it."

Then Waydol roared with laughter, as loud as his challenge before. The levies, Pirvan noticed, didn't seem to be able to tell the difference. Some of them broke and ran for the woods even before the echoes of the Minotaur's laughter died.

* * * * *

Jemar's boat grated on the gravel of the cove's beach. The captain leaped out and ran uphill, toward the hut that showed the blue-staff banner of Mishakal.

Eskaia had been there for the best part of an hour, ever since the pilot boat offered to take her and Delia ashore. How the pilot had learned of Eskaia's danger, Jemar did not know.

Waydol had a priest of Mishakal called Sirbones; maybe he had something to do with it. Likely enough, he was farther forward, though, closer to the fighting that was spreading along the landward side of the cove and creeping closer to the stronghold's entrance. Rubina seemed to have disappeared—or at least no one knew where she was, though Jemar suspected that this was for fear of asking.

The only consolation for Jemar was if the Black Robe had wholly thrown her magic to the side of the Istarians, they would together have swept the sea clean of all foes and be starting their deadly work on the land.

And *now* he could put all of this out of his mind and go see Eskaia. The pilot had also told the boatmasters to start loading the women and children, and some of Jemar's ships already had crowded decks.

The slope steepened quickly, so that a run became a walk, and the walk on a path became a walk up a flight of stone steps. He wanted to keep walking, right through the door and into the hut, to take Eskaia in his arms.

But the door was solid oak behind the blue paint, and locked as well. Jemar knocked, then stood, trying to smell out death or health within. The village was none too clean, so he was still straining nose and ears when the door opened.

It was not Delia, but one of the outlaw women—girl, rather. She could hardly be more than fourteen.

Jemar started to raise a hand to cuff her out of the way, for her impudence in being here at all, then stopped. The girl was smiling.

"Is she—?"

The girl nodded, then nearly went flat on her back as Jemar rushed in, to trip over a stool and nearly stun himself against the far wall of the hut.

"Jemar," came a familiar voice from the shadows at the end of the hut, "is this how you enter a sickroom, and a house of Mishakal as well?"

Eskaia's voice was weak, but under that weakness the old bite had returned. And the pain, the labored breathing, the sense of a desperate struggle for the strength to speak at all—they were gone.

"She is well," a voice Jemar hardly recognized as Delia's came from the other end of the hut. "So is the babe. It will go to full term, though the midwife should be wary of its breathing when it is born, and it may be sickly at first. Also, I forbid your lady to take any more sea voyages until the babe is born."

"Delia, I can hardly walk or ride in a litter all the way home," Eskaia said briskly. "Shall we agree that I stay ashore once we are home?"

"Oh—of course."

That easy agreement sounded so unlike Delia that Jemar turned toward her. Then he stepped forward to catch her in his arms to keep her from falling off her stool.

Delia seemed to have gone from nearly plump to nearly half-starved in hours. Her face was so pale that it seemed to repel color, except for the dark circles under her eyes. Jemar could feel her trembling and the foul sweat on her.

"A pallet!" he snapped at the girl.

"Aye, Lord."

He held Delia. "You did not spare yourself, and—the gods tell me how to thank you. I don't know. Just—whatever I can—we can do to ease you—"

"The pallet will be enough for now," Delia said.

"But Sirbones—"

"He has more important work, as the wounded come in. And Rubina—she does good, not harm, now. But—her touching me now—would not be wise."

"I should think not!" Jemar and Eskaia exclaimed together.

"No, really. Rubina made—chose the wrong color. Her heart—Neutral, at worst. Now—now she betrays Takhisis. The Dark Queen will make her pay. Oh, she will pay."

The girl appeared at that moment with the pallet, and Delia lay back in Jemar's arms with a grateful sigh. In a moment she was stretched out on the pallet, apparently asleep.

Jemar bent and kissed her, then turned to his wife. "I will have you know, my lady, that I have kissed no other woman but you since we were wed. My oath upon it."

"Well, I hope you do not soon have another such occasion for kissing," Eskaia said. Then she actually laughed.

* * * * *

The afternoon shadows had stretched nearly across the clearing when Niebar reached the edge of it. On the far side began a path that led to the rear of the Chained Ogre. It passed a few farms that would surely have watchdogs and the like, but no villages, let alone towns, where seven armed strangers would stand out like a minotaur in a kender village.

Niebar looked behind him to be sure that the horses were invisible from the clearing. He saw no horses, but he did see a kender standing in a shaft of sunlight.

Niebar's first thought was of betrayal.

The second was of the horses! If the raiders came back, with or without Gesussum Trapspringer, and found that their mounts had been "handled" until they wandered off—

"Oh, don't worry about your horses," the kender said. This had the opposite of a reassuring effect on Niebar.

"Are you a wizard?"

"No, and we're standing too close to the clearing to chat, unless there's somebody you *want* to listen to us."

Niebar flushed at being reminded by a kender of the discipline of silence. He let his new companion lead him to a stand of pine saplings, in what must have been a clearing not too many years before.

"You are here for Gesussum, aren't you?" the kender asked. "Because if you aren't, then we'd take it kindly if you explained—"

The kender went on for a while, but Niebar was able to extract from the monologue that he was a Rambledin, that they were a little sorry for their abandoning Gesussum Trapspringer, and that they wanted to help anyone trying to rescue him.

"We can guard your horses," the kender finished. "We can . . ." He went off again on a long list of possible services, half of which would cause more danger than they gave help.

"We can warn you of the tattooed men," the kender said finally. "We can't fight them—they belong to the temples and we'd have to flee if we did, but—"

"The tattooed men?" Niebar said. Involuntarily, his right hand came up and scratched under his left armpit.

"Yes, yes. That's where they have the tattoo. Silly custom, but I suppose the kingpriest asks it. At least they seem to work for him, and I suppose he needs help. He wouldn't be able to spend all day preparing or whatever he does if he didn't. He—"

The knight had stopped listening. The blood was pounding in his ears, and his whole body seemed a little more alive.

Tonight they might do more than rescue the kender and learn what he'd seen during his captivity. They might encounter the Servants of Silence—and Niebar vowed that if it cost him his own life, one of them would leave the inn a prisoner.

It was time that honest folk learned why the kingpriest was, in the name of virtue, turning criminals loose on Istar.

It was also time for him to start listening to the kender Rambledin again. Kender could talk your arm off, then start on your toes, then be insulted when they discovered that you weren't listening to them!

* * * * *

Aurhinius stamped his boots firmly into place and looked over his shoulder at his secretary.

The young man was busy strapping on a helmet in a way that showed he'd seldom worn one. A breastplate leaned against the chair beside him.

"Are you going to wear armor?"

"I won't have many chances, my lord."

"Are you expecting universal peace tomorrow, or my imminent death?"

The secretary flushed. "Well, neither. But—well, it's the biggest fight I've ever been close to."

"Also the first one you've had to reach by boat," Aurhinius said. "Have you ever tried to swim in armor?"

"No."

"I have. I don't recommend the experience. Nine men out of ten who try it end up feeding the fishes. It's a small boat we're taking to shore. While our magic and theirs seems to be holding a balance, that could change. There's also the odd wave escaping from the balance."

"Take the armor if you will, but put it on *after* we're ashore."

"Yes, my lord."

The crew of *Winged Lady* cheered Aurhinius when he appeared on deck. He wished he had given them something to cheer about. Indeed, he felt more like a rat deserting a sinking ship in going ashore than a general putting himself at the head of his men.

It didn't make it easier when he realized that, ashore, he would be beyond reach of this duel of storm magic. The fleet could perish with all hands, but he would be safe to lead his men into Waydol's stronghold.

Or it might be Waydol who perished with his whole band. Aurhinius had asked every god he thought might have an answer, but none of them had told him if he should wish for the success of Zeboim's minions or not!

* * * * *

Tarothin?

The Red Robe's concentration on his spells left him enough physical awareness to know that water was seeping into his cabin. At least it seemed to be from below, so doubtless *Gullwing* was still afloat.

Idiot!

The tone was almost affectionate, and unmistakable.

Rubina. What do you want?

For you to take on yourself the whole burden of the battle.

You jest.

Hardly. What I have put into the storm magic will remain there. The priests of Zeboim lack the power to drive it out. Remember, I am a Black Robe, and I know more of their secrets than you.

But, why—?

Work ashore. The Istarians threaten to advance and cut off our folk. They have no wizard with them, and the minions of Zeboim cannot work ashore. Also, you can now do better at sea alone than with me.

But, Rubina—

Tarothin, I will not miss you long. But I will put into you a memory that you can call up whenever you wish.

If it's the kind I suspect, wait until we have the victory.

Just like a man. Mind always on work, never allowing himself any time for pleasure.

Then there was gentle laughter, without a trace of mockery, and Rubina was gone from his mind.

But her strength was not gone from the magical barriers he was holding against the priests of Zeboim. Indeed, he could begin to see flaws in *their* spells, and if he worked swiftly, he might twist them about . . .

Chapter 21

The sea wind had died by the time Waydol's band had broken free
of the town levies. The mist and fog, however, kept drifting in, but did not always drift onward. Slowly they swallowed the landscape, until Pirvan began to feel as if he
were fighting in a world outside time and space.

It was no warming thought to remember that wizards
had thrown friend and foe alike into precisely such places,
from which they did not always find their way back.

"At least it will slow pursuit," Epron told everyone.
"Bad soldiers who've just had a bloody nose will be cau-
tious about following good ones. Keep your tails up, lads.
We're rounding the last turn on the course."

The cliff that held the actual entrance to the stronghold
was in sight through the trees when a messenger rode
back from the mounted scouts to the north.

"Istarians!" was all he said and all he needed to say.

Before anyone could give orders, the gap in the rocks

spurted armed men. Pirvan counted twenty fully armed warriors, led by that sea barbarian called Stalker and the kender—Imsaffor Whistletrot?

"Thought you could use some help," Stalker explained.

Waydol looked north. "We may need more than you can give. Who else is inside?"

The kender began to recite a list; Waydol cut him off. "Time passes, my friend. We do not need eloquence."

Stalker explained that every man who could be spared from holding the cove if the enemy broke through had come out with him. The ships were loading swiftly, the mouth of the cove was still free of both fog and enemies, Lady Eskaia had been healed—

"I didn't know she was hurt!" Haimya exclaimed.

Waydol rumbled in his throat, in place of repeating his remark about not wasting time—and boarded *Windsword*. The midwife, Delia, was helping Sirbones with the healing. Rubina had disappeared, but had not turned traitor as far as anyone could judge.

"How fare things at sea?" Waydol asked.

Stalker shrugged. "We and they are still afloat. That is victory for us, I think."

If it lasts, it is, Pirvan thought.

Then once again he had no more time for thinking. The Istarians loomed out of the mist, infantry already in battle array in the center, cavalry on each flank. Behind the infantry rode a silver-armored figure, under a high captain's banner.

"Aurhinius?" Stalker asked.

Pirvan shook his head. "Beliosaran. Trying to snatch the glory of the victory for himself, I think."

"He shall learn the folly of that, I think," Waydol said in a voice so low that only those standing next to him heard.

Then he threw his challenge bellow at the Istarians. For a moment they did not even deign to reply. Then the cavalry opened out the distance on each flank, a drum began beating in the rear of the infantry, and they broke into their charge.

They had five times the strength of Waydol's rear guard, and they were all Istarian regular soldiers. They could lose one man for every one of Waydol's they slew and still have enough left to break through into the stronghold and slaughter everyone not aboard ship.

The one thing Pirvan could thank any god for at the moment was that, among Istarians, archery had lately been left to the rangers and town levies. It was too much an elven art, or so it was said, for sworn soldiers of the City of Virtue to soil their hands with it.

No, there was a second thing for which anyone here could thank the gods.

This was a good company to die in, if this was the day.

The square was formed now, and a few of the more skilled archers were already shooting. They had to either shoot low or high, to hit legs or loft their arrows into the rear ranks. The Istarians were advancing with their rectangular shields locked into a solid, arrow-proof wall. The cavalry was working out still farther on the flanks, largely out of bowshot.

The Istarians began chanting their battle cry:

"Uur-ha! Uur-ha! Uur-ha!"

It sounded like a chorus of bears in a vile temper with everything, including one another.

Gaps showed in the line now, and for a moment Pirvan saw the high captain's banner waver. But the banner bearer with the stricken horse passed the banner to another man, and they came on without missing a step.

Then Waydol pushed his way through the square. Pirvan put out an arm to halt him; the Minotaur brushed past as if Pirvan's sinewy arm had been a stalk of grass. Other men took one look at him and opened the gap wider.

Armed but bare-handed, Waydol stood in the open ground between the square of his men and the advancing Istarians. Pirvan mounted, wheeled his horse, wished he dared tell Haimya not to follow, and glared at Birak Epron when he started toward the gap.

Epron remained within the square, but both Stalker and Whistletrot came out at Pirvan's heels. Anyone else who might have felt the urge to go and die with the Minotaur mercifully had no time to act on it.

Trumpets and drums hurled signals about within the Istarian ranks. The infantry halted. To the left, the cavalry put their spurs in and their heads down, then rode for the cliff as fast as the trees and rough ground would let them.

To the right, the cavalry did the same—but their goal was clear to Waydol and those around him.

"Hold the entrance!" Waydol thundered. Birak Epron needed no further orders or explanation. The square broke into a trot, about as fast as it could move without losing form. Pirvan also saw archers shifting about within the square.

The stronghold might last long enough for those within to get to sea. Even some of the square might fight again.

Those who had followed Waydol out to provoke the Istarians were fighting their last battle.

At least that settles the matter of any Judgment of Honor over fighting Istarians, Pirvan thought.

The Istarian cavalry on the right was barely twenty strong, but they were all well mounted and armed with lance or sword. Pirvan backed his horse, couched his improvised lance—and saw Waydol step out into the path of the charge.

The third shatang was in his hand.

The lead rider saw only the foolish defiance of an easy target, couched his lance, and charged.

Pirvan bit back a cry as Waydol let the man come at him. Then he saw that the others were breaking their formation, to allow their captain the glory of the kill.

"Forward!" Pirvan yelled.

His horse jumped forward. At the same time, the Minotaur tossed the shatang from his right hand to his left, raised it, and threw. The lance dipped and tore into Waydol's shoulder as the shatang struck the rider in the neck.

"Struck" was too feeble a word. The shatang drove clear through the man, so that his nearly severed neck actually wobbled on his shoulders for a moment, before he fell from his mount. Two riders behind him fell also, though trying not to step on him.

In this moment of disarray, Pirvan and Haimya rode in among the Istarian ranks, with Whistletrot and Stalker running behind them. The air was suddenly full of war cries, screams, neighing horses, the clash of steel, flying bolas, and the weird roaring of a kender hoopak lustily wielded.

Pirvan nearly lost his mount to his second opponent, but replied by slashing the man's horse across the rump. The horse reared and threw his rider, and Pirvan put a knife into the man's throat as he started to rise.

Haimya had worse luck in the matter of opponents; Pirvan saw Stalker use his last bola to bring down the horse of a rider coming around on Haimya's blind side. The knight waved his thanks.

In moments the Istarians had lost five men and every bit of their remaining order. It was then that Waydol reentered the fray. He held the bloody lance he'd drawn from his shoulder in one hand, then gripped it with both hands and swung it like a club. Suddenly there was another vacant saddle—and the lance snapped like a twig.

Pirvan thought he heard Waydol grunt. He knew he saw the Minotaur reach back over his shoulder with both hands and draw his clabbard. Then all saw what a minotaur who had in his youth fought with a clabbard in each hand could do, even many years later and with one shoulder a mass of blood and torn muscle.

The Istarians who saw this mostly did not live to tell anyone about it. Waydol emptied the area around him of living or at least fighting men and horses in less time than a thirsty man could empty a cup of wine. Several horses who did not go down were running off, screaming from wounds or stark terror, saddles empty.

The other cavalry soldiers began drawing back, whether out of fear or to give the infantry a clear field. Stalker took one of these cautious warriors down with a sling, and Whistletrot jumped up behind another and garrotted him out of the saddle. The man was still fighting when he hit, so Haimya rode over, made her horse rear, and brought its forehooves down on the man's chest.

Then Pirvan saw movement rippling down the line of infantry. It was time to say farewell to Haimya, because they had about a minute more before they went out fighting.

The high captain's banner burst through the ranks of the infantry. Beliosaran was going to lead the final charge himself.

Then more happened in a single moment than any three men could have seen even if each had three eyes. Archers leaped up from the rocks above the entrance to the stronghold. The Istarian cavalrymen on the left, about to dismount and hold the entrance against Epron's square, found death hailing from above.

Birak Epron shook the square out into a line, so that all the archers would have a clear line of fire. They shot, and the surviving cavalrymen joined their comrades.

Beliosaran and his guards dug in their spurs—and Waydol's last shatang flew.

It struck the high captain's horse, and the beast stopped so suddenly that the rider kept going, right over its head. He landed lightly, however, springing up at once and drawing his sword.

He cut a fine, warlike figure for the last moment of his life.

Then Waydol closed and swung his clabbard. The saw-edged blade removed Beliosaran's head as deftly as a girl plucking a grape. The high captain's guards were too far from Waydol to use their lances, but not far enough to be out of range of the clabbard.

Those who weren't cut out of their saddles were too busy to notice Pirvan and his comrades charging them. In a moment the charge went home, and several more of the Istarian guards went down, though Pirvan was now content to dismount them rather than kill them.

The stronghold suddenly had a fighting chance, likewise the square. But the five comrades were now barely a hundred paces from a thousand Istarians howling with rage over the death of their leader.

A ball of fire plummeted from the sky, to strike the ground barely a spear's length in front of the Istarians. Tongues of flame spurted in all directions where it landed. Some reached nearly as far as Pirvan; many flowed over the Istarians.

Pirvan's mouth fell open, but he closed his eyes and wished he could close his nose. He had seen enough dead men still able to writhe and scream, and smelled enough charred flesh.

Only the smell of heated earth and burning grass reached him. He opened his eyes. Flames were rising from the grass and undergrowth everywhere the tongues of fire had touched down. And the Istarians were retreating. In fact, they were running as if the flames were licking at their heels. Some of them were throwing off their armor, and all of them were crying out in fear, some even in pain.

But there was not a single charred corpse to be seen, let alone smelled.

"I think we have found Rubina," Waydol said, "or she us." Then he coughed. Blood spattered the ground at his feet.

Pirvan rode toward the Minotaur, then realized the futility of trying to hold up or lift onto horseback a being who weighed more than he and Haimya together.

"Hang on to my saddlebow."

"No. You folk get—get on inside. There's more Istarians about, and Rubina may not be up to all the work of seeing them off."

"Waydol, you swore an oath of peace, which means you promised to obey me."

"Only in disbanding my folk and sending them away in peace."

"Play the law counselor later," Haimya said, riding up on the other side of Waydol and reaching down. "You *cannot* make us shame ourselves by leaving you out here."

Waydol grunted, the grunt turned into another cough, and more blood joined that already on the ground.

Pirvan met Haimya's eyes above the Minotaur's head. *Lung wound. If we don't take him down to Sirbones, he'll bleed to death or suffocate.*

Pirvan took a firm grip on one massive wrist and placed it on his saddlebow. "Now hold on, friend Waydol, for very surely we will have to dismount and die with you if you stumble over your own hooves!"

Behind them, beyond the first line of fires, another fireball erupted. A pine tree boomed into a pillar of flame, and steam shot up like a geyser as a stream boiled.

* * * * *

Tarothin was vaguely aware of Rubina at work ashore. He deliberately kept the awareness vague. Awareness could lead to influence, and this was no time for Evil to influence Neutral spells.

Not when he almost had the enemy in his grasp. It had been almost easy, once Rubina told him; he would never forget that.

As for the rest—as a Neutral wizard fighting for the balance, he had power that Evil priests fighting against it could never attain.

He gripped his staff and began to repeat the first five syllables Rubina had taught him.

* * * * *

There'd been no more than a dozen archers on the rocks above the entrance, but they'd had the advantages of height and surprise and were picked men.

Pirvan still insisted that they go on ahead, through the entrance, down the tunnel, and into the stronghold. He dismounted, slapped his horse on the rump, and saw it prance away. He hoped it would find a way around the flames—Rubina's fireballs now had three half-circles of fire burning around the stronghold.

"Waydol?" Cold gripped Pirvan as he realized he could not see the Minotaur.

"Over here."

Pirvan scuttled around a boulder. Waydol sat on the ground, head slumped on his chest. Blood now trickled steadily from his mouth.

"Had—had to set—fall. We can bring the rocks—bring the rocks down from inside. My people—know how."

"You can do it yourself, after Sirbones heals you."

"Sirbones—"

"A priest of Mishakal will heal anyone his power allows."

Waydol raised his head. Half his mouth quirked in a smile. "For me—that is a lot of power."

"The longer we wait, the more it will take." Pirvan hoped he would not have to leave a Waydol who could no longer walk, and hunt up some eight or ten bearers to worm him through the tunnel.

"If it must be . . ."

"I do not know what must be, but what must *not* be is you dying out here alone."

"Yes, my lord Pirvan."

Waydol staggered when he rose, and had to put some of his weight on Pirvan, but the knight had carried packs loaded with stones that weighed more, in his training days. He had not owed the stones any debts of honor, either!

* * * * *

Pirvan had no trouble finding bearers after he and Waydol staggered into the stronghold. Enough men ran forward to crew a fair-sized ship. Four of them carried a stout plank door fitted with handles, and on this they laid the Minotaur. The four men and as many others as could get a grip on the door lifted it, and the procession down to the water began.

Pirvan could do nothing more for Waydol, so he went in search of Birak Epron and Haimya. He found them standing in front of Waydol's hut, swords drawn, facing a dozen angry men. From their ragged appearance, most of them were either new recruits or refugees.

"What goes on here?" Pirvan snapped.

"These men wanted entry to Waydol's hut," Birak Epron said. "They could show no right. They said they wanted to bring his goods down to the shore. I think they're after loot."

"Perhaps," Pirvan said, fixing the men with a gaze that made them step back several paces. "Or perhaps they are thinking how much the kingpriest will pay for the secrets of a minotaur who has lived among humans for twenty years."

"Well, by all good gods, why not?" one man said. "Waydol's going home without—"

Birak Epron suddenly had one hand on the man's collar

and the point of his dagger at the man's throat. "Who told you that?"

The man gobbled something that might have been a name. Birak Epron threw the man down like a rotten leg of mutton. "The same one who told the archer who killed Pedoon, or so I've been led to believe. Trying to make trouble to the last, I suppose, but at least this time he hasn't got anyone killed."

"Or at least he won't, if we don't see any of you bastards around here again. The boats are waiting. Be in them before I come down to the beach, or start swimming."

The men ran off.

"I shall have to find the troublemaker and kill him before we turn these folk loose on Solamnia," Birak Epron said. "I know you and your lady are too honorable to do that, but I assure you that it must be done."

Pirvan at this point would have listened to an assurance that they must go questing for the Graystone of Gargath. This quest had stretched his notions of what could and could not be far beyond previous limits—and he did not feel he had led a particularly sheltered life.

Haimya looked at the hut. "I hate to leave it for Istarian looters. They may take everything to the kingpriest even faster than those bandits."

"Time enough to think about that when we've saved the men—" Epron began.

Drums from the ships interrupted him. Then shouts, then a scream from below.

Pirvan studied the stronghold, then the cliffs. There! Small figures scuttled atop the cliff at the east end of the cove, moving like archers. Archers, standing where they could reach some of the ships and part of the houses.

And where they would be as hard to come at as if they'd been shooting from the Abyss itself with Takhisis's permission!

The companions ran down the hill even faster than the would-be looters.

* * * * *

Waydol was in a boat on his way to *Windsword* by the time the three companions reached the beach. Archers were running toward the east, looking for places where they could at least distract the enemy.

From what Pirvan heard, the enemy looked like Istari-ans—rangers, perhaps, or fleet archers. Neither cared whether the bow was an elven weapon, and were among the most formidable archers outside the elven nations. They also had the advantage of height, and altogether they promised to be a problem that Pirvan had not antici-pated and really did not need!

"Can more follow where these went?" he asked, of nobody in particular. Twenty archers up there were doing enough damage. A hundred—

"No." It was Stalker. "Only very good climbers could be up there. I wager one man fell for every one up there."

That was some consolation. So was the stronghold's plainly beginning to fight back. Friendly archers were shooting, not accurately thanks to having to shoot upward. But they had numbers and plenty of arrows; luck might do the rest.

Also, several of the ships in Jemar's fleet were replying. Two had full-sized siege engines mounted on deck, and two more had huge fortress crossbows that could send a bolt the length of a man through a foot of oak. It was one of those crossbows that took down the first archer, snatch-ing him out of sight in a single breath.

This slowed his comrades' fire briefly, long enough for Pirvan to lead his companions up to the blue-doored hut of Mishakal. Several wounded lay on blankets outside it, but Sirbones was nowhere in sight.

"I—I am Delia," said the thin, pale woman holding her staff over a man with an arrow-gouged thigh. "I was—midwife, healer, to Lady Eskaia. She is safe aboard *Windsword*, but Sirbones needs help."

"I'm sure he does," Haimya said. "But Waydol needs help direly. Can you tell us where Sirbones—?"

"Delia!" a voice shouted from up the hill. "Did I not tell you to—?"

"Sirbones, there were so many of them. Leaving them be was worse than healing. Leave be, or I shall have to spend strength healing you that—"

Sirbones appeared on a path just uphill. Before Pirvan could ask him to make sense of this conversation, the archers atop the cliff let fly with their farthest-reaching arrows yet.

Pirvan and his companions knew where three of them went. One glanced off Birak Epron's helmet. A second stuck in the thatch of Delia's hut.

A third struck Delia in the stomach. She gave a faint cry, put a hand on the arrow shaft, then sat down, clamping her mouth shut against the pain.

"Don't touch it," Haimya said. "There it's not likely to kill, with a good healer readily at hand—"

"Ah, but no healer is close enough now," Delia said. Her eyes rolled up in her head, and she fell backward, atop the man whose leg she'd been healing.

"Lady?" he said. "Lady?" he repeated, this time in a wail.

"Delia?" Sirbones asked, hurrying up. He knelt beside her, holding his staff lengthwise along her body. "Delia?" he said again.

Then he rose slowly to his feet, his face working. "I warned her. She—when she healed Lady Eskaia and the babe—she put so much of herself into those spells. There was nothing left for her. Then she went and healed others, giving more and more that was not really there, until a mouse bite could have killed her!"

Blindly, Sirbones groped for support. Haimya let him put his head on her armored shoulder and held him while he wept.

He sobered quickly, but flies had already begun to gather around Delia before he spoke again. "Is it true that Waydol—?"

A thunderclap left that question unfinished. Pirvan looked up to see a dozen small fireballs scouring the top of the cliff where the archers stood. Had stood, rather— these fireballs were not mostly illusion.

Pirvan's gaze followed the blazing corpse of one archer all the way down from the top of the cliff until he hissed into oblivion in the water of the cove. Several more fell after him, and then some rocks, heated until they also threw up steam when they struck the water.

"Waydol is—" Pirvan began, then cursed under his breath as Rubina appeared, seemingly out of thin air.

"I thought I deserved better than that, Sir Pirvan," Rubina said. She was almost as pale as Delia had been, and Pirvan had the notion that her staff was now doing duty as a walking stick. But her beauty was undiminished, and she had donned her black robes for the first time since landing—what seemed months ago.

"It was not meant for you," Pirvan said. "This seems to be a day when one cannot finish saying anything without friend or foe interrupting."

Rubina walked up to Pirvan, shifted her staff to the crook of her arm, then threw her arms around him and kissed him soundly on the lips.

"There!" she said. "No one interrupted that, which is just as well, as I have wanted to do that for as long as I've known you."

She turned to the priest of Mishakal. "Sirbones, by your leave—"

The priest stood his ground. "You do not command here, Black Robe."

Rubina nearly stamped her foot, then shrugged. "Well, you deserve a farewell, too. I am going out through the tunnel and collapse the rocks behind me. Please do not let anyone tamper with the devices until I am through. I can do the work better."

She turned and started uphill. Birak Epron took two hasty steps after her.

"Rubina?" From hardened mercenary captain, he had suddenly turned into a youth whose first love has just slapped his face.

"Oh, forgive me, Birak," she said, turning. "You deserve a farewell, too."

The farewell took the form of an even longer kiss than

she'd given Pirvan. The moment it was done, and before anyone could speak or move, she vanished among the huts.

Pirvan was the first to find his voice, and he used it to ask of Sirbones, "What does she—she is going out there to die! Why? She's done so much for us—"

"So much for you, yes," Sirbones replied. "And so much against the Dark Queen, and the Dark Queen's daughter, Zeboim.

"The Dark Queen will have vengeance on a Black Robe who so betrays her. That vengeance will be horrible, and it will not spare anyone near Rubina when it comes. She goes her way alone, so that no one else will suffer at Takhisis's hands."

Sirbones's words produced an even longer silence than Rubina's sudden departure. This time it was the cleric who broke the silence.

"Let us find bearers for Delia and those who cannot walk, and make our way to the boats."

* * * * *

Tarothin's last awareness of Rubina came in the moment when she hurled a fireball into the tunnel to the stronghold. Half collapsed, half melted, the tunnel was now barred against anything much short of a god.

He called out to her, wanting to reach her with a final message, but he felt the message bounce back from the wall of magic he had erected around himself.

Very well. What was outside already was all that was needed, and nothing that those who fought for Zeboim could send would be able to penetrate the wall and reach him.

At least nothing they could send while they were fighting for their lives.

Tarothin shifted the position of his body and felt an easing of his mind. His time sense was a bit awry while he was this deep in spells, but it should not be long before the Sea Queen direly needed her mother's help.

Chapter 22

What Tarothin did to the servants of Zeboim was one of those things that are simple to describe but hard to accomplish. Wizardry is full of such, but this was one that the Red Robe had not before encountered.

Very simply, he walled himself off from the Evil spells. Then he surrounded the wall with another spell that turned all the power of Zeboim's servants back against them.

He knew several such turnabout spells and would have used one long since, except that such spells risk destroying *all* wizards involved. It was walling himself off *and* repelling Evil at the same time that had needed the help of both Rubina's power and of her knowledge of Black Robe powers.

The result was, as he learned afterward, all that could be expected.

There were, it was believed, seven priests of Zeboim aboard the Istarian fleet. There was one aboard each of three ships, and four together aboard another.

Two of the single priests died without their ships being destroyed. Of one priest they found nothing that could be recognized as having once been a human being. Of a second, they found such remains that hardened sailors turned aside and spewed—into the water rising rapidly from leaking seams.

The third lone priest vanished, no one knew where. All the crew of his ship learned was that suddenly there was a hole large enough for an oxcart in their ship, below the waterline. A well-disciplined crew, they took to their boats swiftly, and also threw overboard enough floatable deck gear so that most of them were saved in due course.

The ship with the four priests suffered a harsher fate.

* * * * *

Darin's first warning of anything amiss was a sudden sharp shock that made the deck quiver under his feet.

Then he saw that where the contending storms had been was only a howling wind blowing toward the Istarians. A howling wind that died as swiftly as it had begun, leaving only patches of foam on rapidly shrinking waves.

Most of the Istarians were already under reefed canvas; Darin saw only one mast fall. But in the center of the fleet, a large ship seemed to rise from the water, as though some monster were lifting it.

Its keel was almost clear of the water when the ship disintegrated. It was not a slow crumbling, like a ship battered on the rocks. It was a shattering, like a ripe fruit thrown hard against a stone wall.

Masts and spars, deck and hull planking, ribs and portions of keel, deck gear, boats, cordage, sails, stores—all arched outward, pieces heavier than any man could lift flying like arrows. Flying, then splashing down among them, were flailing shapes that could only be the bodies of the crew.

Darin prayed briefly that they had not suffered. The Mate of the Deck had already given the order to the oarsmen, and *Gullwing*'s prow was swinging about, toward the Istarians. If any wave followed the other ship's destruction, it would be ready to meet it.

There was a wave, but it was more of a brief swelling of the water. The deck rose under Darin, then fell. Hardly a drop of water came aboard the battered galley. As the wave passed, a sailor came up to report that Tarothin's cabin was now unlocked.

"Did you go in?"

"Unh—no, Lord."

"Shall we go and see if we still have a wizard?"

The man blanched, but knew that Darin was not so mild as to tolerate cowards.

Gullwing still had a wizard, and the wizard, wearing sweat-soaked robes, was fast asleep. In fact, he was snoring fit to open the ship's strained seams.

"Put water by him, and have the galley ready to offer any food he can eat when he wakes," Darin told the sailor. "I will be on deck. We shape our course for the cove."

* * * * *

At sea, the wave from the death of Zeboim's servants was only the hump in the water that briefly lifted *Gullwing*. Closer to shore, when it reached shallow water, it became less benign.

From the boat, Aurhinius could hear more than he could see of the devastation among his ships. That was enough to chill him more than the breeze, but he put the best face on matters that he could. All around him he saw fear that might easily turn to panic; he'd be thrice-cursed if he intended to drown simply because some oarsmen lost their nerve and their wits!

"The battle of magic is over, and I do not think those we had aboard prevailed," he called out. "But I have for long doubted that they were Good or Lawful. There can be a dreadful price to pay for allying oneself with such."

And if these words get back to the kingpriest, so be it!

"I think the Red Robe Tarothin escaped from *Pride of the*

Mountains to fight those who called themselves our friends. He is Neutral, which is to say that he will not pursue us, as long as he has prevailed over Evil."

The men looked relieved, even if they didn't seem to understand the half of what Aurhinius said. He was not sure himself that more than half of it was true or made sense. But this was one of the many times in his years of command when he had to say something, to fill with words a silence that would otherwise fill with terror!

Then all his efforts seemed in vain, as a wall of water rose behind the boat.

It was gray-blue at the bottom and green near the top, and it rose above the boat as high as the aftercastle of a great ship. It swept forward, it swooped down—and Aurhinius felt the boat rising.

"Steer small and hold on to your oars!" he roared over the rush of the water. They might just slide over the crest and onto the seaward side, which would do them no good if there was another wave coming, but—

A foamy crest leaped about them, then they were sliding down the other side of the wave. It swept on, to break in a smother of foam where the shore was level and in columns of spray where it was rocky.

It was the backwash from the wave that overthrew the boat, as all the water flung ashore by the wave sought its way back to the sea. Small, vicious waves hurled themselves at the boat from all directions, the oarsmen sweated and swore, and at last the boat rose, then dropped on a rock normally well below the surface.

The first man overboard was Aurhinius's secretary, and not through cowardice. The rock simply splintered the part of the boat where he'd been sitting, or rather, clinging like a barnacle, and plunged him into the water.

The second man overboard was Aurhinius himself. He might have let a sailor go if the boat hadn't been so obviously sinking. As it was, he was going to be swimming anyway, so why not be useful?

He was more than useful. His secretary had gone under by the time Aurhinius reached him, then came floundering to the surface.

"Help! I can't swim!"

Aurhinius threw one arm around the secretary's chest and began swimming with the other arm and both legs.

"I can. Be easy. In fifty paces, you'll be able to walk ashore."

It was farther than that, because the backwash came and went several times. One sailor had to be revived when they finally lurched ashore, but no one had drowned.

"I *said* the Red Robe had nothing much against us after defeating his real foes," Aurhinius reminded the men.

The boat's stores had not been so fortunate. Much of Aurhinius's campaign wardrobe and armor, as well as his secretary's crate of parchments, pens, and account books, were now down among the shellfish and the seaweed.

Aurhinius hoped there would not be a great deal of commanding to do, at least until he could find some dry clothes. Beliosaran would no doubt enjoy another day of being the lord of all he surveyed, and would probably be more insistent than ever about claiming the ogre's share of whatever victory had been won.

Two horsemen were making their way down the hillside toward the shore. Then suddenly they spurred their mounts so violently that one slipped and fell.

The other came down so fast that he barely stopped short of riding into the sea. He jerked his mount's head about, dismounted, and knelt.

"Lord Aurhinius. Beliosaran is slain, and the Minotaur's folk are fleeing by sea. Your orders?"

The messenger was Zephros, one of those younger sons of a family much in the favor of the kingpriest. He was the last person Aurhinius really wanted to hear what must be said, but that was fate, not fault.

"We have no fleet in a condition to pursue the Minotaur's folk. What of the men ashore? Beliosaran is a grievous loss, I know, but are his men gone? Is the landing party safe?"

"Our men are mostly safe, though the city levies have

no heart for fighting. But there is magical fire all about the Minotaur's stronghold. It burns without destroying, yet bars all from entering."

And we have no more magic to use against it, thought Aurhinius.

"Very well. I will take command and send the men out to search the countryside. Waydol may well have left stragglers from whom we can learn something.

"Also, it would be well to see that no other outlaws repair to this stronghold and make trouble in the north country. The people here have endured enough."

"No more than they deserved, for favoring a minotaur!"

Aurhinius heard honesty in that exclamation—honest hatred. But then, one could hardly expect moderation from people like this young man. How different from the Minotaur's Heir.

The Istarian general wondered if the Minotaur's Heir was still alive. He rather hoped so. Istar would need worthy foes to provide employment for its generals—and to keep men like this sprig of nobility somewhat honest!

* * * * *

The smoke from Rubina's destruction of the tunnel was still rising from the hillside. Pirvan paced the deck of *Windsword* until Jemar the Fair told him rather sharply to leave off, as that was the captain's privilege aboard ship.

Pirvan, knowing how much weighed on the sea barbarian's mind, went below.

The main cabin had been turned into a sickroom for Waydol and Eskaia. Delia also shared it, lying under a blanket in one corner, which was not quite proper according to Sirbones.

Jemar and Eskaia had both told him in plain words what to do with propriety. Had he not yielded, Pirvan and Haimya would have spoken next.

Birak Epron and most of his men were aboard *Thunderlaugh*, so *Windsword* was not quite as crowded as some of the fleet. But there were few places aboard a human-built ship that could accommodate a minotaur at the best of times, and when the minotaur direly needed healing, there were fewer still.

Haimya was sitting beside Waydol's pallet, holding one hand while Sirbones listened to the movement of blood in the other wrist. Waydol was tossing his head back and forth, and every so often he gave a deep groan. Each time he did, Pirvan also saw Haimya wince, as the massive hand closed on hers.

But he would not ask her to leave. He only wished he could take her place.

"Does my heir live?" Waydol gasped. "Have you heard?"

"We know *Gullwing*'s afloat," Haimya said. "That signal came from the pilot boat. But she's dismasted and coming in under oars. The sea is calming, but it may be a while before Darin comes aboard."

Quite a while more for Waydol to suffer, unless Sirbones can use nearly the last spell in him to heal a minotaur.

They had offered Waydol common potions, but he himself had reminded them that if he was bleeding within, they might kill him. Also, the dosage for minotaurs was uncertain. Finally, he *would* be in his right senses when Darin came aboard, and there was an end to the matter.

Pirvan and Haimya had the impression that Waydol could still rise from his pallet and hammer them against the deck beams overhead if they went too much against his wishes. So they waited—for signals from Darin, for the wind to turn favorable, for Sirbones to regain his strength, for they knew not what.

For Waydol's pain to end, was what Pirvan did not dare put into words; that was a wish the gods could grant by ending his life. *If they do, before he speaks again with Darin, I—I do not know what I can do as a Knight of Solamnia. As a man, I wish—*

The cabin door burst open, and the only man aboard who could enter without knocking dashed in, nearly knocking Haimya down.

"Waydol! Signal from *Gullwing*. Darin is unhurt and rejoices in your victory. Also, the wind is fair and we are leaving as fast as the anchors can come up!"

Waydol's bellow was a ghost of its former self, but it still raised echoes in the cabin and made Eskaia clap her hands over her ears. It ended in a coughing spell that brought up bloody foam, and Haimya took a cloth soaked in herb water to wipe the Minotaur's lips and chin.

"Send somebody else down to nurse me," Waydol said. "You ought to be on deck."

Reluctantly, Haimya rose.

Pirvan and Jemar were already on deck when she joined them. Pirvan put an arm around her, but she turned her head away. He knew what that meant—tears he was not supposed to see—and said nothing.

Smoke and flame spewed from one of the huts atop the slope. As the smoke drifted away and the stones rattled down on the roofs below, Pirvan recognized which hut it had been.

"Rubina again," he said. "Making sure that no one will ferret out Waydol's secrets from his hut."

"Out oars!" Jemar shouted. "Deck crew, stand by to make sail." He scurried aft toward the deckhouse.

Haimya's head slipped down onto Pirvan's shoulder, and he felt her trembling.

* * * * *

Only one circle of fire now burned in the distance. Rubina sat on a log outside the stronghold entrance, with a patch of melted rock slowly cooling only a few paces away.

Wearily, she rose to her feet and began to climb the slope to where she could find a view of the sea. She could have levitated there, but not without breaking the spell that maintained the last fire circle.

That she would maintain until the last ship was out to sea.

It was a long climb for a wizard who had spent her strength freely for a whole day. If she had been in the Tower of High Sorcery after such a day's work, it would have been sleep and hearty meals for several days.

She had her doubts about the prospect of hearty meals in this land. She was more certain about the sleep.

Several times she was tempted to throw away her staff and robes. They were mere weight now, and she could end the fire circle with only a few simple words. Simple, at least, compared to what it had taken to raise the three fire circles with which she had begun the day's work.

Yet she had worn the robe and carried the staff for so many years, it would seem unnatural to be without them. She did not care to feel thus, in her last hours of life.

Also, if those hours took her into night, it would be cold without the robes. When she was younger, she had taken much delight in outdoor trysts—she remembered one sturdy soldier, whose name she had never known, and a rose-laden breeze blowing over them both—

The sea spread out before her, so abruptly that she had to dig in her staff and grip a branch to keep from sliding over the edge.

There lay the sea, and on it ships. Two fleets, one to the east and so far off she could barely count it. One to the west, much closer, but just too far off to recognize any particular ships. And a single ship making its way toward the eastern fleet, low-built like a galley, and apparently moving under oars.

She sat down, in sight of the water but a safe distance from the drop. She raised her staff, and cast what she knew would be her last spell, one to briefly improve her vision so that she could make out which fleet was which.

The eastern fleet first. Closer needs less strength.

Her eyes watered, her vision blurred, then cleared—and *Windsword* seemed to be almost near enough to touch.

She even thought she could recognize Pirvan and Haimya standing forward, close together.

She had not wept all day. She did not weep now, until she finished counting Jemar's ships. All ten were there, besides *Gullwing*.

Her work was finished. Why not just take a few steps forward?

Because your friends are now safe from Takhisis's vengeance. The only people left on this coast are enemies. Do you want them safe, too?

That thought ended Rubina's brief tears. It was pleasant to realize that one could go on fighting even after death, if one enlisted the Dark Queen on one's side.

Perhaps the Black Robe was not such a bad decision after all.

* * * * *

Darin would gladly have swum to *Windsword* the moment *Gullwing* was close enough, but Jemar already had a boat over the side.

There was no more news of Waydol to read in the men's faces. He knew there would have been some if the Minotaur was either healed or dead, even if no one had put it into words.

Indeed, the silence seemed to hang over the sea and Jemar's fleet like a mist. The water rolled gently, the air was still, and it was as if there had never been death, terror, or magic here today.

Jemar was first to welcome him aboard the bannership, but then he stepped back and let Pirvan speak.

"Waydol spent himself long after he should have given up fighting," Pirvan said.

"Is that your judgment or the priest's?"

"I trust the priest."

"He is not a warrior. He is—he is not without honor, but it is not a minotaur's honor. Or a warrior's. You are a warrior. What do you say?"

"In Waydol's position, I would have done the same."

Darin gripped Pirvan by both shoulders. "Thank you is only small words. If I find something better to do or say—"

"No haste," the knight said. "Now go below, before Sirbones has to put Waydol to sleep for the healing."

Darin cracked his head on overhead beams several times before finding the main cabin. Sirbones opened the door, and Darin's first thought was that the priest of Mishakal needed a healer himself.

"I must go to work soon," Sirbones said. "I have regained enough strength—I think. I cannot wait longer, regardless."

"Do not be afraid," Darin said. "If my father's time has come—"

Sirbones darted away, with more speed than Darin would have thought he had in his legs.

From the cabin, a hoarse voice said, "What did you just call me?"

Darin bit his lip and wished that he would bite out his unruly tongue. He also wanted to stop blushing, but knew that if he waited for that, Waydol might be gone before he entered the cabin.

So he stepped in and knelt beside the pallet.

Presently he felt a large hand ruffling his hair. There was not much of it to ruffle, as he had close-shorn it before going to sea. *Not much for a funeral offering, either.*

"Now, what did you call me?"

"Father."

"Hmmm. I am not—not the father of your body. But in all else—I will not—not refuse the title."

"The one who teaches a child honor is the father of his soul."

"Did you just make that—ah—did you make that up?"

"I have never read it."

"No, there were not many books in the stronghold, or many lovers of books. Ask Sir Pirvan properly, and I think he will give you the run of his library."

Darin wanted to do many things besides talk of his future education. One of them was to weep. He would prefer to be flung into the Abyss.

"Well, you or whoever said it are all right. So go and fetch Sirbones, my son. If I am not to exhaust him to no purpose—"

A gasp of pain interrupted the speech, and Darin felt the Minotaur shudder. Then a small hand touched his shoulder.

"You stay with your father, Darin. I will go for Sirbones."

It was Lady Eskaia. She wore only a nightdress that concealed so much less than her normal clothing that Darin felt himself flushing all over again. He also remembered that she had been near to death herself.

"Now, don't argue, Darin," she said firmly in a voice that recalled Waydol's in the days of Darin's childish pranks. "I can certainly walk ten paces to find where Sirbones is biting his nails in a dark corner."

She went out, followed by a faint rumbling noise that Darin finally recognized as Waydol—as his father—laughing.

* * * * *

Sir Niebar had changed his plans several times on the way from Tiradot Manor to the Chained Ogre. Each time, it was because of something new that he learned about Pirvan's men-at-arms.

Most of what he learned was how much *they* had learned from Sir Pirvan, about the skills of what they delicately called "their knight's former occupations." Since this included such arts as entering a house from the top instead of the bottom, making watchdogs useless without killing them, and moving in a silence normally associated with incorporeal beings. Sir Niebar was not ungrateful to the Knight of the Crown for those teachings.

He could not, however, help wondering what else Tiradot Manor's men had been taught that they were not confessing. Also, whether Sir Pirvan's friends and enemies would learn of these only at the last moment.

The men-at-arms had also brought a fair amount of specially made devices and potions from the manor's armory. These included spiked boots and gloves for climbing, grappling hooks on ropes, rope ladders, ointments for darkening the skin or concealing one's scent, and potions to sprinkle on meat or biscuit and leave out for unwanted dogs.

Each carrying a pack with their share of the equipment, the seven men slipped in toward the Chained Ogre as clouds shut out the last light from the moons. Only a few lights showed in the houses, and not many more at the inn. The nearest festival was some days off; everyone had work tomorrow and was likely abed for the night.

Sir Niebar's portion of the load was, apart from his weapons and some extra arrows for the archers, a large carrying sack. This was to let Gesussum Trapspringer down to the ground, in case he was in no fit state to climb himself.

As this would be put into use only near the end of the raid, and only in dire emergency, Sir Niebar found himself with the job of sentry. One man-at-arms shot a hook attached to an arrow high into the eaves of the inn. A second climbed up the rope, pulling another rope with him. A third bent onto the second rope a rope ladder, climbed the second rope trailing the ladder behind him, and hooked the ladder over the frame of a dormer window.

The window was open, and the fourth man-at-arms spat on the ground when he learned this. "Sir Pirvan wouldn't have called this a sporting job when he was doing his former work," the man whispered irritably. "No guarding worth the name."

That seemed to be true, but then the innkeeper had no reason to suppose that anyone knew of valuables in the attic. He had indeed probably locked all the attic stairs just in case the kender loosed himself from his shackles and didn't want to jump from a third-story window.

The fourth man-at-arms disappeared up the ladder, along with one of the knights. Sir Niebar and the second knight remained below, as sentries and also in case there was a trap laid in the attic. If they couldn't make their escape with the kender, somebody had to make their way back to a keep and warn the knights.

Sir Niebar kept seeing moving shapes out of the corner of his eye, but they vanished when he looked directly toward the spots. He knew that darkness and an uneasy mind could deceive the eyes; he also heard nothing.

Which did not prove that trained adepts like the Servants of Silence could not be stalking him this very moment—

Light blazed from the attic dormer. For a moment Sir

Niebar was dazzled, for another moment he thought the inn was afire. Then a small figure appeared in the window, silhouetted against the light. Without hesitating, it leaped, aiming for the branch of a tree that stood close to the inn.

A human would have snapped the branch like a twig. A kender, even a full-grown one, merely bent it down so far that he could safely drop the rest of the way to the ground. He landed awry, however, and the rough landing plus his privations had him groaning and unable to rise when Sir Niebar ran to him.

"The tattooed ones—" the kender gasped.

The warning was just in time. Sir Niebar and his companion sprang up and stood back-to-back, swords drawn, as four dark-clad figures burst from the trees. At the same time, a man-at-arms appeared in the window.

"Run!" he shouted.

Apart from waking the whole inn, Sir Niebar saw no purpose in that cry. The knights on the ground were not going to abandon their companions, and there was an end on it. There also would be no chance of taking a prisoner, if they incontinently fled.

So the two knights went briskly to work, and discovered to their mingled chagrin and relief that the four they faced were not finished swordsmen. Chagrin because there was no honor in fighting men who should not have been sent into battle at all; relief because it improved their chances of victory.

They still had to kill two of the Servants of Silence, and a third they wounded badly before he escaped into the night. A fourth might have escaped unhurt if Trapspringer hadn't suddenly rolled over and thrust a dagger taken from one of the bodies into the man's leg.

The man howled, missed a step, and went down like a felled tree as Sir Niebar shifted his grip and hammered the flat of his sword blade across the man's temple. The other knight knelt immediately, to be sure the man was helpless and to bind his wound as necessary.

The kender did a little dance around the prostrate man.

Sir Niebar had never seen a kender in a mood to take a blood vengeance before; he did not care to see one now.

However, the kender's condition spoke for itself. He was now missing fingernails and teeth, as well as sporting the injuries Sir Pirvan had described. It was a minor wonder that he was as fit as he was. It was no wonder at all that he would have shed the blood of one of his tormenters if the knights had not been there.

By now the four men-at-arms were back down from the attic. One of them was thrown; when he landed in the gravel Niebar saw why. A sword or dagger thrust had pierced his heart; he must have died with neither delay nor pain.

Sir Niebar made it his business to make sure that the captive had one of the tattoos, which proved to be the case. Two of the other men-at-arms ran around to the main door of the inn and pushed a large wagon in front of it to discourage opening it. The third knight did similar work in the back, setting fire to a pile of kindling near the door.

Sir Niebar prayed earnestly to Sirrion, god of creative fire, that the kindling would burn long enough to be useful and even beautiful, but not long enough to burn down the inn and reduce innocent people to ashes.

The carrying sack proved useful in the end, for Trapspringer had spent his last strength in the dance. Sir Niebar, as the tallest of the seven companions, carried the kender. Two others carried the dead man-at-arms.

Occupants of the houses on the path back to where they'd left the horses had come awake by the time the companions passed them. But the watchdogs were mostly sleeping off potion-laden biscuit. Most of the people looking out of the houses or running out of them were going out the front as the companions passed the back, and the companions were all dark of face and clothing.

It occurred to Sir Niebar that anyone who did get a good look at them might well mistake them for the very band of the Servants of Silence they had met and defeated, the ones coming for the kender. If so, there would be all the more reason for the farmers to look the other way.

The horses were where they'd been tethered, though

each one now had a kender at its head, ready to "handle" the tethers free in an instant or even cut them with daggers.

"We didn't want the tattooed ones to have your horses and proof of who you were," Rambledin said.

Gesussum Trapspringer's head popped out of the sack. "Miron Rambledin! What are you doing here, if you're doing anything useful, which it would be the first time for you if you—"

"If captivity won't improve your manners, Gesi, the knight can always take you back to the inn," Miron Rambledin said. "Now come along. These good folk have enough to carry without you, and Shemra will be happy to see you—no, on second thought, she won't until you've taken a bath. When did they last let you within ten paces of hot water, if I may ask?"

"You may not," Trapspringer said, but he scrambled out of the bag, swayed on his feet, then collapsed into Miron Rambledin's arms. The other kender gathered around and lifted him, and before Sir Niebar could open his mouth to say a word in gratitude, the humans were alone with their horses.

"Well, it looks as if we have our prisoner," Sir Niebar said. "And Rambledin nieces and nephews will soon be able to tell stories about a real Uncle Trapspringer. Although I hope they do not noise this affair about outside the family."

"Maybe they will, maybe they won't," the man-at-arms who'd spoken up for helping kender said. "But you know how it is with those little folk. What one knows, all do before long. That didn't do us any hurt tonight, Sir Niebar, and mayhap it won't do us harm in the future."

"Let the future look to itself. What we need now is less talk, sound horses, and the night staying dark."

"Aye, Sir Niebar."

In five minutes, the men and horses had departed as completely as the kender, if not as silently, and were riding through the night.

* * * * *

On a stretch of coast that was more naked rock than forest, Rubina was also alone with the night.

She was not alone in this land, she knew. From where she sat, she could see the torches of four Istarian searching parties, going over the battlefield. They seemed to be looking under every brush or even pebble for dead and wounded comrades and strays from Waydol's men.

Twice she heard the clash of steel and the screams of the dying, as they found people who were either enemies or could not prove that they were friends. So far they had not found her, or even come far in her direction.

Takhisis, on the other hand, had not come at all. Rubina had long since expected to be in the Abyss, tormented to the edge of death and then brought back to life for further torment. Perhaps the Dark Queen was healing or consoling her daughter Zeboim?

Perhaps. More likely, Takhisis would come when she chose. Forcing Rubina to walk alone for days, months, even years, for fear of involving others in her fate, would be a subtle torment. The Dark Queen was a goddess, after all, with more time as well as more cruelty than any mortal.

Now one of the clusters of torches was finally crawling up the hill toward Rubina's perch above the sea. Soon she could hear the thump of boots above the boom of the surf. Then she could make out torchlight reflected from armor, and finally she could make out faces.

One of them, in the middle of a ring of soldiers, was none other than Gildas Aurhinius himself. Proving that his night sight was that of a younger man, he was also the first to see Rubina.

"Ho, Lady! What do you here?"

Rubina stood up on legs that seemed ready to turn to water. She left her staff lying wedged in the rocks, not wishing to alarm the soldiers. Aurhinius might be on foot, but he was on foot with some twenty armed guards.

"I wait."

"For what?"

"For my fate."

"Stop talking riddles, woman," another, younger voice

294

snapped. "Men, forward and bind her. This must be the Black Robe of Waydol's stronghold. There is much to learn from her."

Aurhinius turned to the younger man, who wore ornate armor and seemed to be captain of the guards. "Permit me, Zephros."

Aurhinius stepped forward. "Lady—Rubina, is it not?"

Rubina swallowed. She had not expected any Istarian to know her name.

"We try to learn where wizards are, and whether alive or dead," he said mildly. "Sometimes we even succeed. Now, I do not promise that the Towers of High Sorcery will accept you back after this escapade, but I do promise that if you come peacefully, you will in time be free to return to them if you and they wish."

Rubina turned the words over and over in her mind. This was the promise of a full pardon from Istar's masters, if she helped them solve the mysteries of Waydol and the day's fighting.

It was, alas, not a bargain she could accept. Involved were too many secrets that were not hers to reveal.

But in making such a bargain, Aurhinius proved what kind of man he was. The kind of man who should not be close to her when Takhisis struck back. The kind of man whom Istar, Karthay, the Knights of Solamnia, and everyone else needed alive rather than dead.

So the choice was simple. She only hoped that she could find among the ranks of the guards someone to help her over the last step.

She bent, and picked up her staff, at the same time thrusting a hand inside the front of her robe.

* * * * *

Aurhinius thought that Rubina was merely picking up her staff and perhaps offering him her pouches of herbs for safekeeping.

Zephros howled in rage and fear. "She's trying to enspell Aurhinius!"

Some of the guards were light infantry, armed with short swords and javelins instead of long sword and shield. Zephros snatched a javelin from the nearest man, raised it, and threw.

In sporting contests, at least, he had become a deft hand with the javelin. Now he proved that he could throw well in battle—if hitting a standing woman at thirty paces' distance could be called battle.

The javelin took Rubina just below the breasts. Angling slightly upward, it pierced her heart. She barely had time to feel relief at her body's end coming so swiftly, before she felt nothing at all.

Aurhinius tried to keep her from falling, and succeeded at the price of getting her blood on his hands and arms. He turned to Zephros, who had taken another javelin—and now promptly dropped it.

Aurhinius walked down the slope to Zephros, with a look on his face that no man who saw it ever forgot.

"You young idiot," he said quietly.

Zephros cringed at the quiet reproach, as he would not have at a torrent of oaths.

"She was trying to kill you."

"She was a mine of precious knowledge that you have just flooded."

Aurhinius's patience snapped. He gripped Zephros by both arms and thrust his face into the younger man's.

"You can go where you please, tell what you please to whom you please. But you do not serve under me again. If I ever see you in a camp under my command again, I will kill you!"

For a moment, it seemed that Zephros's death would not wait that long. Rage can turn a mother cat into a tigress to defend her kittens; it can also give a middle-aged human general a minotaur's strength to tear apart foolish young captains.

Aurhinius knew that, took his hands off Zephros, and stepped back. Then he spat at the young man's feet, a vulgar gesture he knew, but anything finer was wasted on the merchant princeling.

When Aurhinius walked off into the darkness outside the circle of torchlight, no one made to follow him.

* * * * *

Waydol died just before dawn.

It was as they had feared. The Minotaur had spent too much of his strength fighting after he was wounded, and Sirbones had spent too much of his power healing other wounded. Sirbones did what he had warned Delia against, giving what was not really in him trying to save Waydol, but it was in vain, and the priest of Mishakal nearly followed Delia and the Minotaur.

Fortunately Tarothin was sufficiently recovered, after a long sleep and a hearty meal, to come aboard *Windsword* and administer healing to the healer. "Now, if someone will just tie him to his bunk for a few days," the Red Robe added, "he should be fit to heal anything from blisters to broken heads."

They decided to bury Waydol and Delia at sea—"so that my father will in time make his homeward voyage, even if transformed," as Darin put it. The fleet hove to, the two shrouded bodies were placed on planks, and Tarothin said appropriate blessings since Sirbones was asleep below.

Eskaia was on deck for the burial, though she looked as if she should have been in her bed. However, she had already made it clear what would happen to Jemar if he denied her permission, and everyone else had the sense to hold his tongue.

Darin spoke a few words about his father—"who will live longer than if he had ten children of his body, for all who followed him were like his children."

Then he threw back his head and roared out a better minotaur's mourning cry than Pirvan had expected to hear from a human throat.

But then, he had never expected to meet anyone like Darin.

The drums rolled, canvas scraped over wood, two splashes sounded alongside *Windsword*, and it was done.

Epilogue

The voyage to Solamnia was swift, with good sailing weather. It was not so swift that Eskaia and Sirbones did not have time to recover. When Jemar carried his lady down the gangplank, it was merely for show—and when the cheers erupted, he nearly dropped her into the water in surprise and delight.

After that, there was less celebration and a great deal more work, which Pirvan knew would continue well beyond settling Waydol's men and Birak Epron's sell-swords. The latter could mostly take service with the knights' infantry, but the others ended up divided among Jemar's ships, Kurulus's ship (with some for other ships and post with House Encuintras), and various kinds of land-bound work.

Pirvan and Darin were so busy that they hardly had time to do more than greet each other in passing. But Pirvan noticed that hard work was slowly taking the young man somewhat out of his grief. He also noticed that Haimya had been right: Darin was turning female heads wherever he went.

Fortunately, the women were not turning his.

Minotaurs can make good teachers in more than war and honor, Pirvan thought. Then he corrected himself. One minotaur at least made a fine teacher.

Sir Marod was of the same opinion. Indeed, his opinion of Waydol was even higher than Pirvan would have dared put into words.

"Waydol could have been the minotaurs' answer to Vinas Solamnus. When our founder saw that the notion of honor he was bound to still allowed wrong, he did not yield and do wrong. Instead, he devised his own higher standard of honor, and living up to that, changed the world.

"Alas, that Waydol could not live to do the same. I would fear the kingpriest and his ilk less if we did not also have to fear the minotaurs."

Pirvan nodded. That was the truth by which the knight had to live as an order. He himself would find it hard ever to see a minotaur as an enemy again, unless the minotaur declared himself one.

Sir Marod also kept Pirvan active with business of the knights, so that he not only saw little of Darin but hardly more of Haimya. Indeed, the Knight of the Rose was disposed to keep Haimya at Dargaard Keep until certain matters were negotiated with Istar.

"If you wish, I can also have Sir Niebar and his knights bring your children out here to safety," Sir Marod added.

Pirvan was fortunately able to discourage that idea, without breaching honor, Measure, or common good manners, before it reached Haimya and provoked her into saying unforgivable things about Sir Marod.

This was as well. Pirvan was not entirely sure he would have wished to silence her, once she began speaking her mind. Sir Marod had many virtues, but a knowledge of women like Haimya was not among them.

*　*　*　*　*

Near the beginning of Paleswelt, Pirvan and Haimya finally rode home to Tiradot. Tarothin went with them, to provide some wizardly assistance if needed, and Grimsoar One-Eye wanted to go. However, Jemar had promoted him to command of his own ship, and there was too much work for him.

After a painful farewell to Darin, they rode swiftly. They would have ridden more swiftly, except that Haimya discovered that she, too, was now with child, after many years of thinking young Eskaia would be her last.

Reaching home, they made what was at first a less pleasant discovery. Sir Niebar the Tall and no fewer than seven knights were in residence at Tiradot Manor.

Fortunately, they were paying their own expenses.

"Nothing worth your attention has happened—" Niebar began.

"I will be the judge of that," Pirvan said.

"Very well. I will tell you all, later. For now, I merely say that if at any time anyone had chosen to attack the manor, they would have faced Knights of Solamnia. Then they would have had to choose between abandoning the attack and declaring war on the knights."

Pirvan was not sure that his carefully taught men-at-arms would not have been more useful than the knights in fighting off the kind of subtle attack that was more likely than open war. Neither was he sure that he really cared for having a bodyguard of paying guests around the manor until the knights and Istar finished their negotiations. Both sides loved to quibble; neither side was apt to consider the convenience of the subjects of their negotiations.

But there was a babe growing in Haimya, a splendid harvest to be got in, his children and home to know again. Altogether, there was more than enough to keep a man from sitting and fretting in idleness.

It was early Darkember before the negotiations were completed. Word of this came from Sir Marod himself, riding up with an escort of no fewer than fifteen knights.

"We hope to visit a few of your neighbors," the Knight of the Rose said. "Some of them may need a trifle of explanation as to why they should not trouble you."

"Are you asking me to inform on my neighbors?" Pirvan said. He was not quite amused, but not quite angry either.

"Well, if you do not speak, Sir Niebar doubtless will—" Sir Marod began. Then he could not keep his face straight, and laughed.

"We will visit all your neighbors, but we will say nothing and you need say nothing either. The mere fact of our visit will be enough."

Pirvan poured wine. "How fares Darin?"

"One of the matters we settled was allowing him to enter training with the knights. That was our decision alone, but some among us—I name no names—feared that it would offend Istar."

Pirvan suggested what Istar do with its grievances.

Marod shook his head. "I would have gladly said the same, but I and the other negotiators had responsibilities that you did not. It took some while before we could persuade them that you had done nothing against Istar of your own free will, only through being bound to defend Waydol as a matter of honor and of your orders.

"Then, of course, they wondered aloud why the knights had given you such orders. We expressed curiosity about the kingpriest hiring assassins. What Rubina told Tarothin, the prisoner told Sir Niebar, and your kender friend Trapspringer told everybody, helped considerably.

"The kingpriest is now just barely in the good graces of the merchant lords. I foresee that it will be some years before we hear from the Servants of Silence again, or before he licenses priests of Evil to run wild by land or sea. Even the lawful priests of Zeboim were not happy to hear of their colleagues treating chaos like a toy!"

Marod reached into a belt pouch and pulled out an elaborately sealed parchment square. "All of which is leading up to the fact that the Istarians will hold their peace about this."

Pirvan looked at the parchment, then took it without opening it.

"I did not give it to you to put in a case and hang on your wall," Sir Marod said.

Pirvan opened it. It began with the formal salutation:

Be it Known Hereby, to All Brother Knights

and ended with the declaration:

Sir Pirvan of Tiradot, known as Pirvan the Wayward, Knight of the Crown, is hereby elevated according to the Oath and the Measure to the rank of Knight of the Sword.

It was a lucky day at Tiradot, for that evening a messenger brought word of Eskaia's safe delivery of a healthy girl child. The celebration would have gone on much longer if Haimya had been able to drink more, but she was always sparing of wine while bearing.

She was not sparing of attention to her husband that night, however. When he finally slept, the newly made Knight of the Sword thought himself the most fortunate man in the world.

Saga

DRAGONS
OF
SUMMER FLAME

An Excerpt

**by Margaret Weis
and Tracy Hickman**

Chapter One
Be Warned . . .

It was hot that morning, damnably hot.
Far too hot for late spring on Ansalon. Almost as
hot as midsummer. The two knights, seated in the
boat's stern, were sweaty and miserable in their
heavy steel armor; they looked with envy at the
nearly naked men plying the boat's oars. When
the boat neared shore, the knights were first out,
jumping into the shallow water, laving the water
onto their reddening faces and sunburned necks.
But the water was not particularly refreshing.

"Like wading in hot soup," one of the knights
grumbled, splashing ashore. Even as he spoke, he
scrutinized the shoreline carefully, eyeing bush
and tree and dune for signs of life.

"More like blood," said his comrade. "Think of it as wading in the blood of our enemies, the enemies of our Queen. Do you see anything?"

"No," the other replied. He waved his hand, then, without looking back, heard the sound of men leaping into the water, their harsh laughter and conversation in their uncouth, guttural language.

One of the knights turned around. "Bring that boat to shore," he said, unnecessarily, for the men had already picked up the heavy boat and were running with it through the shallow water. Grinning, they dumped the boat on the sand beach and looked to the knight for further orders.

He mopped his forehead, marveled at their strength, and—not for the first time—thanked Queen Takhisis that these barbarians were on their side. The brutes, they were known as. Not the true name of their race. The name, their name for themselves, was unpronounceable, and so the knights who led the barbarians had begun calling them by the shortened version: brute.

The name suited the barbarians well. They came from the east, from a continent that few people on Ansalon knew existed. Every one of the men stood well over six feet; some were as tall as seven. Their bodies were as bulky and muscular as humans, but their movements were as swift and graceful as elves. Their ears were pointed like those of the elves, but their faces were heavily bearded like humans or dwarves. They were as strong as dwarves and loved battle as well as dwarves did. They fought fiercely, were loyal to those who commanded them, and, outside of a few grotesque customs such as cutting off various parts of the body of a dead enemy to keep as trophies, the brutes were ideal foot soldiers.

"Let the captain know we've arrived safely and that we've encountered no resistance," said the knight to his comrade. "We'll leave a couple of men here with the boat and move inland."

The other knight nodded. Taking a red silk pennant from his belt, he unfurled it, held it above his head, and waved it slowly three times. An answering flutter of red came from the enormous black, dragon-prowed ship anchored some distance away. This was a scouting mission, not an invasion. Orders had been quite clear on that point.

The knights sent out their patrols, dispatching some to range up and down the beach, sending others farther inland. This done, the two knights moved thankfully to the meager shadow cast by a squat and misshapen tree. Two of the brutes stood guard. The knights remained wary and watchful, even as they rested. Seating themselves, they drank sparingly of the fresh water they'd brought with them. One of them grimaced.

"The damn stuff's hot."

"You left the waterskin sitting in the sun. Of course it's hot."

"Where the devil was I supposed to put it? There was no shade on that cursed boat. I don't think there's any shade left in the whole blasted world. I don't like this place at all. I get a queer feeling about this island, like it's magicked or something."

"I know what you mean," agreed his comrade somberly. He kept glancing about, back into the trees, up and down the beach. All that could be seen were the brutes, and they were certainly not bothered by any ominous feelings. But then they were barbarians. "We were warned not to come here, you know."

"What?" The other knight looked astonished. "I didn't know. Who told you that?"

"Brightblade. He had it from Lord Ariakan himself."

"Brightblade should know. He's on Ariakan's staff. The lord's his sponsor." The knight appeared nervous and asked softly, "Such information's not secret, is it?"

The other knight appeared amused. "You don't know Steel Brightblade very well if you think he would break any oath or pass along any information he was told to keep to himself. He'd sooner let his tongue be ripped out by red-hot tongs. No, Lord Ariakan discussed this openly with all the regimental commanders before deciding to proceed."

The knight shrugged. Picking up a handful of small rocks, he began tossing them idly into the water. "The Gray Robes started it all. Some sort of augury revealed the location of this island and that it was inhabited by large numbers of people."

"So who warned us not to come?"

"The Gray Robes. The same augury that told them of this island also warned them not to come near it. They tried to persuade Ariakan to leave well enough alone. Said that this place could mean disaster."

The other knight frowned, then glanced around with growing unease. "Then why were we sent?"

"The upcoming invasion of Ansalon. Lord Ariakan felt this move was necessary to protect his flanks. The Gray Robes couldn't say exactly what sort of threat this island represented. Nor could they say specifically that the disaster would be caused by our landing on the island. As Lord Ariakan pointed out, perhaps disaster would come even if we didn't do anything. And so he decided to follow the old dwarven dictum, 'It is better to go looking for the dragon than have the dragon come looking for you.'"

"Good thinking," his companion agreed. "If there is an army of elves on this island, it's better that we deal with them now. Not that it seems likely."

He gestured at the wide stretches of sand beach, at the dunes covered with some sort of grayish-green grass, and, farther inland, a forest of the ugly, misshapen trees. "Elves wouldn't live in a place like this."

"Neither would dwarves. Minotaurs would have attacked us by now. Kender would have walked off with the boat *and* our armor. Gnomes would have met us with some sort of fiend-driven fish-catching machine. Humans like us are the only race foolish enough to live in such a wretched place," the knight concluded cheerfully. He picked up another handful of rocks.

"It could be a rogue band of draconians or hobgoblins. Ogres even. Escaped twenty-some years ago, after the War of the Lance. Fled north, across the sea, to avoid capture by the Solamnic Knights."

"Yes, but they'd be on our side," his companion

answered. "And our wizards wouldn't have their robes in a knot over it. . . . Ah, here come our scouts, back to report. Now we'll find out."

The knights rose to their feet. The brutes who had been sent into the island's interior hurried forward to meet their leaders. The barbarians were grinning hugely. Their nearly naked bodies glistened with sweat. The blue paint with which they covered themselves, and which was supposed to possess some sort of magical properties said to cause arrows to bounce right off them, ran down their muscular bodies in rivulets. Long scalp locks, decorated with colorful feathers, bounced on their backs as they loped easily over the sand dunes.

The two knights exchanged glances, relaxed.

"What did you find?" the knight asked the leader, a gigantic red-haired fellow who towered over both knights and could have probably picked up each of them and held them over his head. He regarded both knights with unbounded reverence and respect.

"Men," answered the brute. They were quick to learn and had adapted easily to Common, spoken by most of the various races of Krynn. Unfortunately, to the brutes, all people not of their race were known as "men."

The brute lowered his hand near the ground to indicate small men, which might mean dwarves but was more probably children. He moved it to waist height, which most likely indicated women. This the brute confirmed by cupping two hands over his own breast and wiggling his hips. His own men laughed and nudged each other.

"Men, women, and children," said the knight. "Many men? Lots of men? Big buildings? Walls? Cities?"

The brutes apparently thought this was hilarious, for they all burst into raucous laughter.

"What did you find?" said the knight sharply, scowling. "Stop the nonsense."

The brutes sobered rapidly.

"Many men," said the leader, "but no walls. Houses." He made a face, shrugged, shook his head, and added something in his own language.

"What does that mean?" asked the knight of his comrade.

"Something to do with dogs," said the other, who had led brutes before and had started picking up some of their language. "I think he means that these men live in houses only dogs would live in."

Several of the brutes now began walking about stoop-shouldered, swinging their arms around their knees and grunting. Then they all straightened up, looked at each other, and laughed again.

"What in the name of our Dark Majesty are they doing now?" the knight demanded.

"Beats me," said his comrade. "I think we should go have a look for ourselves." He drew his sword partway out of its black leather scabbard. "Danger?" he asked the brute. "We need steel?"

The brute laughed again. Taking his own short sword—the brutes fought with two, long and short, as well as bow and arrows—he thrust it into the tree and turned his back on it.

The knight, reassured, returned his sword to its scabbard. The two followed their guides deeper into the forest.

They did not go far before they came to the village. They entered a cleared area among the trees.

Despite the antics of the brutes, the knights were completely unprepared for what they saw.

"By Hiddukel," one said in a low voice to the other. " 'Men' is too strong a term. *Are* these men? Or are they beasts?"

"They're men," said the other, staring around slowly, amazed. "But such men as we're told walked Krynn during the Age of Twilight. Look! Their tools are made of wood. They carry wooden spears, and crude ones at that."

"Wooden-tipped, not stone," said the other. "Mud huts for houses. Clay cooking pots. Not a piece of steel or iron in sight. What a pitiable lot! I can't see how they could be much danger, unless it's from filth. By the smell, they haven't bathed since the Age of Twilight either."

"Ugly bunch. More like apes than men. Don't laugh. Look stern and threatening."

Several of the male humans—if human they were; it was difficult to tell beneath the animal hides they wore—crept up to the knights. The "man-beasts" walked bent over, their arms swinging at their sides, knuckles almost dragging on the ground. Their heads were covered with long, shaggy hair; unkempt beards almost completely hid their faces. They bobbed and shuffled and gazed at the knights in openmouthed awe. One of the man-beasts actually drew near enough to reach out a grimy hand to touch the black, shining armor.

A brute moved to interpose his own massive

body in front of the knight.

The knight waved the brute off and drew his sword. The steel flashed in the sunlight. Turning to one of the trees, which, with their twisted limbs and gnarled trunks, resembled the people who lived beneath them, the knight raised his sword and sliced off a limb with one swift stroke.

The man-beast dropped to his knees and groveled in the dirt, making piteous blubbering sounds.

"I think I'm going to vomit," said the knight to his comrade. "Gully dwarves wouldn't associate with this lot."

"You're right there." The knight looked around. "Between us, you and I could wipe out the entire tribe."

"We'd never be able to clean the stench off our swords," said the other.

"What should we do? Kill them?"

"Small honor in it. These wretches obviously aren't any threat to us. Our orders were to find out who or what was inhabiting the island, then return. For all we know, these people may be the favorites of some god, who might be angered if we harmed them. Perhaps that is what the Gray Robes meant by disaster."

"I don't know," said the other knight dubiously. "I can't imagine any god treating his favorites like this."

"Morgion, perhaps," said the other, with a wry grin.

The knight grunted. "Well, we've certainly done no harm just by looking. The Gray Robes can't fault us for that. Send out the brutes to scout the rest of the island. According to the reports from the dragons, it's not very big. Let's go back to the shore. I need some fresh air."

The two knights sat in the shade of the tree, talking of the upcoming invasion of Ansalon, discussing the vast armada of black dragon-prowed ships, manned by minotaurs, that was speeding its way across the Courrain Ocean, bearing thousands and thousands more barbarian warriors. All was nearly ready for the invasion, which would take place on Summer's Eve.

The knights of Takhisis did not know precisely where they were attacking; such information was kept secret. But they had no doubt of victory. This time the Dark Queen would succeed. This time her armies would be victorious. This time she knew the secret to victory.

The brutes returned within a few hours and made their report. The isle was not large. The brutes found no other people. The tribe of man-beasts had all slunk off fearfully and were hiding, cowering, in their mud huts until the strange beings left.

The knights returned to their shore boat. The brutes pushed it off the sand, leaped in, and grabbed the oars. The boat skimmed across the surface of the water, heading for the black ship that flew the multicolored flag of the five-headed dragon.

They left behind an empty, deserted beach. Or so it appeared.

But their leaving was noted, as their coming had been.

FORGOTTEN REALMS

FANTASTY ADVENTURE

R. A. Salvatore
Siege of Darkness

The new Drizzt Do'Urden novel
by *The New York Times*
best-selling author of
The Legacy and *Starless Night*

Revenge sought! As a ruling
matron of Menzoberranzan
prepares a venemous assault on
Drizzt Do'Urden and Mithril
Hall, the laws of magic take a
horrific turn. The metropolis of
the dark elves is thrown into
chaos and Lloth, the Spider
Queen, roams the streets!
Hardcover Edition
Available August 1994
Sug. Retail $18.95; CAN $23.95; £10.99 U.K.   ISBN 1-56076-888-6

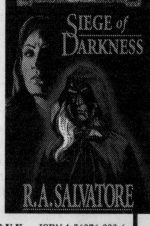

Starless Night
Paperback Edition
Available August 1994
ISBN 1-56076-880-0
The Legacy
Paperback Edition
On Sale Now
ISBN 1-56076-640-9

FORGOTTEN REALMS is a registered trademark owned by TSR, Inc.
©1994 TSR, Inc. All Rights Reserved.

DragonLance® Saga

The sweeping saga of honor, courage, and
companions begins with . . .

The Chronicles Trilogy

By *The New York Times* best-selling authors
Margaret Weis & Tracy Hickman

Dragons of Autumn Twilight
Volume One
Dragons have returned to Krynn with a vengeance.
An unlikely band of heroes embarks on a perilous
quest for the legendary *Dragonlance!*

ISBN 0-88038-173-6

Dragons of Winter Night
Volume Two
The adventure continues . . . Treachery,
intrigue, and despair threaten to overcome
the Heroes of the Lance in their epic quest!

ISBN 0-88038-174-4

Dragons of Spring Dawning
Volume Three
Hope dawns with the coming of spring, but then
the heroes find themselves in a titanic battle
against Takhisis, Queen of Darkness!

ISBN 0-88038-175-2

DRAGONLANCE is a registered trademark owned by TSR, Inc. ©1994 TSR, Inc. All Rights Reserved.